"When man began to multiply on the face of the land and daughters were born to them, the sons of God saw that the daughters of man were attractive. And they took as their wives any they chose. ... The Nephilim were on the Earth in those days, and also afterward, when the sons of God came in to the daughters of man and they bore children to them..."

—Genesis 6:1-2,4

"In all our woods there is not a tree so hard to kill as the Buckeye. The deepest girdling does not deaden it, and even after it is cut down and worked up into the side of a cabin it will send out young branches, denoting to all the world that Buckeyes are not easily conquered, and could with difficulty be destroyed."

—Daniel Drake, Cincinnati, Ohio USA, 1833

RED BIRD

To West,
Please enjoy!
Bf C.

B.A. CRISP

2Portal Publishing
Washington, D.C.   Naples, FL   Oxford, UK

2Portal Publishing
1629 K St. Suite 300
Washington, D.C. 20006

The publisher is not responsible for websites (or their content) that are not owned by the publisher.

Empowerment Enterprises Inc. provides this author for speaking engagements. To learn more, please call 202.508.1463

Cover Art: *Red Bird in Retro,* 2019 (watercolor on panel & Adobe photoshop), Sterling Spencer (1998-), Naples, FL, The Spencer Private Art Library

Library of Congress Cataloging—in—Publication Data

Crisp, BA
  Red bird/BA Crisp.—First Edition Series Book I Quanta Chronicles

ISBN 978-0-578-51314-0 (paperback) 978-1-7343087-0-9 (e-book).
1. Supernatural—Sci Fiction.

2. Adventure—Fiction. 3. Coming of Age—Sci—Fiction. 4. Self-Realization—Fiction. 5. Sandusky (OH) Fiction.

LCCN: 2019918490

Printed in the United States of America

PROLOGUE

A multitude of doubts claw her soul as she forces two fists around a sword. Lift up. Drop down. Fail. Try again. Hazel-green eyes offer hints of gold flecks that settle upon an aurora night sky. What is the past? Where is her future?

Eyes forward. No time for love. Inhale. Count to four. Exhale. She stands her ground. Golden blood paints the rocks below. Waves struggle to lap up the sin that a full moon exposes.

They've arrived. She feels them. They speak to her without words—through the mind's eye.

She refuses to stumble or run. No more fear. The Blues encircle her, their ethereal spears raised toward the forest. "Close the portal!" They yell. Tanks crawl forward. Soldiers fall. Maidens lay black veils over fields of death. From his pine perch, Red Bird watches.

Sword in hand, she dances over the fire until her feet leave Earth, leading a ballet of righteous violence. Her mission? Weaponize truth and rescue reason.

"Sca-Hou," he whispers. "Remember your legacy." She can't see him, but He's there, this trapped being to which she is quantumly entangled. The sea screams. Wind rages. Red bird settles into this strange land to guard the Code. Pain fades. Raga retreats. Peace drifts over the snow. She is home... and knows the password.

In Memory of Sgt. Linda Pierre
KIA
April 11, 2016
Forward Operating Base Gamberi,
in Nangarhar province, Afghanistan

To David
who knew he was taking on one of the biggest challenges
of his life but married me anyway.

To *Blake, Joe, Ryan, Sterling, Bobbie, Dee, Emily,*
Ashley, Lilly, Matilde & Mila
—my inspiration.

To the *beings* who feel alone in this isolated world:
You're not. We're here.

Chapter 1

THE OFFER

Handcuffs hurt. So too, my head.

Any chance of my having a normal childhood got exterminated in phases when I became a Cleveland, Ohio, foster kid. That was eight years ago. I get shuffled through "the system," a failed effort to rid the delinquency in my soul, an 'invasive tapeworm of trouble', so says the judge handling my case. The court considers me an "unruly" child.

I study the racecar-red heels on my feet and nibble my nails as I sit with this cop. My shoes fit better when I wear lace-trimmed bobby socks, like I do today. It's more quiet than usual here at the Cuyahoga County Juvenile Jail, too. Quieter than a tomb, I imagine. I don't see anyone, not even a caseworker or corrections officer. Where are the other kids? The silence makes me feel sick to my stomach and looking for the quickest exit.

Ugly gray-and-pink-speckled linoleum spreads out from under my shoes and it makes me think of the time Katie puked Pepto-Bismol and ground chuck all over Rosie's shoes. Katie had a urinary tract infection but Rosie was too cheap (and heartless) to buy antibiotics—so I stole them. And I don't regret it, either—not even after getting caught, being whipped so hard with a belt that my some of the skin on my back peeled off, and then locked in a closet for three days without food. I still bear the welted tattoos of ugliness as a painful reminder of my fucked-up life—but I'd do it again if it meant saving my best friend.

Speaking of Katie, we are in this together—blood sisters, bound by a needle prick and pressed together thumbs. Nobody breaks that bond—that's in our pledge.

"You going to eat?" the cop asks.

I nod.

I have no idea how this cop caught me. I run fast, even in heels, from a lot of things. But today I can't seem to outrun anything. Not my headache, not my problems, not my childhood. And this, my life, isn't a kid's story. It's a never-ending terror that would mortify any adult with even half a heart.

I just want to be left alone. Why can't people let me live in peace? Peace. Yeah, I haven't gotten much of that these past few years and I'd take a heavy hit if it could be smoked.

My "unruliness" results in a landfill of trouble for me, so I duck school, cops, and the truth whenever I can. Why shouldn't I? It's not like anyone really cares about what happens to me anyway, and I'm a million percent sure I could do better on my own.

People mostly pretend to care about other people. I know this for a fact because I'm able to *feel* others' selfishness and *see* the mini-giveaways in their eyes, their negative energy or impatient desires pinging around on my skin like electrical sparks. Some people might call this ability to pick up other's auras and energies a pile of bullshit but I view it as a tiring curse—and I need a break.

"How old did you say you were?" the cop asks.

"Eighteen," I lie. "I turned eighteen in January. You got the wrong girl."

God, I hope he believes me. Please believe me.

"That's what they all say. You want to talk about Rosie?"

Shit. How did he connect me with *her*? My heart shifts into hyper tick-tock mode. I shake my head. There's a light *thump, thump* behind my eyes. I'm trapped like a windblown piece of litter stuck to a chain-link fence, and I can tell by his accusatory stare, that this guy's not going to hand me any passes to freedom.

Rosie is my foster mom, or at least that's what the court calls her. I have other names for her that aren't so nice—and she doesn't have a motherly bone in her body, foster or otherwise. Even wild animals take better care of their young.

"You stay with her, right?" he asks. "Over at the Trail's End Motel off Brook Park Road?"

"I have a room there," I say. What I don't say is that Rosie makes me pay her to avoid doing stuff she forces the other girls to do—even though the greedy bitch receives a monthly check from the state for all twelve of us.

"Costs money to keep you ungrateful brats fed," she told me—but she barely feeds us.

What really makes me sick is that everyone in Cleveland treats her like a pillar of the community for opening her shit-hole motel to kids like me, the ones out of options and relatives. But it's a scam. She's a scam, a real Queen of the Cockroaches, which is exactly what we call her. I steal to make the rent she charges. She broke our deal. And I hate her, and will always hate her, for what she did.

"Do you know where she is now?" the cop asks.

I sit up straighter. "Rotting in hell?" I try to clap my handcuffed hands for phony hopeful effect. It doesn't go well and I probably resemble an anorexic seal instead.

The cop laughs. "High hopes for Rosie, huh?"

Okay, this guy, he's sort of funny and I smile a little because his energy is good. Plus, cop humor is about as warped as foster kids'—our way of getting by. But I still should have landed a toe kick on his wrinkly twins to take the steam out of him before I tried to run. He's much faster on his feet than I expected, and for a brief moment, when I looked back, I swore his feet left the ground.

I roll my eyes toward the ugly fluorescent tubes stuck in the popcorn ceiling. Their low buzz and slight flicker poke my nerves.

The cop's hands grip the leather gun belt pulled tight around his lean abs. He doesn't have a beer gut like most of his donut-gorging friends who've arrested me before. He's clear-eyed and clear-skinned too. He also sports a goofy gold "eye" ring on his left hand—a green emerald iris surrounded by diamonds, with a black shiny rock for a pupil. Weird—I've seen this ring before. Dr. Awoudi, my psychiatrist, has one too.

The cop stares at me as if trying to figure out which mental path to take so I'll talk. I won't. I glare back.

"What's your sign?" he finally asks.

I blink. "My what?"

"Your astrology sign?"

Damn. No cop has *ever* asked me this before. How could I be so stupid as not to memorize astrology signs? How could he be so smart? "I'm not into bullshit like astrology,"

I say truthfully, trying to guess the correct sign that matches my fake ID. "Humans are nothing more than worthless microscopic slime on the dead side of a galaxy scale anyway. Why bother? Every human's story ends the exact same way. We die."

He raises an eyebrow. "A high-functioning optimist, eh? You could fill in the part where we breathe with happiness and hope."

"Nope. That's about as useful to me as astrology, or prayer, or any other stupid shit people do to pass time on this silly planet until their funeral. How'd you catch me anyway?"

His eyes bore into me, the color of steel railroad spikes. I shift and fidget. I hate sitting, but even worse, I despise people staring at me, testing for mental leaks.

The cop doesn't answer my question. Instead, he strokes gray-amber tufts of rooster-feather-like hair that poke through his chin. This guy? He's smart. And that means I'm screwed—but I'm also sort of impressed by his ability to flip the switch on his aura at will, keeping me mostly in the dark about his intentions. Something weird is going on here but I can't quite wire it together.

I'll bet Katie could get out of this. She turned eighteen a month ago—and aged out of foster care. Lucky her. She was supposed to come get me after what happened. She never showed. I wonder if the cops caught her too. I can't ask or I risk ratting her out if they didn't.

"You're sixteen," the cop says.

Fuck.

"Reality bites," I reply.

The cop stretches his lips upward a little and plops down the crinkly white McDonald's bag that he bought on our way here. The smell of French fries and the odor of stale sweat from kids who passed through

12

here ahead of me swirl over the stained dark-gray folding table. He unclicks my cuffs and clips them back on his belt.

Since free meals are about as scarce as love, I pig out.

The cop plucks my fake ID from his shirt pocket, peels off my picture, and tosses it on the table. His nails are clean and clipped—manicured. That's unusual for cops. I wonder if he has OCD or something?

"Joyce Jones?" he says. "You don't look like a Joyce Jones. And you're Sagittarius. Born December ninth, 1967. Your name is Samantha Ryan Blake. This ID? It's phony."

Crap.

"Where's *your* name badge?" I ask. "What do I call you?" I suck in a breath and take a moment to stare into *his* eyes, hoping to scope a weakness or two and maybe get a rise out of him. "Pig? Oinker? Stinky?"

"You're Sam," the cop says with an indifferent sigh. "You're the only missing kid with campfire-red hair and freckles who stands five feet eight inches and likes to steal. Derelicts call me Pig. You may call me Cameron. Did Rosie give you this fake ID?"

My mom used to call me Sam. This cop's roll-off-the-tongue use of my name, as if he's known me all my life, somehow both comforts and unsettles at the same time. I like the name Cameron. But I'm not sure I like him. It's tough for me to like cops.

Cameron the Cop's nametag is missing. Did some criminal rip it from his uniform during a fight? I don't see any holes torn in his shirt. But I do *feel* holes in his story, as if he has a fake ID somewhere too, but I don't say anything yet.

I stop gnawing on the burger and thwop it down on the greasy yellow wrapper. My throat tightens, tugging my chin down. I nod to admit that yes, Rosie provided the fake ID, not hungry anymore. *Turn it off! Turn it off like a faucet!* I hate feelings. Feelings cause problems and get in the way of survival. And this is definitely no time to feel sorry for myself.

"You deserve better," he says. "Want to talk about it?"

I shake my head.

He sits down beside me. I scoot away, but not too far because I'm trapped between him and the table. People make me nervous when they get too close because the thick muck of their intentions usually suck me into raw deals.

"You sure? Maybe I can help."

"Yeah, right," I say, anchoring my right knee against the wall. "Rosie used to tell me there's nothing worse than a rat—except a cop." But I just gave up the ID scam, so maybe I'm already a rat? No, that can't be right. I didn't give up anything. I got "found out", so there's a big difference.

"Rosie *used* to tell you?" Cameron the Cop asks. "What? She doesn't say that anymore?"

Shit. Hold it together, Sam. *Don't give this cop anything he might later use against you.*

I shift slightly in my chair and look directly at him but refuse to answer.

"Yeah, some cops aren't cool," Cameron says. "I wouldn't call you a rat. I'd call you a fox. A baby fox who caught her foot in a great big trap."

"I always find a way out." I push the fast food away.

"You don't get McDonald's much, do you?"

Again, I don't answer, but stare straight ahead. Rosie says McDonald's is for pretty girls who keep her happy. She can't say that anymore. She's dead—all five foot four, two-hundred three pounds of her—and I imagine by now, she's a rotting blob of maggot-infested stench being claimed by Lucky Willie. Willie's a rather *un*lucky degenerate alcoholic horse gambler, in addition to being Rosie's nearly toothless "companion" who runs her numbers racket. And he possesses about as many brain cells as he does teeth.

"You'll get through this." Cameron rubs his cheeks with his hands and offers me a light half smile.

"Bah! *Riiight*," I say. "Grown-ups lie."

"Sixteen-year-olds lie too," he says. "You don't need help?"

"I won't lie down on anyone's couch." I mentally pinch my brows together as I scan the hall for an escape. But I see only endless gray walls and linoleum laid out before me. Game. Over. The pit of sadness widening in my gut overrides my ability to think straight. I make a conscious effort to fill it in with more grit—which is what Katie says I have in spades.

"You got family?" he asks.

"No."

"Where's your dad?"

My dad is an indistinct memory, yet for some reason my mind conjures him as a pleasantly floating fresh scented puff of camouflage. "Missing in action. Vietnam. 1974. Somewhere along the Cambodian line in a unit called S-FOD Delta, my grandma told me. Why do you care?"

My answer bothers Cameron the Cop, I can tell, but I don't give a crap because it bothers me more that I'm talking. *Yak, yak, yak.*

"What about your mom?"

I shrug. "My mom's in an asylum. My caseworker says visiting my mom is 'not in my best interests.' Besides, she's about as coherent as a cantaloupe and wouldn't recognize me anyway."

Cameron looks away—just like most people do when details get uncomfortable—but his look is a cross between anger and sadness. *Sadgitated*, as I like to say, which is how I feel too—along with being confused and cornered.

The night Rosie died, some lady in blue robes appeared in my motel room—but I don't know how she got there or who she is—or if she's even real, which is worse, because that means I'm probably getting sick like my mom.

Someone left a newspaper on the table. There's another story about UFOs being seen in Tibet, and an article about Golden Temple riots in India. Why is it that where there's gold and religion, there's always a war? India. Maybe I'll visit there someday—if I can break free from here.

"What about your other relatives?" Cameron asks. "An aunt or uncle maybe, someone who could take care of you?"

"The court liaison tried to locate some to take me," I shrug. "I guess they ran too. I'll bet my family line can be traced all the way back to the first Olympics."

Cameron chuckles. "You're smart. You'll be okay."

I roll my eyes toward the ceiling and fold my arms. My head still hurts.

"You're very stubborn," he says.

"And you're very nosy." I give him my best sideways bitch-glare.

Cameron leans his head back against the wall and closes his eyes for a few seconds. Half-circles sit like dark new moons just above his cheeks, making him look doubly tired. It must suck to be over thirty.

I wonder if I can make it to the door, just make a run for it, but I know that door just leads to a holding cell, a 'sally port' they call it, suspended between freedom and captivity, yet another shitty reminder of my limited choices. I wish I could fly away from here, a bird of prey, and shit on everyone's head on my way out.

"Where'd you get those pretty red shoes?" he asks. Cameron looks down at my feet, a smile on his face. He then deftly props a leg up in front of me, as if he knows I'm about to dash and it's a hopeless exercise in futility. This guy is pissing me off because he's 'got my number' as Rosie says—or used to say—before she was dead.

"I didn't steal them, if that's what you're thinking." I sort of *did* steal them, but I don't mention that part. Grandma died when I was eight. Her church friends came to box up the house for an estate sale. I took my mom's red shoes from a closet and hid them in my backpack.

I miss everything about my grandma—the way she always gardened in a sundress and a classy day-at-the-races straw hat that swooped over her green eyes; the smell of homemade chocolate chip cookies permeating my clothes; the fresh flowers she clipped and plopped into crystal vases around her highly cluttered but comfortable old-lady house. And when she'd hug me—which was often—the scent of her Chantilly perfume and lavender talcum powder pleasantly lingering on my t-shirt for hours.

"I wasn't thinking you stole them," Cameron says. "I was thinking we all need something nice to remind us we're human. I'll bet someday you'll turn a lot of boys' heads in those heels."

I think about the word *human*. I haven't felt human in a long time, perhaps all my life. Idiots surround me. Did Cameron just say I might grow up to be pretty?

Dr. Awoudi strides up the hallway, lab coat softly floating behind him almost like a cape, walking with some nurse I've never seen. What took him so long?

"Thank goodness, Samantha." The look of relief is plain on Dr. Awoudi's face. "I'm very happy you've been found."

"I wasn't lost."

He shakes hands with the cop like they're old friends. "Cameron. It's been a long time."

"Too long, my friend. You're looking well."

I crinkle my nose. *Hello, people!* I'm about to be incarcerated for the rest of my life and these two bozos exchange pleasantries as if nothing's happened. I wonder how they know each other.

We follow Dr. Awoudi into Mrs. Myers office.

Mrs. Myers is my 'caseworker', an overworked old lady entrusted with my 'best interests' on behalf of the Cuyahoga County Juvenile Justice System. She's never happy when I run away. In fact, I don't think she's ever happy, period.

Dr. Awoudi pushes oversized round tortoise-shell glasses closer to the bridge of his Romanesque nose and slides his fingers through his wavy black hair. Why is everyone acting so calm? My brain feels like a Mexican jumping bean trapped in a tiny box but I do my best to keep any nervousness from escaping. He flips through some paperwork on a clipboard, more notes for him to add to my already over stuffed court file.

Dr. Awoudi showed up at Juvenile Hall three months ago to administer IQ and personality tests. I don't know why—there doesn't seem to be much of either around here. He's pretty cool for an old guy, I guess, but I'd rather spend time with my freedom. At least his eyes are kind and they remind me of warm half-melted chocolate chips when he smiles—and he smiles more than most people I know.

"Have a seat," Dr. Awoudi says. "You okay?"

I shrug. "I've had better years."

The nurse brought a feminine hygiene kit—standard procedure for runaway girls. Maybe the Cuyahoga Department of Human Services thinks Wet Wipes, miniature copies of the New Testament, and tampons are miracle cures against low levels of conscience.

I plop into another stinky gray folding chair. The nurse pokes the inside of my arm to retrieve blood the way they always do during intake. She'll test me for STDs and to ensure I'm not pregnant. God, I hope I'm not. I give the thought a hard push over a bridge in my brain.

"I've never seen you before," I say to the nurse. "You, new?"

Her badge says *L. Smith*. She nods, but she's too busy watching my burgundy-blue-tinged blood fill the small glass tube and I sense she would rather daydream than converse. Typical. The glint of gold flecks flowing into the tube, along with my blood, seem to startle her.

The nurse places my blood vial in a plastic bag and walks out of the room. I'm tired of strangers pricking me. I bet I have enough plasma stored around Cleveland to feed the entire county for at least a week.

My case file rests on Mrs. Myers's desk. I used to steal peeks when she'd leave her office for a smoke. Everyone's opinion of me is stuffed inside. It isn't exactly a best seller. *Oppositional Defiant Disorder. Prone to promiscuity. Unruly.*

Dr. Awoudi's assessment is the only nice one: *Gifted. IQ 178. Potential wunderkind.*

But this place, these people, they don't cultivate smart. They leave us instead, to rot in crumbling mediocrity where the weight of boredom, meds, and low hopes, keep our chins down and shuffling through 8x10 cells. Most of us later wind up in prison or psychiatric wards severely socially and/or professionally deficient.

It wasn't until Dr. Awoudi arrived, with cool books that he said I could borrow, that I got excited again. I hide in books, able to immerse myself into a fictional world of a characters and to temporarily escape my fucked-up reality. Rudyard Kipling's poems are some of my favorites, particularly his poem, "If". Kipling had genius and soul—but his other work, "A White Man's Burden" about government take over and control of the masses through force, left me bothered. I suppose that was Kipling's point—for the reader to be uncomfortable, to think…and to realize that not all art, or worlds (especially mine), are plushy paradises. "If" gives me hope, no matter how slim.

But Rosie destroyed the books Dr. Awoudi loaned me—said girls like me work with our bodies, not our heads. She tore out my heart when she tossed my hardbound adventures into her motel incinerator. And I hate her for destroying all those beautiful ideas and thoughts she was too stupid to understand. Ashes to ashes…

The Trail's End Motel, where I was sent by the court to live, with Rosie, is the stinky armpit of Cleveland, Ohio, located steps from the Johns-Hopkins Airport. It's flanked on all sides by scrap yards and rows of seedy bars serving oily people—and there's lots of shade in this neighborhood too, which has nothing to do with trees because there aren't any—there's only miles of uneven, cracked, and crumbling concrete that barely supports the latest pipe schemes of losers who will never escape abject poverty's iron fences.

Where the hell is Mrs. Myers anyway? She's usually here to give me a lecture, her gray helmet-head wobbling on her neck while I stare at the white cat hairs stuck to her polyester pantsuit. A near-dead plant in a puke-pink plastic pot collects dust on top of her filing cabinet near the lone basement-like window in this dank office, and a stupid Holly Hobby snow globe rests on her desk. If these cheap trinkets are Mrs. Myers's idea of fun, this woman is about as exciting as watching rust grow on a sewer pipe.

Two or three sets of footsteps clump up the hall toward us. More cops I'll bet, coming to bury me deeper in this putrid pit of a kid prison. A sudden chill unzips my spine and the hairs on my forearms pop up. I focus my brain to try to come up with a plan. I have to figure out how to break out of Juvenile Hall.

Geez, my headache is bad. What was once a light throb above my nose now feels like someone taps an ice pick between my eyes.

"Hello, Samantha. I'm Dr. Evelyn Dennison," says a lady with a British accent.

I slowly twist in my chair to see new arrivals. Two people—a man and a woman. And they're definitely not from Ohio. They're way too dressed up for this rust-bucket, beer-swilling, hick town.

I stand.

"You may call me Evelyn if you wish," the woman continues. She stretches her arms forward to hug me.

I hold out my hand. "I'll shake your hand, lady, but I'm not a hugger."

"Very well," she says, taking my hand—hers is cold. She gestures to the man beside her. "This is my husband, Dr. Sterling Dennison. I'm a psychiatrist, and he's a nuclear engineer. I study culture and human behavior, and he studies propulsion systems and energy."

"Hello, Samantha," the man says. "Lovely to meet you." Warm eyes. Not like hers. Terminally cheerful, maybe.

"So? Why would I care?" I ask.

Dr. Evelyn looks about thirty-something, but she's actually pretty for an old lady. Her ultra-white hair is cut in a classy bob, and she wears an ivory-colored cashmere jacket tailored over a seamless frame, a modern-day Goddess if there ever was one. God, I'd love to have that coat. Her thin chained gold necklace features the same *eye* design that's on Cameron's and Dr. Awoudi's rings. I want it. But what do *they* want with *me*?

Dr. Sterling stretches his thin pale lips into a tight smile. He seems about as uncomfortable as I am. His black hair mostly covers the few wisps of wiry gray that strain from his temples; it reminds me of an overused steel wool pad I used to scrub pans with at Rosie's. And then I notice that he, too, wears the same eye ring. All four of them wear the same jewels. That's not a coincidence.

"What's with the creepy eye jewelry?" I ask. "You guys in some sort of cult?"

The four of them look at each other, then the men glance at their rings and Dr. Evelyn lightly fingers her necklace. My mental antenna throws a spark as I scrutinize this atypical crew. Their dress, the way they stand with confidence. Their manicured hands, polished shoes, clear pupils. And then I see it—what really stands out. Each one of them emanate an intelligence that at least meets, and maybe exceeds, my own. It's highly unusual to be in a room with this much high-functioning brain energy.

"No," Dr. Sterling says. "We earned these years ago."

Normally, I wouldn't let that vague answer go, but this, these fancy folks being here, is far from normal. I decide to play it safe and "dumb down" in order to get more out of them, without giving more of me away than I already have.

"Whatever," I say. "Your hocus-pocus BS is none of my business. Got a cigarette?"

Cameron the cop leans against the wall, hands behind his back, and shakes his head. His blondish-auburn hair almost flickers under the fluorescent light. Why does he seem so familiar? I remember almost everything, especially cops, but lately my memory seems off, and I can't quite find things in my head—like stuff about my past and my life before being tossed into this bureaucratic blender.

The nurse pokes her head through the door and motions for Cameron with a couple of index finger curls. He rubs his eyes.

"Are you crying?" I ask.

"No. Allergies." He follows the nurse down the hall. I hear their voices but can't make out the words.

"Perhaps you're wondering who we are and why we're here," Dr. Evelyn says. She takes a seat in the ugly metal folding chair beside me, her posture back-brace straight. She's probably terrified she might catch a case of foster kid rabies. She's too perfect, which makes me feel distrustful.

Dr. Evelyn either had a very critical mother or got sent off to boarding school at a young age where mean girls likely bullied the hell out of her. I sense she bandages up all that hurt and insecurity under Chanel and uses her fancy degrees as a shield. She's elegant all right, with her best 'day-at-the-races' face, but the inner radar in my gut spins like a blind compass, trying to figure out why they're suddenly here.

"It crossed my mind," I say. "I'm surrounded by doctors, so that can't be good."

Dr. Awoudi laughs and hands me a cigarette, which surprises the shit out of me. He's never done that before.

"I get that I'm in big trouble," I say. "But I didn't expect Scotland Yard to show up."

Dr. Evelyn shakes her head and her beautiful hair swishes along for the ride. "We'd like to talk with you about something very serious," she says.

My hands shake, so I pull them into fists over my chest to hide the thundering of my heart.

I pinch the butt of my unlit cigarette like a clamp between two fingers. Do they know? *Play it cool, Sam.*

"What's in it for me?" I ask.

Dr. Evelyn draws a silver pen from her pocket and clicks her thumb on the cap to offer me a light. *Whoa.* That's cool! I've never seen a lighter pen before. I might pilfer that too. I act like it's no big deal, this bad-ass pen of hers, and lean in to catch the small flame with the end of my cigarette. I drag a deep hit of smoke down my windpipe, which offers a thin veil of cover and calm.

Reaching back into her pretty coat she pulls out five one-hundred-dollar bills. I've never seen this much cash in my life. It excites me to think of all the things I could buy: make-up, cool clothes, or better yet, a ticket to… where? India, maybe? It stings a little, to realize I'm probably not going anywhere except a dank jail cell, and I hate feeling 'closed in' almost as much as I despise being touched.

I punch out my barely smoked cig on Mrs. Myers's desk. The crushed tobacco flakes collapse under my fingers while my curiosity builds.

Dr. Evelyn raises an eyebrow of disapproval, I can tell. She probably thinks I'm a complete degenerate American brat, which isn't far from the truth. How am I supposed to act all proper when I've never had any guidance otherwise, outside of jailhouse rules? I'm not here to impress anyone—but her little look, as if I'm somehow beneath her—not in her league—bothers me, and if she hadn't taken it off her face so soon, I would have been more than tempted to smack it off of her.

"Samantha," she says, "if you hear us, I will give you this money. Deal?"

"Fine," I say. "But I get to hold it." I snatch the cash from her fingers and shove it deep into my lacy black bra. It pisses me off that I still have a lot of room in there.

"Fair enough," she says, almost smiling. I appear too easy for her, and that's right where I want her.

My headache gets worse, which perplexes me because I'm not prone to headaches—not even during my monthly cycle or even after I party hard with alcohol. But I rarely drink alcohol anyway. I don't really care for the poisonous taste of it and only smoke pot occasionally, mostly when I'm able to bum a hit from someone or steal it from other motel rooms. Sometimes the other girls at Rosie's do much worse; heroin, blow, crank—but I don't blame them. It blunts the pain of their own limited options and helps them get through daily doses of being pawed by guys old enough to be their grandfather. I fight the pounding behind my eyes and get back to business.

"I want the coat too," I say.

Dr. Evelyn stands up, takes off her coat, and drapes it over my shoulders. That was easy. Too easy. I have a strong feeling that this lady is an accomplished grifter. I wonder if she steals too—or maybe she's a hustler, able to swindle people out of their life savings using well executed reverse psychology.

The coat feels softer than anything that's ever touched my skin and it makes me think of angel wings, even though I don't believe in that kind of crap. There are no angels on Earth. I've only met assholes and imbeciles since my grandma died. Except for Dr. Awoudi—and maybe this Cameron the Cop dude, though I can't explain why I think that, because cops are usually assholes. Or imbeciles. Or both.

"Give me the necklace too," I say.

"No," she says. "You cannot have the necklace." She sits back down.

Cameron's footsteps come back down the hall; the nurse is no longer with him. Through the doorway, I see him set the vial of blood—my blood—on a table. I stand.

"Why do you have that?" I ask, pointing to my blood. "Why didn't the nurse take it?"

"Strong-headed one," Cameron says. "You ask a lot of questions." He lays his eye-ringed palm on my head—I refuse to flinch even though I hate being touched—and he swipes his eyes again with a free hand. I wonder what makes him allergic. If I knew, maybe I could use that knowledge to aid my escape, instead of being at the mercy of this freak British invasion, who wants God knows what from me.

"Who are you, really?" I ask, feeling both angry and a little scared, so I look at the floor to try to reorient my courage and not give away my discomfort—and growing dizziness. Am I going to puke?

"Look at me," Cameron says gently but all serious-like. He must be almost seven feet tall, and his aura takes up most of the space in this room when he ducks back into this slightly damp office that smells of must and decaying paper. I grudgingly lift my gaze from my shoes to memorize his features—for what purpose I can't say.

He blinks back tears and inhales deeply. "Let us help you. Will you try?"

I nod, but I don't mean it. I don't trust anybody. Besides, who could possibly help *me*? My shit is too deep.

"Good girl," he says. Cameron the Cop's face looks almost pale powder-blue and I see tiny navy-colored veins form on his cheeks like frost crackling. Is he dying? The whites of his eyes seem to turn deep night black for a split second before he swiftly recovers. Surprisingly, he lightly kisses my forehead right between the eyes, and I let him, which is not like me at all! He turns without a goodbye to anyone and *just like that* walks out of the office.

"What the hell was that all about?" I ask.

Before I receive an answer, the tick-tock of the black-and-white clock above the doorway abruptly stops. Mrs. Myers's window rattles and I feel a low underground rumble that vibrates beneath my feet. The lights flicker then go out before backup generators kick on. The faint sound of frightened kids yelling from their cellblocks echoes down the hallway to us.

"What the hell was that?" I ask.

"Blown transformer?" Dr. Sterling says. "Maybe a car hit a pole."

"Where did Cameron go?" An involuntary shiver runs through me, one that's impossible to hide, even under a cashmere coat.

"Back to rescuing promising street souls like you," Dr. Evelyn answers.

I toss her a sour look. "Define 'promising.' And where's Mrs. Myers?"

"She's off today," says Dr. Awoudi.

"Off? She sick or something?"

"Samantha, it's Wednesday, the Fourth of July. A federal holiday."

"The Fourth of July?" I repeat, confused.

Christ! A week of my time is missing. What did I do after I—

No. I can't think about that now.

The gentle smile Dr. Awoudi always wears flees his face faster than a windblown hat. The three doctors toss a concerned look toward each other, then me.

Keep your balance, Sam. Whoa. I'm so dizzy.

"Why am I here? Why are *you* here?" I ask.

"We'd like to make you an offer," Dr. Evelyn says.

"What *kind* of offer?"

I sway and reach for the corner of the desk. *Stay upright, Sam. Breathe.*

"Samantha!" Dr. Awoudi yells.

It's the last thing I hear.

Chapter 2

NOTHINGNESS

A council gathers. People in pale blue robes swoop down from a dusky sky stained with pearlescent stars and strangely colored planets. Three pale moons in different phases keep watch over this odd meeting of translucent beings.

It's neither warm nor cold, frightening nor comforting. Trees taller than skyscrapers, the veins from their flesh-colored leaves pulsating. Hundreds of bubble-sized flickering orbs float over me.

One 'being' glides up to me and gently wipes an open palm, softly as a cat's whisker, across my forehead.

"My sister is ill," she says, turning to face this strange council.

"Human enough she'll die?" A male 'being' asks. I think of them 'beings' because I realize they aren't quite human—they're 'above human,' I think.

Why can't I move? Why can't I talk?

"Yes," the 'She-being' answers.

"When?"

"This," she says, "I cannot discern."

Who are these people? What are they? Where am I?

Whispers, like low whistles when the wind gets caught in seashells, echo around me. This otherworldly group continues its conversation in an unknown language. Strange symbols, etched into a plasma-like obelisk to one side of their meeting space seem to breathe and fold away, almost like a pulsing puzzle—as if it's half alive and trying to figure itself out, while my voice remains lost, left behind on Earth, I think.

But how do I know I'm not on Earth?

Am I dead?

My body *is* lighter, different. I stare down my outstretched arms. My feet aren't touching any ground!

"Plug in her conduit," someone says.

Someone plugs a thin line of light into my spine and it sputters and sparks the way I've seen when welders hold blowtorches to pipes in Cleveland.

"Relax. Nothing matters in matter," someone says.

I fold over. The vastness that I thought was me is not. What is 'me' collapses into heap of material insignificance onto the ground, like a pile of hastily unzipped clothing.

"Nemain," says a male voice.

"Yes?"

"Shall we redeem her and make known?"

The female creature—Nemain—quickly makes a scan of my… soul? Or is it my spirit? I can't tell. She lifts her lips into a light smile, and it is then that I see her third eye, the one that looks like a multi-faceted crystal quartz staring at me from the middle of her forehead.

"You will alight," she says to me, mind to mind, in a language that sounds like dolphin chatter within my head, yet I understand. Her sapphire eyes flicker and remind me of moon-glittered water ripples. "I shall fight for you when the Bezaliel's breach your skin line."

What does that mean? My 'skin-line'? What's a Bezaliel? Hey, wait a minute! I don't understand!

She turns to address the council and they all seem to be laughing even though their lips don't move, nor do their bellies shake—but they're wearing fancy robes so how would I know?

"I wish to lay our plenty upon her, this lost sister, but cannot. The realm rips, and the Infinite Field calls for her return. Lozen needs help."

Infinite Field? Who's Lozen?

"Aye," a chorus says. "And this comes to you how?"

"The Red Bird," she answers, flitting about just off her feet, which I cannot see because they're covered by the shimmer of her pale-blue incandescent robe, as if she doesn't have any feet and the lower half of her is made of…light?

What I do know is that these people—they're not human. Are they even people?

A rumble vibrates in my chest and passes through the council.

"Are you sure they've crossed over?" Another asks.

"Yes," Nemain replies.

"This is serious," says another male being. A look of reserved alarm is apparent in his avocado-sized green eyes and I think he may be the guy in charge. "Take her to the edge of the realm. Lozen has permission to meet you one thread beyond Ninmah's Portal, to escort her back to Earth."

The She-being, Nemain, bows before the Council.

A thousand lights pummel my spirit and I bow too—until insight is lost again, shrouded beneath layers of blood, bone, and skin and I'm stuffed, like a Turkey—back into my body.

Wrapped in Nemain's robes, shielded from cosmic unknowns for which I'm not yet prepared, she flies me to a gate guarded by tall creatures covered in hair, their extra-long arms connected to flesh-colored palms. These beasts stand among other giants, Native Americans I think, except these "almost people" have blue skin, and on some, short chromatic feathers poke out of their chests.

And then one of them, a warrior—and somehow, I know, this is the one they call Lozen—steps forward. Her eyes are black, and her long dark hair with reddish tint is pulled tight behind triangular ears. She secures her strange looking interstellar weapons, grudgingly harnesses me into her arms—and we jump into the abyss where stars dare not fall.

Chapter 3

NASA PLUM HOOK BAY

It's a good thing Dr. Sterling caught me before I hit my head on Mrs. Myers's desk.

I wasn't out long—probably less than ten seconds. Dr. Awoudi said it was just a fainting spell, likely due to low blood pressure and dehydration, which no one believed required hospitalization. He gave me a canteen of water, said it was from his Army days, and told me to keep it before we waved goodbye. I feel as fine as anyone can feel being carted off to another foster home, in possession of a dented Army canteen I'll likely never use.

I told the Dennison doctors that I don't like to talk much, so we travel, thankfully, mostly in silence, the mental gulf between us as wide, I suspect, as the space between two solar systems. I'm sandwiched between them, probably because they're afraid I'll bolt from the car if they let me have a window seat. They aren't wrong.

At least they smell fresh, like perfume and peppermint.

So, back at juvenile jail, I learned that my new foster parents are British scientists who do something for our government, but they certainly don't look like they need the paltry state pittance I come with. They don't even look like foster parents. Most foster parents I've met come with rundown homes containing the putrid smell of fried grease, the scuttle of cockroaches in the walls and stacks of old newspapers used for toilet paper. I wonder what the home of these fancy doctors is like.

I don't like the idea of going to my eighth foster home in eight years but I'm also relieved I'm free, even if I can't account for a week of missing time. Did someone slip something into my soda? I scan my mind trying to locate an incident or event where that could have happened while I was hiding from the police but come up empty.

Did the lights come back on at the Juvenile Jail? And more importantly, have the cops found Rosie's body yet? Her glaring absence and her stench must have led to the discovery of her corpse by now and that's why I'm more than a little stunned that *NOBODY* has mentioned this yet. I shiver a little because if they found Rosie, they also found... no. Turn it off, Sam.

We passed a green-and-white sign five miles back that read, *Welcome to Perkins Township, Ohio, A Crossroads Community. Population 10,000.* But I see no people here—just miles of cornfields and cows. I've never been this far west of Cleveland or traveled farther than Cuyahoga County. At least I don't think I have. At least my headache is gone. I take a swig from the canteen.

Our chauffeur-driven black sedan pulls up to super-sized steel gates at the entrance to *NASA Plum Hook Bay.* Chain-link fence squats on either side, topped with Slinky-like razor wire stretched out as far as my eyes can see, until it disappears over a rolling slope of manicured grass.

Two soldiers dressed in fatigues inspect our vehicle and us. No smiles. All business. Scratchy sandpaper chitchat escapes from their walkie-talkies. The soldiers walk a German shepherd around our car, large guns strapped over Army uniformed shoulders.

Panic percolates past my heart on its way to my head. Are we supposed to be here? Will they let us in? Do I want them to? A desire to run as far and fast as possible rises and then subsides, before rising again in a growing tsunami of distrust. Cameron the Cop said I could trust these people—but since when do his words matter? I don't even know him! Yet he did sort of rescue me from an official investigation of the corpses left in my motel room, which keeps me on the free side of a jail cell, a preferred turn of events at the moment. Besides, if I try to run, I doubt I'll get far, given the G.I. Joe overkill in front of me.

"Three Alpha One, we've got a signal 10-13, request permission for 75-I."

"10-4."

If this place is anything like the Cuyahoga County foster system, I suspect it's a spectacular failure. Pairing bureaucracy with "the best interest of the child" always births a cluster fuck. But I had little choice. The "offer," as Dr. Awoudi put it, was to go with the Dennison's for *special tutoring*, or face juvenile jail for stealing. He didn't mention running from Rosie's or the Trail's End Motel, so neither did I. When he threw in the promise of my own room and access to a library, I opted for the bigger cage. And, hopefully, a way out.

I wonder if Cleveland detectives are allowed in here. I hope not. If the soldiers stall them at the gate, that might give me time to haul ass over a fence. But how? Fly over razor wire? And to where?

I unstick myself from the leather seat to get a better look.

The guard dog unexpectedly lurches at Dr. Evelyn's window, teeth bared, growling, slobbering up the glass and biting air, focused on nothing but her. He'd take off her head if he could. She remains as cool as an icepack—just looks at the dog with her restrained silver-speckled eyes like he's shown bad manners at her tea party.

"Whoa, Sarge! Down, boy!" a soldier says.

Sarge doesn't listen but snaps, lunges, and continues to nip at Dr. Evelyn's window. The sound of his gnashing teeth grinds into my ears like broken beer glass. He wants a piece of her.

Then the dog and I make eye contact—and Sarge stops. He drops his off-with-her-head howl, whimpers, and takes his puffy tan-cream paws off the door. He sits obediently at the soldier's black boots and wags his tail, looking up at us with an almost guilty look.

Dr. Evelyn looks at me with surprise, one French-manicured index finger propped under her chin, before she lifts an eyebrow toward Dr. Sterling.

I ignore them and watch the soldier instead.

"Sorry about that, sir," the soldier says to our driver. "Sarge started acting a bit off about twenty minutes ago, pacing and eyeing up the gate—even tried to squeeze his big mug through the bars. Must be the heat, 'cause this ol' boy never disobeys commands."

The soldier seems nervous, concerned, holding on to a half smile. I can't tell if it's concern for his dog or concern for us. Or maybe even concern for me and what I'm about to get myself into. His hands shake a little and he tightens his grip on Sarge's harness.

"Get him some water," the driver says. "And give him the rest of the day off. Get some fresh soldiers and animals to scour that field across the road. Grid search. If you find anything, contact Major Lynch."

"Yes, sir!"

A soldier in a high tower waves to the gate guard, who motions our driver forward. When we're through, the huge steel bars moan shut behind us. That's it—no going back. My insides feel tingly, but I can't decide if it's dread, excitement, or a combination of both. Who *are* these people? And what is this place, really?

"All clear!"

Hmm. Easy for the soldier to say. I feel more in the dark than if I were spiraling through a black hole.

"Who are you to give orders?" I ask the driver.

"Sam," says Dr. Evelyn, "this is Reggie Chorley, our driver and handyman."

"That doesn't answer my question," I say. "Why would soldiers take orders from the hired help?"

"Courtesy," Dr. Sterling says. "Everyone here makes an effort to treat one another with respect and civility."

"You guys haven't spent much time in Cleveland, have you?"

Our driver smirks at me in the rearview mirror through silver-rimmed wire glasses. His black eyes are penetrating but indecipherable, and his skin is the color of dark caramel.

"What's in the field?" I ask.

Nobody answers.

I try again. "Reggie, what's hiding in the field?"

"Sometimes we get trespassers," he says. "Intruders who snoop around."

"Sam," says Dr. Evelyn, "let's let Reggie focus on driving, shall we?"

"Seriously? Cujo back there wanted to rip your bloody head off and you just want to focus on driving?" I try out a phony British accent as I say this, which makes Dr. Sterling and Reggie laugh. "What kind of intruders?"

"Some people have the wrong idea about what we do," says Dr. Evelyn. "If they try to find out, it doesn't usually go well."

"Not go well, how?" I wonder if they lied to me and this place is really some sort of ultra-security prison for the criminally insane. "Do you give the intruders lobotomies or something? Do they disappear? You shoot them?"

"They go to jail," she says, "for trespassing."

She's lying, but I don't say so.

"How do you know I'm lying?" she asks.

A small shiver tickles my arm hairs because I didn't expect her to pluck that thought from my brain and I don't know how she did. I decide to be honest. "The pitch in your voice rose slightly, your pupils got bigger, and you glanced to the left, which means you just made that shit up—and I don't like it."

"Very well. I shall remain reticent, so you're not bothered by my voice."

"*Grrrr.* You know that's not what I meant. I don't like being patronized either."

I huff and push myself back into the seat, glaring sideways at Dr. Evelyn. She lifts an eyebrow yet again toward Dr. Sterling and smiles. I tightly fold my arms around the brown leather tote they brought for me—a Louis Vuitton. I've never been able to steal anything this expensive, so I have to give these people credit for at least having good taste. It's light though, holding only a few pairs of ugly over-washed gray-tinged granny panties and a toothbrush compliments of Cuyahoga County Social Services. Plus, a stupid Bible, which might come in handy if I ever need kindling way out here.

Trees as thick and tall as Cleveland skyscrapers cluster at attention on both sides of us, acres of reddish-brown, construction-barrel-sized trunks that I'd swear are so big, they're on steroids. They're joined by giant feather-duster-like ferns sweeping their bases. Overcast-colored rocks and spongy-lime moss punch through gaps of earth so dark it reminds me of tinted glass on limousines. Rust-colored pine needles litter the forest floor like nature's confetti. The scent of fresh spruce and rainwater invades my nostrils and I think of Christmas—or at least what I remember of it as a kid, which isn't much. It smells so much cleaner here than in Cleveland. No odor of diesel fuel, or puke, or dumpsters full of rotten garbage. The noise is sweeter, too. No people moaning from the room next to mine at the motel. No overdoses, screams, or wailing police sirens. No blood. I check my fingernails.

A flock of seagulls soars past at window level, their white wings spread as they float and dip on wind currents, their cries free and less invasive than Cleveland's sirens. We pass an apple orchard, weathered, overgrown, and tangled. A lone red cardinal watches us from a low-hanging pine branch, then leaps from his perch right before we pass under him.

The trees give way to open fields of low-sloped ripples of golf course type grass. I saw a golf course once just outside of Cleveland; it too was manicured like this, except there are no little flags *here* to mark the holes. We rise over another small hill and the view takes my breath away.

A stately stone structure bearing majestic pillars of polished ivory greets us under an early evening sun and I think of the ancient ruins of Greece I once studied in my history class—without the crumbling.

I've only seen homes like this in Bratenahl along the Lake Erie shoreline, and even the best of them not *this* grand. I act unimpressed—like Dr. Evelyn—as we round a stone fountain shooting gently curved water from the tridents of bronze mermen. Formal gardens, nicer than the ones I'd sneak into at the Cleveland Museum of Art, show off heavy clusters of roses, daisies, and lavender beside ruler-straight rows of perfectly clipped bushes near the boulder-carved front steps, which lead up a sweeping veranda wide enough to host parade floats.

"Geez!" I say. I can't help it. So much for playing it cool. This place is nothing like the typical blue-collar, cookie-cutter, cinnamon-brick cluster homes I've spent the past eight years of my life being shuttled through.

"The house belongs to the U.S. government," Dr. Evelyn says as she checks the time on her Cartier wristwatch.

"What is it again that you two do for the government?" I ask, staring at the palatial architecture in front of me, the most opulent version of institutionalized bureaucracy I've ever seen.

"Research," she replies.

It's evident I won't be getting solid answers from Dr. Evelyn. But that's okay, because I don't want to give her any either. Yet there's no way she funds European designer taste on a government paycheck or gets into seriously fancy digs like this without connections and smarts.

A warning peals in my head. *Perks come with prices.*

Shut up, Sam, I tell myself.

"It looks like the White House," I say.

Dr. Sterling's royal blue eyes seem to tap dance with wonder and curiosity, and I see, for just a moment, a small reflection of all that might be good in people. But then it fades. "This place was built as a secret getaway for President Eisenhower in the 1950s, during the early part of the Cold War."

"Sterling, shush, don't frighten the poor girl before she even makes it to the front steps," Dr. Evelyn says.

I understand some things about the Cold War, but I don't say anything. I read in class about how the U.S.S.R. and the United States each lay claim to particular East and West sides of the globe, like bullies lining up on opposite sides of a playground to hurl rocks that end up pummeling poor saps caught in the middle.

"Plum Hook Bay was named by the early settlers," Dr. Evelyn continues. "When the government seized it—all nine thousand acres of it—they kept the name."

"Most settlers, known as Firelanders, left voluntarily," Dr. Sterling adds. "Soldiers drove the holdouts off with a court order."

"And guns," Dr. Evelyn says, tapping her knee with a finger. "Don't forget the guns."

"You just told me not to scare her," Dr. Sterling says, leaning forward around me to get a better look at her. "You want the job?"

I laugh a little at his joke, but I didn't know Americans could be forced out of their homes with court orders and guns. I thought that only happened in less advanced places like India's Golden Temple. We have freedom here—until the government decides otherwise, I guess. It reminds me of the court system's "best interests of the child"—which is usually a lie too.

"I don't think I like the government," I say.

"Kiddo, there are a lot of people out there who'd agree with you," Dr. Sterling says, adding a low whistle. "That's why we have gates—and guns."

Dr. Evelyn huffs and rolls her eyes. I guess she thinks Dr. Sterling might be scaring me, but honestly, the gates and guns make me feel better. I bet they keep people like Rosie and her crew of creeps out, more than they're meant to keep me in. Or at least, I hope so.

Staring at this great house, I imagine that if fairytale kingdoms are real, this is how they'd look. But then I remember the stories of Hansel and Gretel and Little Red Riding Hood and my shoulders involuntarily build a little wall on the sides of my neck. I shudder and push dark thoughts away. *Relax, Sam.* But I can't. I don't understand why I'm here and I don't know much about these odd people who stepped in to swoop me away from my fate of a well-deserved lifelong prison sentence.

"We've arrived," Dr. Evelyn says. She pats my knee.

I jerk it away. "Please don't touch me."

"We've made progress," she says. "At least you said *please* this time. Maybe we'll advance our friendship enough to recover your lost week of time too?"

I frown and focus on the windshield. "You won't be getting more freebies from *me.*"

Reggie swings the sedan around the fountain, and we stop. Dr. Evelyn climbs out, so I follow. Two black suits wearing funny radios with little white squiggly cords tucked behind their ears practically march from the overgrown ice house to grab my bag. I refuse to let go. I don't like people touching my things either.

"It's okay, Darren," Reggie says. "She can carry her own baggage."

"Don't we all," Darren says with a look of burned-out irritation on his sun-deprived face, a typical slave frown of overwork and underpay that I often see in Cleveland—people unhappy with life's status quo yet unable or unwilling to mount a change of circumstance.

Reggie winks at me as he unloads the trunk. I stick out my tongue. He doesn't get a pass for being nice. I don't trust him. I don't trust any of them. I wish Katie were here. She always has this way of hugging me with her eyes, to tell me it's okay. This whole situation is awkward, and I'm not sure what comes next—which makes the muscles in my stomach tighten.

A large lady, navy-blue dress, red hair piled high on her head, waddles toward us like a duck on roller skates. Her orange floral apron gets caught in her thighs with each lunge forward. She flashes a smile broad enough to level a cornfield and extends her arms out toward me.

"Good Lord!" she says. "Is this her? Is this the child?"

"Yes," Dr. Evelyn says. "This is Samantha Ryan Blake. Samantha, meet Mrs. Barbara Chorley, Reggie's wife."

"It's nice to meet you, but I'm not a child," I lie, eyeing this new woman with both wonder and suspicion. "I've never known any white woman married to a black man before."

She throws her head back and laughs; her plump frame jiggles. And before I'm able to step away, this supersized lady picks me up and swings me in a circle, my feet lifted from Earth. I catch a whiff of rosemary and roast chicken. Her hug sends my tote and one red shoe soaring up the steps. She lightly kisses my forehead before plopping me back on the ground.

"What the hell! Don't touch me!" I yell—angry as fuck I've just been handled without permission but not really able to do much about it because I'm outnumbered and far from my familiar turf back in Cleveland.

I limp up the wide steps on one heel, pick up my bag, and put on my lost shoe. I'm more than pissed this Barbara lady actually got me off the ground before I saw it coming—and was strong enough to do it. I scan her body for hidden muscles. She looks normal, though clearly, she's a head case. A whacko.

"Honey," she says, "colors make rainbows. If everyone huddled in clumps of one color, we'd all end up staring at some pretty boring landscapes. Look what the rainbow did for you. Here, let me take a better look at your pot o' gold. Turn around."

Dr. Evelyn watches us from the bottom of the steps. I want to say something mean to this strange woman, but she's being so friendly—or perhaps stupid—and I've lost my nerve. "Better do as she says," Dr. Evelyn says. "She feeds you."

"Fine," I say. "You want to pretend I'm a ballerina in a jewelry box?" I slowly twirl for Barbara, wobbling a bit in my red shoes, arms raised over my head, the tote banging against my temple. *Tap. Tap. Tap.* At least it feels better than the raging headache I had back at Mrs. Myers's office, which, thankfully, finally faded. "You want to check my teeth too?" I set my tote down and pull my mouth open extra wide for this crazy woman to inspect.

Barbara giggles. She claps her hands then puts pudgy palms on my cheeks and squishes them —to check for ripeness, I imagine. "You're quite a beauty with all that flame-red hair nestled 'round your cheeks. Mine was once that vibrant too, but the grays slowly invade against my will. Hmm. You need some good cooking to perk you up, though. You're a bit wilted."

I pluck her doughy hands from my cheeks and back away. "Look who's talking. If you were a bowling ball you wouldn't miss any pins. What kind of drugs are you on, anyway?"

Barbara laughs so hard that tears form in the crinkles around her deep-green, amber-spackled eyes. I'm irritated. My insults, thus far, fail to offend her. I'll have to work on that. She seems like one of those comfortable-in-her-skin types whose come to terms with her inner demons. I don't meet many of those. She must have had a great childhood.

"I'm so happy you're here," she says. "Come on, let's show you your room so you can wash up for dinner."

I spot movement through one of the house's big windows. A boy stares into me with so much focus I half wonder if he'll make me levitate. Dark curly hair hangs over his forehead in loose ringlets, and he's sort of pasty pale. He's shorter than me—younger too, around thirteen or so I'd guess—and he holds a single red balloon. He doesn't care at all that I see him. It makes my stomach do a little flip, and not in a feel-good fuzzy way like when I pass notes with cute boys at school.

I point to the window. "Who's the creeper?"

The kid still doesn't flinch.

"Well I'll be," Barbara says. "That little scamp *can* hear me. That's Bennie Bathurst."

"He looks weird."

"Bennie is special," Barbara says. "He's autistic."

"So, he's retarded?"

"Oh, no. Please don't use that word," she says gently. "Bennie's as bright as a fog light when it comes to building gadgets. I've been prepping him for days about your arrival—although he acts as if he never hears a word I say. I see he's confiscated one of your welcome balloons." Barbara smiles and waves vigorously toward the window, which makes the loose skin under her arms flap like bat wings. Bennie slowly backs away from the glass, a robot kid hiding behind heavy scarlet waterfall-like curtains.

"What kind of gadgets does he build?" I ask.

"It's always something," Barbara says. "He made an automatic potato peeler last month that rips the skins off spuds so fast it's as if they're being unzipped, which is helpful around here. Took Reggie a week to figure out what it was because Bennie doesn't talk with anyone except Dr. Sterling."

"Why?"

Barbara shrugs. "Generally, I don't think he cares too much for people."

"Can't blame him." Squinting, I peer deeper into the window. Although I can't see him anymore, I know Bennie still watches us—I feel his eyes, his energy boring into me, even from behind the glass.

"Bennie sneaks out most days and disappears into the forest," Barbara says. "He never hangs out with other kids. He loves animals, too, about as much as he loves gadgets, so I suspect he has a big ol' heart somewhere."

Other kids? Great. The doctors failed to mention that little detail. Strike one.

KABOOM!

The unexpected blast shakes the ground under our feet. I shiver in Barbara's thick arms, but I'm not quite sure how I got there. I try to scream, but my voice has vanished.

"You said they weren't blasting today!" Barbara yells at Dr. Sterling.

"They weren't supposed to be," he says. "I'm so sorry, Samantha. Are you okay?"

I nod, but I'm not sure. When I try to talk, no words come out.

Dr. Sterling kisses Dr. Evelyn on the cheek, then he and Reggie jog back to the car. "I'm going to the station They're testing propulsion systems, Sam, and every once in a while, we get a sonic boom. I hope the noise didn't jar you too badly."

"You both better be back here for dinner!" Barbara yells. "I'm not running a restaurant!"

It takes a moment before my voice slides back into my throat. "What's the station?"

"The NASA side of the farm," Barbara says. "It's like nothing you've ever seen, with all the *Star Wars*–type hoopla going on over there. It's a nuclear reactor testing site, but I wouldn't really know much about that. Never been there. Don't have the clearance. You all right, dear?"

I nod, but it's a lie.

"Here." Barbara reaches into her apron and places two round brown seeds in my palm. "Take these."

"What are they?"

"Native Americans call them *hetuk*, but locals call them buckeyes."

"Do you eat them?"

"Oh, no, dear, they'd make your tummy ache. They're for good luck. The Iroquois Indians believe buckeye trees are unconquerable. Christians call these seeds the eyes of God."

I look again into the window where I saw the strange boy. Bennie is peeking through a crack in the curtain, and I see a thin tear cutting a slow path from his eye to his chin. He sweeps it away with a knuckle, then slowly closes the drapes tight.

I shove Barbara's buckeyes into the front pocket of my jeans and suck in another deep breath. I don't really believe in luck, or in God, but stuck way out here, I might need all the help I can get.

Chapter 4

MEETING THE NOMADS

It's five a.m. Who the hell gets up this early? I pull newly washed white sheets over my head and it smells so good—nothing this fresh and heavenly scented back at the Trail's End Motel.

Suddenly, a trumpet of "Reveille" blasts through the intercom. I'll be ripping out *those* wires when I find them. Fine. I'm up.

I pad across cool granite to the bathroom and practice my best bitch glare in the mirror. I suck in my cheeks and furrow my brow, turn my lips down. Who'd have thought yesterday that I'd find myself being tossed out at a place called NASA Plum Hook Bay?

I spank my face with a hand towel and thump across the floor to stare at a strange painting: a very pale Asian lady seated on a black canvas. She sits cross-legged, smiling, a full moon behind her head. She wears a crown of gold and pearls, and her delicately long fingers hold a pale pink flower with two buds, one fully bloomed and the other closed tight. Some orange-sheet-wearing dudes surround her, twelve of them, and look as if they're praying. But most notably, she has seven eyes. The two normal ones, plus one in the middle of her forehead, one on each palm, and two more on the soles of her feet. Despite the weirdness of the subject matter, I sort of like the painting and it makes me feel peaceful when I stare into her face. The canvass is void of an artist's signature and I'm not sure why. If I painted something this cool, I'd certainly want the credit.

I expected a court hearing yesterday before being brought to my new home—that's what usually happens—but there was none. Dr. Evelyn simply photographed me for "intake" after dinner, which I ate alone in my room, then had me sign some "integrity contract" in which I promised not to run away. As if that would keep me here.

What's their definition of integrity anyway? And the document didn't even have a judge's signature or anything; Dr. Evelyn called it a 'ladies' agreement." Well—since I don't consider myself a lady and she likely just plays one, I assume this means our contract is less than official, and therefore, in my mind, void.

Barbara showed me around a little after intake. I didn't see any other kids, not even that weird Bennie dude, and I looked for him. I followed her to the library—which is huge. It holds a beautiful hand-carved mahogany grand piano, and I crawled underneath last night to read a book about stars I found. That's where I fell asleep—until Dr. Evelyn woke me and told me to go to bed.

But now I just want to hide in my room. I know Dr. Evelyn expects me to meet the other kids today, and I dread this. I'm kind of a loner. And if the other kids are anything like that balloon-foisting, moppy-headed, autistic doofus Bennie, *they* probably want to be left alone too.

I pocket the two buckeyes Barbara gave me, and I step out into the hallway, quietly closing my door. I'm glad it doesn't have a lock. Two uniformed maids (they have *maids* here?) nod good morning to me before continuing down the museum-like hall with their cleaning cart.

The sweeping vanilla-colored granite floor under my feet has wavy caramel swirls. Huge paintings of wrinkly, over-medaled military generals and long-dead presidents hang in busy gold frames on the hall wall, looking down at passers-by. Ha—story of my life. I give the middle finger to one wrinkled white-haired guy in a painting. Then I laugh at the thought of how I'd haul ass all the way to the gate without stopping if he suddenly returned my gesture.

Wide windows draped in thick red velvet curtains stand at attention the entire length of the corridor. A black phone rests on a small marble table sharing space with vases of yellow roses. I sniff one of the buds. It reminds me of my grandma and her garden in Cleveland.

A grandfather clock at the end of the hallway dings to mark the half hour. I'm late.

I try to skate across the shiny floor because it reminds me of an ice rink, but my white Converse sneakers are too new, and they squeak and stop me like Super Glue. I wrap a palm around the black iron stair rail and slowly descend each step. I'm a queen. *All hail Her Royal Highness, Samantha Ryan Blake!* I'm about as close to royalty as a rescue mutt, but Katie always says to "fake it 'til you make it," so, that's my plan.

The smell of bacon tickles my nose. *Mmm.* I haven't had bacon in, like, forever.

Reaching the foyer, I find eight other kids, all of them around my age, standing in formation in front of Reggie, their backs as straight as rulers. But no Bennie. Is he late, or does he get out of this for being a 'tard?

"Blake, you're late!" Reggie says.

I roll my eyes. Goodbye royalty, hello reality. I'm not so sure I'm going to like this Reggie dude.

He holds a clipboard, which he uses to take attendance. I stare at the back of the other kids' heads, scoping for dandruff or lice. We cup a right palm over our chest.

"I pledge allegiance to the flag of the United States of America..."

When we're done, Reggie pulls the big brass latch on the front doors. They must weigh five hundred pounds each, but they swing easily on oversized hinges, which echo in the foyer.

"Out on the lawn!" Reggie barks.

I follow everyone else, which bugs me, because I'm not big on conformity. We jog down the wide steps and over to a lawn at the side of the house, away from the fountain in the middle. The smell of bacon fades, and my disappointment rises.

Nobody talks as Reggie leads us in a routine of breathing, stretching, and breathing some more. Who orders gym class before breakfast? It's still dark out. Grrr. This is child abuse. We never exercised like this when I was in juvenile jail.

Reggie climbs into a golf cart. "Let's move!"

Kids fall into a jog behind him. I run too, but after a half mile, I stop. Everybody passes me, including some barefoot black girl wearing nothing but a green sheet wrapped around her. What's up with that? The last kid to run past—a short pudgy girl who waddles more than she runs, fists clenched tight, inflamed pink cheeks under squinted eyes—nods hello in my direction as she huffs on by.

A row of weeping willows beckons me in the pale gray-pink of not-quite daylight. I inhale deeply and take a seat underneath them, plucking a few clovers. There's a small pile of freshly dug dirt under one of the trees, maybe left by a woodchuck. I've had enough exercise for one day. I think I'll enjoy the sunrise before I head back to bacon and bed. After all, I'm now living in a mansion, which means I've made it to 'easy street'. Wait until Katie hears about this! If she could see me now, I'd bet she'd want to join me—that would be cool. I miss her.

But Reggie isn't having it. He comes chugging back in his old-fogey cart. *Putt putt, neer neer.* I rise and limp a little for theatrical effect.

"Blake! Why aren't you running?"

"Because I'm not being chased by a bear?"

He rolls his eyes and murmurs something I can't hear. Then he barks, "*Move.*"

"No," I say. "You blast me like a rocket out of bed at five a.m. with a stupid bugle and expect me to run a marathon before breakfast? I twisted my ankle. It's sprained. I might file a lawsuit."

Ha! That'll teach him.

"Is that so? You want a ride back to the house, so you can phone a lawyer?" He asks.

I do want a ride. I'm tired of running—from a lot of things—but I'm not telling Reggie that part.

"That'd be great, thanks. I'll sit back here," I say, plopping down on the bench seat behind him.

Reggie presses his foot down on the pedal and blows past some sweaty kids stupid enough to run. I wave my middle finger at them and laugh. Dumbasses. I'm getting bacon.

What kind of power does this golf cart run on anyway? It's super-fast. And then it hits me. We're going super-fast in the wrong direction. *The bacon is the other way!*

Reggie drives me all the way down to the guard gate where we came in yesterday.

"And why are we here?" I ask, not even trying to hide my irritation.

I look for Sarge but don't see the handsome German shepherd that wanted a bite of Dr. Evelyn.

"Hop off and grab my morning paper from that soldier for me," Reggie says, nodding to the gate guards.

"I'm *wounded!*" I reply, wrapping two hands around my right ankle. "Get your own paper. I'm not your slave."

"Hop. *Off,*" Reggie says through gritted, superhero-straight teeth.

Something low, sharp, and mean in his voice makes the hairs on my forearm rise and want to flee, and I jump off the back of the cart to do as I'm told.

Immediately, the cart moves. Away from me.

"Hey! Wait! Where are you going?"

Reggie circles back. I try to jump on the back of the cart, but he pulls away just enough for me to miss. I fall face-first into wet morning grass. He circles around and stops just in front of me. I look up at him and involuntarily shiver.

"You want breakfast? It's two and a half miles back to the house," he says. "Breakfast ends in forty minutes, so I suggest you hurry. And you'd better not fuck up my newspaper. If I have to put up with your high-falutin' city girl attitude, I might need those classifieds."

He whirls his golf cart around, smiles and waves at the soldiers and I quickly flip him off, but surprisingly, he cues up his left arm without looking back to give me the same 'fuck you' salute. The cart and Reggie disappear over a hill, leaving me zero choice but to walk my ass back to the house.

Did Reggie just use the *F* word with me and flip me off? He can't talk to me like that! I'm a guest here! He's hired help. Besides, I'm sure he can be fired for tossing bad language at a fragile foster kid. I usually don't give a nod to being a narc but I just might tell Dr. Evelyn.

I pick up his stupid paper from the guards, who snicker as they sip their coffee and scan the fields. What's so fascinating out there anyway? I head back to the house. Two and a half miles. On foot. I don't walk, either—I run. I want that bacon.

Twenty-five minutes later, drenched in my own yuck, I reach the front steps, beating everyone else back here, except for one really tall, skinny black dude. Whoever he is, he runs like a gazelle. I thump Reggie's plastic-wrapped Thursday morning paper down on a table in the hallway. I'm done with him. He'll pay. His fat ass should jog behind a golf cart sometime so he can see what it's like.

I follow the other kids to the dining room for breakfast. I still don't see the little twerp Bennie. Why doesn't *he* have to run? Lucky boy. I'll bet he gets a pass around here for being a freak. I wish I had autism too, or some other defect I might use to gain sympathy in order to get a break.

Whoa.

The long dining table is draped with a white cloth. My stomach makes an alley-cat growl when I spot pancakes stacked up beside piles of sausage, scrambled eggs, fresh berries, and bacon. Is that homemade whipped cream and biscuits? *Oh my God, it looks so good.* Pitchers of orange juice and milk, as well as butter and syrup, are evenly spaced mid table. The red carpet around the table is practically bald and looks like a well-worn nearly black footpath I used to walk along in one of the Cleveland metro parks.

Dishes clang as kids talk, laugh, or yell. This is nothing like the law and order I saw at Reggie's roll call. It's pretty much a free-for-all now. And I don't see any grown-ups. At least nobody pays me much attention. Good.

I plop down beside a pretty black girl, brush sweaty threads of hair from my face, pick up my fork, and heave six pancakes onto my plate. The detail in this silverware is exquisite. Note to self: *Find a secret place to stash some silver.*

"Hi, I'm Verity," says the girl. "Verity Lane." She waves a pancake on her fork before plopping it with a soft thud on her plate. Her eyes are big and green, the color of limes. Thick caramel-blond waves sweep away from her face into a fuzzy ponytail, but a few tight wisps, like spiraled ribbon, escape to frame proud cheekbones. An oversized cherry-red plastic rosary hangs around her neck—my grandma, rest her soul, would never approve—and she wears a gold hoop in her right ear, a simple silver stud in her left. The henna pentagram tattoo on her forearm clashes with her too-hot pink lipstick.

Verity. What a funny name. Who calls their kid Verity?

"I'm Samantha. Samantha Blake."

"Yeah, you're the new girl. Welcome to the Wrath of Reggie."

"What's with the rosary and tattoo?" I ask.

"Oh, these? I practice witchcraft for prosperity and protection."

"Witchcraft?"

"I'm blending voodoo and Paganism with Catholicism to see what happens. You know, to give myself a leg up in case of an emergency." She says all this a little sheepishly, eyes downcast, hoping, I think, I won't make fun of her. But I'm more focused on her funny accent. She uses d's for t's sometimes.

"What kind of emergency?" I ask, giving her a cautious one-eye once-over as I take a sip of OJ.

She shrugs. "Shit happens. When it does, you need to be prepared."

Great. I'm face to face with a crazy girl channeling Marie Laveau—or Madonna the Material Girl. I wonder if Verity owns a cone-shaped bra.

"I've never heard the name Verity before," I say.

"It means 'true value.' My dad gave it to me before he went to prison."

So, her dad's a convict. Figures. I wonder what he did.

"How'd you wind up here?" I ask, thinking of questions Cameron the cop might ask. "What happened to your mom?"

"My mom likes smack more than me." She answers pretty quickly—typical for foster kids desperate to make a connection, despite knowing those connections will usually be short-lived. It's how we roll. "She got deported to Haiti, where we're from, then she got murdered by a crazy boyfriend who swears he was framed. I kept running away from foster homes, and then I was given a choice: come here for special tutoring or go to juvenile jail for selling weed to an undercover cop. "

I'm not sure what to say after Verity confesses that her mom was killed.

"That's kind of how I got here, too," I say. "Come here or go to jail for stealing." But I don't mention Rosie or the murder.

"No kidding? Miss Sticky Fingers, huh? Remind me to hide my stuff, klepto."

Sunlight begins to leak through the tall windows as I inhale breakfast. I look across the table at two boys with slanted eyes. Each has a single thick braid resting over his left shoulder, stopping just above his chest. They look like the tall Asian version of Tweedledum and Tweedledee from *Alice in Wonderland*. I decide I will forever refer to them as "the Tweedles."

"They're sixteen too, like us," Verity says.

The boys glance over, nod hello, and go back to whispering, heads bent close.

"Pa Ling is from Indonesia and Fensig came from Greenland in the Arctic," Verity continues, dabbing her pink lips on a white cloth napkin and it leaves a bright stain.

Rosie would have smacked her for this back at the Trail's End Motel, and Verity would be charged at least twenty dollars—for the "trouble and time" it would take Rosie to buy a new napkin at Bargain Barn—one that comes in a 4-pack and really only costs a dollar.

"Foreign foster kids?" I ask.

Verity shrugs. "This special program locates kids without families from around the globe. I suspect it's a secret experiment."

"What sort of experiment?" I stuff a wad of pancake in my mouth.

"I'm not sure yet. I've only been here three weeks. But my guess is that Dr.'s Dennison Incorporated are trying to see if they can make normal kids out of us fuck-ups." She laughs, then takes two pieces of bacon and sticks them under her upper lip like fangs. She widens her eyes and makes a "bogeyman" face, her thumbs in her ears and her fingers waving.

Her goofy face makes me laugh too, and I choke a little on my food.

I cross my arms and lean back in my chair. "If I don't like it here, I'm leaving."

"They won't stop you," Verity says. "That's the cool thing about this place. If you participate in their classes, they pretty much leave you alone to do what you want during free time."

"Can I smoke weed?"

"That's a drug they don't want you to do. You can smoke cigarettes though."

"They let us smoke fags? No way!"

"Fags? Why do you use the British slang for cigarettes?" Verity asks.

I shrug. "I don't know." (And I don't.) "It just sort of slipped out."

"Yeah, but don't forget, you still have to run," Verity says. Since I've been here, my smoking got cut in half. Got tired of hacking through workouts." Verity adjusts a sleeve on her blouse, and the gold hoop wobbles in her ear.

"Can we drink Bartles & Jaymes?" I ask.

"Just tell Barbara you want one and she'll open the bar. She'll protest, but Dr. Evelyn will make her give it to you."

"No way! Why would they let us get fucked up on wine coolers but not pot?"

Verity laughs, then props herself yogi upright. "It's the Dennison philosophy. Something about—hold on, let me get this straight, 'An informal atmosphere where emphasis is on individual responsibility and initiative so that we keep enough guts to disobey an order while also building enough personal regimen to think and act for ourselves.'"

"No fake?" I'm almost impressed. But I'm also doubtful. Verity might be the greatest liar I've ever met, possibly able to sell ice cubes to Eskimos, so I stuff my enthusiasm.

She takes a bite of bacon. "No fake."

"Do these other kids speak English too?" I whisper.

"Of course." She looks at me like I'm a freak for asking. "And I speak French and Farsi too. See those three kids there?" She points down the table. "That's Rakito, Tetana, and Priyanka. They speak six or seven languages each."

"Say something in Farsi," I demand.

She does. Or at least, I think she does. How would I really know for sure? I don't even know where Farsi is actually spoken.

"I said it was nice to meet you," she says.

I eye the other multilingual kids. Two girls and a boy. Rakito is the boy who outran the pack this morning—faster even than me, which makes me jealous. He's at least six foot four and is as black as polished onyx. He smiles while the girls talk and reminds me of an owl in an oak tree, maybe full of wisdom because he seems to observe more than speak. Priyanka is looking at him all cow-eyed. I'd bet my red shoes they're doing each other. And Tetana is the pudgy, puffy-faced waddler who brought up the rear this morning.

"What's Tetana's story?" I ask.

Tetana is built like a barrel, but handsome in a boyish kind of way. Her beachball cheeks puff under short black bangs when she runs.

"Tetana's from Kathmandu, Nepal," Verity says. "Her family made bridges from trees without cutting the wood; they actually trained live trees to grow and meet in the middle over river and gorges. She says people can consciously communicate with trees—and even rocks—if they focus enough. Her family was killed by the Chinese Army for giving refuge to the Dali Lama. She was actually on a walk with him when it happened."

The Waddler walks with the Dalai Lama? I don't know much about him, but I know that he's supposed to be some really important Buddhist guru. A teacher once told me Buddhism is a devil's cult. She said people go to hell for practicing religions outside of Christianity.

"Hey, do you speak other languages?" Verity asks.

I shake my head. "I speak English, the *universal* language." I say this a bit too harshly, with a pang of insecure disappointment that she even asked, as if I've over poured salt on my words.

Verity shrugs. "Whatever. Rakito comes from the grasslands of Africa. They found him stealing dinner from a pride of lions. Can you imagine? He supposedly just walked up to the lions and screamed at them until they hid in the bush long enough for him to snag a piece of antelope."

I study Rakito, trying to figure out from where inside his bravery comes. I have to fake my courage, so if this is true, I'm impressed. I don't think I could face down a pride of lions without completely pissing my pants. And what must the lions have thought? I laugh inside as I imagine them looking at Rakito and then one another, completely baffled, like, "who is this fucking guy? Doesn't he realize we're *lions?*"

"Who's the girl wearing the sheet?" I ask. I point toward the other end of the table, at the girl who ran barefoot this morning, her dark hair cropped close to her head, her skin, poreless and perfect, possessed of a faint halo-like white glow. Good aura. She wears a thick gold choker around her neck. But sadness, too, fills the space around her—energy I feel but can't see.

"Oh, that's Saratu. And her 'sheet' is called a *wrapper* and it's handwoven on a loom. She's a nomad from the Sahara. She's homesick. She doesn't talk."

"The Sahara? But isn't that a desert?"

"People live in the desert too, duh!" Verity shakes her head as if I'm stupid. I *feel* stupid. I didn't know anyone could actually live in an oversized sand pile. "Her people watch stars and count sand dunes to guide them through the desert. They feel vibrations of water under their feet. She was the only survivor after her family was attacked by bandits."

I feel a sharp pang of deep anger toward the people who killed Saratu's family. I offer a light wave. Saratu holds up a single palm to me.

"Oh, wow," says Verity. "She like, actually said hi to you. Never saw her do that before."

I don't point out that the girl didn't actually say anything.

Verity continues with her informal introductions. "That cute guy on the other side of her is Genin. He's from a remote Amazonian tribe. He and his entire family once lived in a huge tree house."

"And what happened to *his* parents?" I ask.

"Some sort of clash with loggers. At least, that's what I heard from Priyanka. His entire clan was killed: grandparents, parents, brothers, sisters, everybody." She's half whispering. "Priyanka heard some of the soldiers talking about how they may have been found burned alive and their eyeballs stolen."

"What? Why would anyone steal someone's eyeballs?"

Verity shrugs, impales a sausage link on her fork, bites it in half.

I'm incredulous.

Dr. Awoudi taught me that word. He taught me a lot of words, actually. I keep them on index cards and study them every day until each word is seared into my brain so that I feel less stupid around people. I do this because he once told me that if I hoped to upgrade my shitty circumstances, knowledge and education are key. He also told me to think of learning as a game of 'get smart' so I could outwit "authority" figures.

Genin glares at us; we're talking quietly, but I guess he can tell he's the object of our discussion. He's shorter than the other guys, but wide chested, with tan skin and peanut butter eyes. His eyes seem to ooze with anger, bubbles of lava beneath a smooth exterior. He's handsome—for an over-muscled, abundantly chiseled Latin Rambo type—but he probably knows he's cute, so I don't give him the satisfaction of staring too long, even if he does give me swooshy feeling across the hips.

"Genin survived for a month in the rainforest by eating grubs and spiders. It's some sort of delicacy for his people," Verity says.

"Ew, that's disgusting." I crinkle my nose. "There's no way in hell I'd ever kiss an arachnid-ingesting freak."

Verity giggles, covering her mouth with a royal purple, lace-gloved hand.

"From where on the globe does Priyanka come?" I ask.

"Oh. Well, Priyanka is from India. Her parents were sheepherders near the Pakistan border. A civil war brought her here after her family was killed. I like her nose-piercing. I think I want to pierce my nose too."

Priyanka's coffee-ground eyes flash with a blend of peace and confidence. I wish I had that. I feel like a tangled bundle of curling iron cord all twisted up inside but also afraid I'll suddenly unravel and burn myself or everyone around me.

I wonder if Priyanka's ever been to the Golden Temple. Maybe that's why she seems so calm and collected. She smiles at me and it feels sincere—comfortable, so I smile back, but not as much, before turning away.

Geez, my problems pale in comparison to the kids around this table. I haven't had it easy in the foster system, but I didn't have to flee my country either, like they did—or be forcibly removed after seeing my parents murdered. If somebody told me, "Hey, you have to pack up all your shit and go live in an African foster home now," I think I'd crumble.

"Okay, let's test you," Verity says. "What are the names of every kid here?"

I've got this. I point to each kid. "Pa Ling from Indonesia. Fensig from Greenland. Rakito from Africa. Priyanka from India. Tetana from Nepal. Saratu from the Sahara. Genin from Brazil. And you're Verity from Haiti. Bennie, from God knows where, is not here. And I'm guessing somebody else is missing, because even if Bennie were here, we'd still have one empty seat."

"Wow. You're good." Verity pops her eyes. "Dr. Evelyn said you were super-smart and know lots of big words. Bennie does too. He's from Oxford, England, by the way. Dr. Awoudi found him in an alley behind a bakery. He's been here the longest."

"What's Bennie's story?"

"Hallo, Sammy!" A girl stealthily slips into the chair on the other side of me. I feel like a wrench just tightened my gut. Nobody calls me *Sammy*.

"Jade Sokolov, from Samara, Russia," Verity whispers into my ear.

I ignore her, my focus on the new girl. Jade Sokolov is definitely the prettiest girl I've ever seen in my life. She's way more beautiful than Katie, who used to be the prettiest girl I knew. Her platinum hair, long and paintbrush straight, is pulled into a ponytail that lands at the top of her ass. Deep-ocean Arctic eyes—they remind me of a frozen pond I used to ice skate on in Cleveland—stare me down. Her athletic build and tall stature are comparable to mine, but that's where the similarities end. With my wiry copper hair, tan-red skin, and scattered smattering of fried orange freckles, I feel like Pippi Longstocking seated next to Daryl Hannah.

Yeah, if I looked like her, I could live with making people feel jealous. Pretty gets you anything you want.

"I'm Samantha, not Sammy."

"Uh-oh," Jade says. "You got syrup on your shirt, Sammy. That cost you points."

Everyone stops talking and looks at us.

I shift uncomfortably in my chair. "Fuck off. My name is Samantha."

"Jade's screwing with you," Verity says. "We don't have a point system here. But you do have syrup on your shirt."

"I see you are mouthy and unrefined," Jade says, squinting her eyes as she reaches for the syrup. "Good data points for me, Sammy."

I've met girls like Jade. She looks sport-blazer crisp on the outside, but the filling inside is rotten. She reminds me of Barbie dolls I used to strap to bottle rockets. Three, two, one…lift off!

"If you get in my way, you unrefined twit," she whispers, "you be sorry we ever meet. They've certainly lowered standard to bring *you* here."

"Whatever," I say. "I don't have time for your huff-and-hiss act. Stay out of my way and I'll stay out of yours. By the way, you have a booger dangling from your nose."

Jade quickly covers her face with a cupped palm and swipes at her nostrils. She didn't really have a booger there, but it's cool to know she's just as insecure as the rest of us who share a good laugh at Jade's expense. Verity seems a little scared of Jade, her green eyes wide and skittering in her sockets like beetles that don't know which way to flee when pesticide gets sprayed.

Jade tilts her head back and touches her long neck with spider-like fingertips. "You no match for me," she says.

I raise my own fingers like claws toward her face. "Rrrrr. Pfft. Pffft."

Another wave of chuckles passes through the dining room. But Priyanka cuts it off.

"Oh my God!" she shouts from across the table. "None of the three of you move!"

The kids on the other side of the table slide off their chairs.

"Get up very slowly and crawl across the table," Priyanka says.

When I see what has gotten Priyanka so freaked out, my blood sinks to my ankles.

There's a cobra slithering across the sideboard!

I struggle to make sense of being confronted by one of the deadliest snakes on Earth, right here in Ohio. But my instincts take charge and I abruptly scramble up onto the table, knocking over orange juice and syrup. Verity erupts into screams and joins me, clinging to my arm. Christ— I've now hugged two strangers in two days.

Plan B: If that thing comes any closer, I'll throw Verity in front of it as a sacrifice.

Jade remains completely calm. Tossing me the *I can't believe you're such a chickenshit* look, she casually walks right up to the snake, swats its dancing head out of her way, and confidently strides away into the connecting kitchen.

So, she's not only gorgeous, she's fearless too. How unfair is that? I hate my life.

"Ha! Dat's what you get for flippin' me off out dere," Rakito says. He flashes a bright smile that shines like fresh snow against his coal-skinned face. Pa Ling and Fensig laugh and flip me off in sync. *Nerds.*

Genin reaches into a red satin purse strapped over his shoulder and pulls out a small tube.

"Is that... a blow dart?" I ask. I hope it is. If this guy can live in a jungle, I'm sure he can handle a snake. I think. I hope. Oh, boy, do, I hope.

The cobra surveys Verity and me, tongue flicking from its mouth, testing our fear. My heart thumps, my hands tingle, and I can't breathe. *God, Genin, please kill this thing!*

Barbara rushes into the room, accompanied by a cook. Both scream when they see the snake.

"Go get Reggie!" Barbara yells. "Tell him Bennie's pet cobra escaped and we need a shovel!"

Bennie's pet cobra? Is she for real? What sort of freak foster parents let a kid keep a deadly ass snake?!

There's movement behind a thick curtain to my right. To my surprise, it's Bennie, poking his head out. How long has he been there? And what is he doing? He ducks down, crawls under the table to the sideboard, then stands in front of the cobra doing a funny sway, making the snake focus on him instead of us.

Two things happen at once. Bennie snatches the cobra just behind the head, and Genin blows a dart out of a bamboo looking tube that breaks a beautiful crystal vase into a gazillion pieces, splashing water all over us.

Bennie glares at Genin for only a moment, then he turns to me. He stares into my eyes like he's straining to see what's inside. It makes me feel… funny. Like I've met him before somewhere. But I've never even been to England.

"Ha! You *missed*!" says Priyanka.

Genin shrugs. "This blow dart gun's not like my other one," he says. "It's not broken in yet. It's stiff."

"Unlike your wiener," says Fensig.

Pa Ling gives him a high five.

Genin points the blow dart at the boys, and they run from the dining room, laughing. He gives chase. "At least I have a sausage log!" he yells. "You two got stuck with Slim Jim's."

Bennie takes off as well. Still holding the snake, he goes straight to the front doors. From my vantage point on top of the table, I watch him through the window, the snake now draped over his shoulders, a reptilian shawl on what is no doubt the strangest kid I've ever barely met. He crosses the yard and disappears into the woods.

"That was a fucking *cobra*!" I say.

Verity nods.

Staring now at broken chards of glass, I shudder and feel sick. Broken pieces of glass capture my reflection and stare back. I turn away.

Dr. Evelyn chooses this moment to stroll into the dining room, holding a small clump of fresh-cut daisies and sunflowers. She surveys our chaos, the broken glass and upturned juice. And of course, at Verity and me, who still shake together on the table top. For the first time, I notice that Verity somehow got a piece of pancake stuck to the top of her head.

"Who is responsible for this mess?" Dr. Evelyn asks.

Everyone points to Verity and me, except for Saratu, who's staring with rapt attention at a spot just above my head. I glance up but see nothing.

Dr. Evelyn fixes her disapproving gaze on Verity and me. "Ladies," she says, "your first order of business will be cleaning up this bloody mess."

"But… Bennie… there was a cobra…" Verity protests.

"I wonder if that's what killed Sarge last night," Priyanka says.

My head swivels toward Priyanka. "What? Sarge was killed?" I ask in shocked disbelief. "The German shepherd?"

Priyanka nods. "Rakito said the soldiers found him in the field just outside the gate early this morning. His handler's pretty broken up about it."

Dr. Evelyn thwacks her flowers on the back of a chair. Bright white and yellow petals explode outward and float like miniature parachutes into the syrup drops on the table. "Accountability begins today," she snaps. "Empowered women control themselves and *think*—not react."

Chapter 5

FIELD WORK & WORRY

The sun peeks over a small ridge on Plum Hook Bay, spying on us, creeping over rows of thigh-high sweet corn near a farm field we harvest. It's rays gently tap my forearm while I pluck tomatoes with Verity in a garden bigger than Parmatown Mall. I'm breathing fresh morning air, which inflates my brain cells—and makes me think too much.

I've been here one full week. So far, it's chores, workouts, and classes. But we do get some free time, so I looked for Sarge's grave and found it under one of the king-size weeping willow trees next to the path we run—right where I'd been picking clovers until Reggie left me at the gate. Sarge's handler lays flowers there every day; I wait for the soldier to wipe his eyes and leave before I visit and lay my own. I cry too but I don't let anybody see. I don't know how Sarge died. When I ask about it, everyone shrugs and mumbles something about "natural causes." I can't help but suspect Dr. Evelyn had something to do with this dog's death.

I pinch firm tomatoes from wiry vines and toss them into a basket. Eight years have skated by since my grandma died—since I last saw my mom—and it's been ten years since my dad went missing in Vietnam. Still, daylight greets me each morning, oblivious to the uncertainty that is my life. It makes me feel sad if I think about it too much.

I try to remember what my family looks like, but I don't have any pictures. The photos got lost during abrupt moves to new foster homes. I guess nobody thought to pack a photo or two for me or maybe my former foster parents felt that my having pictures of my parents weren't necessary.

My memory of 'family' is and an out-of-focus patchwork of snippets that fade more each day. Sometimes I dream about my dad, though. He's always dressed in camouflage, U.S. Army nametag visible, his head enveloped in gray smoke, so I can't see his face.

Picking vegetables gives me time to think—perhaps too much time to think. I'm not used to nobody yelling at me the way Rosie always did. Is this what might be called peace? If so, I'm not sure how much of it I can stand. The calmness of it all makes me feel uneasy, as if a dam somewhere along the line of normalcy might break, and we'll all get swept away. Maybe it's because chaos has ruled my life for so long, I don't know how to get comfortable, unlike these other foster kids who seem way more at ease, even if they do seem a bit heavy on the geek.

I lean forward on my knees, stretch in cat-like fashion, and look toward an adjacent field where a lone tree strains its weighty, twisted branches up to embrace a cloudless sky. I wonder if this unique looking tree, with its nearly symmetrical spiral limbs, ever feels out of place surrounded by much shorter rows of green corn that stand at attention like soldiers in formation—their neat rows forced upon a once wild prairie that's been tilled under for the sake of 'progress'. Why was the tree spared? Does the tree now feel singled out for inspection because it's taller than the rest, tangled, and conspicuous? Maybe it grieves as the sole tree survivor? Do trees even think?

I arrange my harvest of blood-red fruit into big round wheat-colored wicker baskets that Reggie occasionally confiscates for Barbara's outdoor cauldron. I never thought a fresh tomato could be as pretty and appealing as my red shoes. Barbara and Priyanka squish the bulbous fleshy perfection out of each tomato and pour it into Mason jars, which they boil, seal and store on shelves in the cellar pantry.

Across the garden from us, Rakito and Genin toss soil-covered potatoes into a green wheelbarrow Pa Ling pushes behind them. Fensig examines each potato and dusts it off with a rag. I learned today that potatoes don't get hosed off with water like tomatoes, or they'll rot in the damp basement storage bin. I also learned that nobody likes to go into the basement. Verity says its *creepy* down there.

Tetana and Saratu crawl along their knees, earthy patches of soil sticking to their clothes as they strip the strawberry patch of its final bounty. Saratu eats more than she picks, but Tetana doesn't complain. Occasionally checking on Saratu behind her, Tetana smiles and shakes her head.

The only kids who aren't here are Bennie and Jade. Why do they get a pass out of all the grunt work? That's unfair. And where are they, anyway? I haven't seen either of them since the incident with the cobra in the dining room last week. They don't come to class, either. I make a mental note to find them and spy on them, so maybe I can figure out how to get out of chores too. I still don't understand what's going on here, or what the purpose is of gathering a bunch of traumatized kids together behind razor-wire fence at a NASA site fronting as a farm.

I slide a cherry tomato across the front of my Rolling Stones T-shirt and plop it into my mouth. It pops under my teeth, its innards splashing around my tongue, tasting cool and sweet. I hope this shit is safe to eat.

I also hope Katie's doing okay. I wonder what she's up to right now—and I wish I'd had the chance to say goodbye. Poor Katie. She was completely freaked out when I left her at the Trail's End Motel and ran away from my mess. She told me to get lost in the cracks of Cleveland until she could figure out what to do. I waited. Why didn't she come get me like she said she would?

And why has no one here ever mentioned what happened with Rosie? Usually if people are dead, other people, like cops and caseworkers, have a lot of questions about who did it and why. But it's as if everything got sealed up in a jar just like these tomatoes will soon be. I haven't mentioned anything about Katie, or about the lady in the pale blue robes, and I won't bring it up unless they do.

Verity kneels behind me, the silver cross at the end of her Wednesday rosary twisting now and then over crumbled lumps of upturned soil as she bends low to pluck tomatoes from underneath the largest plants. Can any of these kids become my friends, like Katie? Friendship and foster kids don't usually mesh—it's like trying to pair plaid with polka dots—but Katie and I clicked, bound together by the blight of a parasitic plague named Rosie. Together, we shared a life jacket against the inevitable current of cruelty that threatened to sweep us away without warning.

A small pulse of pain grows between my eyes. I think too much.

I tug at the buckeyes in my front pocket to ensure they're secure, then scan the woods along the field line. I'll have to figure out the boundaries of this place. Maybe there's a map in the library. But as I reach down to take a swig of water from the gallon plastic jug at my feet, I notice the sky stretch just enough to reveal a glint of silver behind it, as if it's been stretched too tight and torn a small seam. The atmosphere peels back, only for an instant, to reveal a vast space of dark sky littered with so many glinting stars that it sucks the breath from me.

Feeling slightly dizzy, I sway, then recover.

"You okay?" Verity asks.

Her question startles me. I didn't think anyone was watching.

"Yeah. Why?"

"You just look as if you've seen a ghost, that's all."

Whatever I thought I saw is gone now; "normalcy" returned. Maybe it was lightheadedness from standing up too fast.

"I'm fine," I say.

Verity squeezes some doubt at me through squinted eyes but continues to arrange small pyramids of tomatoes on the ground. I get back to work moving them into baskets. The wind decides to kick up a fuss, tags us with dusty gusts, retreats to calmness, and repeats.

A flash of movement near the lone tree in the cornfield pilfers my attention from tomato picking—and she's standing right there, about a hundred yards away! It's Blue Robes Lady from that awful day in my motel room! Her golden hair free falls to her ankles. I blink, shake my head, and look again. She watches us. She smiles and puts her index finger to her lips, telling me to shush from alerting my tomato picking cohorts to her presence.

I quickly and nervously rubberneck my head around to see if Reggie or the other kids notice her too. They don't. And when I glance back—the lady is gone!

I shake off an instant shiver. Am I hallucinating? Seeing things nobody else does only means one thing: I'm getting sick like my mom. The church people said it would happen. I heard them. "The apple doesn't fall far from the tree," they said.

Saratu stands and faces the field where I'd been looking. The crisp breeze causes her wrap to dance at the hemline. Did she see the lady too? If Saratu saw Blue Robes Lady, that would make me feel better—but then again, Saratu's a very strange kid, so maybe not *that* much better.

She lightly steps over two rows of strawberries and tomatoes, stops about a foot in front of me—violating my personal space—opens her arms, and lunges in to give me a long hug.

I'm so stunned I can't hug back. My arms go limp, like withering tomato vines, and the water jug sloshes in my right hand.

She releases me.

Saratu lightly places *her* index finger in the middle of my forehead, and gives it three light taps, as if timidly pressing a doorbell to my mind and hoping somebody's home. She kisses the back of my soil-coated hand. Everyone stops working to look at us, bewildered stares on their faces. But Saratu merely returns to her row and starts gathering berries again as if she never stopped and the hug never happened.

Verity steps up beside me. "What the hell was that all about?" She takes the water jug from my hand, wipes the rim with a clean bandana from her pocket, and takes a gulp.

"Beats the shit out of me," I say.

"Weird."

I nod. My headache has retreated, but now I have a lump in my gut. Something is wrong. It isn't Saratu. It's the air. No. Not the air. It's a *vibe*—the energy around here feels *off*—negative.

Tetana and Fensig both stand up. They look at the sky and then at one another. "Rain is coming," Tetana says.

Fensig looks out over the horizon and drops an entire armful of potatoes on the ground.

"Fensig?" Reggie asks, a look of concern riding along the dusty lines on his face.

"Big storm coming," Fensig says. "Air pressure's dropping. Fast. But something's not right. The air is… different. Storm's going to blow through rough and strong. We'll need to secure the barn door. Look. The horses are already heading in. They know."

A dozen skittish horses trot together back to the sturdy red barn at the bottom of the hill. They nudge and push one another to slip through the door and into the safety of their stables.

Menace.

Dread.

Evil.

Another uncontrollable shiver.

Shadows of low rolling, ever-increasing negative energy sweep over me. Something dark and unseen seems to weave through this open space, pressing into my chest, and stealing my breath bits at a time. I battle against the urge to sprint from this oppressive feeling, this intangible coldness that searches among us. Why the panic? It's a storm, for Christ's sake—nothing to be afraid of. It's not like I haven't successfully managed my share of severe weather. The hairs on my forearm and my head lift.

"What the fuck?" Verity asks and points as everyone stares at me. "Your hair! You look like a punk rocker!"

"Or a mad scientist," Tetana says.

Years ago, just before my grandma died, lightning struck the edge of my grandmother's porch while I sang songs on her bench swing. The static in the air lifted my hair and the bolt of electricity momentarily stole my sight and voice and punched me so hard I was catapulted to the other side of the house. I, a defiant eight-year-old at the time, regained my footing and cursed Mother Nature for daring to interrupt my sold-out imaginary concert.

"Okay, kids," Reggie says, steering away the other kid's stares, as he removes his glasses and wipes his forehead with a navy-blue bandana. He slips his straw hat back on above skipping-stone eyes that scan the sky. "You heard him. Let's get these last crates in and get out of the field so we aren't struck by lightning."

I turn to Verity, who's still laughing at my freakish standing on end hair. "How does Fensig know there's a storm coming?"

"He senses changes in the earth's atmosphere and is very sensitive to electromagnetic fields. Says it's to do with his being from Greenland. He told me it feels like sparks dancing on his skin."

"Stop laughing," I say. But I find comfort in Fensig's weirdness—maybe because it makes me feel more normal for seeing Blue Robes Lady—and for having 'cable-ready' hair.

Dry dirt swirls at our feet and dead leaves tumble by, stampeding away. The temperature swiftly drops a few degrees and a cold chill sweeps through my T-shirt. I stiffen into an unexpected shiver when my hair drops back into place. And then another whirl of air spins by—and this one carries voices. And not *our* voices. Hushed whispers hover above us on the wind, chattering low, like the fuzz of radio waves. I strain to hear words, but the whistle, pop, and crackle interferes, and for the most part, all I can catch are incomprehensible jumbles of foreign chatter. In the end, I make out only one sentence: *"Let not one Lamb enter a den of lions alone."*

What the hell is that supposed to mean?

We scan the sky, wide-eyed and silent, all of us looking up and around, hearing the same thing, until the eerie voices fade toward the lone tree in the cornfield, where three bright cylindrical beams of light, one at a time, pulse into each side of the trunk.

"Look at that!" Priyanka yells.

So, I'm not alone in seeing this light or hearing *these* voices. It's either a mass hallucination or it's real. And it looks and feels real—solid as a billiard ball, this phenomena to which we've all been exposed.

"Run," I say to Verity.

We leave behind nature's bounty and our garden tools just as plumes of dark gray clouds move in from the east, like gallons of crude oil suddenly being spilled into a previously turquoise sea, and it blots out both the sun and my fleeting moment of too much peace.

Silver pitchforks of lightning jab the sky. The lone tree's branches sweep and sway, keeping time with the whipping wind, but I see no sign of Blue Robes Lady.

Bouncing into the house through the kitchen door, we laugh loudly, I suspect, to appear brave—but in reality, we are infused with confusion, a bit of fear, likely some ozone and ions, and adrenaline. Rain sizzles on the rooftop.

I take my turn scrubbing away the soil on my arms in the battered steel farm sink, then sneak away from the others and meander through the wide halls of this labyrinth house. Into the bowels of the darkened library, I go, to research *paranoid schizophrenia*.

A few minutes later, Verity steps in. She looks around to make sure I'm alone, then closes the doors behind her.

I quickly flip the book shut and slide it under some other books piled next to me on the desk, so she can't tell what I'm reading. "What?"

"Please tell me you heard whispers on the wind too," she says.

Bzzzt. The lights dim and flicker before the electricity goes out.

Verity screams.

Again, we're in the dark.

Chapter 6

"SHHH!"

"What do you think they really do on the other side of this place?" I ask Verity.

"I don't know, and I don't care right now," she says through the darkness. "Did you hear voices above our heads in the field?"

"Nope."

"Liar."

The backup generators moan and kick on, bringing a comfortable glow back to the library.

"Looks like we have some light again," I say. My gaze strays to the piano behind Verity, and I wonder what it might be like to play again. But I won't. I'm not ready to glide a single finger across any keys. That's lost to me right now, like my family.

"We may have light, but we're sure kept in the dark without answers around here," Verity grumbles. "And you aren't being very level with me, either." She folds her arms and rolls her head in a little circle around her neck, giving me a glare that might make a bunny wince but not much else.

A throb brews between my eyes. This off-again-on-again headache pesters me. I wish I could send it back to the Trail's End Motel where it started—just banish it, along with the unpleasant memories of that place.

"What do you mean?" I ask.

Verity's hand hooks around her hip as she walks around the desk. She gives the books a shove, and some of them topple onto the floor with a bang.

"Hey!" I say, both surprised and irritated by her unexpected gutsiness. "What are you doing?"

"Oh, come on! You're not being straight with me. What are you hiding?" She scans the remaining books on the desk, trying to figure out which subject held my interest.

"People are entitled to privacy in this country," I say. "Stay out of my business."

Thunder rumbles outside and rain patters so loudly against the windows it sounds like someone's dumping a bag of marbles on the granite floor upstairs. Candles flicker on the fireplace mantel. The rain, the candles, the piano… it's comfort. I like this library.

Though I like it better when I'm alone.

"Don't think you'll get away with hiding your visions from me," Verity says. "You're seeing things we don't. I know you are. Something's up with you, *tifi*."

Tifi. It's Haitian for "girlie"; Verity's heritage slips through when she gets annoyed. A small smile moves to my lips before I realize the gravity of my situation—that I may be a lifetime loony-bin candidate like my mom. But how does Verity know I hallucinate?

"Everybody heard those voices in the garden," Verity continues. "They're all talking about it. Some say it was the spirits of Native Americans who used to live here. You're lying when you say you didn't hear them. And I think you're also seeing stuff we're not seeing, too. I saw you in the garden, looking at that tree. What is it that you see?"

"Where's Bennie?" I ask, trying to change the subject, surprised that she caught me mid-vision.

"How the hell should I know? I hardly ever see that little freak. Why? What does he have to do with this?"

"Where does Dr. Sterling go every day?"

"To the NASA side of the farm." Verity folds her arms across her chest and gives me an accusatory glare. "To work. Stop trying to change the subject. I'm just as smart as you are, you know—in a different way."

"Why do you think they brought us here?"

Verity looks down at the desk. Lightning illuminates her face as she thinks. "I assume it's to assess our adjustment after trauma or something. Or maybe just to restore us—you know, readjust us to society."

I raise an eyebrow. "Do you really think that Bennie, a kid who plays with cobras, could ever be 'readjusted to society'?"

We giggle. Thunder rolls over our heads. It's not threatening, but almost melodic now. I rub the spot between my eyebrows as I feel a light sheet of tiredness pull over me.

"Do you think they knew exactly who we were when they brought us here?" I ask.

"Sometimes."

"Have you ever felt like you didn't belong when you were out there? In the real world, I mean?" I ask Verity.

For once, I'm relieved to be hidden behind heavily guarded gates. I'm unable to escape, I think, but the real world can't get to me either. And I can't decide now if I want to leave this place or not. Everyone keeps telling me that I'm free to go whenever I please, but I don't test their words because other than Cleveland, I really have no place to go—except maybe to Katie's, but after what happened I don't even know if she's still there anymore—and then there's the question of food. On the streets of Cleveland, I survived mostly on junk food I was able to steal from convenience stores. Receiving guaranteed daily doses of homecooked meals from Barbara's kitchen is, admittedly, loads less stressful than living like a rat and wondering from where I'll steal my next bag of Frito's.

"The world is delusional," Verity answers while my mind shifts back to the topic. "But yes, I've had those feelings—that I don't belong in the world. Once, in fourth grade, I used crayons to color fake bruises on my stomach in art class. Later that day, I clutched my stomach and faked a collapse in the communion line during church service."

"Why?" I ask.

"I didn't want to spend another afternoon numbly thumbing every bead on a rosary or mumbling memorized prayers for a Catholic May crowning, I wanted to get sent home, so I could play outside."

She looks away sadly, toward nothing in particular, before she continues. "The priest and a couple of nuns carried me into a courtyard, and there I was, under a cross, looking up at Jesus, and he was looking down at me. The priest—I remember his green and gold robes—sprinkled holy water on my tummy, and I rubbed it until the phony bruises disappeared. Everyone thought it was a miracle. But they also accused my mother of child abuse. Hadn't thought of that. But suddenly, an old beam inside the church gave way, bringing down half of the concrete ceiling. People died that day. Others were left crippled. The congregation freaked and thought I was possessed. The priests held a meeting and they told my mother it was probably best if we never came back. I didn't realize…"

"That you could wield that kind of power," I say.

"Yeah—but it wasn't *me* who made the church fall." Verity shakes her head as if still trying to sort it all out. "I felt something inside when that holy water hit me— a good spirit passing through."

"But that's good, no?"

"Evil was chasing it." Verity shivers. She walks to a club chair, picks up a throw, and wraps it around her shoulders before plunking herself down into the oversized cushions.

"What do you mean by that?" I ask.

"There's something here, on this Earth, I mean. It's here to harm people and its getting stronger."

"You mean like the devil or something?"

"Worse," she says.

Now it's my turn to shiver because I've felt it too, for years, but never shared it with anyone. "Do you ever see things? Like …maybe angels or ghosts?" I ask.

"Never any angels, but I'm pretty sure I saw a ghost in Haiti once when I was about five, right after my dad went to prison."

"Saratu—she has something special in her too," I say. "I sense it. Does what I'm saying make sense to you?"

Verity nods. "If we're the light bulbs, she's the entire electric company. An old soul, as my Grann used to say. Saratu's enlightened."

"Yet on some levels she seems so simple," I say. "Definitely golden-hearted, but enlightened? You think so?"

"Reggie once told me that enlightenment *is* simple."

"*Shhhh!*" a voice hisses. A male voice. "Stop talking!"

Verity and I startle like horses who's bridles are yanked. She throws the blanket over her head and curls into a tight fetal position. I clench my fists and search for the source of the voice. I scope the vents, bookcases, the big globe in the corner.

For the first time I really notice the gorgeous mahogany details in the architecture above our heads: precisely carved, almost lifelike flowers, vines, miniature angels, and a red cardinal on weighty, spiraling branches that stretch partway across the ceiling to fade above the grand piano into a universe of cloudy stars. But I don't see anyone.

My sprouting headache makes it tough to think straight, but I decide to play it cool and act as if I didn't hear any voice at all.

"Verity, are you okay?" I say. "What's wrong?"

"Huh? Are you crazy?" she hiss-whispers from under the blanket.

I peel back a small portion of her cover and wink for her to play along. "Maybe they brought us here because we have something they want."

"Like what?" Verity asks, yanking the scrap of throw I hold from my grasp and white-knuckling it to her chest. She shivers as she looks up into the corners of the library, like she expects bats to come swooping down at any moment.

"Gifts," I say.

"What, like our brains or something?"

"Who knows?"

"*Shhhh!*" the voice says again, annoyed and much louder this time. A book drops from one of the bookcases behind us, where the ladder leans.

"Oh, hell no!" Verity says and retreats back under the blanket. I've lost her.

I slowly approach the shelf, and with a gulp, I tentatively climb three steps up the ladder.

A small pale hand reaches out from behind the autographed Mark Twain hardcover series (he's one of my favorite authors) and tries to grab my wrist. But I latch on first and yank hard on a nearly hairless forearm—Bennie's. He and the books come crashing to the floor in a loud series of thuds before he scrambles under the piano, his dark curls bouncing. I jump down from the ladder and follow.

Bennie turns around and stares directly and uncomfortably long into my eyes. His gaze is penetrating—somehow beyond his years—bold yet cautious, like an over-steeped cup of Dr. Evelyn's Earl Grey tea. I'm overwhelmed by a feeling of knowing him without having any idea how or where or why and it's as if his eyes search my soul for a solution or an answer to something.

"Shhh! You must be quiet," he says in an accent that's not quite British. It's not Irish either. Australian? No. South African? No, not that. What is it? I can't tell. It's an accent I recognize but can't quite place.

"They hear you," he says matter-of-factly. "I scrambled the bugs in your room, but I can't find the bugs they put in the library. Don't talk here. It's a library anyway, so you have to be quiet. And don't worry, you'll play the piano again someday."

How does he know about that? And he talks? *They* spy? Who *they*? My room is *bugged*? I mentally review all the late-night and early-morning noises I've made and the private things I've shared with Verity. I cringe.

I have so many questions, so I start with the first. "How do you know—"

I don't even finish asking before Bennie plants a quick kiss on my forehead and dashes from under the piano in a flurry and disappears. I climb out, trying to see where he went, maybe some secret passageway or something, but he's vanished—like steam—here one moment and gone the next. How the hell did he do that?

I turn to Verity, to see what her reaction is to all of this, and suddenly I'm woozy. The room wobbles; my balance shifts. I'm floating on the inside of a bubble, here but not here. The library splits in two, and now I'm no longer in the library but on the other side of it, standing on the edge of a steep cliff that cuts this room in half.

I'm cold.

Below me, waves thrash and hurl themselves on jagged salt-washed boulders, giving birth to piles of foam that slide off and bob through small crevices into dark caves. Above me, a billion stars dim and pulse, pearlescent glitter from the gods strewn about this strange sky like confetti.

In my hand I cradle the gold handle of a glinting crystal sword decorated with a single red feather. The blade is engraved with strange hieroglyphic-like symbols that fade and reappear.

"Hey! What the hell just happened?" Verity says snapping her fingers next to my ear. "What's wrong with you? Who ran out of here?"

My vision snaps shut. My headache is gone too.

I blink and look dumbly toward her. A small tremble shakes off the final remnants of my hallucination as I return to the present, exhausted, bewildered, anxiety spinning through me like a tornado that touches down and retreats again.

"Whoa," Verity says as she catches me in a sway. "You better sit down before you fall down."

"Shh," I whisper. "Help me pick up these books and let's talk in my room. I do see things, Verity, but they make no sense to me."

Chapter 7

EYE SCREAM

"What's *his* problem?" I ask.

Barbara and I stand by the dining room window, watching the Schwann's deliveryman honk his horn out front, a signal he's ordered to use before he drops off our monthly supply of groceries.

The men in black suits appear, order the man out from his refrigerated truck, and pat him down. A cigarette dangles from the edge of his lips as if it's about to commit suicide and his head nervously bobs and wobbles. One of the suits inspects the unloaded pallets while another signs some paper on the shaky deliveryman's clipboard. The driver practically dives back into his truck, squeals the tires, and spins around the mermen fountain so he can get the hell out of here.

Dr. Sterling told me that the suits are federal agents. He didn't say what kind. I think they look like robotic goobers with stone faces. They're sort of creepy, and they never speak to us. All they do is stand around and look out—for what, I don't know. In fact, the Schwann's guy is the first outsider I've seen inside this overly patrolled 'paradise'.

"New delivery guy," Barbara says as she wipes her hands on her apron. "Likely a local from town who's heard all the rumors."

"What rumors?" Verity asks.

After Bennie scared us in the library last night, Verity and I swore blood sisterhood by pricking our index fingers with one of her sewing needles and touching our palms together. Now Verity, like Katie, is my 'blood sister' too. Of course, we only did this after searching for bugs in my room—not that we found any. But we've joined forces to find out why we're here. Whether we do that by asking probing questions or just paying closer attention, we're going to find out the truth about what's *really* going on at Plum Hook Bay.

We take a break from polishing silver. I despise it because the cleaner smells a little like juvenile jail and reminds me of being locked up, but on the other hand, I *have* been able to snatch two table settings, which I've stashed in a secret hiding place—along with three cups of spare change I've nicked from Dr. Evelyn's office. Once I've saved enough, I'm going to blow the hell out of here.

The first thing I'll do is visit Katie in Cleveland. Maybe I'll even ask her to come with me, to India, so she doesn't have to rely on her married old geezer for sustenance. I can tell she doesn't really like sex with him and only goes along with it for the money. But Katie claims the guy isn't all that bad, that she's his "mistress," a 'geisha girl' who's found a patron. Whatever. She can gloss it up all she wants, but it's disgusting for super old dudes to use their wealth and power to troll after young girls. This guy forces Katie to give him what he feels entitled to take—and she's way more valuable than his cash.

"Hey!" Verity yells in my ear. "You still with us?"

Barbara looks at me suspiciously.

"Sorry," I say. "I was thinking."

Barbara rearranges some fresh flowers in a vase on the sideboard before continuing her story. "Some farmers around here think this land is cursed. Decades ago, they found Native American burial fields at Plum Hook Bay and claim that bad luck arrived once their graves got disturbed."

Verity moves a little closer to me, brushing her shoulder up against mine.

I give her a gentle shove to launch her out of my personal space. "Get off me," I say. "What's wrong with you?"

She ignores me.

"Why did the locals disturb the graves?" Verity asks Barbara.

Barbara picks up a glass and wipes it with her towel. "They were clearing land for farming and I suppose they had no idea it was an ancient burial site. There are some books in the library about how the Natives were buried sitting up, all facing West. Their skeletons were so large the farmers could use the skulls as helmets."

Verity lets out a low whistle, her eyes wide, rapt with attention toward Barbara.

"Do they have any photos?" I ask. "As proof? Or is this just a legend?"

"Some drawings in the books," Barbara answers. "Locals at the time claimed these Natives were each between seven and ten feet tall."

"I think she's right. This place is haunted," Verity says as she shakes her head and shivers, folding her arms.

I roll my eyes.

"What? You don't believe in ghosts?" Verity now clutches the oversized *Mr. T* style gold rosary around her neck.

Where in the world does Verity score all of this religious paraphernalia? This girl must own at least fifty different colored rosaries, and that doesn't even begin to count her collection of crystal balls, tarot cards, a Ouija board, magic wands, the dried herbs hanging upside down in her room, or the small arsenal of gold chalices she pilfered from Catholic Churches all over Chicago.

I don't really believe in ghosts…or even God, for that matter, but it *would* be sort of cool to see an extra-large dead Indian—as long as I'm not alone when it happens. Who on this farm could I trust to help me dig one up? Not Verity. She'd piss her pants before we even got to the edge of the property line.

"I know you heard those spirit voices on the wind last night in the garden," Verity says to me accusingly.

I give her a 'watch yourself' look because I *thought* we swore 'sisterhood' and now she brings up the incident in front of Barbara— yet all the kids talked about it earlier at breakfast this morning, so it isn't really as if Verity broke our bond, I just don't feel like talking about unexplainable phenomena in front of adults who possess both the ability and the authority to force feed us more meds.

"I heard something, but who says they were spirits? And I don't believe in God either."

Barbara and Verity both gasp. Barbara shakes her head. "Child,

God is real." She makes the sign of the cross, kisses a freshly folded napkin, and looks up at the ceiling before she murmurs a quick prayer.

"You mean God is real like the Easter Bunny is real?" I say. "Whatever. If God were real, he wouldn't let bad things happen—like kids going into foster care or bloody wars, or parents going M.I.A. in Vietnam."

"*Bloody* wars?" Barbara shakes her head again. "You sound just like Bennie when you fake his accent. That's funny. But honey, that's not God. That's Satan on Earth." She looks toward the ceiling again, silently pleading, I think, for God to save my soul.

"Ghosts are real too," Verity says. "I've seen them. Ain't you ever seen a ghost or heard God talk to you?"

The less I give these people to use against me, the better. Although I did share with Verity last night that I sometimes experience *visions*. I was too afraid to tell her that I think I'm really hallucinating. And I left out the part about being visited by some strange spirit lady in pale blue robes that nobody else can see. It's not that I don't want Verity to know—it's that, I feel like if I talk with her about it, it'll only solidify the fact that I've inherited my mom's awful disease. Paranoid schizophrenia.

"I think when you see ghosts or talk to God it's called delusional," I say.

Verity shakes her head now too. She picks up a fork and dips it hard into the tarnish remover, and it makes me wish we could go swimming instead. "Never mind the heathen in our midst, Barbara. What else do they say goes on here?"

I frown. "I'm not a heathen. I just feel that people who rely on religion are powerless or maybe lack better ideas, so they just 'go along' and allow themselves to be led like sheep. I've read the Bible—my grandmother made me—and it makes no sense. People use religion as a prop to sell dull points and to keep other people in line—like Pharisees hawking doves and gold on church steps to make their greed appear holy."

"Child? Why are you so angry with God?" Barbara asks.

I drop a fork on the table and sigh. "I'm not angry with God, Miss Barbara. I don't believe *He* exists. It's sort of hard to get mad at a myth."

I'm talking too much. My grandma once told me, *"When you're outnumbered by idiots, keep your mouth shut."*

Barbara looks a bit disappointed with my answer but I don't care. She has no idea what it's like to be me. I don't like people cramming God into my brain as if I'm supposed to numbly and dumbly just accept Him the way a bucket is forced to carry water.

"There's others around here, old timers, who claim UFO's once visited Plum Hook when they were kids," Barbara says, changing the subject. "Personally, I think most of them took too many nips of moonshine." She laughs. Then she furrows her brow and gets serious. "We once had a housekeeper named Gladys who said she saw a nine-foot-tall white Bigfoot following her to the gate. Can you imagine?" She looks at Verity, I suspect to get a rise out of her, but not at me.

Sure enough, Verity's eyes widen, and she reaches into her jeans pocket where I know she thumbs a bright yellow chicken foot she carries around for good luck.

"You believe in God, and Gladys believes in Bigfoot. What's the difference?" I ask, a huff of annoyance escaping me. "It's absurd to heave one's life before the altar of an invisible man—some scraggly, robe-clad, hippie-looking dude who rides around on puffy clouds ready to hurl lightning bolts."

"Sam, stop it," Verity says. "You're upsetting Miss Barbara. She's moved on from the God debate."

But I don't listen. "In every picture I've ever seen of God, he looks like a guy who belongs in a Cheech and Chong movie—ready to roll a fat boy ," I say. "You know what bothers me?" I slowly wave a butter knife in the air. "We are expected to love our neighbor as much as we love ourselves, but we don't. And people are actually stupid enough to believe that God takes sides during wars, elections, or football games! I don't believe in God because humans are hypocrites and God is nothing but a fool's game."

"God is real. Bigfoot is a myth," Barbara says, sadly looking down at the table and biting her bottom lip. Is she about to cry? If so, it makes me feel sort of bad for my rant—but then again, people who believe in God get a pass to rant all they want about Him, while people who don't believe are supposed to simply shut up or get skewered as infidels.

"God is about as real as Darth Vader," I reply.

Barbara shakes her head in frustration and fixes me with a critical stare that seems focused hard enough to summon Jesus Christ himself, but instead of arguing, she continues with her story about the housekeeper. "Anyway. The first thing Gladys did was steal booze from the liquor cabinet and get completely blitzed, and then she rang the sheriff to come nose around. Dr. Evelyn and my poor Reggie were none too happy."

"She was drunk?" Verity asks, giving me a dirty look that silently says *shut your trap, Sam.* "In the daytime?"

"Very drunk." Barbara nods. "Unfortunately, a lot of folks in these backwater towns have bad habits that tend to run higher than their IQs."

"Did she get arrested for stealing the booze?" I ask.

"No, but she lost her job. That was punishment enough."

Good to know they don't arrest people for stealing, they just make them leave. I file this tidbit away in my head and relent on the God debate. Verity wins this one for being smarter than I am, for getting great intel out of Barbara.

"Is that the whole story?" Verity asks.

"No—actually, it gets worse," Barbara says. "Poor thing, bless her heart. About a week after she was fired, both Gladys and her husband got killed in a car accident. The state highway patrol said she was drunk driving on their way to visit her sister in Dayton at Wright-Patterson Air Force base. Her sister's husband was a colonel there."

"The maid just happened to conveniently die a week after getting fired?" I ask. "Doesn't that just seem a little coincidental to you two?"

"Gladys wasn't *murdered*, if that's what you're suggesting," Barbara says. "She was a closet alcoholic who made the poor choice to drink and drive."

The screen door in the kitchen creaks opens, then snaps shut. Verity jumps and clutches my arm.

"Oh my God, Verity," I groan. "Stop acting like such a chickenshit."

Barbara tosses me a sanctimonious look. I've received a lot of those looks over the years so I dump this one, with all the others, into the landfill part of my mind. "I'm going to pray for you," she says.

"Go ahead, waste your time." I cock my head toward Verity. "Prayer is about as effective as her late-night Christian-Pagan-voodoo chants." I peel Verity's fingers from my wrist.

Barbara shakes her head, exasperated with me. I suppose I'm not an easy case for her, but she has no idea what I've gone through, other than what she might have read in my file, which isn't really me at all—but other people's incorrect and subjective opinions put to paper. And if she thinks God is good therapy for me, I swear I'll manifest into a demon child she won't soon forget.

Heavy footsteps thump across the weathered boards, and Reggie steps into the dining room, his massive chest filling the door frame. He removes his frayed straw hat, places it gently on the table, and rests his thumbs under the straps of denim overalls. "I ruined a tractor tire trying to flatten some weeds along a fence line," he says to Barbara. "I have to go to the John Deere store and pick up another. Want to get out of here for a while?"

"Why, Mr. Chorley, are you asking me on a date to the tractor store? You certainly know how to treat a lady," Barbara jokes. "I'd like to go, but I have these two lovely lasses in my charge."

"Well, the girls could come too, and we could stop at Toft's when I'm done," he says. "Provided they finish polishing the rest of that silver to your approval." Reggie squints at me as if he's got no choice but to take me along. I glare back at him.

"Oh, that sounds like a great plan," Barbara says. She neatly puts the small stacks of finished silver back into the big wooden storage box. And then she looks up at Reggie, and her expression turns serious. "Samantha does not believe in our good Lord," she says.

"Is that so?" Reggie looks me over, rocking back on his work boots a little, then gives me a wink and a smile. I roll my eyes. He chuckles softly, and it makes me frown, which makes him smile even more, forging soft crinkles around his eyes, which sparkle like freshly poured tar under the sun whenever he looks at his wife.

"Mmm-hmm," Barbara says as she stuffs a thick arm into an emerald-green-knitted sweater Reggie holds up for her. "I told Dr. Evelyn these kids need church on Sunday, but she says no. Reggie, we have to pray for Sam's soul."

"Okay," he says.

That's it? They're going to *pray* for me? Ha! Praying is a copout to avoid heavy lifting. I guess if Barbara folds her hands together, she escapes the hard labor of actually having to do something that offers me real comfort and service. But she does cook for me so there's that—and she makes sure my clothes are clean. "Planting seeds," I think she called it. Whatever. Religious bullshit never takes root in me. My soul soil is too fertilized with skepticism to keep pests like her from gnawing through what little heart I have left.

And I'm thankful to Dr. Evelyn for having sense enough not to force me into a church pew. Maybe she doesn't believe in God either. I'll have to ask her.

"What's Toft's?" Verity and I ask in unison. High-five.

"You like ice cream?" Reggie asks.

Verity nods.

"That depends," I say. "Do we get to order what we want?"

"Yes," he says, "you can get what you please. Toft's is the best damn ice cream parlor on the planet. Well, it's actually a dairy farm, but they make ice cream."

"Reggie," says Barbara, "please mind your cursing around these young ladies. Lord knows we got enough swearing going on outside with all those Army soldiers—we don't need to be dragging it into the house too, like filthy mud on our tongues."

"Yes, ma'am."

We buff the rest of the silver in record time, then climb into the bed of Reggie's vintage blue Ford. Reggie opens the passenger door for

Barbara, takes her hand, and helps her into the cab, giving her big, floral-dress-covered ass a soft pat as she climbs up. As he comes back around to the driver's side of the truck, he pauses and motions with a finger for me to come closer .

"Don't argue with Miss Barbara about God," he says in a low voice. "Lots of good folk need something to believe in. It keeps them going, if you know what I mean, like a tonic for the soul. What harm does it cause for you, if her beliefs bring her peace?"

Reggie's voice is kind, unlike the tone he took with me on the golf cart when I refused to run. Seems that when it comes to his wife, he has a soft spot.

I shrug. I suppose if simpletons want to believe in God it makes no difference to me, yet still, I'm a bit irritated. "She can have her beliefs, but I can't have mine?"

"That's not what I said. Besides, you won't ever win a God argument with people who insist He exists, so why waste your breath? As for your beliefs, those are always yours—even if you decide to give up on them or change them someday."

"Okay," I say. He's right about one thing: there's no point in arguing. I'll never change Barbara's mind and she'll never change mine. And I'm afraid if I buck him again, he might kick me out of the truck and I won't get ice cream—and that would definitely suck.

Reggie playfully slaps the top of my hand. I slide it away.

We drive through miles of empty land that alternate between farm fields, woods, and open flat slabs of dried cracked mud that remind me of the tanned animal hides that Plum Hook soldiers sometimes dry out by the barn after a deer hunt.

The landscape chases us like a wide brush of green and brown strokes sweeping across a canvas. Freshly cut clover invades my nostrils, and the scent makes me think of my dad, though I don't know why. The wind whips my hair, its strands lashing my cheeks, and I lift my face to the warmth of the sun.

As we enter Sandusky, I notice the avenues run diagonally, like a pinwheel, toward Lake Erie. Who designs a city where every street meets in the middle? We pass manicured lawns and dogs, and in the distance, I spot fancy Victorian homes lining the lakeshore and it reminds me of royalty flanking the edge of a chessboard.

Reggie abruptly slows to carousel speed so he doesn't ruin his truck tires on the sewer-lid-sized potholes or accidently cannonball Verity and me from his truck bed. He drives into the not-so-nice part of Sandusky, a messy nest of abject poverty, a neighborhood that looks too much like Brook Park Road and makes my stomach suddenly hurt.

Cramped western-style mom-and-pop shops slump next to exhausted wood-frame houses with chipped paint and saggy porches. Sheets of plastic or sun-faded bedsheets are taped over missing windows. Tired-looking cars wilt in rust baths on balding dirt driveways.

I lean around to Reggie's open window and tap a finger on the exposed elbow he rests there. "Wow, you turn a corner in this town and things sure go downhill fast," I say.

"Welcome to your personal tour of Lifestyles of the Damned and Desperate," he says. "Lots of good folks in these neighborhoods just trying to make it the best they can. I grew up close by and use this road as a shortcut."

I don't tell Reggie that this pigsty we're passing through is actually better than the neighborhood I used to live in with Rosie but I am a little surprised that he grew up close by. He doesn't look or act like someone who ever had to suffer on these streets.

We turn onto Washington Street, which ends at an amazing park exploding with fireworks of flowers—red, yellow, orange, white, and pink roses in full bloom. The park overlooks Lake Erie, where large ships slide lazily across a summer horizon. I briefly wish I were on one of them, maybe sailing to India, in charge of my own life, not at the mercy of other's schedules, plans, or time, but free to roam and wander at will.

A bronze fountain—a statue of a little boy in a newsboy cap, much like the one Reggie wears, inspects a leaky boot—and reminds me of Bennie.

Reggie pulls into a parking space in front of a three-story limestone building. I don't see any tractors or ice cream.

"Where are you going?" Verity yells, the flush of summer sun and sweat glistening on her caramel cheeks, her elbows comfortably propped on the rail of the truck bed.

"Need to pick something up really quick at my club. I'll only be a minute," he says, disappearing inside. The etching over the door reads, *Science Lodge #50*. I have no idea what a science lodge is and I'm a little surprised that Reggie's smart enough to belong to one.

He comes strolling back out almost as fast as he went in, except now he holds a large manila envelope. I wonder what's in there. Cash? Jewels? Anything I can add to my stash back at Plum Hook?

"What's in the envelope?" I ask.

"Cobras," he says with a smirk.

"Seriously," I say. "Whatcha got?"

"Nothing that concerns you at the moment, Pandora."

I slump into the bed of the truck, a little irritated he won't trust me. But why should he? I don't do much to merit trust—in fact I mostly find ways to vandalize someone's confidence in me, particularly when challenged.

Case in point: I'll find out what's in that envelope later—when he's not looking.

Toft's Ice Cream Shop lies outside Sandusky city limits on Venice Road. The hot pink neon lights, the colorful movie posters, and the wall of mirrors enthrall me. I wish I could fit all of this cheery décor into my bedroom at Plum Hook. I feel like I'm roaming around inside a bubble gum machine—or going into Bob's Newsstand with my grandma on Sundays after church, where she'd buy my favorite orange push-up pop and a comic book. Bob would pat his palm lightly against the top of my head and was always impressed that my grandma had taught me how to read so young.

"I want a banana split!" Verity says as she jumps up on a red vinyl stool in front of the polished glass ice cream case. This makes her sound much younger than sixteen, but foster kids are a little stunted when it comes to those things of which we've been deprived—like love and ice cream.

I order a banana split too.

As a freckled kid in a funny white paper hat and red-striped shirt scoops our ice cream into green glass boats, Verity and I watch the television that rests atop a refrigerator in the corner. It's blaring Madonna's "Borderline" video on MTV. Verity and I think Madonna is the bomb. We've copied her style from the teen magazines Dr. Evelyn brings us. Barbara thinks they're inappropriate—"the Devil's work" as well as "too sexist"—but Dr. Evelyn says we're too seasoned with life to be treated like "vestal virgins." So, Verity and I each wear one fingerless purple lace glove and one big silver cross earring in our right lobes—both items split from a pair.

Verity usually clads herself in the color purple to honor Prince, her favorite musician, and her ancestors from Africa, she says. She told me that Prince made stars out of both Sheila E. and Vanity 6. "I'll be Verity 7," she laughs.

I don't have a favorite artist, except for maybe a local group called, "The Michael Stanley Band." It's not because I don't like music, it's just that music is too beautiful for me to pick just one artist or one song. I love it all—classical, jazz, hard rock, pop, rap. I even greatly enjoy the gospel choirs Barbara sometimes blasts on the portable kitchen radio above the sink—but I don't tell her that.

The ice cream guy hands over my banana split. I'll save the red cherry on top for last.

Some old farmer wearing a navy plaid shirt and a straw-hat yells at the ice cream guy. "Young man! You turn that channel this instant. I've got grandkids here, and *that*," he says, pointing to the TV, "is the devil's music!"

The boy's face turns about as red as the stripes on his uniform.

The old farmer turns half of his glare—he has a lazy eye—at me and Verity, as if daring us to challenge him. His cheeks are pockmarked, like crumbling asphalt, his lips forced down, no doubt baited by the sinkers of boredom, bigotry, and field labor. "Damn group home kids get no guidance and ain't got no hope for growin' up decent," he grumbles. "Can't mix sinners among good God-fearin' folk. It's like tryin' to mix oil and water."

The clink of tin spoons on glass abruptly stops. Everyone's attention now centers on us, the rare and unusual intruders in what I assume is the rigid daily sameness of their lives. The farmer's sermon has served as a moment of cohesion for them: single out someone different, generate a little excitement, and make everyone else feel like part of the crowd.

Anger overrides my grandmother's advice about keeping quiet when surrounded by fools. Verity has given similar advice. She says that when I feel my temper flare I should ask, "What would Jesus do?" I told her I'd rather ask, "What would Paul the apostle do—before he was allegedly saved?" Paul, the self-described chief sinner, would likely kick this farmer's ass.

"Listen, you cross-eyed Bible-thumping fool," I say. "We were here first, and we're watching MTV."

"Samantha!" Barbara gasps. "You have to respect your elders."

"Why?" I ask. "He's not respecting us. He's *rude*."

"You could use some lessons in manners, young lady," the old farmer says, one boot forward, leaning his weight toward me. "And a switch taken to your backside, so you don't go out of the house looking l-l-l-like a wh-wh-whore."

Verity swivels side to side on her stool and stares at the black-and-white tile. Reggie and Barbara stand in silent shock, as if someone painted them in place with glue. The ice cream dude's mouth is wide open, ready for flies.

But I'm not backing down. Not an inch. "I can't imagine being a corn-shucking, quilt-making church wife who spits twenty ungrateful kids out of her vagina for an ugly pig farmer like you. I'd require daily nips of moonshine to keep my s-s-s-sanity," I say, mimicking his stutter.

The farmer looks like he's going to shit himself. I'm guessing no one has ever challenged this old geezer before, especially not a girl. He turns to Reggie. "Boy," he says, "you need to teach her a thing or two about manners."

I don't wait to see how Reggie will respond to this. "What about *your* manners, you chauvinistic old coot?" I ask. "Do you have a cow patty for brains? He's not your *boy*."

"Samantha!" Barbara hisses. I see she's trying to remain lady-like; her fists gripped at her sides, holding back her own demons. But this coot doesn't deserve her decorum. Doesn't she see that? Where's her outrage?

"Why, Barbara?" I ask. "Why do *I* get shushed and have to say sorry, but this fool gets a pass—especially when he started it?" I turn to Reggie to plead my case. "He called me a whore and he called you *boy*."

"Well, if the shoe fits," the farmer says.

Reggie steps between the farmer and me. "Sam, apologize to the man." His voice is deep and there go my arm hairs standing at attention again.

I'd like to wipe off this old farmer's smug look with a mule kick to his nut sack.

"Apologize or forget the banana split," Reggie says calmly, and way too maturely for my taste. His eyes narrow into mine.

I stare daggers back at him, hand on my hip, tipped slightly forward. It's not right for either of us to take this guy's bullshit and just stand down.

"She wouldn't even get the ice cream in the first place if *I* were her father," says the farmer. "But it's obvious you can't be her father. She's probably *her* kid, with that ginger hair," he says, waving a dismissive hand toward Barbara, "given the example she's settin' comin' in here on the arm of a nigger."

Reggie sucks in his cheeks and tightens his fists, but he still doesn't say anything. He actually looks down at the ground. *You've got to be kidding me.* Reggie could pummel this guy forward into 1985—or back to before the Civil War, where he belongs. I've had bad things said about me but hearing someone call Reggie that awful name and cut down Barbara for loving him… it makes me want to start slinging ice cream. And worse.

I step in front of Reggie. "If I were your kid, I'd drink poison or add it your ice cream, you lousy sheep fucker."

The farmer reaches out to snap me up by the collar. But Reggie grabs the farmer's flimsy tissue-pink forearm and stares the man in the eye, a storm of challenge threatening our previously tranquil Toft's outing.

I'm so mad right now I could spit staples into this old farmer's forehead. But the thing is, he deserves some credit for not hiding his prejudice behind phony tolerance, the way most people do, the sort of people who tip their hat but not their hand and say, "Nice day" but mutter *chink, nigger, white trash*, or *spic* under their breath. This is part of why I'm an atheist, because the hidden vitriol of the human spirit always trumps grace. Every. Single. Time.

But I also don't want to see Reggie get into trouble because I'm standing up to a backwater bigot—even if I'm doing it for both of us. So, I add my hand on the farmer's arm too, higher than Reggie's, and I mutter the words I've been asked to say. "I'm sorry." *But I don't mean it, you ugly coot.* "I'm a foster kid and I got trouble learnin' how to treat people nice." *Butthole.*

I look at the farmer and then at Reggie with fake pleading eyes. Reggie looks as if he'll puke, and Barbara rolls her eyes because she knows I'm acting. Verity's head hangs so low it practically touches the counter. I think she's keeping her fear tucked inside so she won't burst with inappropriate laughter.

Finally, the farmer shakes himself loose from Reggie and me.

I look up at Reggie. "Please don't beat me too hard again, Mr. Fred, like you done last time I was rude to my elders," I say. I use the fake name to throw this guy off. Then I turn back to the farmer. "Will you pray for me?" I ask. "Please?"

Barbara puts her hand over her mouth and shakes her head.

"That's better," the farmer says. "At least I know you're workin' on her, Fred. Keep takin' that switch to her, boy. Spare the rod, spoil the child, God says." Then he pointedly eyes Barbara up and down. He clearly disapproves of the mixed-race marriage and makes zero effort to hide his disgust. This perplexes me. All this drama over skin color? I'll never understand why humans insist on rating people by color or culture through thick-headed bad behavior like this.

The ice cream guy quickly changes the channel to the afternoon news and stares awkwardly into the glass case, avoiding everyone's eye contact. He's not comfortable picking a side, and I can't help but think his willful cowardice might even make him worse than the farmer.

The old farmer walks over to a booth to rejoin his grandkids, his lesson of prejudice now wormed into their brains right alongside the blood of Christ, to be passed around with white pride by the next generation.

I return to my red stool and dig my spoon into my banana, twisting my wrist to scoop up gooey sweetness.

The news plays above me. "*New developments in a story we broke in late June. Authorities say the Trail's End Motel Murders have been ruled a murder-suicide after the discovery of a child prostitution ring.*"

A banana slice rests midair on a spoon to my mouth.

My other hand slowly freezes as it cradles the frosty glass boat holding my treat.

My eyes are transfixed to the television screen.

And ice cream curdles in my throat, suddenly tasting sour.

"*Authorities say all children have been accounted for in this bizarre story of a criminal love triangle involving three suspects, all deceased...*"

A spokeswoman for the Cleveland Police Department takes up the entire thirteen-inch black-and-white screen sitting atop the refrigerator, and she mentions something about how all the Trail's End Motel kids are thriving in new homes. Then the screen switches to a view of old camera footage: a crowd held back by yellow police tape in front of the motel. In the background stands Cameron the Cop, alongside Dr. Awoudi. I squint for a better look, but the image changes too quickly, moving on to a latex-gloved detective carrying a plastic bag with a broken green beer bottle inside—out of *my* old room.

Shit.

I'm in trouble.

I need to get out of here.

Fast.

Run!

No. Stay calm, Sam.

Think.

Breathe.

"*...the bodies of three suspects were discovered inside a motel room of one of the alleged perpetrators...*"

My brain goes on spin cycle. A coroner tells the investigative reporter that three people died at the scene as a result of gunshot wounds, a murder-suicide.

Gunshot wounds? There was no gun! I was there. And a murder-suicide? Why is he saying this? And when he said "perpetrator"... did he mean *me*?

My heart flips and flops so fast I imagine it exploding out of my chest and all over my ice cream.

Three photos pop up on the TV screen, side by side.

Rosie.

Some guy.

And...

"KATIE!"

My banana boat drops to the floor in slow motion. I fall forward after it, my jean-clad knees grinding into the shards of shattered green glass.

"No. No, no. ***Nooooo!***"

I rock back and forth, blood leaking through denim and staining the shiny black-and-white tile.

Verity kneels beside me.

"Can't," I sob. "Not possible."

"Let me take her," Reggie says to Verity. He scoops me into his barrel arms.

I want to die. To be dead. Like Katie.

"What are the odds of *that* happening?" Reggie says to Barbara.

"God works in funny ways," Barbara says. "Let's get her home."

"Not Katie!" I scream. *"Oh, God, I'd never hurt her!"*

My cheeks feel cattle-prod hot, tears blur my vision, and my head begins to throb again. Shock and grief flush reason and decorum from my system, rendering me impervious to social mores; I sob louder than the TV news as Reggie carries me to the door, cradling me in his arms, a limp baby under the weight of Katie's murder.

The old farmer rushes over to Barbara, in some effort to both shoo us out and, no doubt, to be nosy. "Nobody is safe," he says. "The devil can even possess people at Toft's Ice Cream Parlor. I'll pray for her, and for you, ma'am."

"Oh, never mind that, you old fool," I hear Barbara reply. Warm summer air from outside sweeps across my forehead. "Just move your sheep-fucking ass out of our way before she grows fangs and I clobber you into next week!"

Chapter 8

STERLING MOON

Slobber stains the front of Reggie's coveralls as he carries my sorry sobbing ass upstairs to my room. I don't really remember much of the ride home. Verity clumps behind us, the *clippity-clop* of her wooden clogs adding to the hurt that already batters my head and heart. Saratu, Priyanka, and Tetana peek around a corner.

It's official. I have no place to go. I'm a case number without a solution, a mendicant pariah dependent upon the state for welfare. There is nothing left for me in Cleveland—or anywhere. Katie is dead.

"I didn't do it," I say. "I didn't kill Katie."

"I know, child, I know." Reggie looks ahead, confident in his direction. "It hurts worse than hellfire to lose a friend. You haven't served in the military, but you and Katie were sure fighting a war back in Cleveland."

Barbara calls Dr. Sterling and Dr. Evelyn. Kids gather at my bedroom door, but Barbara shoos them away and shuts it tight. Verity refuses to leave. She removes my red heels and lacy blue bobby socks, then gets out of the way. She stands in the corner by the full-length mirror, kissing her rosary and thumbing its beads calculator-quick, no doubt adding up the hits and misses of my life.

Dr. Sterling fetches a doctor from the NASA side of the farm, and this dude wearing a white lab coat gives me a shot in the shoulder. Ouch. It makes me loopy, and then I sleep, my mind dominated by a vivid dream.

Verity is ushered toward the door of my room by Dr. Evelyn, who gives her a trinket, as if Verity's some sort of a lab mouse getting a pellet for doing something good.

"Dis 'ting you do, does not feel right," Verity says to Dr. Evelyn.

"Don't worry," Dr. Evelyn replies. *"You'll do your friend and your new country a great service, and it will be years before you must make your decision. I'll be with you every step of the way."*

Both of them look back at me lying on this bed. I try to ask what they're up to, but my body and voice won't work. People in black suits look me over. They ask questions I can't answer, questions about national security, space and time, and I don't feel frightened as much as I am amused. Dr. Evelyn's eyes peer out over a blue paper mask before I feel a tug and a pull "down there." She holds my hand. What are they doing? It doesn't hurt.

Saratu floats above me like an angel draped in rippling orange robes, spying. She looks sad, but angry too, and I've never felt anger from her before. Yet… I don't think she's upset with me. No. She's definitely not. She gets swallowed into the ceiling and disappears.

My dream abruptly switches to a fox running through a snow-covered field. The fox paws at the frozen ground by a tree that hasn't yet lost its leaves. Shots are fired, and the fox lies dead, blood draining from its head, flowing neon pink into a nearby hole. A kit pokes her ears out of the hole, and she, too, cries.

Whoosh!

I zoom through a dark tunnel toward a light and a blue glowing figure. I'm overwhelmed by a feeling of peace, until I'm sucked out of the tunnel—forced to leave because some 'light beings' whatever they are, tell me telepathically that I must go back—because the conduit is closing—yet there is still time, still good 'out there' they say—and to beware of false prophets bearing specious gifts. I don't know what this means.

Another dream has Bennie sitting on my bed with a gray wolf at his feet. He holds my hand as tears stream down his cheeks. Bennie slowly slides a warm palm across my bare belly and it feels oddly good, and I allow this.

The final dream—or maybe it's the same skittish pulp fiction dream just jumping around my brain like a ricocheting bullet—has me pulling Reggie's manila envelope out from under my bed. Inside is a piece of paper with writing. It reads: *L. Ian Windsor, Sr. Oxford, UK.*

Nuclear engineer. DOB: December 8, 1925. MIA. The Tesla Papers. Time leap free energy propulsion. Bigot List Clearance granted 1920.

What is, 'Bigot List Clearance?'

I wake.

Shiver.

It's dark. And I'm alone.

No manila envelopes, gray wolves, or Bennie's lurk in my room. It's empty except for me and my breath—and the sweat condensing from my chest and forehead that moistens the back of my neck and hair.

A sterling full moon strains to stretch its beams through my window. They land on the ache in my abdomen, where a cramp and trickle force me to moan. I click the lamp on the nightstand, reach down, and examine my blood-soaked fingers. Relief. I shuffle to the bathroom for personal protection and a glass of water. I climb back into bed and turn out the light.

Katie is dead. And I'm not pregnant.

Another headache keeps me company as I drift again between dreams and fitful wakefulness.

Someone stands in my doorway.

I sit up.

This is no dream.

"Verity?"

No answer.

"Dr. Evelyn?"

A figure of blue light watches. It has the shape of a person... but it's not really a person. Yet it isn't a ghost either. I'm sure of that because it leans in the doorway, arms folded, void of eyes, or hair, or gender, but instead, appears as a soft glowing silhouette of a not-quite person. Weird symbols leap from its appendages and float toward me—and I wonder if this 'Being' is trying to communicate by emitting an encrypted photonic message that I'm somehow supposed to decipher. The strange but beautiful 'light being' gradually fades away.

Wax-warm peace cascades from the top of my head down through my toes. Pulling the covers over my shoulders, I curl into a fetal position and now feeling euphoric, allowing sleep to drag me back into her abyss.

A little girl with dark curls and honey-hazel eyes meets me at the Skye gate. She wears a red cape and carries a gold-handled crystal-quartz sword with a red feather.

She won't let me through unless I know the password.

Chapter 9

DOLMA KARPO

It's almost the end of July. I've hardly left my room in the three weeks since I learned Katie died. Verity tries to talk with me but I'm not in the mood. She's been keeping up with our research—asking questions, gathering information to share about this place, what they really do, why we're here. But I need private time to tidy this tornado in my head.

How could I have not heard about Katie's murder in Cleveland? Why didn't Dr. Awoudi or the Dennison's or the Chorley's mention it? And what is with this whole murder-suicide by gun cover-up? There was no gun. I know what happened.

As comfortable and fun as Plum Hook Bay might be at times, when it isn't oddly strange, is that nobody has asked me a single question since I've arrived here, about Rosie's murder. Zip. Zilch. Zero. And I find that weird.

There's a rustling sound at my closed bedroom door.

Saratu and the others keep sliding tightly folded triangular notes under it. I kick a big pile of their concern out of the way and some of the notes spin like wobbly flying saucers across the granite floor.

Though I'll admit this only to myself, I'm secretly delighted that Rosie is dead. Thin the herd, I say, especially if the jackals are cruel and depraved. But Katie… she had a decent soul. She could make forest animals want to be her friend. Who would kill *her*?

I scan my face in the bathroom mirror. I've looked worse. My cheeks are dented enough to double as pencil holders, and my hips can't keep my jeans in place without a rope. I've lost at least ten pounds, and I needed that weight.

What I can't figure out either, is why the police haven't shown up here to ask questions. The news showed Cleveland detectives in *my* room at the motel. Surely, they must be curious. My feet pace the bedroom, and my brain runs laps, trying to figure this out. I want to ask Dr. Evelyn about the "murder-suicide," but I can't—I can't risk arming her with information she may not have. All I know is, Katie was very much alive when I bolted from the motel that day. Freaked out, yes, but upright and breathing. And there was no gun.

My head hurts. Tiny orbs of light float before me. If I didn't need my eyes, I might rip them out today because the painful throbbing I feel behind them pushes up against my internal demons and drives them to the surface. No. Not today. No more tears. I'm tired of crying. Besides, emotions get in the way of efficiency. I'd do well to remember that. I turn it off like a faucet.

Tap tap tap. "It's me. Verity."

"Come in."

The bedroom door cracks, and one lime-green eye peeks through. "You decent?"

"Yes."

She swings the door wide open, and she's not alone. In strolls the entire foreign ragtag version of the Muppet brigade: Priyanka, Genin, Rakito, Saratu, Tetana, Fensig, and Pa-Ling.

Priyanka nudges Rakito, who holds a bouquet of white and yellow roses.

"Deese from us all," he says as he flops them toward me .

"The white roses mean sympathy and the yellow ones stand for friendship," Tetana says.

I hesitantly take the bouquet from Rakito's hand and sniff deeply. It's gloriously fresh and alive, unlike Katie or my soul—a small whiff of both sanity and scent uploaded into my scrambled brain.

Nobody ever gave me flowers before. I bite my lip. *Don't let them see you cry!*

"We don't want you rotting in here," Priyanka says. "We are very sorry to hear about your friend."

Everyone nods.

I think about Katie rotting in a coffin, beautiful blue eyes now likely empty sockets being eaten out by maggots. I want to cry again but can't, because I think I've drained the entire reservoir of tears from my head. "Thank you."

Their thoughtfulness also makes me want to hug them, but I know I won't.

Verity smiles, and I assume she understands what I'm going through even without knowing all the details, because friends just seem to learn your vibe. I eye up the others, studying faces to gain glimpses into their thoughts. They look down, up, and around, and their fidgeting hands lightly rub arms locked across chests, or stuff themselves into tight pockets. They don't know exactly what to say, but their awkward sincerity, which I also *feel*, is a sign that I can relax.

"Come swim with us today," Genin says at last.

"Swim?"

"In the river," Verity says. "It's hot outside, and if I have to watch Pa Ling and Fensig roast any more ants under a magnifying glass, I'll go nuts!"

"That's just gross," Tetana says.

The boys laugh and punch each other in the shoulder, as if burning innocent insects alive for sport makes them medal-worthy. Buttheads. I'm about ready to decline their well-meaning invitation when Saratu silently cuts through the others, takes my hand, smiles, and points to the door. "Big sister. You go."

The room snaps quiet and jaws drop. Every head swivels toward Saratu as if she just farted and shattered a vase. As far as I know, those are the first words she's said since she's been here.

"You can talk!" Verity shouts.

Saratu's dark fingers intertwine with my pale ones. It reminds me of a Reese's peanut butter cup. I give her a tight hug. She hugs back and taps my shoulder like a bongo drum. It makes me laugh. But then...

I groan and bend over, cradling my temples in my palms.

Genin takes my arm and helps me sit down on the bed. "What's wrong?"

"Bad headache," I say. "On and off since before I got here."

Saratu puts her index finger between my eyes again, but she doesn't tap three times the way she did in the field. "Bad," she says. She shakes her head. "Bad people."

"What do you mean?" I ask.

Genin moves between us and nudges her out of the way. "I have a cure for headaches. Here." He holds up a fat joint.

"Man, where did you get that?" says Rakito. "You know that's the one drug they don't want us doing."

"I know, right?" Genin grins. "What's up with that anyway? They'll let us try LSD, shrooms, or blow, but we can't smoke pot? That doesn't even make sense."

LSD? This is news to me. I never thought to ask for that—or shrooms. And where are they getting this stuff? I know Barbara can't be serving it, because she summons Jesus Christ whenever we even request a drink from the bar, along with giving us a big sermon about booze being the devil's brew. Of course, when we tell Dr. Evelyn, she lightly scolds Miss Barbara for interfering with her "work".

Perhaps Dr. Evelyn is studying the effects of alcohol on teenage brains—or maybe she's looking into new therapies to cure us enough so we may reenter society. But why can't we smoke weed?

"Tibetans have cultivated cannabis for centuries," Tetana says. "Monks consider it sacred."

"Native Americans use weed in their rituals, and for medicine too," Verity adds.

Saratu cocks her head at the pale Asian lady painting in my room, then leans in closely to inspect the Asian lady's arsenal of eyes. I want to ask her what she means by "bad people." Does she mean people like Rosie, whose woeful treatment is imprinted on my brain? Maybe Saratu is able to channel memories from people's heads, sort of like Dr. Evelyn's done with me a couple of times.

Saratu looks at her palms, checks out the soles of her feet, touches her forehead with a finger. She stretches her arms to the ceiling and opens them wide like a flower in slow bloom, spreading and wiggling her fingers. Then she bows to the Asian lady painting. What is it with this kid? She seems to nonchalantly walk over or around life's hot sands, literally and figuratively—to just 'let go' and ignore drama, unlike the rest of us who seem mired in scrutiny, personal pain, and distrust.

"Saratu, what are you doing?" I ask.

"She's acknowledging the greatness of Dolma Karpo," says Tetana.

"Dolma who?"

"The second-most-worshipped deity in Tibetan Buddhism," Verity says. "She's known as 'White Tara,' the liberator—a healer of bodies and souls."

"Verity, why didn't you tell me about White Tara before?" I ask. "You've been in my room at least a million times and never mentioned this."

Verity shrugs. "I don't know. You never asked."

Tetana interrupts us. "Saratu insisted this painting be brought to your room before you got here."

"Why?" I ask.

"I have no idea. She used to meditate in front of it every day when it hung in the dining room, then one day she just got up, tugged on Dr. Evelyn's sleeve, and pointed upstairs. It was Bennie who somehow read her mind. He whispered in Dr. Sterling's ear that Saratu wanted the painting brought here. God knows how he figured that out. As Reggie moved it, she hovered close the whole way, wouldn't allow a black suit or a soldier near it either. She totally spazzed out that day."

I look Saratu up and down for any remnants of spazzy she might have left. She seems calm. So, I look at the painting too. "What's up with all the eyes on this… White Tara?"

"Dolma sees everything, including your mind," says Tetana.

Saratu points to the painting. "Good." She then points to the joint Genin holds. "Good too."

Everyone laughs.

"Light it up," I say. "If she says it's good, I'm game. But where'd you get it?"

Genin pulls out a red lighter. "Believe it or not, we got it from Reggie. He grows his own pot plants in the woods. We spied him throwing burlap bags full of ladybugs all over them a few weeks ago. He dried the leaves out, even made some oil from it, and stored it all in the barn."

"No way," I say. "Why would he smoke weed?"

"He probably just tells us he meditates, but he's really stoned off his ass!" Priyanka says smiling wide, her head rolling over on Rakito's shoulder.

The room erupts with laughter.

"I bet he sells it to the soldiers," says Pa Ling. "Maybe he's the secret drug dealer of Plum Hook!"

I doubt Reggie is either a weed smoker or a drug dealer, but I don't say that. I decide I'm going to research Mr. Reggie a bit more deeply— go recon.

But for now, I force a deep hit of dope into my lungs. I hold it to kickstart the hum of my high, all systems go, like the purr of a shiny new scooter, and then I release my choke. A cough and smoke come tumbling out of me along with my problems and my headache.

Thoughts of Katie give way to just being here, in the moment, following Saratu's lead.

Chapter 10

SHOULDER WARS

Twenty minutes into our trek through the woods, we climb a high slope along a footpath. Lake Erie is about three miles away, its foamy waves teasing the shoreline of Sandusky in an endless game of tag. As I absorb this pristine vista, a fleeting feeling of knowing every law of the universe—of being connected to every rock, tree, animal, and part of the sky—fizzles inside me. And then the tyranny of my left brain runs interference, forcing enlightenment to bid quick retreat.

Displaced razor-wire fence butts up against the fields in all directions, a reminder of civilization's unnatural intrusion upon Plum Hook Bay. But I still can't see the NASA side of the farm, the part none of us kids have been allowed to visit. It's purposely hidden by the tangled arms of pine trees, so dense that I briefly doubt that even an ant could belly-crawl through.

The Huron River, at least half a football field wide, slices right through the middle of this governmental land grab. Wild cherry trees post closely together on her banks, lined up at full attention for nature's parade, brimming of fruit, their branches bent eagerly toward the water, forming small leafy caves from overly loaded rich red cherries.

We dip into one of these "caves" for shade and privacy. Saratu, Verity, and I spread out a dark-green Army-issue wool blanket. It's scratchy against my legs, and I'm glad I don't have to sleep with it. It's almost as rough as the cheap sheets Rosie made me use—the irregular ones she'd buy at Bargain Barn.

Saratu plucks a few cherries from one of the branches, gently examines them, rubs them along the bright pink sheet she chose today, and pops them into her mouth one at a time. A trickle of wine-colored juice dribbles down her flawless extra-strong dark-chocolate chin.

Priyanka and Rakito make camp behind two beige boulders, away from us, hidden on their own blanket, a private party of two. I hear Priyanka giggle, and then I don't hear any sound from them at all. Those two fit together like pot and lid; sometimes they finish each other's sentences. Rakito pulls out Priyanka's chair for dinner and takes her hand to guide her over rocks, and she makes him special treats, like frosted cookies with his name on them, and helps him with some 'business plan' he has for returning to Africa.

I can't even imagine what that sort of love must be like. I can't keep a boyfriend longer than two months. Of course, most guys' moms wouldn't let them visit me at the Trail's End Motel. And I'm also sure boys were warned to stay far away from "a girl like me." Still, my loneliness and struggle to make a meaningful connection, like the one Priyanka and Rakito share, hurts. So, I stuff the bad feelings down with weed, sex, and attitude.

An unexpected lump grows in my throat. I shake my head to jumble the bad memories roaming around my brain, in the hope they'll go away. None of that matters now. My past is gone and my future uncertain.

Still, I'm surprised that it isn't even a big deal, except to Miss Barbara, that Priyanka and Rakito have sex. Everyone just expects them to marry as soon as they're old enough to defy Dr. Evelyn's wish that they go separately into the world and gain "life experience" first. Dr. Evelyn even gets birth control pills for Priyanka.

Dr. Evelyn says its unnatural to expect abstinence from teenagers once they've 'done the deed'. Dr. Evelyn refers to birth control as "vitamins" and says any of us girls can have them if we ask. Why can't other adults be this normal about teenage sex? Why does anyone make sex out to be some sort of grave and unforgivable sin where it's primarily the girls who are expected to feel shameful about it, and shunned, unless we're married, but the guys get a free pass and 'high-fives'?

Miss Barbara says it's because girls are supposed to be the guardians of male morality. I think this is an oversized crock of smelly shit disguised as Puritanism and designed to allow dirty old men off the hook when they cross the line with girls like me.

She also said that Reggie was her first and only 'love' and that she waited until her wedding night to lose her virginity. She didn't say whether or not Reggie did the same, but what is the big deal? Unless of course, that deep down in every society's psyche, maybe women really are nothing more than chattel.

The other kids strip down to their underwear and cannonball into the water, a symphony of splashes. Droplets hit us like buckshot, and laughter spreads.

Pa-Ling climbs out, arms hugged tightly across his tan gooseflesh chest. "It's frrreeeezing!" He yells.

"Ha! You got shrivel dick!" Fensig says, pointing at Pa Ling's underwear. "I can see the fruit of your loom!"

"Don't you mean root of his tomb?" Tetana jokes.

Pa Ling cups his guy parts with both hands, smiles, and shrugs, before diving sideways back into the water to dunk Fensig.

"Come on, girls!" Tetana says, swimming up to the river's edge. "Don't leave me alone with these two douchebags!" She splashes us, her cheeks pink, her eyes glistening with a late-morning summer high.

Saratu tumbles into the water, her sheet clinging to her like the fine stone-carved folds of a Roman statue.

Verity and I remove everything except for our bras and panties, and Verity tiptoes ahead of me into the ice-bucket-clear water.

I plunge my foot into the water's edge. It's so cold that for a moment I swear I could cut diamonds with my nipples. But my headache is gone, and I feel content. Happy, maybe? Is that possible? But Pa-Ling is right, the water's freezing!

Why would the river be this cold in August? A gentle current polishes tiny tan and slate-colored pebbles as gray crayfish—Ohio's redneck version of mini-lobsters—scuttle over my toes to get out of the way.

"*Brrrr!*" I shiver and yank my foot from the lazy current. Then, feeling impish, I push Verity. She screams, latches on to my arm, and takes me with her into the river.

We dive and resurface to float on our backs like otters, holding hands. Hot sun bakes my face and cool water washes over my skin, baptizing me against my problems, sinking them to the bottom of this muddy river we've stirred up, where they get squished between my toes, buried in the muck.

"Shoulder fight!" yells Fensig.

Genin swims to me. "Climb up around my neck and wrap your legs tight under my arms," he says.

Tetana climbs up on Fensig. "Come on! I *dare* you." She laughs. "They call it 'shoulder wars.'"

We get into position in chest-deep water. Tetana and I wrestle on top of the boys' shoulders until she falls over.

I win!

Verity then climbs up on Pa Ling, and I beat her too.

Saratu declines to play. She just watches us with serene bemusement from the river bank where she's propped up on an elbow, drying out.

Genin's hands cup my waist when I climb down, and he slowly rotates me to face him. His chest and shoulders feel like the granite floor in my room when I place my palms on his chest. Warmth swooshes through me. I smile and swim away, but not before he plants a quick half kiss that lands partly on my lip and mostly on my now tingly cheek.

"Ooooh!" Verity coos. "Genin and Samantha sittin' in a tree, K-I-S-S-I-N-G!"

Genin and I now float as far apart from each other as possible as pink flames of embarrassment smother my cheeks. I remind myself that this kid actually eats hairy spiders—and likes them. But I'm not sure why we both feel so shy. It isn't as if I've never PDA'd—made out with a guy in public, tongue and all—but I guess being in the great outdoors, so remote, among a few friends… well, it seems weirder to do now.

Priyanka and Rakito resurface from behind the boulder and toss themselves into the forgiving water. Priyanka swims to me and gently tosses a splash and a teasing smirk. "What is this I'm hearing about you and Genin?" She winks and dog paddles in a circle around me. She seems comfortable and non-competitive with the rest of us girls, which makes her easy to be around. My shoulders relax.

The boys high-five Rakito, but his eyes rarely stray from Priyanka. He looks at her as if she's a goddess in our pond. I wonder if somebody will ever look at me that way. It might be cool if I really like the guy, and it would definitely be completely creepy and stalker-ish if I don't. There's nothing worse than getting the wrong kind of attention from a repulsive sort of dude. And I know what that's like.

I shove those thoughts away. Today is too good to let the bad invade.

A flash of blond shows up at the edge of the riverbank in front of our cherry tree. She can't go unseen, Miss Prissy-Ass, Jade Sokolov, standing there in khaki shorts and a white tank top with a bow-and-arrow set strapped over her shoulder. Wisps of spider strand silk hair waft lightly around her face. She studies us in her stone-faced way, a beautiful half-angry statue about to call down the dark forces of wrath, I think, to drown us if she could.

"I play chicken fight," she says, pointing her bow at me.

Jade strips off her clothes, revealing lacy lavender panties and a "too small for her tits" matching bra. Her waist is tiny, her arms and legs toned. She reminds me of the naked ladies I once saw in a dirty men's magazine at Bob's Newsstand—only better. The boys' mouths drop open and their eyes stick on Jade like plump leeches, sucking up the animalistic energy that sparks the air with a discomforting swirl of teenage angst and runaway hormones.

Priyanka smacks Rakito so hard in the stomach it leaves a handprint, which isn't easy to do on black skin. I've never seen Priyanka wear jealousy so tight; the wrinkles of poached attention poke through her normally placid façade to draw an unmistakable frown between her eyes.

"Owwwww!" Rakito says, doubling over. He apologizes to Priyanka, and I can tell he means it. But seeing Jade practically naked, well—even a girl can't help but gawk at nature's masterpiece, a specimen of carefully sculpted ice, inside and out. Jade probably even shits frozen crystals.

I paddle toward Genin until a pang of jealousy zips through my stomach too, forcing me to tread lightly in both my heart and on the water.

"Genin," Jade says, "you be shoulder war partner?" She puts a fingertip to her lips and pauses to let the guys' gazes linger on her totally-perfect-make-me-want-to-puke frame before she dives in and swims over to him, popping up way too close.

He looks at her all loopy like a drunken tourist. Barf. I hate this chick. Evidently, she's been watching us in the woods and now seeks his attention to make me jealous. The worst part is, it's working.

Play it cool, Sam.

"Hell yeah!" Genin says way too fast and stupidly.

Lust-struck *moron*. Now I hate him, too.

Priyanka narrows her eyes until they could double as razors. "Rakito," she says, a bit too coolly. "Put Sam on your shoulders."

Our long fingers intertwine, Jade's and mine, as the two boys circle. Saratu chews up a small corner of her pink sheet while she watches from the riverbank, her attention focused. The others splash and cheer. I push, but can't budge, Jade—she's like a heavy door with something lodged behind it. Her forehead crashes against mine, and Fourth of July sparklers go off in my brain and enrage me. We spin. Her hand snatches fistfuls of my hair as we lock on, eye to eye.

Patoowee!

She spits right in the center of my face.

"I don't like it when you play with my toys," she hisses. "Nee-yet, I don't like share. You understood?"

Jade plucks me from Rakito's shoulders, and I tumble into the water defeated. When I come up for air, she cradles Genin's cheeks in her hands, taking her spoils.

Bitch.

"You cheating little whore!" Priyanka yells, atypical of her usual calm. "You can't spit and pull hair! That's so against the rules! Sam wins by default!"

"Yeah!" Verity says, lending support, hand on her hip for effect.

Jade turns to them and laughs. "If you say so." Then she looks toward the riverbank, alarmed. "Hey! Stop, freak witch!"

Saratu dangles Jade's bow over the river. She purposely drops it into the current, and Jade's weapon bobs slowly downriver before it goes under.

Pa Ling dives in to save Jade's stupid toys, but Jade swims straight at Saratu.

Saratu gets tangled in her sheet and falls backward on the slick bank when she struggles to get up and run. Jade reaches her, drags her into the water, and holds her under.

"Here is water," Jade says. "Maybe you find next time, so family won't die. Maybe you tell Sammy's friend Katie she says halo!"

Rage...

A fuzzy crackle in my head.

Is this the sound paranoid schizophrenia makes? I try to quiet the sparks and sputters popping off in my brain but my anger against Jade mounts like a hive of swarming, pissed off hornets.

In chest-deep water, I plant my feet against the muddy bottom and propel myself toward Jade, yanking her from Saratu, who resurfaces, chokes, coughs, and finally spits up water so she's able to breathe again.

Saratu's alive.

Thank God.

Priyanka, Tetana, Verity, and I help Saratu back to our blanket, but everyone stares at me, including Jade, and my nerves suddenly feel like overloaded electrical wires.

"How the hell did you jump that far so fast?" Genin asks. "That had to be like twenty feet you covered in two seconds."

I shrug. "I don't know."

"You cannonballed *out* of the water like a flying squirrel," Tetana adds, eyeing me suspiciously.

"Where is Pa Ling?" Verity interjects as she watches the water. "He hasn't come up for air."

We scan the river. The boys dive back in, comb the shoreline with their eyes, arms spread wide to feel for him under the murky river.

"Did he float downriver and get out somewhere else?" I ask, pressing down my panic.

"Pa Ling! Pa Ling! Where are you?" Fensig calls. Fear vibrates from his throat, and he tries to hide his accidental high-pitch crackle by deepening his voice an octave.

Five minutes pass.

Jade stands there like a tree stump, seemingly unbothered by Pa Ling's failure to resurface, which makes me even more pissed. "This is getting serious," I say to Priyanka and Verity. They nod and glance uncomfortably at each other.

I feel the worry emanating from their skin like a soft vibrational current, and it lightly lifts the hair on my forearms. The boys sound nervous and shrill as they call out for our friend, Pa Ling, their voices too high for their bulk.

Seven minutes.

Still no Pa Ling.

My hands tingle, and lightheadedness makes me want to faint again, like I did the day I came here, but I force myself to breathe and stay upright. The thought of another untimely death pours despair into my already skittish and shrinking heart.

Eight minutes.

Saratu strolls downriver, away from us, following the current. She taps her feet on the compacted, bare-brown bank every few yards. She backs up now and then and repeats.

"What is she doing?" Verity whispers.

"I think she's trying to locate Pa Ling using her feet the same way she tried to find water in the Sahara," I say.

"You leapt at Jade like a panther," she whispers. "How did you do that?"

"I don't know. I was angry."

"That wasn't even human," she hisses. "You scared the living shit out of me."

Nine minutes.

Ten minutes.

Fifteen minutes.

Murmurs of panic.

Sixteen minutes.

Saratu closes her eyes. She taps the soil with her toes. She backs up. She stops and points at swirling water moving around the large boulder in the middle of the river.

"He's there?" I ask.

Saratu nods.

I see nothing.

Please let me see him!

A mass of black hair, like the splayed wings of a dead crow, suddenly breaks the surface.

"Pa Ling!"

I dive in and grab his arm, yank him to me, and roll him over. I try to brace a leg on the muddy bottom, but it's too deep here, which surprises me. I arrive at the riverbank to drag his wiry but heavy frame onto solid ground as Verity gently takes his head into her hands.

Tetana yells to the boys downriver that we've got him as Verity begins to pound his chest. And all the while Jade just stands there as if she's watching a very boring movie and is about to flip the channel. Jerk.

"Pa Ling!" I shout. "Can you hear me? Oh my God, Pa Ling! Please answer me!"

I open his mouth with my fingers and put my lips over his to blow air into his lungs every time when Verity nods, after she thumps her palms fifteen times on his chest.

Tetana takes over for Verity. Thank God Reggie made us learn CPR even after we kept French-kissing the dummy just to piss Reggie off. He coated its lips with iodine and hot sauce and made us promise to take CPR seriously "or else."

Long fingers lace through my wet hair as Pa Ling embraces me, flips me under him, and shoves his tongue in my mouth.

Instinctively, I ram a knee into his balls. He howls in pain, clutches his wrinkly twins, sits upright and loudly laughs between coughs.

"You fucking little faker!" I yell.

He jumps up and high-fives the guys who've rejoined us.

I spit at the ground, trying to get his kiss germs off my lips.

"That isn't even funny," Tetana says. "You had us worried sick! But wait. Pa Ling? How badly did Sam injure your vagina?"

Everyone laughs. Pa Ling playfully punches Tetana in the shoulder, a soft-braided smile on his face.

"How do you do this? Stay under so long?" Rakito asks. "Magic?"

"Yeah, man, I'm with him," says Fensig. "Did you hide somewhere along the riverbank?"

"No," Pa Ling says. "My father taught me to swim before I could walk."

"But did he teach you to hold your breath for seventeen fucking minutes?" Fensig asks.

"Yes. It's in our blood. I'm part of the Sama To'Ongan tribe of Bongao—a Bajau. My feet barely touched dry land before I was brought to Plum Hook. I even had a pet shark, Loki. He'd let me hold his tail so we could free dive."

"Why would you befriend a *shark*?" Priyanka asks.

"It was our way. Bajau, we become like one with animals, all the same energy. But the government banned our dives when the commercial shrimp boats came, and we were forced to work for the shipping companies, checking their nets. Some of my tribe drowned in those nets, including my older brother."

Pa Ling looks out over the Huron River to avoid our faces, his smile gone, eyes darting like a fast-moving storm. "The sea changed. It's darker now, less forgiving, and less alive."

"Jesus Christ, man, I didn't know," Fensig says. "I'm sorry, dude. That's heavy."

"What happened to your parents?" I ask.

Pa-Ling shrugs. "I don't know. About a year ago our tribe was forced off the islands to work at sea. A relocation plan. One night my father pushed me overboard off a shrimp ship, a rusted-out hellhole—because he said he felt some sort of evil overtaking the boat. He told me to avoid the nets and swim for my life. I prayed very hard to Umboh Tuhan, Lord of the Ocean, for guidance back to our abandoned village. Loki helped me find my way. I lived mostly alone there for about eight months before Dr. Awoudi found me."

"'Mostly alone'?" Genin asks.

"I had the company of Barong," Pa Ling says.

Verity gasps. We turn to look at her.

"Well?" I ask impatiently, knowing she can hardly wait to spit it out. "Who is Barong?"

Pa Ling nods at her to tell us.

"In Indonesian mythology Barong is a panther-like creature. He's considered the king of spirits, leader of the hosts of good, and enemy of Raga, the demon queen," Verity says.

"Uh, are you okay dude?" Fensig asks Pa Ling, pretending to check his pulse.

Pa Ling yanks his wrist away. "She's right," he says frowning. "Barong is a tiger, my brother and my spirit child. He stays with me for life to protect me against Raga, the evil one."

I look at Genin and roll my eyes but he looks away. Does he actually believe in this shit?

Fensig pulls Pa-Ling toward him for a hug. I've never seen American boys hug like this. It's an embrace born of understanding and shared experience, like brothers, and rooted, I think, by deep bonds of friendship, which makes me feel envious. When I look at Genin again, he softly smiles at me, and it's an unexpected look of understanding and kindness so now it's my turn to look away when I feel myself blush.

We've all lost loved ones way too early, and with them, we've lost a part of ourselves, our heritage, our ancestors, and their lessons. They're now just unrecoverable memories that will get folded away in time, to die, just like our childhoods. That thought makes me feel closer to these kids. We've all had to swim through more sewage than most adults wade through in a lifetime.

"Queers," Tetana jokes, breaking the tension.

We laugh nervously as the boys pull apart and then lock palms above their heads in a show of brotherhood.

"You've explained *how* you stayed under so long, but not *why*," Fensig says to Pa Ling.

Pa-Ling shakes his wet hair like a dog. "There's a hole in the river."

"A hole?" Tetana asks.

"A tunnel. Maybe a cave," Pa-Ling says. "I went down about forty feet. There was a light down there, at least another thirty or more feet below me, but then the light went out and everything got dark."

We look at the large silent boulder. It's a thick, arrowhead-shaped rock about twenty-five feet high steering water around its base, a linebacker of limestones.

"Seriously, dude? A hole? And you had an opportunity to get into it but you didn't?" Fensig asks, a smile creeping across his lips at the joke, which makes Genin laugh a little.

"Weird," Rakito says. "Natural phenomenon?"

Pa-Ling shrugs. "I don't think so. Something is down there."

I shiver.

"What you think is down dere?" Rakito asks. His heavy African accent is a reliable sign of both his concern and curiosity.

"I wonder if it has to do with the NASA side of things," I say.

"It was definitely weird," Pa Ling says. "I couldn't get my bearings. If it wasn't for Saratu negotiating with whatever it was, I'm not sure I would have found the surface again."

"*Saratu?*" Genin and I say at the same time.

"Negotiating? You mean, she was like, talking to someone?" Priyanka asks.

"Yeah," says Pa Ling. "She was there, by the boulder, underwater. I could see her. She used a strange language I couldn't understand—but whatever is down there seemed to understand it."

"Did it sound like the spirits on the wind on the day of the storm?" Verity asks.

Pa-Ling shakes his head.

Everyone stares at Saratu, who sits on the riverbank, calmly examining cherries again. She's completely composed, despite having been literally dragged through the mud by Jade—and apparently having done some out-of-body swim lessons with something hiding under the river.

We approach her.

"How you make Pa-Ling see you underwater?" Rakito asks. "Magic?"

Saratu pops a cherry in her mouth, smiles without showing teeth, and holds out her palm to offer Rakito some. But she doesn't answer his question. She's lost again in whatever world she inhabits when she can't or won't relate to the real one. I remember how I saw her floating above me in a dream the night I learned Katie was murdered. I thought it was part of my dream, the one in which men in black suits watched while a scrubs-clad Dr. Evelyn performed some sort of weird procedure on me. Was it a dream? I know that Saratu wasn't happy as she faded into the ceiling.

I slide a palm back and forth across my stomach for comfort before clutching my elbows to steady my nerves.

"Pa-Ling, Saratu wasn't in the water," I say. "Verity and Priyanka took her back to the blanket after rescuing her from Jade, right after you dove under the water. Then she walked along the bank while we all looked for you."

Pa-Ling shrugs. "She was there. I saw her. She communicated with whatever was down there."

Jade acts disinterested, which makes me think she either knows about this hole and Saratu's gift, or she thinks Pa Ling is full of shit. Or maybe she's just a raging psychopath who doesn't care if one of us dies. But I have a feeling she knows something we don't—like that we're all being mind-manipulated on this freak farm. Maybe that's the experiment. Without warning, she sucker-punches me in the side of the face before taking off down the footpath toward the house.

"I have a different hole to deal with right now," I growl to the others, "and it begins with *ass*. I'll have to get back with you on the creepy river episode later." And I take off after Jade.

"Come on! Girl fight!"

Multiple footsteps pound through the woods behind me, crushing twigs and crispy leaves.

But the sounds fall farther behind as I gain on Jade. I reach her on the hill just beside the house and grab her ponytail. She twists and peels herself free. I purposely fall back as she sprints to the house and whips open the screen door to the kitchen. I go in after her.

A startled maid, the cook, Barbara, and Dr. Evelyn stand up in unison from the rustic wooden table near the sink.

"What the hell?" Barbara says.

We dash through the kitchen into the dining room, which is already set for lunch. The aroma of yeast rolls and roast beef rises in tiny steam swirls of bliss. Jade stops at the other side of the table and moves in the opposite direction every time I lunge to one side or the other. Her eyes narrow, and she smirks. "What's matter? You lose slutty friend and now you fight *me*? This Katie. She wasn't really friend, she low-life. Sold you out."

I hurl a water goblet from off the table; she ducks, and it smashes on the glossy wood-paneled wall behind her. Barbara yells something about all the broken vases, pitchers, and glasses we break and wants Dr. Evelyn to switch to plastic. The other kids enter from the main hall—apparently, they came through the front door. They're wet and still in their underwear. I'm sure this is all a bewildering spectacle for the adults.

Dr. Evelyn tilts her head with a curious look yet holds Barbara and the cook back from breaking us up. Her arms are out in front of both of them as if to say, *Let's see where this goes.*

"Stop running away from me, you coward," I say.

"Oh, I no, how you say, scaredy-cat," Jade says. "I snap neck clean with two fingers if I want."

"Prove it, bitch." I leap onto the table.

Priyanka and Verity grab the roast beef platter to get it out of the way. Genin saves the mashed potatoes while Saratu clutches the bread basket. Rakito tries to move some glasses, but I fling myself off the table toward Jade, taking a table settings with me. The two of us roll on the floor. I kick and punch with everything I have, but so does Jade. Her fist lands like a sledgehammer on my face, and I use an elbow to knock her off of me before pouncing on her back.

Orchestral music begins to blast through the intercom system, the one usually reserved for morning reveille. If the intention is to soothe us savage bitches with dead-guy tunes, it's lost on us. And is that the *Star Wars* theme? Who the hell queued up this music?

Barbara yells for us to stop, but everyone else bends over with laughter, including Dr. Evelyn. I suction myself to Jade's back, a rabid squid, until someone pinches my shoulder by the neck, and I fall like a plucked tomato.

Reggie.

He yanks me up by the elbow as some bulky army-looking dude with a gray buzz cut and weird black-ink snake tattoo on his bowling-ball-sized bicep does the same thing to Jade.

"You take that one, Major, and I'll take this one," Reggie says.

"I'd say that's a fair exchange, Colonel," the major replies.

Colonel? Did the buzz cut guy just call Reggie *Colonel?*

Reggie hauls me outside through the kitchen door. "Get on the golf cart."

"Can I at least have some clothes?"

He steps to the side of the house, by the cellar doors, and finds an empty burlap sack. He uses his Swiss Army knife to cut some slits, then throws it to me.

"Seriously?" I say. "You're not earning any points for originality."

"Put. It. On." He grits his teeth.

Flour settles over my arms as I put on the makeshift shirt. I brush it off the best I can as I step onto the golf cart. Reggie—the colonel—climbs into the driver's seat.

"Hold on," he says, yanking the wheel toward the barn. "It's going to be a long night. Ever castrate a pig?"

"Loaded question," I say. "Why did the army dude call you Colonel?"

"Loaded question," he replies.

Chapter 11

SQUEAL

I slip into a pair of jeans and a "Reagan-Bush 1984" T-shirt Verity brought from the house. It's a strange clothing choice, and I give her a questioning look.

She shrugs. "I didn't want to waste a good concert T-shirt."

I hide behind a splintered door leaning sideways against a combine on the dusty barn floor. The smell of hay and straw makes me sneeze.

"Bless you," Verity says.

Reggie never blesses me after I sneeze—because, like me, he doesn't believe in that sort of God-like fluff. And why would God bless me only after I sneeze, anyway?

"You can go back to the house now," Reggie says gently to Verity. "And tell Miss Barbara that Sam says thank you for her pants."

"But—"

"No buts. Go on now."

As Verity slips out of the barn, she looks back at me cross-eyed with her tongue out.

Reggie positions a chair under the single oversized bulb that dangles from a long cord in the center of the barn. He's readying his interrogation. Hogs snort and rustle behind us, and the smell of slop and pig shit mixes with what's left of Verity's "Love's Baby Soft" perfume. I fight an urge to gag. I have no idea what Reggie has planned, but it no doubt involves another "down home" lesson. Those never quite stick with me.

"Go retrieve a piglet from one of the sows," he says.

"Why?" I plunk down in the chair. After saving Pa Ling from drowning, running all the way back to the house, and fist-fighting with Jade, I'm tired.

Reggie looks wider and taller from this lower perspective, a sturdy and reliable tractor that's been pushed through hell but somehow keeps plowing. He stink-eyes me—then unexpectedly kicks the chair out from under my ass.

I fall with a thud to the floor, disturbing dust that billows before settling again. The hairs on the back of my neck stand at attention just like they did my first day when he left me at the gate. "Hey! What did you do that for?"

Reggie grits his teeth, and I can tell he's controlling his breathing, trying to keep his composure. I guess I test his patience.

I don't argue; I already know that words are basically useless with him when he's pissed. And I won't get out of this until I do as he says, so I may as well get on with it. I get up and stomp my way toward a pen, brushing straw off my Levi's. It takes a few minutes for me to scoop up a squirming piglet, and as I return with it to the chair, one really angry, screeching sow repeatedly bangs against her gate behind us.

"If she escapes from her pen, I'm leaving you in the dust," I say.

"If she escapes from her pen, it won't be me she's looking for," he says. "Sows have great memories. Now—sit down and hold the piglet by its hind legs, face up. Keep its head down toward your knees."

I turn the squirmy piglet onto its back; its semi-shiny pink underside almost glows under the light as the little guy wriggles, snorts, and grunts. I lightly tickle his tummy, but not too much—I'm a little worried about his mom breaking her gate.

Too bad these cute little guys get so big and become bacon.

"That's a lady pig," he says. "We need a boy pig."

"What difference does it make?"

"The difference is, you can't castrate a lady pig."

"What does that mean?" I ask.

"We castrate the boy piglets because they have a terrible odor in their meat if you don't. You wouldn't touch your bacon if we let hogs keep their balls."

"Why didn't you tell me to grab a boy pig in the first place?" I huff. "How do we castrate a pig?"

"What you're going to do is make an incision through the piglet's scrotum over each testicle, then you'll pull out his balls and use this knife to cut them off."

"Like hell I will!" I drop the piglet and stand up. It squeals away from us and races back toward its pen, a tiny pink blur.

Reggie lowers his eyes and shakes his head. "Go get another one."

"Why do I have to do this? Jade started it," I say, fists on my hips.

"Because Jade already knows how to castrate piglets. In fact, she's one of the best at it."

I make a face. "Of course, she's the best. She's the best at *everything*. Is there anything Jade can't do?"

The flicker of a smile creeps across Reggie's lips. I've made my jealousy too obvious and it appears to amuse him. As he always says, *Pay attention to your own self.*

I go back to the frightened piglet and ease her back into the pen with her mother, taking a moment to peer into the sow's eyes to let her know I meant no harm. She stops squealing and plops down on her side, offering her terrified offspring a comfort suckle.

If I dare climb back into this particular pen to scoop out a boy pig, she'll likely go nuts and try to pin me between her body and the wooden slats until I'm crushed to death.

I'll choose more wisely this time. I observe the other sows before settling on one toward the back of the barn. She's still weak from giving birth only a few days earlier, and she's giving more attention to the slop than her offspring. When I swipe a boy pig from her pen, she doesn't even notice until I'm back in the chair. But when she does take note, she starts slamming the side of her pen, riling up the others. The result is an offkey band of screeching, pissed-off pigs.

Unfortunately, the ruckus behind me reminds me of that day in the motel room, and my stomach spews acid. This whole scene makes me feel light-headed and ready to puke.

When I have the piglet in position, Reggie hands over a knife with a polished, well-worn wooden handle. It unfolds like a switchblade. "Use the muscles in your legs to hold that piglet down, or he could bleed out when you cut him," he says, guiding me. "Now, use your thumb to push up on both testicles—right there. That's it."

A sudden flap of red feathers startles us, and we look up to see a cardinal perched on a rafter. His head bobs, and he joins the pigs in song, adding his chirps and whistles to their snorts and squeals.

Another unexpected and dreaded locomotive type of pain thunders through the track of my brain.

A woman in a pale blue hospital gown stands before a mirror over a white sink. She takes this very knife I hold and slits her wrists lengthwise. Burgundy blood spurts onto the glass and stains the sink in a million red-rain spatters. The woman falls to the white tile floor as a river of life flows away from her. Reggie stands behind her, a look of shock and horror reflected in the mirror. He couldn't save her and uses his body to block Barbara from witnessing the suicide of their only child.

Reggie snaps his fingers next to my ear. "You okay?"

I'm back in the barn.

I nod. My headache leaves the station of my head about as fast as it arrived and for that I'm glad. But this vision of Reggie makes me feel overwhelmingly sad.

"Good. You had me worried there for a second, like you drifted off to another world," he says. "Now, make a small incision through the skin of the scrotum over each testicle in the direction of the tail. Be sure the cuts are low on the sac to allow fluid drainage."

The knife in my hand hovers over the belly of the piglet. It's one thing to stab at something in blind rage, quite another to break the skin of an innocent. "I don't think I can do this," I say, lowering the blade to my side.

"I think you can," Reggie says. "Breathe and focus."

The smell of oil, old timbers, and straw permeates my nostrils. I slowly exhale and bring my hand down, mating metal to flesh. The blade cuts through the piglet's skin.

A tiny droplet of bright red blood bubbles up, a blister of life's condensation. The smell is fresh, and it oozes with an energy that overtakes the staleness around me. The piglet lets loose with a high-pitched, surreal squeal that reminds me of a screaming infant in complete agony. But I remain firm, thighs tightly clenched.

A swaddled baby is placed in Verity's arms at a hospital. It's a girl. Dr. Evelyn is there, as is some black guy who kisses Verity's forehead and poses for a picture. But the baby is white. Can two black people give birth to a white baby? I try to see the newborn's face.

Reggie gently places his hand on my collarbone and I snap back to reality. "Good," he says. "Now pop the testicles through the incisions and pull on them slightly. But keep your thumb pressed against the piglet's pelvis."

I do as he says, my focus arriving full force and unbreakable because keeping this piglet alive with minimal damage is priority number one. How different it feels to cut into an animal with control instead of rage—it's peaceful for me—even though I'm one-hundred percent certain it's not peaceful for the pig.

"Go ahead, slice the cords to the testicles," Reggie says.

With a single flick of my wrist I cut both cords.

Reggie sprays the fresh wound with a rust-colored antiseptic. "Never seen anyone cut two cords at once," he says. "You might be better at this than Jade."

"You think so?"

Reggie nods. "When you focus, you're able to accomplish damn near anything you set your mind to. Okay. This one's done. Go find us another. We have eleven more to go."

I take the newly castrated piglet back to its mother.

I pick up another piglet and return to the chair... and so it goes until we finish. Twelve little piglets lose their balls this moonless night, but at least all of these pigs live to tell the tale —unlike the other "pigs" I left behind in my motel room.

Chapter 12

SCATHA

Thank God for Sundays. No chores. No classes. A full day of free time. It's early and still dark, a grayscale photograph sort of dawn that slowly stretches and yawns before lifting sunshine to unfurl it over the fields. Draining what's left of the sleep from my head, I sift through the contents of my swollen mind. It's mostly junk that I toss away to make room for the new stuff—like how to castrate pigs, and the boxing moves I've learned from Reggie: Jab. Cross. Hook. Uppercut.

Reggie strung up bales of hay last night to teach me "the art of pugilism." He made me do it *or else*. He didn't specify what "or else" meant, and I didn't want to find out—especially after I discovered what we do to the pigs. Now *there's* a sound I never want to hear again.

But that's the least of my problems.

Rosie's death at the Trail's End Motel was closed as a murder-suicide. Which means I'm off the hook—grand prizewinner of some surreal secret pardon, compliments of whom I'm not yet sure. But it also means I still don't know how Katie died—and maybe I never will. I also don't why the authorities never came here to question me about Rosie. The investigation was open for a month, plenty of time for the cops or a caseworker to come nosing around.

I close my eyes. Bennie's breath is on my ear.

"Samantha, I know you're awake. Scay-How, look what I've got!"

My eyes spring open as his not-quite-English-accent fades away, like the end of a good song. I turn my head toward the sound of his voice, but he's not really there. I must be dozing and dreaming, a half-comatose twilight where the cosmic and conscious roll around together, distorting reality just enough to momentarily fool me into thinking dreams are real. What's a Scay-How anyway? I roll over and pull the white sheet over my head. It's Sunday. I don't have to get up.

A mewing sound startles me. This is no dream. Squinting into daybreak, I see trace outlines of furniture, shut my eyes again, and listen.

A long whine, sort of like a puppy but not quite, forces me fully awake. Slowly, I peer over the side of my bed.

A small ball of breathing fur and the glint of yellow eyes greet me.

I pull the sheets up to my neck with a squeal and hit my head on the headboard. My heart bangs against my chest. There's a *rat* in my room! Plum Hook Bay has rodents!

Get a grip, Sam. You've castrated pigs, for Christ's sake. Look again.

I stretch out my trembling arm to click the lamp on the nightstand. What if this thing jumps up to bite me and I contract rabies? Twenty-two shots in the stomach, that's what I heard, and frothing at the mouth.

And why am I so afraid of rats? It's not as if I haven't encountered my share of them back in Cleveland, both with and without tails. I even successfully trained a couple of them to steal for me.

I exhale loudly, trying to sound both perturbed and unafraid, and force my eyes over the cliff of the mattress. I hope this thing, whatever it might be, is more afraid of me than I am of it.

But it's not a rat.

It's a…

…baby fox?

"How'd you get in here?"

She's reminds me of a disheveled pile of autumn leaves and she's loaded with frightened screeches that sound louder than a Cleveland fire truck. I close my eyes, then reopen them. The fox is still here, the inkwell-black-dipped tips of her ears perked up like antennae.

I reach down and scoop her into my arms. She's a girl all right. I learned how to tell the difference with the piglets. She's light and little, too, maybe only a few weeks old. I stroke her soft fur and pull myself out from under the covers. She smells outdoor fresh, like just before the morning sun sucks dew off the grass.

"Shh," I say. "It's okay. You'll wake everyone. Where'd you come from, little one?"

I look her over for scratches, wounds, or other evidence of harm, but find none. She's healthy. Loud. Squirming. What I do find is an ivory tag attached to the bright green bow tied around her neck. It reads: *Happy Re-birth, Scatha. BB*

Happy Re-birth? What is that supposed to mean? And who is Scatha? Me? Why would anyone call me that? But just minutes ago, Bennie called me "Scay-How." I heard him, the light tremble of his voice rolling through my early-morning head fog. Could that have been his way of saying Scatha? Or was I dreaming? Bennie wouldn't give me a gift. I haven't even seen the little twerp since he spied on Verity and me in the library and then blasted out of there like a rocket.

I build a secure pillow cave for my new kit, then pad across the room to put on a T-shirt and jeans. As I splash cool water against my face, a memory of my mom suddenly forces its way forward from the murky depth of my mind. She's teaching me how to swim, and I laugh, wet head thrown back against her freckled chest on an inflatable tube, her arms protectively around me as we pretend to float to Mexico via Lake Erie. *I'm sure we can make it, Mommy!* I was four. Her gold necklace poked me between the shoulders, and I looked back at it…

An eye necklace.

My mom wore an eye necklace!

I catch my breath.

Yes. I see it in my mind almost as clearly as if it rested around my own neck. This is no hallucination. This is a memory!

I pull back my nest of copper hair and move away from the mirror.

Verity bursts into my room without knocking.

"What the hell?" I say. "You always barge into someone's private space?"

"I heard you howling," she says. "I thought something bad happened."

"You don't knock first? Bursting into someone's room can get you killed. And if you really thought something bad happened, I know you—you'd go get somebody else to step in here first, as a shield, you big chickenshit."

She frowns. "Why were you howling?"

"I wasn't."

Verity punches her hip with her fist and rolls her head around on her neck. "Whatever. I *heard* you. You were loud, too."

Sheets stir on the bed.

"Oh my God! Is Genin in your bed?" Verity's eyes go wide. "Hi, Genin! No wonder you were howling, Sam. How rad is that?"

I throw my hairbrush at her. She ducks and laughs.

"Genin is not in my bed," I huff.

She shrugs. "Too bad. You could use a good lay on your birthday."

"My birthday isn't until December."

"That's not what Barbara told me. She said your birthday is today."

"Well, Barbara is wrong." I flip the sheets back to reveal my new friend.

"Whoa, a fox?" Verity steps closer. "Oh my God, so cute. *Waaaay* cuter than Genin. Where'd you find him?"

"She. It's a girl fox. She was beside my bed this morning. I think Bennie snuck in here and left her as a gift."

"Bennie? Why? He doesn't even like you. He welcomed you here with a cobra, remember? Took one of your red welcome balloons too. Bennie hates everyone." She ruffles the hair on the top of the fox's head. It seems to like her. Not surprising.

"Beats me," I say. "I think it's weird too but look at this." I pluck the tag from the bow around the fox's neck.

"BB. It's got to be Bennie," Verity says. "Weird. But you didn't actually see him deliver the fox?"

"No."

"How would he have gotten in here?"

I shrug. "Secret passageway?" I pick up the fox and stroke her fur, quickly scanning my room for potential secret passageways.

Verity fingers the silver pentagram she wears today, a gift from Dr.

Evelyn for studying a bunch of books about religion, which Verity actually likes. Religion makes me snore. *Zzzzz.*

"Scay-how," Verity says. She's one of the most famous warrior Goddesses in Scottish mythology."

Of course! That's the accent I heard when Bennie spoke to me in the library. He's Scottish, it's in his lilt, even though Verity claims that Dr. Evelyn says he's from Oxford.

I look at the tag that reads Scatha. "It's not a very cool name," I say.

"It is if you're Scottish. Legend says she came from the Isle of Sky and trained only the worthiest warriors."

"To fight what?" I ask.

"Unfortunately, that's where the legend gets fuzzy. Her story was never written down, only told orally, centuries ago. She's known as the 'shadowy one'—a powerful prophetess and martial arts expert, which is weird, since she's supposed to be from Scotland, not the Far East." Verity furrows her brow as if trying to unravel a mystery before she continues. "In the fourteenth century she appears again in Irish folklore, but that story focused more on a male warrior she trained, who later became her lover. It's alleged they fought some great battle together against a supernatural force of evil that turned out to be her sister, but not before the warrior cheated on her—with this sister."

"Figures. We get one good female warrior and some guy elbows her out of the history books to take the credit."

Verity's attention returns to the fox. "Hey, did you know Native Americans believe a fox stole fire from the sun? Foxes are thieves too, just like you!"

I glare at her. "I only steal what I need."

"Yeah, you're a real Robin Hood all right." Verity puts a gold-bangled hand to her hip. "You steal because you hope nice stuff will make you feel more normal. It won't, you know."

"I do not. Anyway, you read too much bullshit." I feel my irritation rising. It hurts to be called a thief, even though it's true, so I decide to switch subjects. "Myths are no better than religion—they're just made-up stories for people to explain shit they don't understand."

"Myths and religion have usefulness in our world," Verity says, suddenly serious. "They help us understand life and *feel* something, in the same way art or music can." Her lime-green eyes search mine, as if to find some common ground. But there is none so she looks away.

"Heal your mom, then," I say. "In fact, if religion is real and you think all your hocus-pocus crap works, heal *my* mom too. And make us rich. And bring Katie back from the dead."

"It doesn't work that way," she says. "What's eatin' you today, birthday bitch? Bad night?"

"Of course, it doesn't work that way. If life did work that way, we wouldn't be here. Just tell God and your little voodoo spirits I'm out of patience. I believe in logic and science."

The pup lightly licks my forearm and it feels like wet sandpaper. Her shiny red fur gets brighter with each sun ray that leaks through the pines and slips through the window. I think about what Verity said. Maybe we *are* all somehow connected on this stupid little terrarium, but I don't believe it has anything to do with a fire-and-brimstone God of the type Barbara consumes every day like an over-sized bowl of Wheaties.

"Okay then, non-believer," says Verity. "Why don't you explain what happened with Pa Ling and Saratu at the river? Using only 'logic and science.'"

I think for a moment. Verity knows I see weird things, but I haven't been completely honest with her about that—I haven't told her that I suspect my 'off-kilter' brain chemistry is to blame and that I'm probably sick like my mom. Verity thinks I have a special gift, like I'm an oracle or something. She'll be disappointed to learn that I'm just a run-of-the-mill lunatic and Delphi isn't calling.

"Pa Ling stayed under too long and hallucinated," I say. "Then he surfaced too fast, which caused his eyes to see things that weren't there due to lack of oxygen, accompanied by high adrenaline and pressure on his brain."

"Is that what you tell yourself when it happens to you?" Verity asks. "That you're 'coming up too fast' when you see shit that the rest of us don't see? Or when you fly through the air? You did fly yesterday at the river, you know. We all saw it. You sprung up out of the water like some sort of heron. God, you sound like Dr. Evelyn when you lie. You don't get it, do you? Religion and science reside on the same coin of 'knowing,' silly girl, just on flip sides." She eyes me sort of nervously, I suppose, to gauge my reaction.

I decide to lighten up a little and pitch her a soft smile. Her lips turn upward a little too. No need to entangle Verity with my personal concerns and pulverize her day into ruins just to make myself feel better—and actually, seeing her sad would make me feel worse.

I stroke the fur of my new gift. Verity's analogy, I must admit, is intriguing. Science and religion placed on the same coin, sort of like heads or tails—different, but functioning together the way Barbara and Reggie do.

As for my visions and my alleged flying… I don't know how to explain what happened. I didn't even think about it, I simply reacted and the flying just happened, like breathing. But there must be an earthly explanation for it, and I'll bet the answer is hidden on the NASA side of this farm.

"Well, if God appears to me," I finally say, "you and Barbara will be the first to know."

"Good," Verity says through a small chuckle. "Until then, we'll keep praying for your soul."

"While you're at it, why don't you light some candles and a do a midnight naked pagan dance in the woods, too?" I cock a smirk toward her.

"You know, that's not a bad idea," she laughingly says.

Verity looks as if I've given her a new idea to mix in with all the other "hoo-doo" she practices in her attempt to keep evil at bay and it reminds me of what Reggie said about Barbara's practice of Christianity acting as 'soul tonic'.

Studying religion may be Verity's way of coping with life's jerk-offs, a hobby that keeps her semi-sane, the way Saturday morning cartoons once did for me when I used them as a temporary escape from my reality at the Trail's End Motel. But of course, I can't give Verity that. Instead I spout off, "You're too much of a chickenshit to even walk down to the kitchen by yourself at night for a glass of water, let alone to go out in the woods and dance naked."

Verity reaches out to pet the baby fox, but stays silent, biting her bottom lip.

I suppose I shouldn't be so hard on her for being loaded with enough beliefs to fill a sleigh. At least she believes in *something*. I wish I could embrace her sense of magic. What happens in the real world is never as good as my hallucinations or hopes.

Priyanka appears in the doorway. "Good, you're up. Dr. Evelyn wants to see you in her office right now."

"Why?" I ask, suddenly wary. I can't think of anything I've done that warrants a summons to Dr. Evelyn's office. Maybe the cops are here? Maybe they're waiting in Dr. Evelyn's office to read me my rights and cart me away in handcuffs, a murderess in the midst of all these helpless foster kids. I can see the news footage now: me going outside the gates, jacket over my head to hide my shame, looking hard enough into the ground to leave pupil-sized drill holes in my wake.

Priyanka shrugs. "Beats me. What did you do this time?" Then she perks up. "Whoa! Where'd you pick up a baby fox?" She steps into my room for a better look.

"Bennie, I think." The fox wriggles against my chest.

"Bennie? Seriously?" The diamond stud in Priyanka's nose glitters as it catches a glimpse of daybreak. "He hates everybody."

Priyanka is from the Punjab province in Hussainiwala, India. She once told us that girls from her village marry early, around fourteen or fifteen, and they don't even get to pick their husband—that couples start as strangers but *learn* to love. Yuck. I don't get it. I'd never marry somebody chosen for me. What if they smelled or had bad teeth? Or worse, a needle dick? And why get married anyway? It's like being a prostitute without perks.

"Better make sure that fox doesn't have rabies or something," Priyanka continues. "Oh, and happy birthday." She trots down the hall.

I shake my head and study the fox. She looks healthy to me. And it's *not* my birthday.

Verity removes a yellow chicken foot from her pocket, holds it above her head, and murmurs a chant.

I roll my eyes. "You're the only Catholic-pagan-voodoo-witch-Christian I know," I say. "You're such a weirdo."

She stuffs the chicken leg back in her pocket and pulls out a pink container with a white lid. She unscrews the top and pulls out a green wand as she tilts her head toward the ceiling, prayer-warrior ready.

"What is that?" I ask.

"Holy water is boring," she says. "I prefer 'holy bubbles.'" She blows through her little wand and litters my room with a battalion of floating suds that drift and pop on the furniture.

"You're crazy," I say. I stroll out of my room carrying my baby she-fox, slight concern pinching my brows as I wonder why Dr. Evelyn wants to see me.

"Not as crazy as you," she calls after me.

Saratu runs up to me in the hallway. She smiles, claps her hands, and jumps up and down, evidently excited.

"You like the fox?" I ask.

She nods as if she hasn't eaten in weeks and someone just offered her a piece of fruit.

"Want to hold her?"

I carefully place the kit in her arms. This girl has one of the biggest hearts I've ever felt. Tears load up her eyes as the kit licks her cheek. She reaches into the folds of her sheets with one hand and offers me a yellow piece of paper. I unfold it.

Will you be my big sister? Circle YES or NO.

I've never been someone's big sister before, and I'm unsure how much this role requires. I'm concerned, too, because I'm already over the weight limit for my own baggage.

Gosh, she's a weird chick, this Saratu, but I'm drawn to her—can't help myself. She has such vulnerability—and humility—yet also possesses an incongruous strength. Put Saratu in Cleveland and she'd either be crucified within the hour, or she'd gather a few dozen followers and start a new religion. Perhaps that's her gift: a huge heart that enables her to sense life on a grander scale than the rest of us. Maybe deeply troubled people and orphaned puppies learn to do that; I don't know.

But there's only one question for me now: Can I handle the responsibility of acting as her big sister?

I refold the paper, place it back in her tiny palm, and cup my hand over hers. I nod.

She beams.

A zap of electricity shocks me like one of those prank buzzers, and I jump back, startled, and look at Saratu to see if she felt it too, but she acts as though nothing just happened. She gently hands my fox back to me, and her bare feet pitter-patter down the hall with a tiny skip, leaving me standing here in a swirl of wonder and confusion.

Despite the unexpected electrical shock, Saratu's happiness makes me feel sort of good about myself. I'll figure out how to be her big sister. Anyone who thinks sheets are a fashion statement *needs* a big sister anyway. But I'm surprised she didn't ask Tetana to take the role; they're practically inseparable. Maybe she did. Maybe Saratu is collecting 'big sisters'.

I rap lightly on Dr. Evelyn's door. "It's Sam."

"Come in, Samantha."

She's seated at her desk, a rustic picnic table with iron legs and a faded gray top that reminds me of driftwood limbs I used to collect at Edgewater Beach. Stacks of papers, folders, and a red rotary phone take up one side. Fancy framed awards and certificates protected by glass covers hang like badges of credibility on the wall behind her. Her space is light, organized, and much fresher and interesting than Mrs. Myers's office. I detect the wispy scent of roses too, but it always smells good wherever Dr. Evelyn decides to be.

She spins her fancy padded office chair around before pulling navy-blue reading glasses from her nose and tapping them on her bottom lip. I'm relieved to find no cops waiting with her.

"Where'd you find the fox?" she asks.

"It's a gift. I think it's from Bennie."

"Bennie? Does he talk with you?" Her eyes narrow, as she seems to hope I'll say yes.

"No. I haven't seen him since he got Verity and me in trouble with the cobra." That's a lie, but I don't want Dr. Evelyn to know what he told me in the library.

"Don't let the cobra fool you," she says. "It doesn't have any venom. Bennie practically spoon-feeds the damn thing. Why'd he give you a fox?"

So—she doesn't know I'm lying. Or at least, nothing in her body language or expression suggests suspicion.

"Beats me," I say. "I'm just as much in the dark as you are."

"Boy or girl?"

"Girl."

"That's too bad. Girls are much more difficult than boys. And meaner too." She winks. "I'm surprised he gave you a gift. Bennie hates everybody—except Dr. Sterling." She taps her glasses on her chin and swivels in her chair. Her fresh platinum hair swings with her but not a strand falls out of place. "Well, happy birthday," she says. "You have a delivery."

"From who?" My heart throbs a little in my chest because it's not my birthday, I don't understand why everyone insists that it is, and nobody is supposed to know I'm here. I also didn't ask anyone to order me anything.

"From *whom.*" She corrects me.

Dr. Evelyn is a stickler for grammar, and I've picked up a lot of bad linguistic habits. My speech is a combination of Cleveland street slang and Heartland auto-plant hillbilly strung together with big words that Dr. Awoudi taught me.

A rap sounds on her door. My heart plunges.

"Come in, Reggie."

Relief.

Reggie ducks and squeezes his shoulders together a little as he steps through. He's dressed in his usual denim overalls and floppy straw hat, and I realize that this ensemble doesn't really suit the man I'm getting to know a little. The truth is, he's sort of a smart dude when it comes to this foster parent gig.

Reggie stands off to one side, his hands behind his back. "Where'd you get the baby fox? They're almost impossible to catch. You didn't take her from her mother, did you?"

"I think Bennie gave her to me," I say, pulling her close, wondering if Reggie will take her away and put her back where she likely belongs, in the wild. "I don't know what happened to her mother."

"Bennie? Well, I'll be." He smiles. "That boy is about as strange as drinking Scotch from a dirty sock, but he sure has good taste in gifts and girls. Didn't think he had it in him. Never gave any of the other girls a gift. He must really like you. You like him too?"

"Ew. No." I shake my head extra hard to ensure Reggie gets the point. "Bennie and me? No way!" I don't even have a thing for Genin anymore, not since he blew it with his sticky-tree-sappy behavior with Jade. "That's just gross. I don't even know Bennie."

"Evidently you made an impression on *him*." Reggie laughs and looks at Dr. Evelyn like they're in on a secret.

"Well?" Dr. Evelyn says. "Do you have it with you?"

"Yes, ma'am." Reggie brings his big hands around in front of him and holds out a partially unwrapped present.

"You already opened it," I say.

"Had to," Reggie replies with a light shrug. "It's protocol for any packages coming through these gates. They must be inspected in a locked room at the Sandusky Post Office. I tried to re-wrap it, but I'm not good at that kind of stuff, like Miss Barbara. And she had her hands full making your cake, so she couldn't do it. I figured you might not want to wait. Here you go."

I trade him the fox for the package and rip off the paper.

It's an ugly doll. The box smells heavy with tobacco smoke.

"What is it?" Dr. Evelyn asks.

I crinkle my nose and squint my eyes, looking up at her with half-confused disgust. "It's a Golden Girls Warrior doll. And her name is Jade!" I can't even get a good gift for my *non*-birthday. Well, except for the fox. Thank God for the fox, and maybe for Bennie too.

I hold up the blindingly neon-pink-and-yellow box. Inside is a fuzzy-red-haired lady warrior wearing a green-and-gold cape and holding a silver sword. She's painted with too much cobalt-blue eye makeup and her thighs are over-muscled, like a body builder's. I don't understand who would send me such a ridiculous, hideous ill-fitted gift, or why, and evidently it shows on my face because Dr. Evelyn's laugh bursts forth like a gush of garden hose water, and Reggie joins her.

"I don't get it," I say. "Anyone who knows me knows I've never even liked dolls! And I'm too old for one anyway." I plunk the box down on Dr. Evelyn's desk. Taped to the back of the box is a little card, so I rip it off and peel it open.

Happy fourth birthday. Love, Mom.

"Is this a joke?" I say, tossing the note down on her desk.

"No," says Dr. Evelyn. "Your mom has brief moments of clarity, and Dr. Awoudi feels it's important to let her know you're safe."

"She knows I'm here?" I ask.

"Not exactly," says Reggie. "She was told you're living with a very spiritual family in Sandusky. Which pleases her."

I make a face.

"She asked Louie to send you a birthday gift she saw on TV. She still thinks you're four years old."

"Who's Louie?" I ask.

"Her nurse."

"How come I never got any gifts from her before?"

"Because Avril never had a nurse as nice as Louie," Reggie says, rocking lightly on his boot heels.

"Can I visit her?"

Reggie frowns. "Probably not a wise idea until you're older."

"I'm seventeen. Define older."

"It's not you I'm worried about handling it," he says. There's a wisp of warning in his voice to shut it down, so I do. I've gotten used to being told that I can't see my mom, and it's become normal.

I look at the ugly doll again. I always imagined my mom having better taste, but then again, I don't remember much except snippets, and I have to fill in the gaps. I guess the doll isn't *that* ugly, and it *is* a gift from my mom. But the name… I don't want to have to stare at that every day. Jade. Bleck!

"Dr. Evelyn, may I please borrow your Sharpie?" I ask, using my too-many-sugar-cubes-in-the-tea voice, and she knows it too, but smiles anyway.

She plucks the marker from a short crystal vase and hands it to me.

I lay the box on an empty part of her desk and hide the name "Jade" beneath layers of black chemical-smelling ink. I write "SCATHA" over the top and hold it up for inspection.

"I changed her name," I say.

Dr. Evelyn and Reggie exchange a look. I don't understand it, but I do notice, and file that information away "being good data points for me," as Jade once said when she called me unrefined.

"You feel all right, Sam?" Dr. Evelyn asks.

"Of course. Why wouldn't I be?"

"You don't participate in any therapy sessions."

"You said they weren't mandatory. I like therapy about as much as I like church. Neither does any good. Besides, Reggie needs help around the farm, and I'd rather work with him." Did I just say that? Ugh. I should have simply admitted that I'd prefer some LSD and a pass from chores to experience preferable 'alone time'.

"Hard work is often the best form of therapy," Reggie says. He's obviously pleased that I'd rather hang out with him than her, but now I'm studying Reggie more closely, who stands there with a shit-eating grin, and I think he might be high because his eyes look about as glassy as polished rocks.

Dr. Evelyn gives him a little eyebrow raise of disapproval. "Now that you're a high school graduate, you have more time on your hands," she says to me. "I think you need some options."

"I don't like the sound of that," I say. "You're using your ultimatum voice, which always leaves me with two yucky, no-win options. What sort of options are we talking about?"

"Therapy with me one hour per week, or an afternoon of church every Sunday with Barbara and Reggie."

"Oh, come on!" I moan. "You say today is my birthday and if so, the choices you offer are a prison not a present!"

"Take. Your. Pick." She says sternly. "By the way, Dr. Sterling, Reggie, Barbara and I also got you a little something for your birthday." She pulls a small white box from a drawer and slides it across the desk.

I lift off the cardboard lid and pull out a fluffy cotton square to reveal a gold charm bracelet with three charms. The first is a book that says, "Better for the Earth." The second is a small shield that says, "Say no to violence, abuse, and greed." And the third, a wolf, reads, "Protect wildlife."

"Thank you," I say. "I like it a lot." And I do.

"Here, let me help you put it on."

Dr. Evelyn secures the clasp. I jangle the bracelet in front of the fox, who's still tucked into Reggie's log-like arms. She reaches out to paw at the charms. He passes the fox back to me.

"What's it going to be, Samantha? Therapy or church?" Dr. Evelyn asks.

I sigh heavily and roll my eyes at Reggie, but Dr. Evelyn can't see. "Therapy," I groan.

"Great. I will see you Wednesday at two o' clock. I hope you have a wonderful birthday." She gives me a Mona Lisa smile that expresses either feigned happiness or suppressed irritation, I can't quite tell.

"Miss Barbara made you a beautiful cake," Reggie says, following me out the door. "Lots of pretty flowers. She and Priyanka put a lot of work into it, and Verity helped too. Dinner should be fun."

"Got any weed?" I ask Reggie.

He looks surprised. "What? Weed? As in marijuana? Me? No. You know you can't smoke that here."

"Uh-huh," I say, giving him a doubtful glare. "But you can?"

"Hey, what's your fox's name?" He asks, I suspect, to change the subject.

I haven't given any thought to a name, but she does need one. "Hope," I say. "As in, I hope therapy gets canceled and the church burns down."

Chapter 13

BUCKEYES AND BLOOD

ennie sprints over the hill toward the house. One brown ringlet flops against his forehead, and he puffs to keep it out of his face. Tears trickle down his cheeks as he scrambles toward us.

Jade's head bobs over the ridge after him. She uses an elbow to clobber him into the grass and knocks whatever he carries from his hands. It splinters into a thousand tinkling chimes, where hundreds of nuts and bolts scatter in the green grass like glistening stainless-steel dewdrops. Bennie howls as he gathers up a few of the broken parts of whatever gizmo he's built, his face now 'summer beet' red.

Reggie and Rakito watch from the barn; they're too far away to intervene in Jade's bully session of Bennie. Tetana and Priyanka sit on Reggie's tractor by the screen door that leads to the kitchen, cigarettes dangling loosely between their 'peace-sign' fingers. Saratu and I are on a blanket near the tractor, where we've been playing Crazy Eights. Rising to our feet for a better look, Saratu gently lifts Hope into her arms and protectively wraps her within the folds of today's turquoise sheet.

Jade swats Bennie hard across the back of his head, spiking spiraled brown tufts to attention. She screams at him in Russian, but I can't understand what she says because they're still too far away. Bennie finds his feet again and runs toward us, then past us, and struggles to open the screen door behind me.

One thing I know for sure is that thirteen versus seventeen is not a fair fight. But what in the hell did he do to piss her off so badly? Maybe he deserves what he gets.

Jade reaches him again, grabs hold of his starched white shirt collar, and whips him around so that his knees skid on the gravel driveway beside us.

Barbara comes to the screen door. "Jade! Stop tormenting that boy or Dr. Sterling will have your head!"

Jade ignores her.

Bennie stands. Dark-bluish blood drips from his gravel-chewed knees.

I quickly step between Jade and Bennie to block her path to him.

"Move out of way," she says, focused on Bennie, not looking at me. "You have no business getting into ours, and if you do, you eat gravel too."

"A real female Rambo, this one," I say to Saratu.

"Oh my God!" Priyanka points toward the hill.

A silver-gray dog limps toward us with an arrow stuck in his front right leg. He lifts his snout to the sky and lets loose with a long wail that sends a chill of sadness through my soul. For a moment I think its Sarge, the German shepherd, but this isn't him. Sarge is buried under a willow tree by the footpath. This must be the wolf Barbara told me about when I got here. So, it's true. Not that I doubted Barbara, but Bennie, to me anyway, seems more like a wolf's dinner choice than playmate.

Bennie sprints to the apple barrel by the house and grabs the top handle of a small khaki-colored metal box along with a handful of Barbara's buckeyes. He dumps it all into his front shirttail and scrambles toward the wounded wolf, leaving the salvaged pieces of his... whatever it once was, lying on the gravel.

Rakito races from the barn to fall in step beside Bennie. They arrive at the growling wolf where Rakito slowly bends before the canine, his palm held up in front of its snout. It quiets and lies down—snap, just like that. Together, Benny and Rakito work like battle-field surgeons to save the wolf and remove the arrow. Maybe Rakito really does talk to lions, like Verity said.

"That's right, you little coward, go save wolf." Jade laughs.

"What the fuck did he do to you?" I ask, squinting with disapproval while I clench my fists.

"He breathes," Jade answers.

I roll my eyes at her, fists on my hips. "Seriously, Jade, what did he do? Did he sic that animal on you or something?"

"He's coward," she answers, staring up the hill at him with an evil scowl. "He needs to be treated like man to grow like one."

"He's thirteen!"

"No matter. He's baby now. He's weakling—not like he once was. I shoot wolf with arrow for fun to see if Bennie act like man. He fail." She shrugs and stares at the ground. "I break his little machine because he ignore me when I find him in woods."

"He's autistic," I say. "Or are you too stupid to realize that? And you shot his wolf with an arrow, for *fun*? Did you shoot the soldier's dog too?"

"It's mutt with teeth so I bite first. Good rule for life." A pleased smile creeps into the corners of her mouth. But something else she said strikes me as odd. "What did you mean when you said, like Bennie 'once was'?"

"Neyet," she says. "It's no matter for you in this world. He needs to mind his business and find another planet to bother."

"I think your language wires are crossed. Don't you mean another person to bother?"

Jade's eyes lock on to mine—cold, measured, but unable to penetrate very deeply because I refuse to let her in. "I make no mistakes," she finally says.

"Then that means you won't be messing with me," I say, daring her to cross me again and feeling the same rage percolate through me I always feel when Jade shows up.

To injure an animal and a little kid for sport... it makes me want to tear her arms off. I clench my fists so hard my fingernails slice my palms. I fight the urge to pounce on her.

Jade lets loose with a scoff. "You twit. I see now. You like this little boy, no? Is that why you get mad? You have crush on mutant dickweed?"

Her sneer makes my stomach burn, and a pulse of pain pokes me between the eyes.

"You." She points to me. "Him." She points to Bennie. "Are danger to us all..."

Jade pulls the bow from her shoulder and aims it at Bennie on the hill. My scales of courage are suddenly tipped in favor of fear that she'll hurt Bennie, or worse, and, on some instinctual level, I can't let that happen.

"Oh no you don't!" I seize her ponytail and yank her to the ground. My fists furiously hammer at her face to release my rage and maybe pound some sense into her.

"You little bitch!" Jade spits. "You no match for me!"

We roll into a small ditch that runs alongside the driveway.

Jade wraps her legs around my waist and flips me under her where I now stare up at a partly sunny sky, my waist pinned between her thighs. Puffy white clouds drift lazily by, oblivious to the commotion below, moving along a much higher and undisturbed path, and I wish I were able to soar among them. The other kids scream, cheering I think, for me to kick Jade's ass.

I swing at Jade the best I can, but she's fluid. Hand-to hand combat seems like an easy dance for her. But if I pay attention, it's equally easy for me to memorize things, whether it's foreign languages, math—or, in this instance, her jujitsu. I right-cross her and manage to jump on her back. Bad move. She rolls over. Her size and experience put me in the dirt and back under her fists.

Think, Sam! What did Reggie teach you?

Icy-blue veins in Jade's neck begin to throb, reminding me of the pulsing river that rushes through Plum Hook Bay and eventually drains into Lake Erie, unless the beavers use dams to cut off the flow.

That's it! *Cut off the flow!*

I solidly wrap my long piano fingers around her neck, imagining I'm a cobra, depriving the evil inside her of its host.

Don't.

Let.

Go.

Jade's eyes bulge. She claws at me like a trapped bird, but refuses, surprisingly, to offer even one micro-expression of fear. She just gazes into me with uncaring, blue-black, deep-ocean colored eyes that won't let me see anything worth saving. Where is her soul? Her compassion? I can't feel it within her as I often do in others, particularly if I touch them, which I hate to do because it takes so much out of me. A darkness nests within Jade's eyes, one I want to forever extinguish and it looks too much like what I saw back at the Trail's End Motel.

Her face turns pink, red, then blue. The veins in her neck pulse against my finger pads, desperate for oxygen and swelling as I meet Jade eye for eye, sharing equally, our mutual hatred.

"Die, bitch." I say this so calmly that I don't know from where it comes.

In the sky above Jade's head, an ancient castle looms high on a cliff above the sea. It's a fortress, my fortress—where only men of renowned are able pass the traps I set. The dragon comes.

Jade's face cracks. There's her fear. That's better.

"No!" She's suddenly yanked from my grasp.

Reggie pulls her up out of the ditch as easily as plucking feathers off a chicken. Rakito offers me his hand and pulls me out of the pit too. This time Reggie's glare falls on Jade and not me, and my rage subsides as quickly as an extinguished matchstick.

Jade gasps, bent over like she might puke. The imprints of my palms, a temporary light pink tattoo around her throat.

Gone is the castle on a cliff.

Verity gives me her best suspect frown, hand on her hip, head cocked, ready to pepper me with accusations about seeing visions. Or perhaps to chastise me for almost murdering Jade. The other kids seem nervous. I think Jade and I frightened them. I feel it bouncing off of their skin.

I glance up at the sky to avoid Verity's glare. I feel a tiny bit guilty for getting so bloodthirsty and I hope to never again glimpse the dragon in my vision, though I can still see it now, in my mind's eye. It's not the sort of dragon I've read about in fairy tales or seen in pictures of Chinese festivals. It's way worse.

A far-off flash of plane wing catches the sun. Four small airports stand ready to serve Sandusky and surrounding communities, although only military planes are permitted in NASA's immediate airspace.

But…

…something's not right.

The glint in the sky moves too fast. It gets brighter, closer. As it comes toward us, it's round, like a bright crystal beach ball, the color of a full moon and almost translucent.

"What the hell is that?" I point and ask, getting everyone's attention.

The glowing ball of light, about the size of Reggie's Ford, stops and hovers above our heads. And just as with the bluish figure standing in the doorway of my room, on the night I learned Katie died, this thing has no real features—no metal, windows, engines, or pipes. No heat either. And it's completely silent.

"Reggie?" I repeat. "What the hell is *that*?"

"I don't know," he says. "Never seen anything like it before in my life."

"Good Lord Almighty," says Barbara. "Sweet Jesus, protect us all. Reggie? Is that NASA's?"

"Let's hope so," he says. "If it isn't, we've been breached big-time."

Barbara makes the sign of the cross before yelling into the house for Dr. Evelyn. Sirens scream in the distance. Seems NASA already knows something got over their fence—or maybe it escaped from the other side where we aren't permitted to be.

"Oh my God," Dr. Evelyn gasps, hand to her mouth, as she pushes open the screen door. She stops next to Barbara and looks up in awe. I can tell she has no idea what this thing might be, which sends a chill from the back of my brain, down my spine, and out through my toes.

"You know what it is?" Barbara asks.

Dr. Evelyn slowly shakes her head, not taking her eyes off of the thing. "Not. One. Clue."

Guards suddenly appear, lined up along the roofline of the house. And to my surprise, they react without much thinking and fire off their weapons.

Smoke.

Noise.

Chaos.

Duck.

Cover.

The blast of firepower vibrates through my body, shakes my internal organs and rattles my bones. The unexpected bullets also cause me to freeze out in the open, at risk of being used for impromptu, trigger-gleeful target practice from gun-toting baboons who call themselves trained soldiers.

"Cease fire! Cease fire, God damn it! We've got kids down here!" Reggie screams, waving his arms like a madman at the soldiers. "We don't know what the hell that thing is! You hit it and it could blow. Get on the radio, call the other side, and find out what the hell is going on, you idiots!"

Reggie's in full command, putting himself between the foster kids and the bullets. Never saw anyone do that on the streets of Cleveland. It was tuck and roll down Euclid Avenue and hope the other guy gets it first. My legs involuntarily wobble like Barbara's gelatin molds.

The light comes a little closer, grows brighter, a bit bigger, like a translucent eyeball in the sky carefully checking us out, but its pupil is not quite opaque and the entire thing looks practically holographic, yet it's not quite fake enough to convince me it's not real.

Reggie slides in front of me.

"Don't move and don't run," Dr. Evelyn says. "Stand still."

"You mean act like it's a fucking bear?" My knees wobble, and I look at her as if she's gone daft. "I think this thing might be slightly more advanced."

Without warning, the glowing orb slowly meanders over our little group, until it gains some speed, and with barely a sound, except for a small *swish,* pinballs around our perimeter, zig-zag and zip!

Kitchen windows shatter, and so too, do the windows on Reggie's beloved Ford. I watch him wince.

Screams.

Ours.

We duck, dive, and scatter like spooked chickens. Except for Reggie. He stands statue straight, eyes closed, focused on his breathing. How much weed did he smoke today? The light zips around him, bigger and brighter, a shiny gold globe now littered with spark mist. Every now and then it pulsates with a dim reddish glow and I think it's scanning us, looking for something... or someone.

I yank Reggie behind a lilac bush.

The light shifts direction and careens toward Saratu and my fox.

No!

Saratu doesn't run. Cradling Hope in her right arm, she holds her left hand toward the light, palm out, chin high, unafraid, brave, as if she's resigned to this thing coming at her and will just accept whatever it has planned.

"No!" I scream.

I leap.

Pulling one of Barbara's buckeyes from my pocket, I throw it at the strange light—but miss.

A blue laser beam shoots out of this freakish sky ball and engulfs both Saratu and Hope. It lifts them off the ground and pulls them upward toward its underside, its brightness momentarily blinding me.

Gone. They're gone!

The strange light in the sky raises altitude and hovers over us before folding in on itself like some sort of puzzle that gets smaller, and it silently disappears, sucked into an invisible hole of air as if it never existed!

I search the top of the hill for Bennie and his wolf but they're gone too.

"Saratu? What happened to Saratu and Hope?" Tetana asks as she climbs out from under the tractor with Priyanka. "Where'd they go?"

My legs still wobble, but I refuse to drop. I slowly inhale and expand my belly, the way Reggie taught me to do when I get upset. Hold it for one, two, three, four... hold. Exhale. Do it again.

Reggie and Rakito inspect the ground where Saratu once stood. I join them. Nothing—even my buckeye is gone. Maybe I didn't miss. The grass is as undisturbed as freshly laid sod. But it's greener than the rest of the grass around us, and taller by almost three inches, as if the orb somehow expanded the cells within each blade of grass, making them taller and more colorful than the others outside the orb's boundary. I press my hand over the affected grass but instead of leaving a handprint, the blades spring back to strict attention.

"Where's Benny?" I ask, desperately not wanting him to be gone from us too and hoping he had time to take cover. I fight an overwhelming urge to sprint over the hill and into the woods, to scream his name and search for him until he's found.

I'm surprised to see that Jade is just as stunned and frightened as the rest of us. She scans my face looking for an answer I can't give. Then she turns and runs inside, slamming the screen door behind her, and I think that maybe there's more human in her than I give her credit for not having.

The grownups are scared too. Barbara hugs Reggie. He searches the sky as deep lines of concern sprout up around his downturned mouth.

"Are they dead?" Priyanka asks, clinging to Rakito. "Are Benny, Saratu, and Hope dead?"

"I don't know," Reggie says. "I don't know."

As awful as that sounds, we trust that Reggie won't lie to us about things as serious as life and death, even if we don't like his answers.

"Oh my God," Priyanka cries. "Where are Pa Ling and Fensig?"

"They're hunting in the woods with Genin," Rakito says tenderly. He looks down at a shaking Priyanka and pulls her close to him. "We need to find them."

"Not now," Reggie says.

Verity plunges her arms around my waist. This time, I don't push her away but hug back, not letting go. Five of us are missing, nearly half of us, a clusterfuck of a foster home if there ever was one. It's also an incident that surely won't escape outsiders. I need to get out of here. Maybe Jade is right: bite first. That thing, whatever it was, lit up the sky like a dozen lightning strikes. I fight an urge to puke when uncontrollable thoughts of Saratu and my fox being vaporized creep into my brain.

Tetana sobs uncontrollably, her chest heaving and quivering. She picks up pieces of Benny's gadget. She's closer to Saratu than any of us, so I understand her heartbreak. I fight against the growing lump in my throat too—grateful to still be here—but also hoping against the odds that Saratu and Hope aren't dead.

After Tetana's gathered up the bits and bobs, she slips them into the apple barrel and slumps up the steps, past Dr. Evelyn, and steps into the house.

Dr. Evelyn looks at me with a weird expression. For a second it reminds me of Rosie's accusatory glare right before she'd beat me with a belt. "What?" I ask, feeling guilty, but I don't know why—because I didn't do anything.

"How did you do that?" she asks.

"Do what?"

"It's not possible for any human being to leap the way you did. No, not leap—you *flew* toward that thing trying to save Saratu."

I shrug and look at Verity, and we both act as if we don't know what Dr. Evelyn's talking about. Nobody else volunteers anything either. Maybe everyone's too scared, or maybe they don't trust her. And maybe they don't trust *me*.

Reggie wraps his large hand over my shoulder, and it feels like a warm compress, an unexpected source of comfort. "I want everybody in the house until we can sort this out," he says. "Dr. Dennison, call the other Dr. Dennison and get him and his men over here."

Dr. Evelyn looks at Reggie almost with disdain, as if he somehow got in her way. But she turns and walks up the steps, and just like Jade, she slams the screen door behind her.

"Call the cops," Rakito says to Reggie.

Reggie shakes his head. "They can't help us."

Chapter 14

OFF WITH HER HEAD!

"You have to break their necks with one strong crack before you chop off their heads with a hatchet," Reggie says. "Just pick one up and hold it against your body, press its wings down with one hand, and wring its neck with your other."

It's been a week since Saratu and Bennie disappeared, and Reggie has kept me busy the entire time. Busy, and close. He has no idea what happened to Saratu or my fox, and nobody at NASA seems willing to share any morsels of value that might help us find them. But he did say that Bennie's wolf survived Jade's arrow.

Reggie also told me that any news out of the NASA side of the farm is on a 'need to know' basis, a compartmentalized "bigot list" he called it, used for government security, which I think is total bullshit when it comes to missing kids or pets. This secrecy likely means NASA either got caught completely naked—or they know *exactly* what that zippy light in the sky was and are moving to obliterate their tracks under silence.

Eleven bleach-white chickens run mad around my feet in the holding pen down by the barn. I can't even catch one, let alone snap its neck. Two hundred more chickens roam freely with the cows, horses, pigs, and sheep out in the pastures. I hope Reggie doesn't expect me to hunt down and kill them *all*.

"Why do *I* have to do this?" I ask.

"We need dinner."

"I don't know why we just can't go to a grocery store like normal people."

"That's *not* normal," Reggie says. "That's complacency. And convenience."

"It's a damn chicken. What's next? Are we going to grow our own Twinkies and Fritos?"

"Ah, convenience foods," he says. "The processed opiate of the masses. Industrialized farming will ruin the health of the people one day. You'll see."

Reggie walks over, reaches down, and grabs a chicken so fast I'm not even sure how he did it. There are a lot of things that surprise me about Reggie. Like just this morning, I saw him take down a soldier in front of the house when the guy got smart. One quick move, and *plop*—the soldier crumpled onto the grass, until his comrades slapped him awake and carted him off to whatever chore it was Reggie had ordered him to do. With his height, his broad shoulders, and a gut to match, Reggie reminds me of the old miner song, "Big John," except for the fact he's black. He's like a comfortable walnut farm table—rustic with years of dents, scars, and scratches, but still durable and solid, able to hold a meal or decent conversation too.

But it's not just Reggie's size or abilities that startle me—it's his odd combinations. Here he is a big, tough guy, but then he also grows and smokes dope. And he practices yoga. It's like pairing yogurt with jelly beans: they don't go together. Sometimes he's in Rambo mode; other times a Buddha-like quality washes over him. He's taught me how to breathe and stuff like that, too. I think he thinks it might calm me after Saratu's snatching. And I admit, I do like to temporarily clear the mental smog building up in my head. I sit in the morning with him sometimes, now, before the other kids awaken.

Reggie also taught me to recognize all the edible plants in the woods. Wild poke leaves, elderberries, rhubarb, asparagus, cherries, dandelion greens, chickweed, pawpaw fruit, black raspberries, high-bush blueberries, and Jerusalem artichokes—which are actually wild sunflowers and taste sort of like potatoes. There are ostrich ferns too, and a crazy variety of morels—mushrooms. Reggie tells me some of them make people high, or so sick they could die—but he refuses to tell me how to tell the difference. So of course, I don't eat any of them.

Reggie also hides things sometimes. It's not as if he lies to me—it's just that he omits details from some of our conversations—yet there may be a reason for this and I think it may have to do with being here. He's got the clearance to go to the NASA side of the farm with Dr. Sterling. But I don't understand how the government ever gets anything done if the right hand has no idea what the brain, eyes, or mouth are doing. I suspect it operates about as efficiently as Frankenstein, and I know how well that story played out.

But today I'm just happy we're finally permitted outside. We've been on house arrest for the past week while soldiers, scientists, and black suits combed through Plum Hook bagging every last flea. The weird zippy light in the sky also spooked government officials enough to ink permanent scowls across important foreheads, and though these men and women have been scrambling around like they know what they're doing, I can tell it's all for show, the way Barbara sometimes covers a flimsy card table with one of her fancy lace tablecloths when we play Scrabble.

To make matters worse, the body-snatching orb wasn't just confined to our side of the fence. It was seen in Sandusky, and in every single Ohio village within a twenty-mile radius. It brought news people and UFO hunters right to our gate from as far away as Europe. People want answers.

Large metal warning signs went up: *NASA Plum Hook is government restricted space—it is unlawful to enter this area without permission of the Installation Commander. All personnel and the property under their control are subject to search.* And in big bold red letters at the bottom it reads: *USE OF DEADLY FORCE AUTHORIZED.* And even so, some people get too close to the razor wire anyway, and gun-toting soldiers chase them off.

The Department of Defense confiscated an additional four hundred acres of land—calling it a matter of "national security." This meant kicking more people out of their homes, which sparked public protests and led to a lot of yelling. I overheard talk from some of the military types, the ones with too many medals on their chests—

walking pincushions I call them—of faking nuclear disaster to force surrounding populations into a mandatory evacuation. I'm glad that hasn't happened—yet.

"What do you think happened to Saratu and Hope?" I ask Reggie. It's certainly not the first time I've asked, even though he always gives me the same answer.

"I don't know," he says, looking at the blade on his axe handle. "If I did, I would tell you. But until we do know, stay close, okay?"

"I might leave," I say. "Run away and never come back."

"You're probably safer here than anywhere in the world right now. But if you do run, you might need this." He reaches into the pocket of his faded overalls and hands me a shiny gold compass. The back is engraved with the words, *'From BB'*.

"Bennie? Why did he give you a compass?"

"It's not from Bennie. An old friend gave it to me." He studies the distant field with a furrowed brow. "He kept me from getting lost once. Saved my life."

"Those were my dad's initials too," I say, following his gaze into the empty field. "What's your friend's name? My dad's name is… was… Brice Blake."

But instead of answering, he holds up his palm, so we can "experience the calm," as he always says when he wants people to shut up.

I hand the compass back to him, but he won't take it. "Keep it," he says. "It served its purpose. It's my gift to you."

Nobody has ever given me such a nice gift "just because." If it were *my* compass, I certainly wouldn't offer it to Reggie, or anyone else, especially if he smarted off to me the way I do to him sometimes. Its gold needle floats over a black background, pivoting wildly from north to south, east to west. I tuck it into my front pocket next to Barbara's buckeye.

"Hold out your arms," Reggie says. "Pull the chicken close to your chest when I hand it off to you."

I do as he says, and soon I'm cradling a chicken in my forearms like a baby. "If you ask me to burp this damn thing, I'm dropping it and going back to the house."

He ignores my remarks. "Now snap her neck with one strong twist," he says encouragingly, "but don't hesitate or you'll piss her off and she'll peck the shit out of you." Reggie always curses when his wife isn't around, and it makes me laugh, but today I'm a little nervous, with a wad of crumpled worry caught in my throat.

I close my eyes and slide my hand over the chicken's pillow-soft head. She stabs her yellow beak into my skin—one strong, unexpected icepick peck—and I drop her. She flaps away, leaving a wake of white feathers. A single drop of blood pools around my thumb, a small vent releasing some of my pent-up angst.

"I can't do it," I say. "I don't want to kill something for no reason."

"You have a reason," says Reggie. "It's called dinner. There's a natural hierarchy in life, and some animals are sacrificed so others may live."

"It doesn't seem right. Who are we to decide a chicken's fate? I thought we were supposed to protect weaker species, like guardians of the Earth or some shit like that. Besides, I like my animals standing up." I shake my tree-hugger, granola-girl charm bracelet at him—the one that he and Dr. Evelyn gave me for my non-birthday.

Reggie laughs. "You like bacon too. We feed these chickens, shelter them, and offer a safe place for them to roam free from predators. There's a difference between senseless sport kills and need. We're a higher species on the food chain."

"I wouldn't refer to human beings as a 'higher species,'" I say. "What about that old farmer who called us names back at Toft's? He's most definitely *not* a higher species. Why didn't you kick his ass? You just stood there taking his abuse while I did all the talking."

Reggie smiles softly. I can see he's not bothered that I just called him out for shrinking from a fight and acting like a coward in front of his wife. "To control your emotion is a skill only the greatest warriors master. Fight wisely."

"Whoa. Okay, that's deep, Obi." But I do silently marvel at his words. I also experience a fleeting moment of déjà vu unfurling itself before it swiftly curls up again.

Reggie picks up another chicken and puts it in my arms. "And

I wasn't talking about humans," he says. "Now go ahead—you can do this. Breathe. We need seven chickens for dinner. The sooner you finish, the sooner you get free time."

"What do you mean, you weren't talking about humans? You just said we're a higher species on the food chain."

"I did say that, didn't I?" He winks at me. "Okay, let's do this."

I close my eyes. Inhale. Exhale. I open my eyes. I want to get this done so I can go back to the library and do some research.

"I can't," I say.

"You can. You did a pretty good job squeezing Jade's neck a week ago. You'd have killed her if I hadn't intervened on that clamp-clutch I taught you."

"Jade's a heartless bitch. She deserved her medicine. This? It's different. These chickens never hurt anyone."

"Why do you think the chicken you're holding is so fat?"

I shrug.

"We kill the fattest ones because they don't allow the others to eat," he says. "Sometimes they peck other chickens so hard they kill them, and then they stand on the dead ones to take more than their share of feed."

I stare at a bald spot of dirt between two patches of grass. It looks like a skid mark, nature's finish line. I silently agree with Reggie that some animals deserve to die, but the ones I met in Cleveland walked on two legs and didn't have beaks or feathers. And I don't miss them. In fact, I'm glad they're dead and feel sorrier for the dirt that has to accept their sorry carcasses for fertilizer. I suppose I should have a little remorse about Rosie and that other guy's death but I don't. Good riddance.

I close my eyes. I feel puffy cotton-ball-like chicken feathers float through my fingers. I tighten my grip and exhale once more. The chicken's heartbeat *tap tap taps* against my finger pads.

Crack.

One snap. Dead weight. I lay the chicken's body on the wooden stump.

Reggie hands me the hatchet. "Remember, a small, quick, clean swoop to take off her head.

Thwack!

The chicken head tumbles to the ground, her soul to the abyss.

Red blood spurts from her flapping body like a gusher from a Texas oil well. I gag. The chicken's beak opens and closes on the ground as if she's trying to tell me something, to utter last words. Then the chicken *body* squawks. I didn't know they could do that without a head and it completely freaks me out!

The carcass suddenly rolls upright, jumps off the stump, and starts chasing me around the pen—**without a head!** It does a somersault and keeps going, all the while making a weird cluck-gurgle sound. I dodge and roll to get out of its path, then jump up on the bloody stump and punt the headless carcass with the toe of my sneaker. It cartwheels across the grass, leaving a trail of red splatter. Finally, it stops moving.

I vomit.

Tears of laughter stream down Reggie's bearded cheeks. He has to cap a hand around his knee to keep from falling over.

"I don't think it's very funny," I manage to say, wiping puke off my chin with the back of my hand before retching again, tears stinging my eyes.

"You look like a preacher leading 'chicken church' up there on that stump," Reggie says between gasps. "I forgot to tell you, sometimes they do that. It's just a reflex. You have to strike them below the voice box."

I jump off the stump and pick up the next fattest chicken. "You kill them your way," I say, "and I'll kill them mine."

Chapter 15

NIGHT TERRORS

It's bedtime at Plum Hook Bay. And I'm exhausted—mostly from over-thinking about what happened to Saratu and my fox, and Katie's murder, combined with all of the physical labor and military-type training Reggie puts me through on the farm. I'm also completely dreading therapy with Dr. Evelyn.

I switch off the light next to my bed. Darkness descends. My eyes slam shut like the squeaky screen door that leads into the kitchen. I briefly think about my dad and grandma before I drift off to sleep and freefall into the Sandman's abyss:

The county put a few of us here with Rosie, who owns the Trail's End Motel. She gives us a room and receives money from the state, and in return she keeps us delinquents off the streets of Cleveland. Win-win, except when she's being a bitch.

This grimy motel stuck between two scrapyards near the Hopkins Airport might suck but it's a much better option than being locked up in Juvenile Jail, forgotten in the cracks of a sorry "system" and treated like a stubborn stain.

And Saturday mornings are the best here in this slime pit of a motel. No school. And since there's a TV in my room, I watch Scooby-Doo, still my favorite cartoon even though I'm sixteen. The only bad part is, I'm hungry, and Rosie won't unlock the door or bring me food until she comes to from her drunk, and that's likely to be sometime this afternoon. She puts locks on the outside of doors of foster kids she thinks might run away. Katie used to sneak me food, but she's gone now. She turned eighteen and 'aged out' of this pathetic 'system'. I sure miss her.

Keys jangle. This early? Maybe Rosie brought me McDonald's. A pancake platter with scrambled eggs and a large Coke sounds so good right now.

She opens my door and walks in with him, and no breakfast. "He's going to be your babysitter," she says. "You better behave."

Babysitter? This is weird. She's weird. He looks weird too. Long skinny fingers rub rough stubble along his chin as he grins at me like that Jack Nicholson guy in The Shining.

I'm way too old for a babysitter, and she knows it—and I know her game. She thinks it's time.

I stand up and move to the other side of the bed, near the bathroom, away from them. But there's no place to go. Privacy obliterated. I don't get a "do not disturb" option.

"Why don't you just lock me in here like you usually do?" I ask.

"Shush! You be nice to this man or else. Here. Take this pill. It's a vitamin."

"But I don't want to take a pill!"

Rosie raises her palm and holds it in the air over my head. I roll my eyes and put the pill in my mouth.

The man puts some cash in Rosie's chubby fingers, and she stuffs it in her bra faster than Zorro sheaths a sword. Rosie loves money. And her tits are so big I wonder how she fits anything else in there.

The blinds flanking the window behind the TV curl halfway up, allowing a single sun ray to peek through. It shines on the bed like a dingy spotlight, highlighting the dust in the air, and raises the footlights of my suspicion.

"Why wouldn't I be nice?" I say.

"That's my girl." Rosie's ass bounces like a Jell-O mold under black polyester pants, her butt cheeks desperately stuffed into bulging panty lines. She exits and locks the door behind her.

"How old are you?" the man asks

"Sixteen."

For a moment, I fold two undernourished arms across my chest and stare at the TV. Then I decide to glare at him instead, this stranger in my motel room. He smiles wide, shows off rust-stained teeth that appear to be saving a fleck of tobacco for later. Gross. His grimy black tank top, faded jeans, and oversized belt buckle of sparkly fake diamonds clash against his breadstick arms. Weakling. Dirty blond hair grazes his shoulders, covered by an oily-looking Cleveland Indians baseball cap. Even from across the room, he smells like car parts, body odor, and gasoline.

"What's your name?" he asks.

"You're supposed to be my babysitter; you tell me. I don't even know your fucking name."

"You can call me Guy."

If Guy is his real name it's just as plain and ugly as him.

"Your name is Guy? How convenient. My name is Girl."

I feel awkward holding court in front of the door to my tiny mustard-colored bathroom. I turn my face toward the TV again. But I don't really care anymore about what Scooby is doing because this stupid Guy takes up all my space, fouling up the air—not that it was that clean to begin with. I quietly push the white pill out of my mouth and smash it like a booger, rolling it between my fingers until it disappears. I don't know what Rosie gave me, but I do know she wants me fucked up alone in my room with Guy, likely so I won't remember much of what he's about to do, which means I'll never be able to tell.

"You can keep watchin' cartoons," he says.

He sets a six-pack of Rolling Rock on the nightstand, plops down on my bed, and pats the empty space beside him. "Come on, now. We'll watch it together, girl."

I slide onto the bed belly first, feet on the pillows, head on the other end away from this twang-tossing hillbilly geezer called "Guy." I teeter as close to the edge as I can without falling off.

"I'm hungry," I say.

"Here, have a beer."

"I don't drink beer this early." I look at the green glass bottles on the nightstand and roll my eyes. I can't believe this doofus is offering me a beer at nine thirty in the morning. "This is stupid. I'm too old for this."

I stand up again.

"I want out of here—or I want you gone." I say.

Having a strange man sitting on my motel bed in this shithole that passes for a "foster home" is about as unnatural as horse piss passing for champagne.

"Relax. You don't have to get all jittery on me," he says. "I agree. Yer too old for a babysitter. Can't we just git along and try to treat each other as equals?"

I nod.

"Good. You ain't never tried beer before?"

"Not with a guy your age. And not this early."

He plucks a Rolling Rock from the carton, pops the top with his belt buckle, and hands it to me. "Maybe you should. We pay better. Take a swig."

I sniff the bottle and tip a small nip. I spit it out on the worn shag carpet where the occasional loose thread sometimes snags my big toe. "Yuck! That's gross!"

"Rolling Rock is an acquired taste," he says, laughing.

"Acquired? That's probably the biggest word you know." I hold the bottle toward him. "This… is like a mixture of peroxide and piss."

"Ya have to drink it fast," he says. "Pinch yer nose and you won't taste it."

"Why? Why do I even have to drink this?"

"It takes away yer hunger. You'll see. Come on, I dare ya! You finish one beer, I'll give ya ten bucks."

"Ten bucks?"

"Yep."

"I want twenty."

"Wow. A six-pack is only three bucks. But seein' how's ya drive a hard bargain, fifteen is the best I can do." He reaches into his back pocket and tosses a ten-dollar bill and five ones on the bed. I snatch it up and place it on the dresser by the TV. Then I force the fizzy piss liquid down my throat with big gulps, pinching my nose and chugging as fast as I can.

Hiccups. Mine.

We watch cartoons.

I feel floaty.

"How 'bout a little kiss right here on my cheek?" he asks, tapping a stubbly spot.

"Yuck. You're old."

"I'm only thirty-eight. Besides, y'all agreed we'd get along."

I shrug. Chugging beer is an easy way to earn fifteen bucks. I don't feel as hungry either. Maybe he's on to something, this Guy. I crawl toward him and pucker my lips to his prickly cheek. Without warning, he snatches the back of my hair and twists it hard until it's firmly wrapped around his oily fingers.

"Ow! Hey! What the fu—"

Guy shoves his tongue down my throat until I gag and a reflex forces him back. I try to scream, and I want to puke, but I can't do either. He flips me under him on the bed, crushing me with his weight, and thrusts his hand up my summer nightgown, my favorite one, the one with daisies and fireflies. His mouth smashes against mine.

It's not really a kiss.

It's not really a kiss.

It's not really a KISS!

I kick but I'm pinned beneath him, his belt buckle painfully pressing into my bare belly. He raises a palm.

Whack!

I.

Do.

Not.

Want.

To.

Be.

Touched.

"Don't you move, little girl," he growls. *"Don't you dare fucking move, you understand? Look at me, you little slut. I paid good money for a piece of this virgin ass."*

Virgin? Is that what Rosie told him?

Guy spits on my face. I stare into his crazy-angry-bloodshot-shit-brown eyes, as beer-infused saliva drizzles down his chin. He smiles as if he's come to Sunday dinner and I'm on the menu. He loosens his belt buckle and unzips his pants, then rips open the top of my gown. The buttons pop, pop, pop. I hear them bounce off the wall, fleeing somewhere to land on the bed and floor. My favorite nightgown no more.

Guy slides grodie fingers over braless boobs, the ones Katie calls my "mosquito bites." He bends his head forward, licks my left nipple, and it feels worse than a wasp stinging my heart—vile and wrong.

"Fuck you!" I yell. "God damn it. Get the fuck off of me!" I spit at him but miss. He punches me, hard, on my left cheek. Dizzy crackling tiny needles of light invade my vision, and I seriously wonder if this is how Wile E.

Coyote feels after Roadrunner hits him on the head with a hammer. This man's violence and hate permeate this room where I don't belong— have never belonged. Guy seems to think my confusion and his control is funny. He grins wider, looking eviler and way worse than any Saturday- afternoon Vincent Price horror flick I've ever seen. My grandma would say he has the devil in him. If l still lived with her, she'd call the pastor and they'd cast Satan out of this "Guy." She'd call the police, too—but pastors and police don't exist here at the Trail's End Motel. The lump in my throat grows thicker but I'm too frightened and ashamed to cry.

Guy yanks my panties off with so much force they rip. My legs shake as if they're spinning in a science class centrifuge. He slaps me again and presses my arms down hard into the bed. I'm afraid he'll push me through the mattress. Am I going to die?

No!

Please.

No!

"Noooooo!" I yell. The tears arrive and burst over my lower lashes to cascade down my temples and land on the now crumpled bedspread.

More tears. Unanswered screams. I know people hear me but don't want to get involved. Denial is the worst form of abuse. I hate this place. I hate him. I hate them, the people who hear me but do nothing and turn a blind eye. I hate me too. What did I do to make him think he could do this? No! I did nothing. This. Is not my fault. Not my fault. His battery acid hate is cruel and care-less—and I am its undeserved, unwilling recipient.

Float. Disconnect. Turn it off—like a faucet.

He enters me.

He grunts.

He rolls off.

Defilement.

The knife through my body stops, but my soul wound is deep and will leave a permanent scar—one I'll be forced to hide like a regrettable tattoo,

*under some conventionally appropriate mask of bravado so I can avoid
being plastered with another negative label. "Foster kid" is bad enough.
We're already singled out as lowlifes. People forget that our circumstances
are not our fault.*

*I know how caseworkers and the public view rape victims—like
voyeuristic sideshow freaks, able to rise only as high as their pretension
allows. There are no victims, Rosie says. Girls like me are whores—a
commodity who will never be able to reach normalcy. What is 'normal'
anyway? I don't think anyone really knows.*

*Guy yanks me up, Raggedy Ann style, and props me where he wants. I
kneel on the bed before him. He's on his knees too, pants off. Blood trickles
between my thighs.*

"I hate you!" I scream.

*"Shut the fuck up, you love this. Tell me you love it. You scared, girl?"
He yanks on a fistful of my hair. "I said, are you scared? Answer me! Don't
you think today is a beautiful day to die?"*

A vile serpent is he, this Guy.

I nod.

*My answer pleases him, and he attacks again. I catch a strong whiff of
body odor, blood, and beer.*

Evil.

Evil.

Evil.

*"This is so good, don't want to waste the moment by coming too soon,"
he says. "Touch. This. You said you was hungry, so you better show me your
appetite."*

*He puts my hand on his dick. It looks like a pinkish worm wearing a
bloody helmet. I don't want to put my mouth on him.*

"Yeah, that's for you," he says.

*He forces my head down with his grimy fingers and thwacks my cheek
with his thing. I keep my lips closed. He yanks me up by the hair again
to his face, where his beer breath pants against my cheek. "Open your
fucking mouth and suck me off or you will be one sorry little bitch, do you
understand? Now do it real nice just like Rosie told you."*

He pushes my head back down. I gag and choke as his other hand holds down the back of my hair, a heavy wet rag. Teardrops pummel the bedspread like a dripping faucet—and nobody cares.

Guy thrusts his hips back and forth. I hate the disgusting slurping sound this makes. My shoulders and neck grow tight. My lips swell and burn before going numb. I taste metal and blood.

"That's it, that's it… yeah, that's a good little girl. Yeah baby, suck it. When we go for round two, I'm putting this right up your tight little asshole."

I look up at him in surprise when he says this.

"Yeah, that's right, I got you all damn day before I kill you, real slow like. Keep sucking."

The TV plays a commercial. A little cartoon boy asks an owl wearing a graduation cap how many licks it takes to get to the center of a Tootsie Roll Pop. The owl takes the lollipop and gives it three licks before he bites it off the stick. "Three," he says.

Deep anger suddenly overrides my fear.

I like this owl.

***

There is a chunk of skin in my mouth.

Guy is on the floor by the door of my motel room, trying to get out, but he can't. Door's locked—on the outside. How wonderful for me—and how horrible for him. At least for a moment. And not long enough for my taste.

He writhes around on the worn carpet moaning like one of those baboons on Wild Kingdom as he clutches his bleeding crotch. I cock my head to one side and stare, fascinated that this grown man howls like a sissy girl.

On the way down, he knocked over the blue lamp on the nightstand, leaving behind broken hunks of porcelain, a field of dead, useless light gone dark. Ruined. And he got a lot of blood on my flowery bedspread. It's a bright scarlet red that reminds me of the cardinals outside that sometimes perch on my window ledge. Rosie won't be happy. She'll have to pay for this broken lamp. Correction: she'll make me pay. She charges me for everything, including toilet paper and shower water, and she makes me do chores like cleaning up after the losers who don't get locked in their rooms.

I touch the wet red mess on this bed, and stare at my fingertips. I look back at the strange man whose blood is on my hands. He reaches for me. "Please help…"

Snatching the last beer from the nightstand, I throw the bottle at him. It hits the wall above his head and breaks, shards of green glass and golden liquid tumbling over him as droplets splatter the carpet.

Scooby Doo is back on TV. He always solves the crime. "Rut-roh, Shaggy." I eject the tip of Guy's dick from my mouth like a spitball. It lands on the blue carpet under the TV and reminds me of chewed bubble gum.

Bang! Bang! Bang!

"Samantha! Oh my God! Samantha! Are you okay? God, tell me you're okay!"

It's Katie.

She jiggles the door handle, but it's locked.

Guy whimpers. He's in shock. Going unconscious, I think. He tries to talk, but no sound comes out. I grab his fake oversized diamond belt from the floor, slowly crawl over to him and strap his hands together tight, high on his chest.

"How 'bout another kiss?" I ask.

Centimeters from his face, I study the large pores on his nose, several pockmarks, and a small scar near his chin—likely a souvenir he picked up during an attack on some other girl. I pick up the biggest piece of broken beer glass I can find—and I cut my hand a little, but I don't care because it doesn't hurt me as much as he did—then yank his hat from his head and throw it to one side.

"My grandma always said a gentleman removes his hat in the company of a lady," I say. "You weren't raised right." There's a cold calm in my voice, flash-frozen vengeance oozing from every pore of my body.

Two voices outside now. Rosie and Katie. They argue.

"Samantha!" Katie shouts. "For God's sake, answer me! Rosie, open the fucking door! Hurry up!"

"Please," the man whispers. "Help me."

They can't hear him. His voice is too soft, and the TV too loud.

I lean in, lightly suck his bottom lip, and then shred it off with my teeth. I twist my head like a famished animal—a lioness on the savannah of Africa. Blood spurts from his mouth, a broken faucet. He howls much louder than I thought he could. He wriggles around and falls sideways, but I strapped his hands pretty tight. This Guy is not going anywhere—except maybe straight to Hell.

I spit his bottom lip out too. "I like Wild Kingdom," I say. "Have you ever seen it? I watched a special on primates once. Sometimes the alphas bite off the faces of other apes they view as a threat."

I'm glad I'm naked. It will be easier to clean up.

Broken glass cuts through Guy's flesh easily, almost like the scalpel I use to dissect frogs and cats in biology class—except dissecting a human requires a few more tugs and pulls.

Sitting back on my heels, I study his now lifeless body. Killing someone, it turns out, is hard work and now I feel sort of sick. I struggle to hold back my swirling nausea until it breaks through my mouth and I vomit beer all over the blood, the carpet, and this Guy.

Katie screams, clawing at the door from the other side. Why is she so upset? I've got this. "What have you done?" she cries. "What have you done, Rosie? She's way too young! Oh my God, open the fucking door!"

Rosie the bitch won't open the door. She doesn't give two shits what happens to me and I wish her dead too. She thinks the tables are turned against me in here, some twisted lesson to bend me into compliance. She wants me broken like the beer bottle and extinguished like the lamp. Won't she be surprised?

"I told you if you didn't do as I said, I'd break her," Rosie snaps back. "This is your fault. You tried to set up your own territory and take her with you. You don't do that to Rosie!"

Katie sobs. "I paid you triple not to do this. He's brutal. You knew that, and you put him in there with her anyway. You broke our deal!"

Rosie's keys jangle in my door. "No, YOU broke our deal taking off with that rich old coot and stiffing me. You owe me. Besides, that brat in there needed put in her place, acting all high and mighty 'round here, not pulling her weight like the rest. Can't have the others startin' a mutiny, bringing heat on me."

A stir in the corner of the room distracts me from the argument outside. From nothing appears a lady in blue robes. Except... I can almost see through her.

She smiles from the other side of the bed—it isn't an icky smile like Guy's—and she says I'll be all right. But her lips never move, and her voice isn't a voice—more of a feeling she telepathically washes over me like being drenched in holy water, baptized in good spirit, and perhaps even some borrowed strength. How'd she get in here? Who is she?

The door opens. Rosie steps in first.

A flash more brilliant than lightning. The glint of shiny metal.

Rosie screams.

Rosie's blood, too, is on my hands today.

It is written:

"If any person ensnare a child of Anunaki, putting a ban upon them, by order of Anu, that human shall be put to death, the honor of Scatha restored."

***

"Samantha! Samantha! Wake up!"

I throw fists in the air as I shoot up in bed stiffer than knee-high cornstalks.

Someone grabs them and doesn't let go. "Shhh. You wake up Plum Hook Bay," Jade says. "Stop swinging. Sammy? Sammy? Hear me! You safe."

"You were dreaming," Verity says. "We could hear you all the way down the hall. Jesus, Sam, you're drenched in sweat."

"Night terrors?" Jade asks, her thick Russian accent bringing me back to reality. "Bad memories or something?" She releases her grip on my fists and walks over to the window, where she stares outside. Moonlight cascades like a waterfall over her beautiful white hair, and she shudders before cradling each of her elbows in her palms. I have a feeling she has her own night terrors.

Verity hands me a lit cigarette. I take it and inhale deeply.

My body trembles with an involuntary shiver. I remove my wet nightshirt and wipe sweat from my face.

Verity sprinkles something around my bed.

"What the hell are you doing?" I ask.

"Creating a boundary of protection," she says. "It's consecrated salt. It keeps away demons." She finishes up and climbs into bed with me.

"You left Jade outside your salted rim of protection," I say.

"Jade has a bow and she knows how to use it."

"I wouldn't get in stinky bed with you two cooties anyway," Jade says. "You're both, how you say, dee-scus-ting."

I reach for the glass of water on my nightstand, and notice a single red balloon tied to my headboard.

"Did you guys bring me this balloon?"

"I didn't," says Verity. "Did you, Jade?"

"Do I look like balloon type?" Jade now faces us with her hands on her hips. "And I don't even like Sammy. Besides, where in hell would I get balloon?"

Bennie.

He's alive!

No one knows where he went after we all saw the strange light in the sky. The others—Fensig, Pa-Ling, and Genin—returned not long after, and they hadn't seen him either.

Bennie is out there—hiding somewhere. Maybe he, too, has found a protector in the red bird—or better yet, his wolf. That would be more fitting for a little autistic scamp like him.

Woods near a path I've never taken. Bennie, walking backward out of a lab, along the river—Whoa, what is that he just passed? Damn it, I can't go back. He's on the path, over the hill, and now he's at the barrel by the kitchen retrieving his broken gadget, sneaking away after...No. People cannot fly.

Verity snaps her fingers by my cheek. "Hey! You in a trance or something?"

Jade squints at us. She looks at the White Tara painting, then at me, and stomps out of my room with a long sigh.

Chapter 16

PLUM HOOK BAY

Dressed in black, with charcoal on my face and my compass comfortably tucked inside my black sweatpants, I sneak through the woods behind the house. I clutch a flashlight, but keep it turned off so I don't alert the camouflaged goons on the roof.

It's one a.m.

Thank God Reggie taught me how to do an elbow crawl to go after the best blackberries at the bottom of a bush; this place is teeming with gun-slinging soldiers and men in black suits, all of them pacing three stories above, scanning the horizon, and occasionally splintering the night with a smoky cough or low conversation.

Barbara claims the locals think this entire place is haunted, which elevates my racing heart rate. I push further into the forest anyway. Maybe she's right. There is definitely an eerie vibe here.

What if that housekeeper, Gladys, really did see a white Bigfoot out here? Or saw *something* she shouldn't have? Seems a bit too convenient that the alcoholic maid died in a car wreck barely a week after getting tossed from her job. Goose pimples rise on my forearms like the little yeast bubbles in Barbara's homemade bread. I don't really believe in White Bigfoot, but I hope I don't run into him either.

It occurs to me that maybe a Bigfoot killed Sarge. Then again, they didn't find a mark on that dog, and I'd think a Bigfoot attack would leave about as much evidence as a lion kill. Jade wants me to think she did it with her arrows, but I don't buy that either. Dr. Evelyn is my main suspect, though I admit my evidence is flimsy and circumstantial: the dog growled and barked at her at the front gates. That's all I've got. It's not like Sarge took a chunk out of her ass—but I could tell he would have.

"Ouch!"

A briar lashes my hand as I push deeper into a part of the woods where I've never been. I suck on my finger to stem the bleeding. The black eye I got from Jade last week throbs a little, like a mini heartbeat, above my cheek. I christened her with a black eye too, which takes the sting out of mine a little. I'll be lucky if I don't break any bones while cooped up on this freak farm for foster kids.

It's chilly, dark, and damp as I move deeper into the trees, searching for Bennie. He has to be out here. It's like I can almost *feel* him and his energy the way I see auras. Crickets chirp and a few bats flit and wobble overhead. Dew licks the ankles of my sweatpants.

Mimicking soldiers I've watched training for weeks over these ten thousand acres, I continue to walk, dodge behind trees, or crouch low and check my surroundings to ensure I'm not being followed. But after walking for an hour, I still haven't seen a soul, not even the soldiers Reggie's claims are out here doing night patrol.

Light cloud vapor hovers around the moon but the stars still shine through. I stare as far as I can into space watching them sparkle, and they remind me of diamond dust carelessly scattered over light years of black velvet and wisps of translucent cosmic ribbon. Will it ever be possible to someday roam among the stars, or are we forever doomed to ramble in cramped biological vessels over this broken Pangea, this precarious aquarium called Earth? Pangea—another word I learned from Dr. Awoudi. He always told me that education held the key to my better future. Play the foster system game, he'd said.

The clearing ahead ends at a cliff. Creeping to the edge, I peer over into the valley below.

Holy.

Shit.

Jesus, Sam.

Calm down. Breathe.

The Plum Hook Bay NASA "Station," as I've heard them call it, is nothing like the Plum Hook Farm I've come to know. This place is a stark white futuristic city, all shiny metal and polished stone, like a space station on another planet. Grayish-white smoke spews from two massive hourglass-shaped concrete towers that give off an eerie vibrating hum. Fog lingers in little patches before it fades away. A landing strip hosts a swarm of soldiers in dark uniforms circling around something big, but I can't make out what. Men bark orders. There are tanks. Engines growl. My heartbeat increases.

Whooosh!

Oh, shit. Oh, shit.

Something flies over my head, but I don't see what. An orb? No. There's no zippy light. A cardinal? Not this time of night. And whatever it was felt way too big to be a bird.

There it is!

A dark triangular plane hovers silently over the landing strip, making zero noise. The only reason I even know it's up there is because the spotlight shining up from the runway glints off of it now and then. The silent black object rises about fifty feet, and…

Poof.

It slingshots into the darkness above and disappears.

I've never seen a plane hover or move so fast in my life.

If NASA built this thing, I suspect that they could also build the orb-looking craft that took Saratu and Hope. Maybe this place builds all sorts of machines using the same silent engine technology. Is this what Dr. Sterling works on every day?

I have lots of questions, too many, and the only way to get answers is to get closer. But that won't be as easy as sneaking up on a chicken. They have guard towers here, the kind I've seen in prison photos, and cameras too, the big clunky kind usually hung in store corners to catch shoplifters. If I'm spotted, I'll bet this entire place will go into squawk-and-flap mode.

Thank God my gym uniform is black. And—bonus—it makes me look skinny.

Using thick pine trees for cover, I move toward the boundary of the compound, I see signs looming over some of the buildings: *Westinghouse. Lockheed. NASA. The U.S. Department of Defense-DIA.*

Haliburton. Central Intelligence Agency. DARPA. The Atomic Energy Commission.

My eyes dart back to another sign. *Windsor Technologies.* It features a wolf in front of a moon logo.

L. Ian Windsor, Sr. Oxford, UK. Nuclear engineer. DOB: December 8, 1925. MIA. The Tesla Papers. Bigot List Clearance. USAP.

That's all I remember from my dream. Windsor Technologies. *Think, Sam.* But the recall fails to come.

An American flag sways high on a pole. In front of, on a trailer, lies a rocket with *United States Air Force* painted on its side. Men in suits stand with armed soldiers on lookout towers over my head, all of them carrying big guns.

Five extra-long black windowless vans pull up to the doors of a building, and a lady and several men wearing pale blue scrubs with surgical masks walk out to meet them. A hospital, maybe? I'm not sure. Some Army guys wearing gas masks unload another lady plastered to a stretcher. She has long dark hair and an IV punched into her forearm, and a thin hose running under her nose. Her blue bicep has a metal band with a red feather around it.

The woman in scrubs, a doctor I guess, attaches something to the hose, and they wheel the patient inside. Two more stretchers unload— but these hold yellow body bags with tags. Shaking her head, the doctor unzips one, lifts a rather larger than normal ice blue arm from within, examines it, then stuffs it back into the body bag shaking her head.

Then she steps back and pulls her mask down.

Oh my God.

I push up hard against the back of a tree and swipe sudden sweat from my forehead with a shaky hand.

It's Dr. Evelyn!

What the hell is she doing here?

And who are the dead people? Trespassers? Whoever they are, they're extremely tall—at least eight or ten feet. Could they be the Native Americans Barbara talked about? But what would NASA want with long-buried dead? And surely those bodies would be skeletons by now, if not mere piles of dust. And the lady on the stretcher, going in, but not likely coming out? She wasn't dead—at least not yet. Who is *she?*

Cold sweat trickles down my neck. I have to get out of here.

I look off to one side, away from this quasi-dystopian lair passing for "advancement." Behind me, as far as I can see, and slightly buried in the ground, are half-barrel, igloo-looking type buildings—metal white sheds with ridges. People could live in these. Maybe they do. Or maybe this is where they store dead bodies!

Dr. Evelyn glances up from her work—and toward *me*. I crouch lower against the tree but she pauses and squints her eyes as if she somehow *knows* I'm here… then quickly looks down again at another body bag before she motions for it to be opened.

Whew.

My heartbeat thuds like a savage drum beat in my ears.

I make the sign of the cross and silently mutter a Hail Mary, courtesy of my grandma's insistence I be raised Catholic right down to being baptized, 'communioned', confirmed, and taught to memorize prayers I don't really mean and rarely repeat unless cornered. Playing the odds, I guess. Verity and Barbara would be pleased. And hell yes, I'm scared. If I could, I'd teleport myself back to my room, pack a bag, hitch a barge to India, and keep my mouth shut.

The metal igloos are about fifty feet apart from each other, weird half-moon shaped buildings standing out like soft glow balls among a darkened landscape. I crawl up to the nearest one. No windows. One door. Locked. I put my ear next to it. Nothing.

I crawl to the next building. Same thing.

A noise behind me, and I stiffen. Soldiers? *Breathe. Tell them you got lost.*

What I've heard is… a song?

Who would be playing music so loudly out here at this time of night? I expect the "Safety Dance" song by Men Without Hats, to alarm both soldiers and suits, send them swarming toward me like a bunch of pissed-off hornets that just got their nest whacked—but they go about business as usual and unalarmed, which means they're used to this.

Tiptoeing deeper into the igloo camp, searching for the source of the music, I creep from one building to the next, placing my ear against each. There must be at least a hundred of these identical buildings, a labyrinth of labor lined up in rows, no doubt put together on the orders of some overachieving general, now dead, whose painted likeness probably hangs outside my bedroom back at the house. What purpose they serve I can't say.

Wait.

A light!

No, two lights.

I see two small yellow lights atop an igloo.

I move toward it.

A deep growl.

The hairs on my arms spring up like porcupine quills.

Bigfoot?

Run!

Instead, I trip over a branch and fall into the dirt like a clueless dork. It's also very dark, so I can't see much, but I do see something etched above the door of this igloo; *Silo #57*.

And I see the beast, too—on the roof of the building.

It's not Bigfoot.

It's a wolf. Bennie's wolf, maybe?

It leaps, lands three feet in front of me, and growls.

With a scream, I curl into a fetal position—so much for being brave—squeeze my eyes shut and make a wish to disappear. I press my face to the ground, crumbly dry dirt sticking to my lips like stale cake crumbs. I suck in short, shallow gasps and then spit out the soil I've accidently inhaled. If it's Bennie's wolf, it isn't limping as I'd suspect after taking one of Jade's arrows.

The wolf crouches low beside me, his snout pressing against my face while his stinky breath steams up my cheek.

The music stops.

I hear a *bzzzz*.

A click.

I peek.

A door opens.

A shadow, a small figure, emerges. A troop of at least four soldier boots come stomping toward us, no doubt compliments of my scream. Way to go, Sam.

"*Damn it,*" I whisper.

"Randolph! *Dialdi eta retiro! Ezka duel zun,*" The voice commands.

I don't understand this strange language.

The boots come closer. *Tromp, tromp, tromp.* Then a click of guns.

I leap to my feet and swiftly 'tuck and roll' the way Reggie taught me, into Silo #57, before the door slides closed.

Chapter 17

SILO 57

I'm in a lab.

Or a psycho's lair.

It's the weirdest 'kid cave' that I've ever seen in my life.

On one side, scattered electronic circuit-type things and metal components share space with multi-colored wires. Books are piled into small columns on a red-checkered tablecloth spread out on the floor. Whiteboards contain weird mathematical equations with symbols I've never seen and remind me of seriously complex sheets of piano music that I'd suspect even Beethoven would find difficult and I certainly couldn't play—and I'm a decent pianist.

Glass test tubes, vials, beakers and flasks sit patiently in wooden holders on a stainless-steel table, placed with all the care and precision of a model train set.

On the other side of Bennie's space is what looks like a mini Ripley's museum. A shadow box propped on a large desk displays pin-impaled insects. Spider corpses are pressed behind glass frames and mason jars sit along unfinished shelves, containing... well, I don't know what they contain and can only imagine, but they float, preserved in amber liquid.

Behind the jars are neatly stacked animal bones, or at least I hope they're animal bones, and they rest in brown baskets under a long bench. It's hard to tell around here what's human or not, especially given the impromptu horror show I just witnessed starring Dr. Evelyn, but I don't see any human skulls in the baskets. It offers me little relief. I'm not sure I can trust anyone who collects bones or thinks that wolves, cobras, and spiders make great pets—but he didn't shut me out of the silo.

A variety of reptiles, bats, birds, and mice rest or play in the cleanest cages I've ever seen. And looking up, I see a huge ant farm, trapped between two massive panes of glass suspended from the ceiling with long thick chain. Each reddish ant, and there must be hundreds of them, is bigger than a fifty-cent piece and has black pincers that look as if they could snap steel cable, or at least shear off a finger. I shudder and stick mine in my front pocket. I never knew ants could grow this big. No way these creepy crawlers are native to Ohio or even the U.S. for that matter. How did Bennie capture them?

The cheesy disco music is gone. Classical music hums in the background now, a calming opiate of soft piano keys keeping time with the faint smell of bubbling chemicals he's got cooking on a little white stove. Freshly cut pine tenderizes my lungs too—and even though there is death here, there is life too, and while I'm a bit nervous and distrusting, this whole scene also makes me feel alive and deeply curious.

Bennie sits on a tall steel stool before a bank of computers, his back to me, in the middle of the room. A red cardinal perches on a piece of driftwood nearby, monitoring everything Bennie does, as if it knows just as well as I do that this kid is far from normal. I didn't know that wild birds could be tamed. Is this one his pet too?

And then I spot the cobra, the one that got Verity and me in trouble with Dr. Evelyn in the dining room weeks ago. It's curled up in a Longaberger basket. Wow. This is real. I'm not hallucinating—but there is a small part of me that wishes I were.

"I see you saved your snake," I say.

Bennie ignores me.

"Cool cardinal," I say. "What's his name?"

"Edwin."

"You named your cardinal Edwin? That's gay."

No response.

I frown at the back of Bennie's head a little unsure of what to say next. His dark semi-spiraled ringlets glisten with freshly washed shine under the soft light hanging above him. His computer screens, thin TVs that emit a bluish glow, flicker. I've never seen anything like them—or him.

"What are you doing, Mr. Roboto?" I ask. "What's with the wolf out there? Who names a wolf Randolph anyway? He looks good as new too. I'm glad he recovered from Jade's arrow. What language did you use to call him off—is it some weird *Star Trek* stuff you made up? What is this place?"

Bennie stiffens a little in the shoulders. Like me, I don't think he's a big fan of Jade Sokolov. But then again, I sound like one of those babbling, wannabe Valley Girl types I so despise and perhaps that's his issue. *Shut. Up. Sam.*

Bennie still doesn't respond.

Finally, he turns to me. "Here," he says. "Hold this."

I instinctively hold up my palm expecting him to hand me a tool he might need extra hands for, but instead, he drops a huge hairy spider into it.

"Oh my God!" I yell.

I reflexively attempt to fling the thing across the room, but it's stuck to my skin like Velcro!

"Don't move," Bennie says. "If you move, you will die."

"What the fuck?" I complain, trying to keep my voice low—steady my breathing… one…two, three, four. It doesn't work. The gray-silver spider slowly ambles up my wrist en route to my elbow. I've never held a spider before. I'm freaked out and super stressed that Bennie just dropped this damn thing into my hand as easily as sharing a piece of candy—and I was stupid enough to fall for it! Have I learned so little from my time as a runaway on the streets of Cleveland?

"Look at her," Bennie says, lowering an index finger to stroke the spider's head. "Isn't she beautiful? I named her Cutie Pie, after one of the radiation detectors we use. By the way, you were doing the Safety Dance all wrong."

"Get. Her. Off. Of. Me."

Smaller than a tarantula, but not by much, "Cutie Pie" doesn't look like any arachnid I've ever squashed. No wonder Jade kicked Bennie's ass—I bet he made her hold a spider too.

I stretch my arm out stiff. The spider watches, multiple eyes of cold glossy sapphire BB's gazing fixedly at my face.

"You were doing the Safety Dance wrong," Bennie repeats.

"Off. Now. I don't dance."

"I can teach you how to do it right. Look at the screens over my shoulder."

I look at the screens.

The first one shows my skin up close. I see pores, a couple of rust-colored freckles, and white hairs—an otherworldly forest. The second screen shows deep-blue, almost royal-purple veins and floating blood cells with golden flecks (do people have golden flecks on their blood?). They remind me of little inner tubes riding plasma rapids, and occasionally, they knock into each other before drifting off camera like slow moving spaceships. On the third screen is a bunch of numbers and some strange symbols.

"What the hell is all of this?"

Bennie stretches out an arm and touches my black eye with a wet fingertip he's just dipped into some sort of salve from a tin. He startles me and I jerk back like a frightened cat. "I hate being touched," I say, my cheeks firing up with heat.

"I know. I'll be quick," he says. And with one swipe he's done.

"How would you know I hate being touched?" I ask, skeptical he would have access to such knowledge when I've barely interacted with the kid since I've been here.

"I remote viewed your file."

"Huh? What the hell does that mean?"

Bennie shrugs as if it's simple. "I transcended my form and joined forces with an electrical current running through the woods to Dr. Evelyn's office, jumped off, read your file and then caught another cosmic current back here—like hitching a ride on a train. You ever been on a train?"

I shake my head, confused.

"Oh, that's right," he says. "You haven't yet—but you will when you're in London. And you used to watch the train that would run past the back of your grandmother's property by her garden. You'd wait for the red caboose because a man would throw you candy every Saturday morning at 10 am."

"But...how?" I shake my head. "That wasn't in my file."

This kid creeps me out.

"I already explained it. I built Cutie Pie," he says, changing subjects. "This spider has tiny cameras implanted in her, and she can send information about a person to these computers in real-time. She's uploaded with radioactive poison, too. If someone smashes her, they'll die like that." He snaps his fingers. "Cool, huh?"

"No, not cool. Killing people is *not* cool." Even as I say it, I realize I'm probably not the best person to be offering such a moral lesson.

"Is Cutie Pie a robot or something?" I ask.

"She's a real spider," Bennie says. "She's bioelectromagnetic."

I shake my head with more confusion. "I have no idea what that means, you screwed-up little Frankenstein."

"Be careful," he warns me. "You're not so normal yourself. You have to promise not to kill me if you want me to remove the spider. Otherwise we converse with the spider still on you."

"Why would I *kill* you?" I ask. "I mean, for real?"

I'm not angry enough to kill him, and besides, anyone in the business of murder knows you don't move in for a kill if the other guy has better weapons.

I look at him quizzically, a hard puzzle this kid.

Bennie talks way older than thirteen too. He scares me almost as much as seeing Dr. Evelyn examine dead blue people in yellow body bags. He should be playing with G.I. Joe's or riding a bike to Bob's Newsstand to enjoy a freeze pop—not here in some secret NASA nuclear facility studying blood samples and making friends with cobras.

"You're a master warrior," he says. "You know how to kill and you train people to kill."

I feel the blood leave my cheeks. His unexpected words pump up my heart too.

"Fine. I won't kill you," I say. "What choice do I have anyway, you warped little creep?

Bennie smiles a little and gently peels the spider off my arm. He places it in a silver jewelry box and slides it into a safe under the desk. Then he turns and studies my blood cells on his strange TV screens.

The numbers on the third screen change, disappear, reappear, lots of zeroes and ones along with other strange symbols I don't understand. Bennie touches the middle screen with one finger, swipes it, and the view zooms into a single cell.

How did he do that?

The spider, the computers, and Bennie—they're all way beyond 1984 technology. Yet there's all this archeological Indiana Jones relic stuff here too.

"Did the government give you this stuff to play with?" I ask.

"No. Do you know your blood type?" He asks.

"O-negative. It's in the folder you said you remotely viewed."

"I know," he says. "Just wanted to see if you knew."

I make a face. I wonder if Bennie's intelligence is a natural gift or if he's some kind of government experiment, perhaps vaccinated with smart medicine—or bio electromagnetically enhanced, whatever that means.

"Do you know your Rh factor?"

"My what?"

"Do you know if you code a protein on your blood cells that is also found in primates?"

"I…" I have no idea what he's talking about. "You *don't* code the protein," he says, still facing his screens. "Fascinating. I thought you were all destroyed or gone forever. But I had a feeling when I saw you…"

"You thought who were all destroyed?"

He still doesn't turn to face me. "About ninety-five percent of the global population, humans, have this D protein, or positive Rh factor in their blood. The other roughly five percent are Rh-negative. But there are few others who fall into neither category. They're very rare indeed. Less than forty souls in the entire world have what's called 'Golden Blood.' Did you know that governments put Golden Bloods on secret registries?"

"What is Golden Blood?" I ask.

"A vortex sentence if they figure out what you are."

"What do you mean?" I think about how Dr. Awoudi had nurses extract my blood when I arrived at juvenile hall, and Cameron the Cop took that blood. My heartbeat ticks up a notch. I've had my blood taken lots of times since my grandmother died.

"You're a walking weapon," Bennie says. "A hybrid."

"A hybrid? You mean like your spider?"

Bennie nods. "Sort of," he says. "You wouldn't have died. From the spider bite, I mean. You're resistant to its poison. In fact, you're resistant to a lot of things. But make sure you get enough iron. You'll suffer from anemia if you don't—it's typical for our types, a genetic anomaly of our breed."

"You have this 'golden blood' too?"

Bennie nods again. "Euskari, Samantha."

"I have no idea what you just said, goober."

If I'm being played, this kid is the best actor I've ever met. I search his frame, up and down, for clues that he's lying, but I can't find any giveaways in his expression or body language—nor can I *feel* him lying.

"The language is Basque," Bennie says, matter-of-factly, as if everyone in the world speaks it. "It's a lost language humans are unable to master because it mutates," he says. "It's an updated version of Sumerian, which most consider a deader language than Latin. Shame."

"What? Language can't mutate."

Bennie zones out on me, his dark melted-chocolate-brown eyes completely focused on the screens. Is this autism coming to roost? When I asked, Dr. Sterling once told me that Bennie's "indefatigable" mind is his way of testing the limits of his capacity. He rarely sleeps. He rarely plays. Maybe drifting off is how he gets his rest. He leans over and presses his eyes on a microscope, puffing away a ringlet of hair that's fallen into his face.

The door to the silo slides open, and Randolph lumbers in. The wolf lies down at Bennie's feet, rests his head on black-and-silver oven-mitt-sized paws, and looks up at me concerned. But then he yawns and closes his eyes. Who names a wolf Randolph, or a cardinal Edwin, anyway?

"Randolph is Old Norse and means 'shield wolf'. He is my soul guide for this time. The red bird is the spirit of the Source beyond Ninmah's Portal."

A small shiver skips over my spine. "How did you...?"

Bennie looks away from his microscope and offers me an almost but not quite sly smile. Seems that maybe Dr. Evelyn or perhaps Dr. Sterling taught him some of their mind tricks—or maybe he's taught them!

"Who's portal?" I ask.

"Ninmah isn't a who, it's a place."

"Where?" I ask.

"You can't get there from here," Bennie answers. "No one can. It's hidden behind Shambala—and no one can find that either."

"That's not what I asked," I say, a little impatient.

Randolph, surprisingly, falls asleep—and even snores.

"You won't find Saratu or your fox in the river. They're not there."

"Why would I look for them in the river? Wait—you know where she is?"

Bennie shrugs. "I'm smarter than you, but I don't know everything."

I furrow my brow. He *is* smarter than I am, and that bothers me. I like to be the best at everything. "Did you give me the fox?"

Bennie nods.

"Thanks. Best non-birthday gift I ever got."

"Rebirth day," he says. "And she's not a gift, she's *your* soul guide."

"What do soul guides do?" I ask.

"Keep you out of trouble," he says. "Yours has more than its share of work to do."

I frown.

Bennie switches gears. ""Those egoists over there at NASA just split open a door to Hell and made a huge mistake."

A sprouting fear begins to grow in my gut. I sense the doom of which he speaks as it winds its way through this area like it did that day out in the field—but I don't understand what it might be. "And?" I ask.

"Physicists made a huge mistake," he says. "They cracked a big part of the code that controls the entire multiverse."

"Multiverse?"

"It's complicated." He says. "Have you ever heard of something called 'dark matter'?"

"I think Einstein called it spooky action at a distance," I say.

"Right." Bennie raises an eyebrow. "Humans give it the name 'dark matter' because they can't define it, don't know its composition, or understand how it works."

"So?"

"Dr. Sterling figured out how to split a neutrino. His work accidently cracked the lid on Pandora's box, which began a huge argument between solid engineers like him, and theoretical physicists. Those physicists have no idea what they'll unleash if they actually succeed in getting the top off of Dr. Sterling's lid. It will destroy our worlds."

"Worlds? And what's a neutrino?"

"There's more than one world. They're stacked," Bennie says. "Neutrinos are oscillating forms of dark matter that hold truth, unmeasurable bits of energy that power and protect worlds... or destroy and kill them, depending on who wields the Source."

Bennie turns quickly toward me. He reaches for my arms, but I pull away.

"Are you remembering?" he asks.

"Remembering what?"

Bennie's eyes flicker in a way that reminds me of a lizard, but only for a second. It coincides with the sensation that we've somehow met before. "No." He says. "You're not yet fully restored."

"What are you talking about you dork?"

"It means your memory is riding through the information vortex and that others may not yet know you're here, on Earth, I mean. If you can't remember, you're not fully restored."

"I have visions from another place, another time I think." I'm surprised at myself for sharing this so freely. It's not like me at all, particularly when he's blabbering like someone who might need mental help. But I feel a connection to Bennie, not because of anything he's said or done—but because I *feel* he has a 'good soul' more interested in helping than hurting others—but like my sketchy memories about my family, maybe I'm off base about Bennie too.

"Everything you know will eventually come back to you," he says. "And you'll need to be prepared. Boy, will you need to be prepared."

I expect more of an explanation but get none and he switches gears again.

"Religion is really a divisive invention, don't you think?" Bennie asks. He lifts a hand to the cardinal, Edwin, which hops off its driftwood to perch on his finger.

"What does religion have to do with any of this?" I ask.

"Religion has a hand in everything," he says. "Every ancient religious text on this planet is part of the True Word. What humans fail to comprehend is that the Word is actually a scattered code for the Source."

I roll my eyes.

Bennie lightly strokes Edwin's head with his other finger.

"The Word isn't contained in one book like the Bible," he says.

"It isn't?"

"Big human mistake," he says. "It used to be one book, one intergalactic code for everything, created eons ago. But now it's hidden on Earth, scattered like confetti. Too bad that only a small portion of the Word was poorly reconstructed and misinterpreted by humans. They couldn't understand it but took what little they had and converted it into Earth's rudimentary religions."

"I'm not religious, and I don't believe in God," I say.

"Good. You're not suckling the sap."

I look at him quizzically.

"I deduce that when you claim no belief in God, you mean the bearded white man who sits on clouds demanding to be worshipped and feared, a Supreme Being to whom you must confess your sins, repent your ways, and fall in line?"

I nod.

"Well," Bennie continues, "that's not what Gods are like. Unfortunately, most humans are too ignorant and territorial to figure out that if they stopped fighting over their Gods and compare their sacred texts, they'd discover a key that enables them to traverse black holes as easily as turnpike tunnels by bending space and time."

Perhaps I'm not the craziest one on this foster farm after all. His wild claims, I must admit, sound sort of sci-fi cool. At a minimum, it's way more interesting than the boring Bible stories I was force-fed as a kid.

Bennie's nearly perfect peppermint Tic-Tac teeth appear when he smiles widely for the first time and he explains, "Earth-bound scientists think it takes millions of universes to create enough energy to space travel, but they're wrong. The intergalactic code—the Word—is a precise measurement of the ultimate Truth, sans all the complicated theory. But when humans 'go rogue' and play with neutrinos, chaos brews, and universes collapse."

"Are you sure you're only thirteen?" I say, staring at him as if he needs medication and a room next to my mom's in the loony bin, stat. "Now I know why you don't hang out with the rest of us. You'd get your ass kicked."

He lightly shakes his head. "Think of the stacked universe like a book," Bennie continues. "This universe is page one. Rip out a page and the story won't flow. Rip out a bunch of pages and the entire galactic book becomes kindling. What we're being forced to deal with now are split neutrinos that work as if they're poking holes in the pages of a book, which causes other worlds to leak into ours like ink blots, smearing everything until this reality is blurred and no longer makes sense."

"Since when has reality *ever* made sense?" I quip.

Bennie briefly stares into my eyes before he turns away. I sense he's shared all with me he's willing to reveal tonight. I'll have to learn about

"Golden Bloods"—and everything else—on my own. Or with Verity's help.

And before this night, I thought all I had to worry about was getting away with murder.

***

I climb through the window into my room just as the sun pokes over the fields. Staring into the bathroom mirror, I wonder: *Who am I? And what did Bennie mean when he said I'm a walking weapon, a hybrid?* I don't *look* like a hybrid. Not that I would know what one looks like.

Hey, wait a minute.

I touch my cheek. The black eye Jade christened me with last week is gone! What the hell did that little twerp use on my face?

Chapter 18

LIVE FIRE

"**B**lake! Rack your slide and keep that damn gun pointed downrange!"

The gun range is about the size of a football field—an expanse of faded brown grass salted with brass bullet casings and snow. It supports propped-up paper people spaced at various distances. We stand "on the line," a long ledge divided into individual shooting lanes by weathered vertical slats of wood. A few orange leaves left on the trees behind us struggle to hang on, like nature's candle flames twisting and flicking with each breath of cool air. When the wind huffs, they lose their grip and waft along the updraft and pillow down over the shooting range, next year's fertilizer.

My cold fingers are slightly swollen and pink-red at the tips.

Sergeant Major Brock Lynch walks behind all nine of us. Drops of mad hornet spit fly from his mouth when he shouts, and he shouts a *lot*—mostly at me. There's a narrow gulch between his eyes shaped like a tiny pirate sword, which makes him look mad all the time. I'm pretty convinced the old coot has never known a single moment of fun his entire life.

Somebody said he fought in Vietnam along the Cambodian line. Not too many dudes worked that border, so I want to ask if he knows my dad—but I don't know how to relate to Lynch. He's a rugged survivalist type who prefers carbines to kids, I think, and I'm… well according to Bennie I'm some sort of hybrid Golden Blood freak. Plus, I'm a terrible shot, so I'm already pretty low on Lynch's gold star list. I've failed to hit a single target—this gun flings back in my hands every time I fire, somersaulting over my head like Bruce Lee—and I've twice pinched my fingers just trying to load this thing. Blisters bubble up on the webby flesh between my thumb and index finger.

What sort of place allows fucked-up foster kids to shoot real guns anyway? I mean, what if one of us snaps? Did the doctors think a few rounds of live fire would be good therapy?

"Jesus Christ, Blake!" Lynch yells. "Cease fire!"

Weapons land on the ledge in front of us, pointed downfield so we don't accidentally shoot each other. Lynch paces, his fatigues rustling with each step. Two red-shirt-wearing range instructors smirk, and the kids snicker too, all except for Jade, whose expression is set to another rerun of "iceberg bitch."

Verity's next to me, and she reaches over to help, but Lynch barks at her.

"Stand down, Lane, and return to your position!"

Verity hangs her head like she's just been thwacked with a rolled-up newspaper. Jerk-off.

Reggie shovels fresh snow along the back of the range behind us, about fifty feet away, and watches.

Snow—in August.

We thought there had never been snow in Ohio in August before, but a history book in the library confirmed it did snow here in August once before, in 1816. Why it decided to snow again today in August 1984 is anyone's guess. And it's not just the snow: almost overnight the tree leaves turned bright yellow, red, and orange, then broke away from their limbs, leaving the forest a gnarly, naked, thickly twisted land of deprivation. The soldiers waved it off as a "freak storm," but they're acting more fidgety than trained professionals should. Lynch tries to weed the weak from the warrior, cultivating the proverbial grenade garden of soldiers to render his unit pest free.

Lynch stands in front of me, ramrod straight. "You've been out here twice and still can't control your weapon." Wiggly earthworm veins pop in his neck as if searching for a way out. I'll bet that even his own internal organs don't like him.

My cheeks feel hot against the cool air. Lynch's wood-burning words have stoked my irritation.

"Sokolov!" he shouts, without taking his eyes from me.

"Yes, sir!"

What a kiss-ass.

"Show little Sammy girl how a real lady shoots."

"My name is *not* Sammy!" I snap.

"It is until you learn to shoot." Lynch's stainless-steel, drill-bit eyes, bore into me, blowing off my anger like sawdust shavings.

Jade loads her weapon, racking her slide as easily as Rambo, and cradles her hands around it until it's an extension of her arm. She looks through the sight of her semi-automatic forty-five—a big gun for a girl, soldiers say.

Jade closes her right eye.

"Aim for the cranial vault," Lynch says.

Jade slowly squeezes her trigger. The sound of the gunshot vibrates through my chest, a morning gong…

… clad in saffron colored robes I peer through the jungle. Beyond the trees, mountains rise above the mist. A white crane with red-tipped wings glides near a waterfall searching for a fish. A man in a wide-brimmed straw hat arrives via the river in a homemade boat of palms. He uses a bamboo stick to steer toward our temple on the riverbank. He brings me the war's wounded—mostly kids—and calls me "Sister."

The thud of metal snaps me back to reality where Jade has fired off fifteen rounds. They've formed a single tightly grouped opening in the middle of her target's head. It looks as if she punched a hole in it with her fist. Bitch.

Jade looks sideways toward me and surrenders a feline smirk. I look down. I want to punch her again. I feel jealous and angry toward her for one-upping me at almost every turn—then reveling in my insecurities.

"Show Princess Sammy how to properly grip her weapon," Lynch says.

My forehead crinkles and steams up with anger but Reggie says I can't act like a smart ass with Lynch during shooting class—or he'll make me sleep in the barn with the pigs.

Jade goes through the exact motions again, slowly, then hands me my gun. "Make friends with gun," she says. "You're, how you say, 'slap happy' with trigger. It's why you miss. You flinch." She stands behind me and folds her fingers over mine on the gun. She isn't being nice, just methodical. She's doing as she's told, following orders.

"Now that's hot," Pa Ling says.

Guys laugh. Girls roll their eyes.

"You wouldn't even know what to do with a girl," Fensig says. "You'd jizz right in your underpants if one even said hi to you."

"No, he wouldn't," Genin says. "He's free-ballin'. Goin' commando!"

"And how would you know, queer?" Tetana asks.

"Can it!" Lynch yells.

The silence is swift.

Everybody here is afraid of Lynch, even the soldiers. He's some highly decorated war hero who talks with presidents. Why he's spending time out here with us is anyone's guess. Maybe he got demoted.

"You need tight grip," Jade says. "Not that tight. Take control. No flinch. Flinch make you miss target."

We slowly pull back the trigger together.

Bang! A direct hit.

"Show her again," Lynch says.

I shoot another hole in my target right next to the first one. "Maybe I could get good at this," I say to Verity, feeling slightly less like a loser, and smiling for the first time this morning.

Jade sniffs and tosses us both a look of amusement. "Don't get hopes up. You mutts are runts of outfit. How you say, 'expendable.' Like, I call you to start car and bring 'round in case it had bomb."

Lynch and the others laugh, which spikes my mad meter even more. Reggie, still watching, sips steaming chicken noodle soup that Barbara made, from a green thermos.

"You need to toughen up your insides, kid," Lynch says, spitting a chunk of tobacco at the ground. "You're too sensitive, emotional—and that can get you killed."

Lynch is clueless about me. He of all people should know that strength comes in different sizes. My insides are about as hardened as the cold metal on these guns but I don't tell him that.

I glance at Reggie again and wonder if my lacking "Annie Oakley" skills disappoint him. Jade called me a runt and 'expendable.' I don't want to be expendable. I've already been mostly discarded the first half of my life, and now I might be completely expendable too? Not acceptable.

"Sir," I say. "Permission to shoot unattended?"

Lynch shakes his head. "Sammy, if you think firing off two shots while Sokolov swaddles your gun qualifies you for a SWAT team, you're a lot dumber than I thought. But..." He sighs and tips his camo hat. "Permission granted."

"I want to try for my dad, Lieutenant Brice Blake. He was on the Cambodian line too," I say.

For the first time since I've known Lynch, he lets slip one teeny-tiny, almost miss-able expression of surprise. He slightly lifts up the camouflage hat perched on his head and scratches a spindle of gray hair before he pulls it down again so the rim hides his stare. Then he looks up at the cloudless sky, bites a thin upper lip, and locks both hands behind his back, as if he's been handcuffed.

I got him.

He knows my dad.

But he's too smart and too cool to give up that knowledge "on the line" in front of his men and a bunch of kids.

"Blake, are you going to shoot or what?" he barks. "You either step up to that line and show me you can fire a weapon, or you stand down! Do I make myself clear, Lieutenant?"

Lieutenant?

He shakes his head in confusion and looks toward Reggie, who stands a little straighter—alarmed?—as if something just happened and he's not quite sure what.

"I mean, Blake!" Lynch says. "Do I make myself clear?"

I nod. "Yes, sir!"

"I didn't know your dad was in the army," Verity says. "Was he killed there?"

I'm not going to focus on her questions right now. Lynch watches me, his steel blue-gray eyes like magnets drawing me in for closer inspection, but ready to repel me too if he doesn't like what he sees.

"Remember when I told you my dad was in prison?" Verity whispers. "He got thrown in the brig in Vietnam and was dragged out of the jungle along the Cambodian line, dishonorably discharged for protecting somebody—refusing to talk. But then he went MIA. Later my mom got word he was moved to some federal prison, but they wouldn't say where."

I bury my surprise. She never mentioned this before. And I'm ashamed that I never asked. But then, I never mentioned my dad either, as if their absence in our lives is an acceptable circumstance that shouldn't matter because they aren't our moms. And that's bullshit. Girls need their dads, too. At least they need *good* dads. Maybe this is why the world doesn't have more female physicists, assassins, or sci-fi writers—because girls grow up mostly with moms who get stuck squeezing pennies to make lemonade instead of learning how to build lasers.

"Later," I say.

I rack the slide. I'm angry. About everything that's happened to steer me away from a normal life and family.

The unforgiving metal still feels foreign as I melt my palms around its grip and press my thumbs to one side of the trigger, near the safety switch.

What havoc humans wreak with guns. If someone gets mad at the world and decides life is worth little, guns are able to extinguish souls faster than the Gods can fashion one, I think. And what fear humans instill in each other by wielding something as small as a finch, but so deadly in its construction, in order to feel like Gods, when no good God, I think, would encourage violence.

Yet guns also bring feasts to the family table and have saved innocent lives by countering a threat of violence. Maybe guns keep societies from languishing in the Stone Age. Or do guns lead us back to the Stone Age?

I struggle too, with notions of how God and guns fit together. I've watched some of the soldiers pray before they practice killing people. It's confusing for me . If God is love, how do guns serve as an extension of such love?

But I push all that aside. Right now, it's just me, a gun, and an orange target.

Ready.

Aim.

The gun slowly rises away from my chest, at the end of straight arms.

Rosie.

Guy.

Murder.

Blue Robes Lady.

Cameron the Cop.

Dr. Evelyn.

Bennie.

Saratu.

Hope.

Yellow body bags.

Mom.

Dad.

Golden Blood.

Katie.

Fire.

My weapon is empty. I lay it upon the ledge and turn to face my judgment.

Jade's mouth is agape, and everyone else stands slack-jawed too, looking downrange at my target. I aimed for the target's head all right. It's just not the head we all expected. This one is... lower on the body. Right above his balls.

"Ha! Look!" Priyanka laughs. "She hit the cranial vault!"

The girls erupt with laughter. The range instructors wince, as do the boys.

"There may be hope for you yet, Blake," Lynch whispers.

"Beginner's luck!" Jade yells. "Permission to challenge the underling, sir!"

"Who you callin' an underling?" Verity says. "God, Jade, you got issues."

"Have at it," Lynch says. He's clearly amused, and I think a little proud of me. But this isn't my weapon of choice. I prefer swords.

Wait—why would I think that? The closest I've ever been to wielding a blade is a steak knife—and I rarely get steak.

"It's a contest," Priyanka says. "Jade's challenging you to a shoot-off!"

"No." I eject the magazine from the gun and carefully place it back in the box.

When I fired this weapon, I zoned out everything and everyone, allowing myself to be completely swept into a Zen-like disconnect from emotion. This feeling of nothingness was nice—even peaceful—and I want to feel it again. Too bad it's so short-lived. And I don't want to ruin the moment by thrusting myself into competition—at least not today. But still, how realistic is it to think that target practice is a "must have" skill for kids?

I turn to Reggie and bow slightly.

He bows back.

"What's the matter?" Jade says. "You chicken?"

"No."

Our eyes lock on to one another, each searching for weakness. After a moment Jade turns away, a slight blush in her cheeks, pissed off. Probably because I don't bite back. As Reggie says, "*to control your emotion is a skill only the greatest warriors master. Fight wisely.*"

Jade reloads her weapon and takes aim.

I squeeze my eyes tight and wish with all my might her gun jams.

She flinches—and misses.

Gasps all around.

Annoyance, and a look of distraction, roll across her usually placid face… and I just can't resist. I reach out and yank her black sweatpants down to her ankles.

There's pointing. Laughter. Jade drops her weapon on the ground and Lynch roars like a rabid military maniac, lunging for the gun to get it out of the snowy dirt. Jade tries to come after me, waddling, and trips.

"Run!" Verity yells.

I launch into a full sprint right through a pile of freshly shoveled snow, past Reggie, who slaps his knee with amusement.

Feet.

Leaving.

Ground.

It's only a couple of inches at first, but I glide above the snow, like I do in bad dreams when I'm chased by a white-faced man in a black cape and top hat, crazy Einstein-like icicle-white hair poking out from underneath. He tried to smother me once as I slept, pluming his bat-wing cape at the end of my bed before hovering over me and then slowly compressing his weight until I couldn't breathe. I don't stick around for that guy anymore when he shows up in my dreams—not now that I've learned to fly.

But I'm not in my dreams now. I'm flying in real life, unaided by technology.

And the moment I think about that, gravity snatches me back. I land hard, tumble through powdered snow, and slide heavily into a small ravine. A black shadow moves toward me from a nearby boulder.

Not Jade.

Headache.

Dizzy.

I drift away, the camera of my life pulling back again before it fades to black.

Chapter 19

REALITY BYTES

I t's therapy day.

Out the window of my room, I watch dark clouds descend like rolling lava on skeletal flesh-colored cornfields. Thunder rumbles in the distance; Grandma used to say, 'God is bowling' when she heard a storm grumble. We've had a mix of sleet, snow, and rain for seven days, and it pelts my soul. I feel troubled, trapped, and miss the sunshine. I not only miss the sunshine, I miss a lot of things—the city, a real school, a family…

I've been on bed rest ever since Genin found me passed out in the ravine three days ago—which means I've been holed up in my room, visited occasionally by Dr. Evelyn, queen of cranial code cracking and yellow body bags. I'd hoped she'd forget therapy (even faked a deep sleep yesterday), but she jumped in because I'm captive and conscious again. And now I pace back and forth in my room feeling like an enclosed tiger.

"According to Dr. Awoudi, you've very skilled at ducking questions," Dr. Evelyn says. She peers into my file, a thin one *she* created, not the monster file I had back at Mrs. Myers's office. "But I hope we can be open with one another." She looks up at me. "The kids said you didn't run from Jade, but that you flew the other day at target practice. I'd like to discuss why they think they saw such a thing."

She's lying. They wouldn't say that—at least I don't believe so.

"How the hell would I know?" I say, folding my arms and turning away from her, feeling irritated. "Ask *them*. Maybe *they* need more meds."

I'll give up nothing and do my best to keep Dr. Evelyn from plunging into my head. It isn't pleasant in there and what goes on in my brain is none of her or anyone else's business.

"Why do you despise therapy?" she asks.

I calculate my next move for this unsolicited match. Dr. Evelyn rolls up the baby-blue sleeves on her expensive looking blouse, and her silver charm bracelet slides down a thin, pale wrist. *Jingle, jingle.*

Round one.

"I hate examining myself," I say, looking around and trying to figure out how to get out of this, away from here, and her. "I don't see the point. Why can't people leave their shit piles behind them and move along—you know, get on with life? Besides, people who gorge on their problems only end up using them as pitiful excuses to pass as victims."

You examine dead people in yellow body bags on the NASA side of the farm. I can't say what I'm thinking though or she'll know I was on the NASA side of Plum Hook Bay, where us kids are forbidden.

"Why so hostile? Cup of tea?" She asks, fanning her hand out over the afternoon spread Barbara left. The small tower of little cucumber and cream cheese sandwiches look good but Dr. Evelyn isn't getting an inch of cooperation from me.

I shake my head. "No thank you." I'd rather smoke a joint, I think. I wish I had one to calm my vibrating nerves.

Dr. Evelyn sighs and rolls her head from side to side, then pours a cup of hot lemon-ginger tea from the dainty rose-petal-fine-china teapot. She adds a bit of milk. Who puts milk in tea?

The long quiet is maddening. Nothing from her. No questions. No answers, no words—just occasional slurps of tea as she intently watches me until I can't take anymore silence. "You already know I'm a runaway foster kid," I say. "What else is there? How about this: Do you know what happened to Saratu and Hope? Why don't you answer some of my questions for a change?"

"I wish I did," Dr. Evelyn says. "Frightening. None of us had time to think or respond. But we do now. I've heard it said that there is valuable space between a reaction and a response. In this instance, biding our time is smart, especially if others hide things from us."

Hide things? Like how you're hiding what you do on the other side of the farm late at night—plucking limp, lifeless arms from yellow body bags and examining them?

I study Dr. Evelyn and wonder how she manages to always look so freshly pressed and chipper at the crack of dark thirty. "Who would hide stuff from us?" I finally ask. I don't even try to hide my sarcasm. "And by the way, I think 'biding time' is an excuse for people to do nothing."

She shrugs. "Many people hide things. Sometimes it's necessary. NASA for example," she says as she cocks her head toward the field. "It's a classified facility. It's forced to hide from the world because our scientists work very hard on new technology that could save or enhance lives. The research they do is on a 'need-to-know' basis and requires high security. Some things must remain secret to prevent war or promote peace."

"It ludicrous that human beings build weapons to prevent war or promote peace under the ruse of enhancing lives," I say. "It's like playing beer pong with Sarin."

"How do you know about Sarin?" Dr. Evelyn asks.

"Reggie told me," I say.

"Hmm," she rolls her eyes. "I have to wonder what Reggie is thinking when he feels it necessary to teach you about poisonous nerve agents."

"Well?" I say. "I could go get him right now if you want, and you can ask *him*. He can go through this torture you call therapy."

"Ha. Ha. Nice try." She gingerly places her cup on its saucer. "But to answer your question regarding Saratu and your fox, I'd say maybe." Her voice hosts a trace of shaky worry-fear and lacks its usual self-assured cadence, which surprises me and I stop pacing. "I know it sounds harsh to hear that good people sometimes become casualties of progress. We do our best to minimize such damage but also learn to accept it as a painful part of protecting the greater good among our respective countries and its people."

Her lukewarm and indirect way of telling me I should learn to *accept* the disappearance of Saratu and my fox as a 'casualty of progress', angers me. I've had to *accept* that my grandma died. I've had to *accept* that my dad's M.I.A. due to some stupid war in a faraway place that took him away from me. I've had to *accept* my mom's illness. I've had to *accept* being raped in a faux foster home by a douchebag. I've also had to *accept* the offer I was made in Mrs. Myers's office to come here. I'm tired of just accepting.

"I find it really hard to just *accept* that my friend and fox were killed for national security," I say. "Acceptance can go fuck itself. You have my file. You already know about my psycho mom, my cancer-ridden grandma, and that my dad died somewhere in Cambodia. Is that why I'm here? You probably think I inherited my mom's illness, right? You hope to study me like some sort of zoo monkey?"

Dr. Evelyn shakes her head. "Life certainly threw you quite a few daggers, didn't it?" She reaches down into her orange tote, pulls out my thick manila file—my real one from Mrs. Myers office—and offers it to me, arms outstretched.

I despise Dr. Evelyn, I suspect, because she appears too remote from her feelings, her narrow gray eyes fixed upon me and as cold as a polished silver pot someone forgot to fill with warm tea. She's definitely not the type of woman who'd bake cookies or sing me to sleep or even hug a kid the way Barbara so naturally does. I feel no depth of emotion from Dr. Evelyn—just placid efficiency and evasion, peppered with a dash of entitlement, as if the right side of her brain's been scrubbed.

I grudgingly yank the file from her arms. It's heavier than I remember—mostly physicals, IQ tests and scribble-scratch left behind by a series of "Dr. Assholes" from the juvenile justice system, their ink-blotted diagnoses ultimately writing me off as a lost cause that stamps my life "unworthy." This file always arrives ahead of me too, wherever I go, a warning for 'authorities' I guess, of my impending arrival.

Curious, I turn to my blood type. It says O-negative, but there's nothing about my Rh factor or "golden blood" in here. I toss the file on my bed where some of the paperwork peeks out from under the oversized manila, and face Dr. Evelyn again.

"What makes you angrier than anything in the world?" she asks.

"Therapy," I say. "You expect me to bare my soul while you conceal yours?"

Dr. Evelyn ignores my question. "What is the worst thing anyone's ever done to you?"

I experience a micro flashback of Guy making faces on top of me, tearing the flesh between my thighs, making me beg and bleed, telling me it's a good day to die. I squeeze my eyes shut to rip the scene from my head, but feel Dr. Evelyn watching me, her prey. I square up my shoulders as my anger unfolds in every direction of my mind, and spins around my head like the goofy gold needle on the out-of-control compass Reggie gave me.

"I don't like this game," I say, staring down on her. "I want to know why Saratu disappeared and what really happened to Katie. Why do I have to hold a candle up to my core while you and this freak farm keep us all in the dark? I'm nothing but a fucking case number to you. Why do you even care about what I think or how I feel? Answer *my* questions: why are we really here? I'm interested in what *you* know."

"Rosie was a cruel bitch."

Stab. Burn. Dr. Evelyn certainly knows how to launch sudden and unexpected missiles to the heart, which seriously blow me off balance.

"How would you know?" I'm surprised by her swift change of gears and stumble to recover. "You might be too."

Dr. Evelyn registers a look of hurt, but she quickly casts it off like flicking a tick from her sleeve. "Dr. Awoudi showed me the Trail's End Motel interviews. I saw the children. I saw where Rosie held you captive. If murder were legal, I'd have killed her too. Since you're not the type to pussy-foot around, let's share a raw discussion, shall we?"

I work to mentally stuff Rosie's bloodied corpse back into the perfect little brain basket I made. "Are you going to spit it out?" I hiss. "Are you going to accuse me of killing Rosie? This would be perfectly typical, getting blamed for something I didn't do. You're just another quack who averts her own issues by probing mine!"

I pace from one side of Dr. Evelyn to the other, caged in this gilded playpen. I long for the outdoors, ache for it, even though it's cold and snowing—in August. I check my breathing, keep it flagpole steady so my thoughts don't tumble out of my ears the way hundreds of baby spiders scramble from the womb after their pregnant mother gets squished.

"I'm not accusing you of anything." Dr. Evelyn says. "I already know you killed Guy. What you need to understand is that self-defense is not murder. Survival is not murder. An eye for an eye is honorable and brave."

Sway.

Stay upright, Sam.

I feel as if Dr. Evelyn just landed a perfect right cross and upper cut to my brain. I stagger before the thumping in my head begins.

Stone tablets appear. A cave with strange carvings. Torches light my path. A space half known, a time forgotten among no time, cast into a bubble, straddling a fence between two worlds, unsure of where I fall. A battle cry:

> **"The battle-birds were filled in Skye**
> **with blood of foemen killed,**
> **an eye for an eye,**
> **to avenge Scatha the skilled."**

A warm flush swipes my cheeks and confusion punches the breath out of my lungs. Dr. Evelyn rises from her chair. I back up but don't turn away, eye meeting eye, both of us reading the thoughts and visions of the other like a film on fast-forward. My stomach muscles tighten and my fingernails slice into my palms again creating small, bloody quarter-moon imprints.

"Tell me what happened that day in the motel," Dr. Evelyn says.

"No."

"Tell me about Guy."

Verily in those days, I procured the freedom of the sons and daughters of Ninmah, upon whom slavery had been imposed, and established justice in accordance with the Word to bring peace upon the land, to banish complaint of the mouth, to turn back enmity and rebellion by the force of arms, and to bring well-being to the sons and daughters born between men and gods.

I struggle to breathe the way Reggie taught me—slow and steady, but anger slowly roasts me over the slow fire of Dr. Evelyn's interrogative spit. I mentally teeter between two realities, wondering if I'll finally land for good on the 'mentally unstable' side and hoping it won't be so.

"Samantha?" Dr. Evelyn asks. "Are you okay?"

She stretches out her hand, grabs my forearm, and places a white pill into my blood smeared palm as she searches my eyes. "Take this pill," she says. "It will make you feel better, calm you."

"No!"

The Trail's End Motel comes rushing at me like an unexpected and blood-curdling tsunami of memories. I can't move out of the way—there's no place to hide. I bang my now throbbing temples with my fists as I struggle to stop the incessant noises in my head. Sweat oozes from my underarms and spreads across my chest, almost like the freakish slow-moving mid-summer snowstorm outside.

Dr. Evelyn reaches into her orange tote. "Here," she says. "If you don't want to take the pill, this will make you feel better."

Has she gone mad too?

"Nooooo!"

With a fist, I knock the unopened green bottle from her hand and it crashes into the tea set. Both bottle and teapot explode on the granite floor. The foamy brew fizzes and I rage inside. My heart wound is split wide open, oozing hurt, and is now unwillingly exposed by the emotional peroxide Dr. Evelyn poured. It burns beyond measure, all these feelings that bubble up within me.

"What the fuck is wrong with you?" I ask, tears streaming down my cheeks.

"You attacked your killer in self-defense," Dr. Evelyn says. "You've wadded this bloody mess up in your head like you're guilty of murder, yet what you did was justified and brave. Samantha, look at me."

I struggle to blink sense into Dr. Evelyn's angle, her agenda. Is she baiting me so I admit what I've done and go to jail? Or is she actually trying to help? Is she a mad scientist or concerned professional? Do I mention that I saw her at NASA playing with cadavers? I don't know what to do, and I don't like not knowing what to do because it leaves me without solid footing—vulnerable. I can take care of myself! I'll be fine. Breathe. Think. Recover.

I turn to face the Asian lady painting, the Dolma, to plead with her about what I should do. How do I get out of this? Out of here, away from therapy? But White Tara offers only the same silent serene smile as always.

"Who killed Katie?" I ask, practically choking on spit that slides too fast down my throat.

"I don't know," Dr. Evelyn says. "I wish I did. We do know it wasn't you."

Her charm bracelet tinkles as she reaches for me. I jerk away. I'm exhausted. And I definitely don't want to be touched.

"We?" I ask. "Only two people should ever know about a murder, and one of them should be dead, I think."

"Reggie, Dr. Sterling, and me," she says. "And it wasn't murder. It was 'justice'."

"Does Mrs. Myers know?"

"No. Mrs. Myers is about as clueless as a mop left to stale in an abandoned building."

A small smirk crosses my lips. I do appreciate how the Brits come up with their clever and classy descriptions of people and behavior. "Does Dr. Awoudi or Cameron the Cop know?"

"Yes."

"Why hasn't Dr. Awoudi shown up with Cameron the Cop to arrest me and take me back to jail?"

Dr. Evelyn gently rests her hands on my shoulders and turns me to face her. "They haven't shown up because we *are* the authorities. Sometimes when you're put in a corner, it's wiser to fight back than end up lined in chalk. I've never killed a person who didn't deserve it."

I let her words register. How many people has *she* killed? I want to ask, but I don't.

"Stop touching me."

She doesn't.

I study this polished woman, as calculated and put together as an ivory chess set. Dr. Evelyn may examine dead bodies, but I'm skeptical that she's actually capable of squeezing a single drop of barbarity through her British blue-blood pores. Although come to think about it, she wouldn't be past using poison—or any other method that might preserve her French manicure. "Kill someone? You?" I ask in disbelief. "You're a walking *Vogue* cover living at the top of the socioeconomic food chain!"

"Yes, me," she says. "But only when justified."

I wonder how she defines *justified*. Do all of those corpses she studies in yellow body bags that she unzips on the NASA side of this farm represent her idea of 'justified'?

"Get your hands off of me," I say. "What do you mean *you're* the authorities? And how do you know that the prick back at my motel room told me his name was Guy?"

"I'm able to pick up pieces of your thoughts," she admits. "It's a gift. Though it doesn't come naturally to me like it does for you. It had to be developed. Hours of practice, focus and occasionally, drugs. People's thoughts settle on me like pollen grains if I concentrate. And yes, we are the authorities... sort of." She frowns as she says this.

I want to launch her out of my brain and my personal space. I can't quite read her the way I do the others. Is she foe or friend? And she needs to take her hands off of me. Now. Basque glides off my tongue as if I unfurl a whip. "*Zer enoo zuk.*"

I can tell by the swift look of fear that scuttles across Dr. Evelyn's forehead that she doesn't understand a word of the language that Bennie and I share. She doesn't have our blood. The voices grow louder in my head as I search for a clearer signal.

No. You cannot enter here, waiting for the Nephilim to grant you Earthly entrée. Return to your realm Bezaliels.

"Sam..." she says. "What language did you just speak? Sam? Are you with me? What's happening to you?"

"Remove your hands from me you vile human."

I push Dr. Evelyn as hard as I can but she holds on and we both tumble over the chair, taking it with us to the floor. I kick, punch and tear at her bobbed hair.

"I don't like to be touched," I scream.

A million cheering voices in my head tell me to kill her, but these voices are unlike the hushed whispers blowing through the fields above our heads when we picked tomatoes. This is different. This is much worse. This is an evil indifferent to life of any kind, including mine—but it will use me, I fear, to get through, because I'm guessing, that it's not from this world, unable to take biological form, and maybe requires a host.

Dr. Evelyn links her arms through mine and locks her legs around my knees, immobilizing me. I'm definitely more than a little surprised that she too, knows the art of jujitsu, and delivers it in a much more calculated and experienced manner than either Jade or me.

"Let me go! Is this it? I go to jail for murdering a monster?"

Every part of my body and mind feels inflamed and tainted. Unholy. My shoulders hurt too, as if I got my wings clipped on this stupid, filthy, dying place called Earth. I want to scrub its lice from my soul, along with the other scourges I picked up when I got tossed into this gutter of a planet, the boondocks region of all galaxies. I'm a displaced strategist involuntarily drafted into an unseen war by those who'd never cross the front lines into this atmosphere, but who instead, hang at ultra-high altitude, watching chaos unfold. I remember. I am Scatha, the lost warrior. And I **DO** have a family!

I stare at the lamp by my bed and focus my anger on it because I'm unable to heap more pain on Dr. Evelyn and I want for her to hurt the way I do—to understand. It jiggles a little at first before it lifts about two inches off the nightstand. It zooms across the bedroom, where it violently meets one of the big windows and both shatter. Icy wind from the freak August storm punches the sheer curtains hanging in the way, bringing nature's wrath inside to join us.

"Oh my God," Dr. Evelyn says. "Reggie? Did you see that?"

Reggie and Barbara stand silently in the doorway. I was so zoned that I didn't hear or see them arrive. Barbara covers her mouth behind her husband, scanning the demolished tea set and broken window with a look of distress. She makes the sign of the cross.

"What the fuck is going on?" I shout. "Let me go!" I try to wriggle free from Dr. Evelyn. No luck.

Bennie... help.

I know he hears me.

"We won't hurt you," Reggie says, crouching beside us on the floor. "You're not going to jail. I promise. No one knows where you are or who you are. Understand?"

Tick-tock. Tick-tock. Tick—

The grandfather clock in the hallway hushes. The other lamp light flickers and dims before getting bright and then settling again into a soft glow.

I choke and cough up more tears, staring into Reggie's eyes, trying to read his soul, but I'm interrupted by Blue Robes Lady who appears behind his shoulder. She's not smiling. She leans over Reggie. Does Dr. Evelyn see her too?

Blue Robes lady waves her index finger at me and mouths, *No.*

Reggie turns to look. "What do you see?"

"Let me go!" I scream.

"I'm going to ready an injection," Dr. Evelyn says.

"No!" Reggie snaps. "It's part of her problem, these quick-fix shots—always a pill or a potion for what ails us, even if the side effects are worse. She's had enough to kill a cow."

Barbara hands Reggie a glass of water she's fetched from the bathroom—after first blessing it and once again making the sign of the cross.

He pours it over my head.

The unexpected splash of cold shuts off the remaining crackling fuzz and rush of voices in my head. The lady in blue robes climbs into the Dolma painting and disappears behind a monk.

I nod. Dr. Evelyn loosens her grip.

"Consider that your baptism," Reggie says. "Nobody is going to jail. As far as society is concerned, you don't exist."

"Story of my life," I whisper. "How is that even possible?"

The buzz in my head slowly returns, like adding fizz to a soda, and my headache rages fiercer than ever. I double over, fists to temples.

Reggie plucks a fat joint from his shirt pocket and lights it up. "Here," he says. "Smoke it quick."

"Reggie Chorley!" Barbara says with a gasp. "Are you contributing to the delinquency of a minor? Oh, good heavens, husband, why are you carrying hard drugs around? What else are you hiding from me?" Her cheeks turn flush pink with embarrassment . She churns her apron over in her fists and glances cautiously around the room.

"I'll explain later," Reggie says gently. "You need to trust me on this one, Barbara."

Barbara unclenches her jaw. Seems her husband has a natural knack to both calm the natives or command the hair on our forearms to rise as needed—that must be *his* gift.

None of us understand why Reggie suddenly urges me to smoke pot, right here, right now, in front of them. But Dr. Evelyn releases one of my arms, and I clear tears from my face with a shirt sleeve. Black mascara, light-pink blood, and snot dirty my cuff, a palette of pastel teenage angst now openly worn on my sleeve.

I take the joint and inhale deeply. The blast of weed immediately clears my head. Poof. Headache, crackle, and fuzz—gone.

Damn, Reggie grows some good shit.

Barbara carefully steps around us to pull heavy burgundy velvet drapes across the sheer curtains and broken window, shutting out the wind, snow, and cold.

Reggie helps me to my feet, then does the same for Dr. Evelyn. She brushes pretend dust from her slacks. "If you work for Septum Oculi, almost anything is possible," he finally says.

"Who's Septum Oculi?" I ask, blowing smoke toward Dr. Evelyn, who crinkles her nose and waves it from her face with a look of disgust.

"Septum Oculi is an organization, not a person. We work to ensure governments don't do stupid things to hurt the people they're supposed to serve and protect. We guard the Western world under the

Komokuten Agency. Other agencies manage the north, east, and south. We all answer to a central agency known as Vor."

I eye Reggie and the others with suspicion, a like a skittish rabbit drafted into another involuntary hellhole. The revelation that these people are Septum Oculi from the Komokuten Agency, under the rule of Vor—whatever the hell all of that means—makes my head twirl—or maybe it's the weed. I've always known that whatever was going on here had to be something really fucked up—because stepping into the worst sort of shit just seems to come naturally for me.

"I've never heard of any of these agencies," I say.

"We work undercover as CIA, KGB, or other types of governmental officers," Reggie says.

"As in top-secret sort of stuff?"

"Yes, but we have a higher clearance. It's called CTS, short for COSMIC Top Secret."

I laugh out loud, which propels me into a coughing fit. "That's completely cheesy," I say when I catch my breath. "COSMIC Clearance? You couldn't come up with anything better?"

"What do you see that we don't?" Reggie asks, deadly serious.

My arm hairs spring up again. The smile flees from my face. How does he do that? I fear if I tell these "high-clearance" people that I see shit they don't, it'll just confirm what the quack doctors have said all my life—that I'm schizo-freak like my mom.

"You go first," I say. "Septum Oculi? Komo what? What the hell do you guys want with a bunch of screwed-up kids, anyway?"

"It was a protection order handed to us straight from Vor. It's very rare for them to break protocol and reach out to us directly. We think it may have something to do with NASA making contact."

"Contact? As in aliens?"

"Not exactly. We suspect the U.S. government discovered a new kind of energy it can't control, which puts us in danger. And I don't mean just us, here; I mean every person on the planet."

"Go on," I say.

"Dr. Sterling supervises a team of scientists, engineers mostly. They work on harnessing nuclear energy so it can be used in research and development for future technology. Frankly, I don't understand much of it. But something happened."

Dr. Evelyn chimes in. "The Atomic Energy Commission barged in and confiscated the entire program."

Reggie nods. "They kicked Dr. Sterling and his team off the project and moved them to a nuclear jet propulsion program headed nowhere. And that's about when people started getting hurt."

Barbara picks up broken glass and porcelain, gingerly placing it in a hand towel, ruminating over each jagged hunk of what was once her beautiful English rose teapot. But I can tell she also listens, ears tilted toward us like antennae, and catches every word.

"Hurt how?" I ask. I feel a strong impulse to leap out of the room and into another life—to leave them here to sort it all out. But I know I can't. I have no place to go.

"Some of the scientists and soldiers… we find them dead, or they disappear," Reggie says. "We don't know exactly why, but we do know some agency wanted foster kids here as either bait or breathing test kits." He looks at me with a focused expression, and something in his eyes, but not the man himself, makes me uneasy.

"Because foster kids are throwaways," I say, anticipating Reggie will protest that my words are untrue—but he doesn't. I'd initially hoped on some level that Verity was right and these people wanted to rescue and restore us. But I know now that this isn't the case. At least not on the NASA side of this circus tent.

"Partially," Reggie says, rubbing his hands over his face as if trying to wash off the repugnancy of it all. "Some foster kids are viewed as expendable. Truthfully, they prefer people from asylums, and sometimes they prey on the developmentally disabled. Easier targets, even if they put up a fuss." He pauses, then continues cautiously. "Beings with troubled pasts are easily discredited by governments as mentally unstable." He stares into the middle distance as if he remembers something unpleasant before adding, "Or they suffer 'practical accidents'."

Beings?

"Um, that flowed out of you a bit too easily," I say. "How many times has our government used civilians as unwitting test subjects?" I check my wrists and look down at my legs. Seems I've suffered zero effects from Dr. Evelyn's near-death grip—but I also wonder how much the government, or her, has tinkered with my body, blood, and mind.

Reggie shrugs and glances at the Dolma painting. "Likely more than we'll ever know. But our government isn't the only one. A foreign intelligence officer once told me that every time the public puts on head phones or watches television, it's all the time any operatives need to keep good folks distracted and divided, so that no one is the wiser when other human beings are sold like lab equipment."

His comment makes me think briefly about the Toft's ice cream incident and the argument about music, television, and skin color. It all seems so trivial now—inconsequential compared to what's at stake here and a good reason for Reggie to stand down from fighting a bigot.

"I'd wager my career your rare blood is a draw too," Dr. Evelyn says.

"Get out of my head," I say. I send her a double-dare glare, one that would slice her to pieces if it contained any steel. But she smiles.

"I wasn't in there," she says, checking her hair in a mirror. "You mentally tossed that to me. By the way, your mother sees visions too." She smooths the spots on her blouse I roughed up with her gracefully manicured soap-commercial quality fingers.

"My mother's batshit crazy," I say. "Mrs. Myers said she's about as coherent as a cantaloupe."

"Your mother isn't 'batshit crazy,'" Reggie counters. "Unfortunately, she sprinted into a major problem as a young CIA field officer."

Everyone stops what we're doing to stare at Reggie.

"I do wish you two would tone down the cussing," Barbara finally says, putting a hand to her hip. But I barely hear her. I slowly shuffle toward the bed and sit down, stunned.

"My mom? A CIA agent?"

No way.

All I've ever heard about her has been mostly negative—save for a few faint scraps of pleasant memories at the beach or in the park. For the first time in my life, thoughts of my mom pole vault from shame and revulsion to higher hopes, and it causes a small pang of regret in my stomach—I guess because I miss her, even though I don't feel I know her that well or much about her, and wonder if she actually really loved me at all—and if she were so sick, why didn't she fight to get better and take care of me, instead of letting me land here?

"What happened to my mom?" I ask.

Dr. Evelyn and Reggie share a look of concern.

"Colonel, no," Dr. Evelyn protests. "Maybe we shouldn't—not yet."

"This kid has gone through enough," he says. "I feel she is ready to know what really happened."

Dr. Evelyn trades looks with Barbara and waves a hand at Reggie to continue.

Barbara picks up slivers of broken glass, concern crackling across her forehead as Dr. Evelyn stoops to help.

"Your mother discovered information about the Atomic Energy Commission she wanted her supervisor to see," Reggie says. "Unfortunately, he was killed before she got to him and was later accused of his murder. She fled with you. A couple of years later, someone slipped her a nuclear dose of LSD and stole her files. The dose should have killed her. But it didn't. She had the benefit of a special type of blood that seemed to stave off a sure death sentence. Her failed assassination attempt surprised some higher ups at the AEC who wanted to study her. She was remanded to a military psychiatric hospital under protective custody."

"What information did she have?" I ask.

"Rumor has it that she discovered a secret program globally experimenting on unsuspecting humans using widespread invisible energy fields for things like crowd control or what we term 'urban slumber', an induced sort of stupor to keep people calm and mentally committed to false causes—an experimental effort to prevent humans, without their knowledge, from rebelling against what they're expected to do—and to be content leading lives of mediocrity—or to fight among each other to distract them from what's really going on in this world."

I don't know what to say. Reggie's words make me feel both sad and angry—violated too. Sad for humans. I'm also sad for my mom and me, and sad for all the great memories she and I missed.

"It isn't all a lost cause," Dr. Evelyn says, interrupting my thoughts as if she senses my widening despair. "There is still a lot of good 'out there'." She sweeps an arm toward the window to make her point. "People still have hope, display bravery—justice prevails, and the creativity and resourcefulness of humans still inspires. Many of us somehow push past our fear, like you. Generosity and compassion too, is abundant among humans. They are not a lost cause."

She's right, I think. Although I tend to view the human condition as collectively and perilously ignorant, I also feel that some people I meet are *aware and awake*, able to overcome invisible waves of control forced upon them. I offer Dr. Evelyn a light smile and she smiles back, a bit relieved it seems—but I still hide the feeling that she can't be trusted.

"Can I see her?" I ask.

"Likely not," Reggie says. "It's too dangerous and her mind is not the same."

"Do you know what happened to my dad?"

"We know a little. While serving with the Army, someone gave up his unit's position to the enemy along the Cambodian line in Vietnam. His trail runs pretty cold after that. He was declared missing in action because they never found a body. I'm sorry."

Reggie looks at Dr. Evelyn and then at his wife before drawing in a deep breath. "There's more."

The edges of the room expand and contract with my heartbeat as I'm thumped by all of this information. I nod for Reggie to continue.

"You inherited this special blood, not from one, but from both parents," he says. "This is extraordinarily rare and of great value to governments because, well, it doesn't fit any earthly profile. Some think your blood type may hold information to the missing link in human evolution—but the people who've studied you aren't certain." Reggie glances at Dr. Evelyn when he says this.

The '*people*' who've studied me.

This unexpected and blood-curdling knowledge makes me feel violated again—but who exactly, I should target, I'm not sure. How does anyone fight a shadowy enemy like 'government'? I'm a hybrid freak girl holding half a story against a faceless ghost, which means my odds of winning any sort of redemption are about nil.

"You're telling me I'm not human?" I ask.

"No," Reggie says. "You're human—but a much more upgraded model of human, almost as if something or someone inserted unknown material into your ancestral genetics."

"What does that mean?" I ask.

"Good question," Reggie says. "We don't know. What we do know is that your mother has learned to somehow use her cardiovascular and nervous systems to transmute energy—to negatively impose this energy on those who might mean her harm or harness it to help or even cure others."

I look at Reggie quizzically. "I don't understand."

"Do you remember Dr. Sterling's science class lessons on photosynthesis in plants?" He asks.

I nod.

"It sort of works that way but instead of converting nutrients to energy through the sun, we think your mom may use her blood to transmute energy so she can communicate or effect changes in people through her mind," he says.

I shake my head in an effort to absorb what he shares, listening closely as I stare at the ceiling. "What is the Atomic Energy Commission?" I finally ask.

"An organization that used to study science and technology," Reggie says coldly, and it sounds like he's not a fan.

"What do you mean they *used* to?" I ask.

"The organization was abolished by Congress ten years ago. The public thought nuclear testing harmed the environment and lacked sufficient safety standards. What hardly anyone knows is that the organization wasn't really abolished, it was just renamed the Department of Energy—DOE."

My mind still grapples with the fact that this DOE thinks nothing at all of using human beings as lab rats. "Who runs this *DOE*?"

"No one knows," Reggie continues. "It's a very elite group with big power."

I take a moment to smooth the wrinkles on my bedspread before I look at all of them.

"So, let me get this straight," I say. "We have eleven screwed-up kids living on a nuclear freak farm where strange zippy lights in the sky pluck us up without notice. We have a dead housekeeper, Gladys, who claims she saw a white Bigfoot, and the alleged graves of giant Indians buried god knows where all over these farm fields. And now you toss in the DOE, my mom being a CIA agent, your creepy eye rings, plus a legal guardian who lets me smoke dope. This is a disaster of a foster home."

Dr. Evelyn and Barbara look at each other and shrug in agreement before Dr. Evelyn raises her brows. "You told the kids about Gladys, Big Foot, and the Indian burials?" Dr. Evelyn asks.

Barbara nods.

Dr. Evelyn looks at me. "I'm surprised you haven't already raided the graves for treasure."

"I may do some exploring," I say.

"Oh, Lord no," says Barbara. "Don't go angering their gods too. That's all we need!"

"Sam," Reggie says, "let's refocus a moment here. If you don't want to tell us what you're seeing that we can't see, you don't have to. But maybe if we trade information, it could help us find Saratu and Hope."

"How?" I ask.

"Whatever you're seeing may somehow be connected to what's going on over there. Perhaps you're somehow picking up or tapping into DOE's energy source, similar to the way your mom can channel energy."

"I see a golden-haired lady in blue robes," I say. I blurt it out, just like that. "She looks like she's from Bible times. Her skin is the color of the limestone rocks down by the river and her eyes sometimes glow gray. She stood behind your shoulder a few minutes ago and told me not to kill you."

Barbara gasps. "Sweet Jesus of mercy." She makes the sign of the cross for the third time and covers her mouth, backing away from both the painting and me.

"Where did she go?" Reggie asks.

I sweep up a deep breath, cock my head toward the Asian lady panting, and let the truth tumble out, "She shrunk herself, floated toward the Dolma there, and hid behind one of the monks."

Reggie turns to inspect the painting. He scratches the canvas with his fingertip, lifts each corner of the frame, moves it an inch or so from the wall, and takes a peek behind. He picks off a dust ball and drops it into what water remains from glass on the floor. It melts away to reveal a fine red wire, no bigger than a thumbnail.

He glances with concern at Dr. Evelyn.

"Are you sure?" she asks.

"Am I sure?" I say. "Hell no, I'm not sure. I don't understand what I'm seeing at all. Who is she?"

"No, not that," she says, holding up a palm to shush me as she looks at Reggie.

I frown. It took a lot of courage to finally blurt out that I occasionally see Blue Robes Lady and now nobody seems to care!

Reggie gives her a nod, and Dr. Evelyn wraps her right hand tightly around the eye of her necklace until her knuckles practically glow white.

"Thankfully, this listening device is dead," Reggie says to Dr. Evelyn. "Someone snapped off the chip on the other end and it's missing. Sam, did you do this?"

I clutch both of my elbows with my fingers and shake my head. "No." But once again, I discover that Bennie is right and someone put a bug in my room, just as he'd said in the library. From the shocked look on Dr. Evelyn's face, I can tell it wasn't her.

A memory stirs. It's foggy and far away.

Standing on a ridge, I lift a sword over my head. It's cold, dark, and damp. Lights in the sky—hundreds of glowing golden bubbles. I hear something—strange music. Hope sits by my feet staring upward. We watch the stars looking for...

"Sam? Samantha! You still with us?" Dr. Evelyn asks. She claps her hands by my right ear. I blink and nod. "Reggie," Dr. Evelyn says, almost excitedly. "It's possible. Admit it."

Reggie stares at the ceiling, his lips pursed, then looks at Dr. Evelyn once more, then at me before locking eyes with his wife. He nods.

"Would someone please tell me what the hell is going on?" I ask.

"Camaeliphim," Dr. Evelyn answers.

"Camaeli-What? Sounds like a disease," I say, looking at both of my arms and ankles to ensure I don't have some sort of rash.

"It's not a disease. It's a very special group of people we heard might exist—a highly classified epigenetic experiment to enhance the natural athletic and mental skills of rare blooded human beings," she explains, before her voice lowers and she adds, "or to take them the other way— make them compliant slaves."

"And you think us kids…"

"No," says Reggie. "We're not certain. It's been a rumor among governments for decades, but we've never seen any evidence. At least… not until you and Bennie got here."

Something in the painting moves. Camouflaged in the silver moon around the Dolma's head, I see Bennie's baby offspring version of Cutie Pie, its creepy little camera eyes watching this whole scene. Reggie likely missed it, due to the glare on his glasses or his attention being drawn to the bug-hiding dust bunny. Clever. Mini Cutie Pie—no doubt the daughter of the real deal—crawls over the frame and hides behind the painting.

"I have to go," I say. "I need some space—time to think. May I please be excused?"

"No," Dr. Evelyn says. "She can't be left alone. It's too dangerous.

She's still weak. And I need more time."

I don't like her attempt to deny me my freedom, and I especially loathe the thought of more therapy, considering this session wasn't exactly a success. If we proceed in doctor-patient fashion, Plum Hook Bay might well crumble like an Atlantis falling into the sea.

"Let her go," Reggie says. "If she is Camaeliphim, they won't risk poking a cobra—at least not yet. She may be too valuable or too dangerous."

"Whoa—wait one minute," I say. "Dangerous? What the hell is that supposed to mean?"

"You may be a walking weapon," he says.

I groan loudly and push through them toward the threshold of my room, dig my hands deep into my front pockets, and start for the great outdoors. I wonder who's really nuts around here and, for the first time, I doubt that it's me.

Chapter 20

THE SHADOW SPIRIT

On a snow-covered log I sit, deep in the woods along the river where we swim, my ass wet and cold. I stare at the boulder where I rescued Pa-Ling and pull up my collar, thankful, finally, for some fresh air. It feels good to get out of the house even though it's freezing outside. The large rock in the water reminds me of a lone Stonehenge standing tall against the unrelenting chill. Did Pa Ling really see a glowing light coming from a cave beneath us? If Saratu was guiding him back to the surface and "negotiating" with whatever was down there, what was it?

My mind drifts more than the snow blowing past me. I think about what Dr. Evelyn and Reggie said, me being Camaeliphim, a genetic experiment of some sort.

I wonder, too, if this manipulation is responsible for my screwy visions and crackling headaches, or if those are effects of the medicine Dr. Evelyn may be sneaking into me.

The endless questions I have about my life, this place, these people, and the events of the past few weeks play a fast game of tag in my brain, where answers are never "it" for long. All I know for sure is that I want to find Saratu and Hope alive and get the hell out of here. I haven't yet figured out where we all might go, but I'm working on it.

Heavy flakes force everything into hiding—except for my high-speed thoughts, a small herd of skinny deer, and a few brave cardinals, their scarlet feathers bright checkmarks against the snow-covered landscape. Even the river covered up and went to sleep. The quiet reminds me of what it might be like to walk around in an empty freezer. My breath, scratchy droplets of ice crystals that form in my throat, keep beat with a cough. The echoes of my booted steps munch on new-laid snow. It seems that even Mother Nature has gone manic, turning August into January and rushing us through a year's worth of seasons within a matter of days while she outruns her own straitjacket.

Some of the pine trees sport lime-green buds, peeking out from under the darkness of gray bark, but they seem afraid to venture further. Chunks of silvery ice sit frozen on the river, unable to continue their slow march toward Lake Erie, stuck in place until the river decides to wake up, stretch, and run again. The sky, an endless horizon of ash-colored clouds, thinly veil Plum Hook Bay. The air settles down a bit heavier each day, a slow compression of eeriness that permeates every pore of this place.

Dr. Evelyn and Barbara seemed scared of me, and even Reggie looked at me differently too, for a minute, like maybe he was nervous to be around a genetically modified freak. I guess sending a lamp across the room using nothing but concentrated anger stretched their brain bands. And mine too, for that matter. I never knew I possessed such a gift—or is it a curse? If I'm able to launch lamps with my thoughts, what might happen if I wish someone's head to explode? I scan the snow, mulling my newfound skill sets. A tiny mouse scampers across a drift before it disappears.

Maybe I was genetically manipulated when I entered foster care years ago. I read something once in Dr. Evelyn's office, when nosing around for spare change, about some research study called *MK Ultra*. Plus, Reggie mentioned I've been scrubbed from the court system too. On paper I no longer exist. Normally, I'd be happy to have the trail of my life covered over about as heavily as the paths in these woods now covered with snow.

I mean, getting lost seems like a perfect opportunity for personal reinvention. I could become anyone, I suppose. But my case file forces me to confront a discomforting prospect: If I no longer exist, what's to stop a government from performing an irreversible lobotomy on me? Or worse, killing me? But what if Reggie's right and they can't kill me? They *have* to be able to kill me. All people die. Or should I say, all *beings* can die—or at least I think that all beings can die.

Everything I ever learned in biology class doesn't dispute that organic matter, including humans or even hybrids made with human material, must have an expiration date.

Staring at the ice, I command the pestering thoughts in my head to quiet down. It doesn't work so I try to breathe like Reggie taught me. It grows darker both outside and, in my head. Darkness no longer frightens me like it used to, because humans, I'm learning, are definitely way scarier.

A cardinal comes to perch on a thin limb over the river. His head twists, bobs, and scopes around, maybe confused about why a genetically altered lowlife would sit alone post-sunset, freezing her ass off deep in these woods. If Bennie is around, his chirpy little creature, *Edwin* (who names a bird Edwin, anyway?) certainly doesn't make a good spy. The cardinal preens his feathers, tail popping up and down like a seesaw. He lets out a repetitive light-hearted garble that startles me.

CRACK!

I jump from the log and slip down the riverbank, snatching a low-lying limb to keep from plunging through the ice into bitterly cold water. The ice under the cardinal's perch suddenly creaks and rumbles as if someone hides underneath and forces it apart. Bubbles spit up next to the boulder like slow boiling tea. More whip-like cracks echo and bounce through the forest as a sewer-lid sized hole forms.

"Oh, shit," I whisper. Bluish light steadily glows under the bubbling water and a chunk of ice rockets straight up, sending a plume of red feathers floating to the ground.

I leap behind another fallen log before I'm next, then slowly poke my head up. I pray to a God that I don't believe in that I won't lose the hairs on my head the same way the cardinal just lost his feathers. How am I going to tell Bennie about his bird? The kid will be crushed.

Someone stands across the river from me, on the opposite bank.

It's... me?

I shake my head, and my alter ego—the me on the other side—does the same thing. I hold up my palm like I've seen Buddha do in pictures, as a show of peace. (I hope.) The other Samantha does the same thing a mere split second behind me. Then she reaches in her pocket moments *before* I do and pulls out a buckeye. She's now moving *past* me in time. I'm so freaked out. I don't understand what's happening.

She ducks down, then lifts her head—and now she's a lady with red hair, dressed in army fatigues. She turns, the clothes peel away, and she runs deeper into the woods, draped in animal skin, chain metal breast plate, red feathers in her hair, an armband, and a sword that turns from steel to fire-colored plasma, drips of it melting the snow beneath her feet in steamy swirls. She stabs the sword forward into nothing and makes counter-clockwise small circles until she creates a mirrored portal hosting a black hole. She steps into it and disappears!

Bennie is likely the *ONLY* person I know who might be able to explain what I'm seeing—unless this is a full-fledged hallucination. But if it is, would I be able to ask myself that question? Do crazy people know that they're crazy?

A struggling sunbeam, stretches its last grasp at twilight before being swallowed by a cloud and the blue light in the river slowly escapes from the newly formed hole in the ice, rising upward wide and bright like a searchlight. A figure moves within it, a shadow spirit stretching its arms overhead, like a diver ready to reverse springboard into the sky. I see only the outline, but I can tell it's an extraordinary being, perhaps ten feet tall. My breath escapes in one long sigh of surprise.

I pick up a red feather by my feet and add it to my pocket of consolation prizes, along with Barbara's and Bennie's buckeyes.

My compass vibrates so I pull it from my front pocket to take a look. The arrow spins clockwise, then counter-clockwise. It stops on north, then south, then zips around like it's dizzy, unable to locate direction.

Great. Now my compass is schizophrenic too.

WHOOOSH!

I dive into the snow behind the log, heart thudding, an instant and startled reaction to this unexpected noise.

The light, now the size of a large tree trunk, arches upward into the night sky, the super-sized shadow spirit gone. Three golden orbs, like the one that took Saratu, but much smaller, softly ping against the wall of the beam until they, too, launch themselves into the heavens and disappear. The beam gets sucked back into the water, and ice quickly closes over the hole leaving the surface untouched.

I'm alone again.

Falling back into the snow, I stare up at a clear night sky. The veil of clouds has been swept aside to reveal heavy clusters of stars, like spawning far-off winking grapes of diamonds bending some invisible vine. I've never seen such studded heavens.

I also can't shake the feeling that Saratu is near. I *feel* her. But she doesn't appear, doesn't speak. And it's not like I have a ghostly sense of her. It's more like... a comfortable low hum of energy vibrating through me.

Come on, Saratu. Talk to me. Say something. Please give me a sign. Some clue as to where you are.

But there's nothing, and the serene hum-vibration fades.

And then the smell hits me. The putrid scent of sulfur and body odor blended with rotting garbage. I force down the urge to spew as I hesitantly peer over the log again, straining to see.

There's someone on the other side of the river. Crouching. The figure pokes a finger into the snow, then reaches up to a tree branch and plucks a few dangling pine cones. *Crunch. Crunch. Crunch.*

I blow out a breath for courage and stand straight up. "Bennie, is that you? Are you munching pine cones, you 'tard?"

The figure stands up and it's so large that at first, I mistake it for a Polar Bear until I realize it's not—that maybe it's a man?

Oh my God. "What the hell *are* you?"

This thing, whatever it is, is way too tall to be Bennie. Way too tall to be *human*. It twists its white fur torso toward me and fixes me with half-burned, post-ember-charcoal eyes. All black, no whites.

White Bigfoot!

Gladys the dead maid was right!

Seeing this creature in the flesh is likely the reason she took up drinking—to steady her nerves and gain courage to call the authorities.

This beast is intimidating as hell and looks straight at me!

Oh, hell no.

I haul ass toward Silo 57.

Hooves gallop behind me, and fear strikes my brain with such clammy coldness that I effortlessly bid my feet to leave Earth, hoping to God this abominable snow creature can't fly and gain ground on me! But it's not his hooves I hear.

Large horses carrying extra-tall blue-skinned Native Americans race under me—or at least I *think* that's what they are. The riders' long hair flutters behind them, red feathers bouncing, battle cries unfurling in a language I don't understand. A form of Basque, maybe a different and more ancient dialect? I decipher only bits: a war is coming, and they're on their way to a battle, to shore up a front line somewhere. I look for my alter ego but don't see her among them. My heart drops to my stomach as the galloping hoofbeats subside and the war party leaves the ground, rising upward to join me.

Terrified of being kicked out of the sky by wildly flailing horse hooves, I decrease my altitude. Tree branches lash my face like a gazillion tiny switches as I struggle to hold course and maintain a safe distance from this oversized Smurf-colored otherworldly Native American war party. I mentally steer myself onto a clear path, like I do in my dreams, but I'm tired. This is the longest I've ever flown, and the clouds are coming back, and soon there is no moon. It's hard to see, I'm lost, and I'm quickly losing altitude because I'm thinking too much about actually flying.

Mayday!

But a distress call is futile.

My boot kicks someone in the head, and we both go flailing over snow, twigs, and rotten leaves. I somersault, land on my boots, and crouch into combat mode, picking up a pine cone, ready to fight— although a pinecone is a paltry and ill-thought weapon against either White Bigfoot or a blue-skinned war party. I should know better.

"What the hell, Samantha? Christ, you busted my lip open!"

I relax.

"Verity? What the hell are you doing way out here?"

"Looking for you. Barbara said you were upset and... well, I kinda already know what happened because I sort of spied through your bedroom door. I wanted to make sure you were okay."

"You came out here by yourself?"

"Believe me, I didn't want to, and I was just about ready to go back, but then I saw a light and heard you—so here I am. And you're *not* making me go back alone. I had a tough enough time following your tracks. What are you doing way out here anyway?"

Verity pulls off her purple knit hat and presses it against her bloody lip. Her distress is evident—she violently shakes, her teeth chattering—her intense gaze filled with questions, and perhaps seeking assurance that we'll be okay out here, even though I suspect we're lost.

Verity looks around and moves closer. "You didn't have to punch me."

"Sorry," I say. I don't mention that I actually kicked her rather than punched her. She doesn't need to know I was flying.

"Shit happens," she says as she shrugs and shivers. I can tell she's nervous. "What were you running from?" She looks up, down and all around, searching for the nearest threat. She's such a loveable chicken, but she does have the courage to follow me out here like this, her concern for me overriding her fear, so I have to give her some credit for loyalty.

"White Bigfoot," I say.

She rolls her eyes. "Yea right! Stop fucking with me. And why are you pointing a pine cone at me?" She gives me a '*have you lost your mind*' look.

I chuckle inside because I'm telling the truth and she thinks I'm joking. I lower my arm and drop the pine cone.

"You can't do that!" she says, racing to pick it up. She slaps it back into my palm. "It's bad karma to drop your third eye."

"What?"

"Your third eye. It's bad luck to just drop it on the ground."

"It's just a pine cone."

"It's not *just* a pine cone. It's a symbol of enlightenment. Did you know that the pope's papal staff has a pine cone at the top? And just outside of St. Peter's in Vatican City is the Court of the Pine Cone, which houses a huge bronze sculpture of a pine cone—the *Pigna*? Pine cones are found in almost every religion and region on the planet. A pine cone, like a buckeye, helps protect us." She snatches up another pine cone for herself and stuffs it in her coat.

"I don't have time for another one of your religious history lessons, especially out here," I say. "I'm going to see Bennie. And you're coming along." I yank her forward by her puffy purple coat sleeve.

"But I—"

"No buts. I don't know what's up, but something is, and I'm not wasting my time taking you back to the house when you're potentially piecing shit together that I might be able to use. Come on."

Chapter 21

CAMAELIPHIM

Verity studies my skin like I'm one of Bennie's science projects and uses a shaky index finger to make temporary indentations on my bare forearm—checking, I think, to see if I'm real or made of Silly Putty.

"What are you doing?" I ask, jerking my arm away, feeling annoyed. She knows I hate being touched.

"I just can't believe you of all people might be part angel," she says. "You don't even believe in God. Geez, you're a Nephilim."

"Dr. Evelyn called me Camaeliphim, not a Nephilim. I'm a genetically modified lab freak. What's a Nephilim, anyway?"

"Never heard of Camaeliphim," she shrugs. She doesn't answer my question about Nephilim.

Bennie and I got into a big argument when I showed up at Silo 57 dragging Verity along, both of us nearly frozen by the time I figured out how to find this place. Thankfully, for once, my compass worked. I swore to him that Verity would never have the guts to come here by herself—especially after I told her about seeing White Bigfoot—he relented and promised not to sick a radioactive spider on her. Then he added more logs to the fire and served us tea.

He plays with some chemical concoction as Verity and I talk, a foamy brew that looks sort of like root beer but smells like burning wood and unwiped ass. He dips a large metal spoon into the froth and closely examines the bubbles. Then he stops, looks up, and puffs a ringlet out of his face. The dark circles under his eyes look worse than I've ever seen. His pet cardinal watches, head bobbing, tail twitching, a chirp now and then. So, it wasn't Bennie's bird that became a feather duster in the woods right before I saw White Bigfoot. I'm happy about that—but sad for the other bird.

"You wouldn't know about Camaeliphim," Bennie says to Verity. "You won't find it in any of the religious texts they give you to study."

"It's so weird to hear you talking," Verity says. She walks toward him, checking him out as if he's a zoo exhibit.

Bennie ignores her, so she hoists herself up beside him on an empty stainless-steel worktable and swings her legs. "I know Camael is a Dominion angel," she says, almost bragging. "He was one of seven archangels who cast Adam and Eve out of the Garden of Eden, on God's order, with a flaming sword. He worked with a Cherubim angel named Jophiel. Christians don't recognize Camael because he was banned from the Bible."

"You never told me what a Nephilim is," I remind her.

"Christianity created archangel hierarchies," Verity says. "Seraphim, cherubim, dominions, powers, thrones, virtues, and principalities." She thumbs a royal-purple rosary around her neck and winks at Bennie before she continues. "Nephilim are the offspring between humans and Watchers," Verity continues. "Watchers used to be archangels too, before they tried to overthrow God's kingdom. Dominions cast them to Earth, where they mated with humans. Unfortunately, Nephilim corrupted humans—used them as slaves or killed them for sport. God wiped the slate clean with Noah's flood by wiping them out."

"Interesting story," I say. The truth is, I'm sorry I asked. I turn to Bennie. "What the hell are you cooking? The smell gives me a headache."

"It's not my experiment giving you a headache," he says. "It's *her*." He points his spoon at Verity like he's casting a spell. "Also, she's wrong about the Nephilim being wiped out."

"What do you mean?" Verity says.

"Some survived," he replies.

"Did not."

"Did too."

"Stop it, both of you," I say. "Bennie, you go first."

"Mother Teresa over there," Bennie says, nodding toward Verity, "like every other religious scholar, studies seriously incomplete interpretations. Remember when I told you that all world religions possess only a piece of the story?"

I nod.

"Humans formally recognize twenty-six sacred texts around the globe," he explains. "But there exist another thirty-six. Twelve of them have never been released to the public but are housed in a vault at the Vatican. The other twenty-four are not books at all, but codes and maps disguised as archeological relics and they're geo-cached all over the world. There's a race among the Nephilim and governments to find them before the people do."

"And whoever pieces them all together wins a key to world domination," I say.

Verity looks back and forth between the two of us like we're bonkers.

"Not just the world," Bennie says. "The entire multiverse."

"The multi-what?" Verity asks.

"The multiverse."

"What the hell is a multiverse? That's not in the Bible." She rolls her head and plants a fist on her hip.

I now have a ringside view of Bennie and Verity about to spar over religion versus science. This might be better than watching MTV. I wish I had popcorn.

"A set of stacked and parallel universes," Bennie says.

Verity looks at Bennie as if he's lost his mind, then looks at me like I just joined him. "Did he take his meds today?" she asks. "And why do you look like you believe him?"

I shrug.

"How cozy," Verity says. "Me standing in a room full of sharp instruments with two crazy crackers, one channeling Einstein and the other carrying demon spawn."

I chuckle. I suppose Bennie and I sound just as ridiculous to her as she does to us when she prays while straddling a broomstick.

"Think of the multiverse as bubble wrap," Bennie says. "Each bubble is its own galaxy. If one gets popped, it sets off a chain reaction where they all pop, and everything, including God, ceases to exist, right along with heaven and hell and all of your precious little saints—who, by the way, were never all that pristine to begin with."

"That's not even possible," Verity says. "God is the alpha and the omega. He's omniscient and omnipotent. You cannot destroy God."

"True. God is the Source of all," Bennie says, "a highly advanced force billions of years old that created all manner of beast and being. God uses the multiverse to 'be'—to keep everything in balance."

Verity covers her mouth with a palm, and I catch a whiff of her Love's Baby Soft perfume. For one of the few times in her life, she's speechless, her lime-green eyes wide like hungry Venus flytraps.

"There isn't a being alive that has both the intellectual and spiritual capacity to decipher God's code in a way that won't cause the multiverse to fold in on itself. That's why the code was split up and tossed here on Earth, to hide it from the rest of us—to prevent chaos."

"That's not in the Bible," she says, eyes narrowing at Bennie.

"See?" Bennie says, pointing the spoon at Verity again. "She's part of the problem."

"How am I part of the problem?" Verity jumps off the table and puts her fists on her hips.

"War is profiting that hides behind principle," he says. "While you humans argue over which ridiculous dogma is real, those who profit from your stupidity laugh all the way to the Big Bang."

"Never mind her, who are the Septum Oculi?" I ask.

Both of them frown at me, displeased, I assume, by my interruption of their debate.

But Bennie answers. "An intelligence group," he says. "They work as a team to keep the globe safe. The Septum Oculi guard the Western world but consider Komokuten, an ancient all-seeing angel warrior, their mascot—hence the eye jewelry they wear."

I think about my mom's eye necklace. Does she still wear it? My mom must be Septum Oculi too.

"I call bullshit," Verity says. "Komokuten is one of the Four Heavenly Kings of Buddhism from the Far East, and they're each considered mythical."

"Again, you miss the point," Bennie says. "You have only part of a very poorly told story. Think of the Komokuten and the Four Heavenly Kings as guardian angels, the way Dominion angels are to God in Christianity. And—who says we aren't talking about the *same* angels? Perhaps everyone on Earth worships the exact same god without realizing it, but they use different names and local stories to aid cultural meaning and relevance."

Verity looks both awkward and in awe. I get the sense that a small light is beginning to blink in her brain somewhere—but whether it's a new idea or a warning light, I can't yet tell. She twists a blondish ringlet around her finger as she ponders everything Bennie just laid upon her psyche as if *he* were the Oracle at Delphi.

"Go on," she finally says.

"Septum Oculi are highly trained special forces that study the Four Heavenly Kings to help protect Earth. By the way, Verity, Buddhism's not really a religion and there is no God to worship. It's a lifetime *practice* where a person channels personal energy into emptiness, the great cosmic enlightenment. Humans have no idea how close they get to seeing truth when they study Buddhism."

Verity and I both roll our eyes. I don't know much about Buddhism, but it sounds like a bunch of hokey monk-chanting gibberish to me and another attempt to keep the masses in line—to divide and conquer, just like Reggie said in my room.

Bennie continues to stir his concoction in small circles.

"What about Camael?" I ask.

"According to myth, he's an angel of war. But not just any angel." Bennie says. "He's God's secret agent in charge. He went dark years ago when the Nephilim and the Watchers joined forces to put a price on his head."

"A price on his head? Everyone knows you can't kill an angel," says Verity.

"Not true again," Bennie says. "With the right type of holding cell you can completely destroy one—or just study it." He looks toward the

NASA complex as if he can see it through the silo wall.

Verity and I shiver, and I take a deep swallow that almost hurts. I'm not going over there. That's where the government takes its yellow body bags.

"When you say, Septum Oculi keep the globe safe, what do they do, exactly?" I ask.

"It's an espionage alliance," says Bennie. "They have more power than the CIA and KGB combined. They don't follow government or global orders. They fly above the law."

I'm not surprised. That explains why nobody came calling for me after I redecorated my Cleveland motel room in rapist blood red. "How do you know this?" I ask.

"Camaeliphim aren't genetic freaks created via lab experiment," Bennie whispers.

I'm confused again. "No?"

"I know you've wondered," he says. "We're so much more."

"We? Me too?" Verity claps her hands, hopes raised, eyes loaded with excitement.

"Not you," Bennie says. "You're one-hundred-percent human just like most everyone else here. You're special, because you're a receptor, but you're purely human."

Verity's cheeks droop, and I feel a twinge of pity toward her. If anyone deserves to be part angel, she surely does, given her unwavering faith in and defense of God. It's certainly not a role I'd audition for.

"What does that mean, a receptor?" I ask.

"It means beings from other realms are drawn to her positive energy, the photons and vibrations of her DNA. She senses high-level information, even if she's not yet tuned enough to correctly decipher the messages. And Verity, your father wasn't dishonorably discharged from military duty because he was a criminal. He's being held in a brig, an English battleship, not far off the coast of Indonesia."

"What? Why?" Verity and I both ask in unison.

"Ten years ago, some American soldiers fighting along the Cambodian line saw something they shouldn't have," Bennie says.

"Each was required to sign a denial and never speak of the incident under threat of court-martial and charges of treason. Verity's father refused to sign—said 'the people' had a right to know and he wasn't going to have the government discredit him and his men as liars."

"What? My dad went to prison for refusing to sign a piece of paper that asked him to lie?" Verity asks, a pained look on her face. Tears involuntarily spill from her eyes. I know she misses her dad and thinks about him as much as I do mine. I feel her hurt and anger as if it were my own.

"What did the soldiers see?" I ask. "Did Verity's father and my father serve in the same unit?"

"No," says Bennie, "Your fathers weren't in the same unit, but their outfits did meet up and join forces to fight against whatever was out there that day. Even the Viet Cong, the enemy, joined them. Dr. Sterling said it was so horrid that the only soldier who returned stateside alive, was a shell of himself—his hair turned completely white and his limbs paralyzed. He was also blind, mute, and deaf."

"Was?" Verity asks.

"Dr. Evelyn gave him a lethal dose of morphine to put him out of his misery," Bennie says.

My blood freezes.

"What?!" Verity yells. "That seems like overkill to me."

"Um, that was the point," Bennie says as he stirs the pot.

So, Dr. Evelyn definitely has the capacity to kill. And I'd bet she's responsible for all those yellow body bags.

"Relax," Bennie says. "The guy asked to be put out of his misery. It wasn't cold-blooded murder."

"I disagree," Verity says. "It's not Dr. Evelyn's place to decide a life."

"She didn't," Bennie says. "The laws of nature decided and she just followed the order."

We both look at Bennie confused but he doesn't elaborate.

"How do you know so much?" I ask.

"I heard a saying once," Bennie says. "*A wise old owl sat on an oak, the more he heard the less he spoke, the less he spoke, the more he heard, why aren't we like that wise old bird?* If people think you're autistic, they think you're dumb too, so they tend to talk too much in front of you."

Verity looks at me with high-minded defiance, her doe-eyed lime-green naivete replaced by a determined jade. "I'm going to law school," she says coldly.

Bennie lays his stirring spoon on the table, stands in front of me and studies my face like I'm a specimen under one of his microscopes. "*Nirkin kaz egen,*" he says. "*Verity zin hau. Camaeliphim ez dir natura. Ez NASA, et tu Camealiphim. Zite keen eta.*"

It's Basque, and I know what the words mean: *Verity won't understand. Camaeliphim aren't lab experiments. There is an ancient scroll that claims God granted Camael permission to take a band of Dominion angels to Earth so they could mate with humans too, as the Nephilim did. They created alternative hybrids to counter Nephilim and any humans helping them.*

"Hey, no fair!" Verity says. "What language is that?"

We ignore her.

I'm surprised Bennie threw me such a curveball after spewing so much science. I respond to him in Basque. "You're saying we're related to angels? You believe that we're some sort of spiritual hybrid? Seriously, what are they putting in your Tang?"

"Helllooo!" Verity says, waving her arms to get our attention. "It's not very polite to leave friends out of your conversation by switching to a language I don't know. Although I don't know *why* I don't know it. Hey! Did you guys make this up to shut me out?"

Bennie and I shush her, and she hops back up on the table again, angrily folds her arms, and glares at us.

"Is my dad alive?" I ask Bennie.

"I don't know," he says. "His lifeline goes cold and he can't be traced, alive or dead, here or in other realms. I'm not able to see him in my mind's eye like Verity's dad."

"What do you mean? How?"

"It's known as *translocating* but your government calls it 'remote viewing', remember?" Bennie says.

I nod.

"If you let your mind go, and forget concentrating too hard, you can mentally and accurately visit people, places, or events," he continues. "You can even move around in different dimensions or visit the past and future."

"Could I fly?" I ask.

"Yes," he answers. "Time isn't the linear construct humans believe it to be. But humans do use time linearly because it works well here on Earth. Time makes sense for a race of beings who can't grasp multi-dimensional concepts without going mad."

It's not the goofy answer I wanted to hear, but it confirms what Reggie shared about my dad: nobody knows. I also wonder if I can use this 'remote viewing' to see my dad? I wonder if I *have* been using it without realizing it, when I see visions of Blue Robes lady or seem to get caught between two worlds, watching some future or past unfold?

"Whatever I saw at the river was not an angel," I say. "It was a monster covered in fur—White Bigfoot. And it smelled like shit. I almost barfed. NASA lab experiment?"

"Likely a Deva, a nonhuman who helps Dominion forces. They shapeshift and manipulate electromagnetic fields, even the ones in your brain. Beings usually can't see them unless they're very young children, hybrids, or receptors. Where were you along the river?"

"Down by the boulder where the rest of us swim." I don't mention that I saw a version of myself there, too.

"NASA Plum Hook Bay has the strongest electromagnetic hot spot on Earth, plus the lowest level of seismic activity on the globe, making it perfect for nuclear testing, *and* what humans like to call 'paranormal phenomena.'" Bennie shifts his weight from foot to foot, looking at me as if he knows I saw more than what I've shared. "Wait here."

He walks to a massive steamer trunk at the back of his lab—the size of a walk-in closet. As he lifts it open, a whirl of old dust spins away in tiny tornadoes. Bennie crawls right into the trunk, the soles of his shoes pointing toward the ceiling, and starts tossing its contents onto the floor: costumes, fake jewelry, props, make-up, wigs, and various theatrical surprises.

Verity jumps down from her perch to examine everything. "Whoa," she says. "I didn't know you were into theater."

"I'm not," Bennie says from inside the trunk. "These are decommissioned spy disguises from the 1950s, back before tradecraft turned technical and made human intelligence worthless." He emerges from the trunk holding a round silver tin and looks closely at Verity. "You're pretty."

"Why Bennie Bathurst, thank you! Such a sweet compliment, especially after being so rude. You're not at all the zombie fart Sam says you are. And thank you for telling me about my dad, although I'd really like to know how you know all this stuff."

"I can't tell you yet, but I will someday, beautiful lady." The way Bennie says this to Verity causes a lumpy sad feeling in my stomach.

"What the hell?" I say. "Can we cut the smoochy ass-kissing and get back to business?"

"Can I look through the trunk?" Verity asks.

"It's all yours, Pandora." Bennie offers her a toothy, totally out-of-character smile. If he weren't so scrawny and pasty, with oversized liquid-ink brown squid eyes, he might be cute. Perhaps nature will be kind once he passes through puberty.

Verity leans into the trunk—and to my surprise Bennie shoves her into it, closes the top, and secures the latch. She screams and bangs on the lid.

I run over and try to pry it open, but it's locked again. "Bennie! What the fuck?"

"She's a much stronger human than she realizes," Bennie says. "She'll be all right until we finish our business."

And then he does something even more shocking than locking Verity in a trunk: he makes a fist and punches me full-on in the nose with a brutal and quite effective right-cross!

I reel backward and smash against a table. Bright sapphire -blue blood spiked with golden flecks gushes forth from my nostrils. The cardinal flaps and chirps around my head, losing a feather here and there as I struggle to stand up. I can't believe this little shit had that sort of strength in him!

"You little bastard!" I scream as I regain my balance to go after him. But Bennie holds up his left hand like Saratu did the day the orb took her, and I'm suddenly frozen in place, two inches above the floor, unable to move even an eyelid. My mind races up and down the length of my body looking for a way out but it's kept contained within my flesh, locked up under muscle and bone.

"I smashed your microchip," he says. "It's disabled. Would you like me to remove it from your person now?"

I can't give him an answer because I can't move. Realizing this, Bennie drops his hand. Gravity returns, and I wobble a bit in the knees, but don't fall when my feet find ground again. I pinch my nose and tilt back my head to stem the blood flow.

"I think you broke my nose."

"I did." He shrugs. "I'll fix it."

"How?"

"The same way I fixed your black eye. Here. Lie down on this table."

I do as I'm told. Bennie puts on a headlamp, picks up a long pair of ultra-thin tube-like tweezers, and uses them to look up my nose. I never imagined in a million years this would be a hole on my body any guy, even a Noid like him, would be interested in exploring. I hope I don't have boogers.

"Now hold still. This is going to be very uncomfortable," he says. "You ready?"

"Yes."

Behind Bennie's shoulder, hovering near the ceiling, Blue Robes Lady appears.

Then poof, she disappears, and Bennie's tweezers hold a rice-sized microchip connected to a hair-thin quarter-inch wire.

"Here," he says dropping it into my palm. "Want a souvenir?"

"Who would do this to me?" I ask.

"People like them." Bennie points toward the NASA complex.

"But why?"

"Somebody's tracking you for study. Or… biding time until you're of use."

"Of use? For what?"

"For mind control? Perhaps to kill or steal." He examines the chip in my hand. "Yeah, this is definitely government-issue. It's a bit fried though, as if your mind and body rejected it years ago."

"How many other kids have these implants?"

"I'm not sure. Not everybody gets one. Only the lucky ones," Bennie half jokes, looking for a moment just as 'sadgitated' as Cameron the Cop did before he left me in the custody of Drs. Dennison.

Reggie called me a walking weapon. Who did this to me and why? Is it my blood? Or am I a pieced-together pile of corpses like Frankenstein, brought to life by some bio magnetic-electrical zap? I shudder. I'm not liking any of this.

Yet somehow, I know that Bennie, dark circles and all, suffers the same way I do. It makes me feel connected to and a bit sorry for him. We're in this together, two lab rats joined by rare blood.

Bennie picks up the tin he retrieved from the trunk.

"What is that?" I ask.

"Dimethyltryptamine. Amazonian Indians call it Ayahuasca yage. It's an ancient psychedelic drug used in very sacred rituals. Dates all the way to pre-Sumerian culture. As a salve it cures almost anything, even bloody broken noses. As a brew it helps you maneuver through parallel or even very remote worlds millions of light-years away."

"Are you on it now?" I ask.

"No. Why?"

"Oh, no reason at all. Other than you just locked my best friend in a steamer trunk, then punched me in the face, levitated me, and pulled a microchip out of my nose."

Bennie runs a hand through his hair, which reminds me of Dr. Awoudi. He tilts his head up to look at the monster-sized ant farm hanging over our heads, removes his headlamp, and huffs the loose curl off his forehead for about the billionth time since I've known him. "I'm not the one seeing ladies in blue robes," he says, and he laughs for what I think is the first time ever.

"Fine. So how do we use it? Do I just rub it on my nose?" I ask.

"Yes. Rub some into your skin and then drink some of the brew I made. Oh, and Verity will need to drink some too."

I lean over and take a sniff of the stuff. "It smells like smoked ass. I'm happy to fix my nose, but what possible reason do we have to actually drink your poison?"

"So, you may go down into the hole by the boulder and get into that cave, and then tell me what's there," Bennie says. "Don't worry, the CIA tested this stuff on humans. It works. I think it might be even more effective on hybrids. Dr. Evelyn tried it too."

"Well, that explains a lot—about Dr. Evelyn anyway," I say. "We get high on psychedelic drugs while you tinker around top side? Hell no, I won't go. Why don't you use your remote viewing skills to see what's in the cave?"

Bennie shakes his head. "I've tried. For some reason, when I arrive at a certain point, I'm locked out."

I move toward the trunk to rescue Verity, but Bennie grabs my wrist. And there it is again, the same electrical zap I felt the day I handed Saratu my baby fox. Only this time, Bennie and I both jump back, and he releases me. He felt it too. I'm not crazy. Or we both are.

"What the hell was that?" I say.

"I don't know." He looks as confused as me and curiously rubs his arm. "Wait. Before you let her out of the trunk there's something you should know about our kind."

I plant a hand on my hip and cock my head impatiently for him to get on with whatever he needs to say. "Camaeliphim descendants, those like us, have souls that Nephilim don't."

"I'm not following your logic—or lack of it," I say.

Bennie continues, briefly glancing at the trunk as if to ensure Verity can't hear. "We're able to see into alternate realities in a way humans can't."

"Riiiight," I say, shaking my head. "Okay, Rabbi Einstein, check this out: Why create Golden Bloods like us to fight devil spawn when God or angels could take out Nephilim? Why fuck around with the Earthly gene pool to make hybrids? All God has to do is cast some fire and brimstone, right? Game Over."

I reach for the latch on the trunk.

"Stay with me," Bennie says, lightly touching my arm. "Religion is a ruse to keep galactic masses in line. God isn't fire and brimstone or even a *being* but a *force*. I know this isn't easy to believe, but a highly advanced society moved to Earth eons ago, one in which modern humans have no concrete memory. This society instituted an epigenetics study that created a race of other highly intelligent beings. Earth was their nursery, a secret Breeding Base I, a new legion created to protect God. But it didn't work out the way they had hoped."

"What happened?" I ask.

"They were betrayed and followed here by a group of Watchers who contaminated the breeding containers. The Watchers then claimed the new creations, humans, as slaves."

"Why did these space dudes require human slaves?" I ask, shaking my head in disbelief for the baker's dozenth time.

"Because Watchers aren't biological beings like us and can't tolerate long periods of oxygen. They can't 'work the land' to search for the Code of Everything. They need human slaves and Nephilim to do the work for them."

"And Camaeliphim?" I ask. "Where do we fit into this?"

"Camaeliphim are genetically modified beings between Dominion angels and humans. We use photonic energy from plant systems to weave in and out of the universe and we thrive on oxygen. But this same oxygen is toxic to Watchers who are primarily silicon-based beings."

I cock my head at him, a little doubtful, but Bennie shares more.

"Humans and animals are coded to require oxygen harvested through their systems on this planet, a catch-22, because breathing and other bodily functions actually minimize the risk for silicon-based species like Watchers wanting a home here. Unfortunately, many humans, but not all, have also been programmed by Watchers to systematically destroy anything oxygen-giving, like trees or plants."

"Why would they even need this planet?" I ask. "They have the entire galaxy—billions of universes to bother, if they wanted."

"For the gold," he says. "It powers them up. More importantly, they hope to take physical form so they may help Nephilim find and rebuild what we call, The Word. If they're able to do that..."

"They own everything," I say. "Including God."

"Yes."

"This is where the Word comes in," Bennie continues. "It's a galactic cookbook, a code for everything. The Ebians ensured it was dismantled on Earth to keep the Watchers contained."

"Ebians?" I ask.

Bennie stands straight, his flecked green-gold irises fixed on me and no longer the dark brown I know. "They're the original Earth seeders. They made us, Camaeliphim, to counter Nephilim."

I shake my head. I'm not sure what to believe. I'm also afraid of losing my tether, getting lost in Bennie's words, doomed to float forever between lucidity and lunacy, carried along the cosmic currents of this strange kid's dark matter, spiraling, spiraling, spiraling...

He seems to sense my struggle.

"Think of Camaeliphim as the buckeye seeds you carry in your pocket," Bennie says, interrupting my thoughts. "Native Americans say nature made buckeye trees impossible to destroy. Camaeliphim, like buckeyes, connect with nature, so like Nephilim, we're nearly impossible to destroy. We keep the multiverse in balance and require harmony to survive. Nephilim require war, decay, and violence to advance, using technology, from which they feed. But they can, with great focus, be powered down."

A multitude of doubts claw at her soul as she forces two fists around a sword. Lift up. Drop down. Fail. Try again. Hazel-green eyes with gold flecks settle upon an aurora night sky. What is the past? Where is her future? Eyes forward. Keep them dry. No time for love. Inhale. Count to four. Exhale. She stands her ground.

"Whoa," Bennie says as he catches my elbow with his hand. "You should sit down before you fall down. Straddling two worlds will do that to you."

I ignore him but won't forget he noticed—and more importantly, how he recognizes my foray between worlds. "How does my government fit into this?" I ask.

"The U.S. government just split neutrinos, which nobody thought was possible," Bennie says. "Think of neutrinos as pixie dust. It's everywhere. It moves through you even now, like a filter, rebalancing positive and negative energy. The problem is, once split, neutrinos decay and switch sides, playing for the Watchers and Nephilim, speeding up destruction."

"How?"

"Split neutrinos cause realm rips—huge holes in our universe that we don't know how to fix. Parallel dimensions above and below leak or bulge into this world, further distorting reality," he says. "It also seriously skews our electromagnetic fields. Elephants, butterflies, birds, to name but a few, use them to navigate, and so, too, do Camaeliphims and Dominion angels. If this planet loses its electromagnetic field, we will be shaken from it like a bad case of fleas."

"I've never heard you talk like this. Verity's right. Are you off your meds?"

"Rumors on Earth claim I'm the smartest Camaeliphim in our black hole," Bennie says with a wink.

"Black hole?"

Bennie chuckles lightly, a small sigh escaping his lips. "This galaxy, this Milky Way? The entire thing already resides inside a black hole. It's part of the reason physicists have a difficult time coming up with a Theory of Everything—they can't see beyond, only out. It's the equivalent of peering through a keyhole into one room with the hope of seeing an entire castle."

"You look tired," I say.

"We get tired. This vase in which we're confined eventually breaks down. We die, just like pure humans do."

Bennie lightly tugs my arm and pulls me close. He removes a strand of hair from my face and places it behind my shoulder. He smells of Ivory soap and fresh air—comfortable, yet it also gives me a case of flittering ladybugs in my stomach. I know him, a fleeting moment of déjà vu. His intensity and intelligence seem way older than thirteen, and there exists, at least at this moment, an internal power that smolders within him. I find it almost commanding and hard to resist, but I pull away.

"You have a Raga to contain," Bennie says.

"Raga? Who's he?"

"Raga's a she. Mahrah's Nephilim daughter. Think of Mahrah as Satan or Lucifer. Mahrah's been contained in another realm, the Source Vortex, where no beings reside. We believe that he once mated with a human to help the Bezaliels."

"Bezaliels?" I know this name. I've heard it before—in a dream.

"Ah, you're not as far along as I thought. It's the true name of the Watchers. 'Watchers' replaced the term Bezaliel's in the Bible as propaganda, a dark ruse to fool humans into thinking these fallen entities are protectors and friends."

"Where is this Raga?"

"She could be anywhere on this planet, likely keeping a high profile. "

I look at Bennie quizzically.

"Raga feeds upon attention, depends on it for Earthly survival. A large following of human beings, those who worship fame and fortune, enable her to draw energy. She's dangerous because anyone, human, hybrid, or interdimensional entity can be tempted by her false vibrations. She lives here by stealing your soul and invading your mind. She spins you around in the head to keep you grasping for things that don't matter.

"Have you ever heard of the term 'urban slumber'?" I ask. "Reggie mentioned it to me back at the house—says it's a secret program where some governments use energy fields to control masses of humans. Maybe Raga, like God, isn't a being—but, instead, a Force—the opposite of God's Source—like the flip side of religion and science residing on the same coin, as Verity once told me. Do Dr. Sterling and the others know about Raga?"

"Humans? They don't know this story. Septum Oculi is an elite but important earthly team primarily composed of humans that stamp out terrorists. They don't actually realize how much they help a multitude of parallel universes. For them, Camaeliphim is a locally grown lab creation. And with the exception of Reggie, they're mostly blind to other realms. Raga is an upgraded breed of Nephilim. It's rumored that she can't die. And yes, I have heard of urban slumber. It's a smart theory you've got, but it's not the same. Raga is now a 'being' made manifest somewhere here on Earth, and that's a first for the Bezaliel's."

"Then what hope is there?" I ask, sliding fingertips along my right forearm to cast off increasing dread and wondering what sort of gadget Bennie used to immobilize and levitate me.

"Raga can be thrown into the Source Vortex beyond our conscious horizon, where the First Force banished her father. There's no escape from there."

"Huh?"

"No one knows what that means," Bennie says. "The Source Vortex is likely hidden in the Word, but until the missing pieces scattered all over this planet are found and pieced back together again, humans move toward permanent darkness century by century."

"Who is Scatha?" I ask. "What does she have to do with this?"

Bennie smiles. "You're remembering."

He walks over to the trunk—Verity has been banging on the lid this entire time—flips the latch and opens the cover. Verity sits up like Dracula and whacks Bennie hard in the leg with a wooden cane.

"You're both totally bogus to leave me wigging out in a dark trunk!" she says. "Rule number one, turkeys: *never* lock a token black chick in a trunk or subject us to musical marathons of Air Supply, got it? What were you two doing, anyway, making out?"

"What?" I say. "Ew, no!"

Bennie looks at me funny.

Verity climbs out of the trunk with a hot pink feather boa wrapped around her neck, and Bennie lends her a hand. "What the hell happened to your face?" she asks me. "You walk into a wall?"

I stuff the tiny microchip into my jeans and put both hands in my front pockets. "Bennie punched me when I tried to get you out of the trunk."

"Bennie? Bennie punched *you*, Princess She-Ra, in the face? Whatever. What were you two discussing in that strange language?"

"It's Enochian," Bennie says.

"You told me it was Basque," I say.

"Basque is an Earthly dialect of Enochian."

"Enochian?" Verity says, then sneezes. "That makes so much sense."

"How does that make sense?" I ask.

"Hardly anyone in the world masters Basque," Verity replies. "Linguists don't even know its origin. It's not Latin or Arabic or Indo-European-based. It's a language that completely stands on its own. Even today only a few people in a remote mountain region between Spain and France speak it fluently."

"And Enochian?" I ask.

"Oh, there's this guy John Dees, and his assistant Edward Kelley, who lived way back in the fifteen hundreds," she says. "Kelley had visions and spoke a strange language which Dees captured the best he could in a journal. He dubbed it 'Enochian,' the language of angels. Kelley claimed he had conversations with them. Scholars blasted Dees's work as a fraud, though."

"Dees was blasted as a fraud because the language constantly evolves, and his critics were too human to understand it," Bennie says.

I have no idea what they're talking about, and don't care to ask. "Verity, Bennie wants you and me to drink that psychedelic brew on his hot plate over there and channel ourselves into the cave under the river."

Verity puffs feathers from her face and throws one end of the fluffy boa over her shoulder. "Cool. But I can't."

"Why?" Bennie asks. "You chicken?"

"Yes, that's part of it. But also, your brew's got chagropanga leaves in it—I can smell it—and I'm allergic." She sneezes again. "But I can guide you both down to the cave if you two drink it."

"How can you guide us?" I ask.

"When I was little, I saw voodoo queens and shamans in Haiti use this stuff all the time by the waterfalls during Festival. I tried it once and saw all sorts of things—like it moved a cosmic curtain so I could peer into some great unknown, but I also broke out in hives and couldn't breathe.

I almost died. So, if we do this, we do it my way, got it? I play the lead, and you two cosmogony crackers follow my direction. Agreed?"

We nod, but if Verity almost died drinking this crap, I don't want to take one swallow.

Bennie hands me the tin of salve and I rub a handful over my nose.

Verity screams.

"What?" I ask.

"Your face! It's completely healed!"

"Yeah? So?" I say. "You believe in miracles, right?"

"I do, it's just—I've just never seen a real one performed in the flesh, on a heathen hybrid!"

Chapter 22

ASTRAL WEAVERS

"I don't give one goddamn who you have to get over here," Reggie yells from Dr. Evelyn's office as I enter the kitchen with Verity. "Call in the National Guard or the Air Force, I don't care, but find somebody who knows what the hell they're doing."

A door slams, and Sergeant Major Brock Lynch blows past us and out the side porch, his cheeks the color of the cardinals pecking at the sunflower seeds in the feeder outside.

I've never heard Reggie lose his cool like that before. "What the hell do think that was about?" I ask Verity.

"I don't know, but hurry up," she says. "I just want to get what we need and get the hell out of here before Colonel Reggie stops us and asks lots of questions."

Before leaving Silo 57, Bennie and I made Verity spit shake, cross her heart, and swear to secrecy that she tells *no one* about the real meaning of Camaeliphim. I suppose it helped a great deal when Bennie told Verity that her witchy woman, saintly pseudo-pagan voodoo-Christian services were needed to save the world.

She clutches my arm, and I let her, because I fear she might barricade herself in a closet if I don't keep her close. We throw a few Little Debbie snacks and some Fritos in a burlap bag, plus some Lucky Charms cereal (Verity insists), and we head down the hallway to the library for a book Verity thinks will come in handy. I close the library's doors behind us, and she finds the book and opens it on the big desk.

"*According to Ohio folklore, in 1755, eighteen-year-old James Smith was captured by the Iroquois in Pennsylvania and was brought to live among their tribe in Northern Ohio as part of their custom of 'adopting' a male if one of their warriors died in battle,*" she reads. "*Smith claimed in journals that much of his time was spent near a river natives called Canesadooharie, located five miles southwest of Sandusky, and there he discovered buckets full of black pearls."* She looks up. "Sam, it's the Huron River, where we swim! It branches off here. Look at this picture."

There it is, Smith's crude drawing of the boulder. I make a mental note to look for black pearls the next time I swim—if I ever jump back into that water. God only knows what sort of chemicals NASA might be dumping in there to infect us, or what might live beneath the surface.

Verity flips a page and summarizes what she's reading. "Smith says in his journal that many tribes, including a race of red-headed giants, met along the banks of the Canesadooharie every year to conduct a special ritual. He describes a boulder in the middle of the river thirty feet high, where Native Americans engaged in extended meditation."

"Let me see that." I look over Verity's shoulder and silently read along. When Smith asked why the area was considered sacred, Iroquois and Wyandot elders told him it was a burial place for the gods, a place of great energy where spirits roamed in peace and sometimes guided warriors on battle paths through visions and crucibles. They buried their dead here, too, among those "not of our kindred."

"What does that mean?" I ask, pointing to the last line.

"Remember how Barbara said Ohio settlers found giant corpses? The local natives claimed the Indian mummies weren't part of the tribes," Verity says. "Maybe they came from someplace else way before Native Americans got here."

"Or maybe they came from another world," I say.

"Or heaven," she says, looking up toward the ceiling. "We should get back to Bennie and prep you both to drink that yage. We need to get you into that cave before anyone figures out that the place in the river might be key to something."

"Yeah, like our early graves."

A rustle sounds from behind one of the large club chairs across the room. I jump in front of Verity—to do what, I'm not sure, but someone is in here with us, and I don't think it's Bennie. Verity trembles behind me, her teeth practically chattering as she clutches her book.

I reach for one of the decorative swords hanging on the wall and jump up on the desk. "We know you're in here! Show yourself."

"Really?" says Verity. "That's all you've got? Yawn. How about using some cool celestial warrior moves or something? Or maybe you can fly over there, like Peter Pan!"

"Shut the hell up. You crossed your heart," I hiss.

Very slowly, a pair of eyes rises from behind the chair.

"Genin?" Verity says. "What are you doing in here? I didn't know cavemen could read." She puts the book down and brushes her arm, pretending she was never scared and gives Genin a smart-ass smirk.

"I'm going with you," Genin says. "If anyone knows how to guide an expedition through a psychedelic forest, it's me."

I lower the sword. "You can't go with us, Genin."

He gives us a cocky smile and ties a red bandana around his forehead. His shoulder-length wavy black hair falls around his neck, shiny, like newly preened raven feathers "Sure I can. If you don't let me go, I'll tell. Besides, you two ladies need someone protecting you if you're planning to drink Ayahuasca yage."

"I can take care of myself," I say, anger rising about as much as his penis pomposity over his stupid idea that I need protecting.

"Sure, you can." Genin laughs. I want to slap him, but sometimes I want to kiss him too. He slides out around the chair, a Bowie knife strapped to his camo-covered hip, his chest broad and taking my breath away. If his entire tribe is as hot as he is, I hope to meet them someday, provided they're not dead and missing their eyeballs, like Verity claims.

"How do you know about yage?" Verity asks.

"I'm from the Amazon, remember? I cut my teeth on yage," he says.

"What's it like?" I ask.

"Trip of a lifetime, once the puking subsides. Come on, let's go. I came from the river. Bennie's already there. He told me about your little plan. Of course, I had to put him in a headlock and give him a wet noogie until he spilled his guts. I'll be going into that cave with you."

"Bennie wouldn't talk to you," I say. "Besides, he could easily stop you from harming him if he wanted."

"*Riiight*," Genin says. "Bennie is a wimp; he couldn't crack a walnut. And he did talk to me. That little pantywaist coughed up your plans without even trying to cite his name, rank, or serial number."

The only reason Bennie would tell Genin about our plan is if Bennie knows something we don't and needs Genin there—though I can't yet figure out why. And Genin is too caught up in his G.I. Joe role-play to even consider that Bennie might have played him.

"Bennie is going to stay sober with you," Genin continues. "He doesn't want to drink the brew. You two dorks will stand guard while me and the Viking princess descend into hell's gates. After she puts on the ant gloves."

"Ant gloves?" I ask. Though I'm still thinking about Bennie not drinking yage. It's so typical of him. I should have known. The little twerp likely has a fear of puking and considers it beneath him—too human. Or perhaps he's unsure of how he might react and won't risk a loss of control.

Verity looks at Genin as if he's gone daft. "When we drank yage in Haiti, we never put on ant gloves."

"Yeah, and you're allergic to the leaves now, aren't you?" Genin asks.

Verity nods.

"If you'd taken the venom, you'd be drinking the yage. Anyway, it's a rite of passage for young warriors to stick our hands into gloves filled with bullet ants for ten minutes. It strengthens our immune systems against the poison."

"That's the stupidest thing I've ever heard," I say. "Why would anybody do that?"

"All the boys in my tribe do it." He says it like it's no big deal to be attacked by ants. "We're about nine years old when it happens the first time, so you're getting a late start. And you're a girl. Usually this rite of passage is reserved for dudes, warriors who'll grow up to protect their tribes. Real men among men."

I roll my eyes. But now he's got me thinking about the ant farm back at Bennie's lab, the one that hung above our heads. Are those bullet ants? Surely, he wouldn't buy into Genin's macho warrior crap.

"Yeah, okay, Rambo," I say. I brush past him toward the door. "But if you get in my way, I'll punch you in the face, got it? Come on, Verity. Let's go."

I hear the large old grandfather clock upstairs outside my room gong five times. We'll miss dinner, but I think we're all too excited to care.

"I love strong women," Genin says to Verity. "They're such a turn-on."

***

We trudge through knee-high snow in our bulky snowsuits toward the river. Verity walks and reads at the same time, branches smacking her bright purple hat every now and then. Breath tumbles out of our mouths like steam, and the light begins to fade under the shadowed tangles of tree limbs. My throat feels as if I've inhaled a dozen menthol cough drops, and my lungs slowly harden to ice blocks.

"Listen to this," Verity says. "It says here that James Smith once saw a grass mound containing the bones of three skeletons so large, he could fit the skulls over his head like a helmet."

Could there really be giants out in the fields somewhere? I'm surprised to find I'm now more interested in knowing the giants' history than I am in stealing the valuables that might be buried with them, which is something I would have seriously considered doing back in Cleveland.

"The elders of my tribe told us of giants too, living outside Ecuador and Peru," Genin says. "They were supposedly peaceful pale-skinned people hiding deep in the forests. I never saw any, though—it's just a myth. They acted as spirit guides to help hunters and protect the terrain. I didn't know they had the same legend in Ohio."

"Seriously?" I say. "Nothing cool ever happens in Ohio, at least not beyond this freak hole. This entire state is full of mediocre Midwestern kooks."

"Ouch. Harsh," Verity says. "I lived in Southside Chicago, and this place sure beats the hell out of most places. I think Buckeye folks are adventurous and brave."

"You've never been to Cleveland," I say.

I nudge her aside and greet Bennie by the riverbank. He carries a lid-covered bucket and a bamboo stick about three feet long, and a large canteen hangs from his shoulder. He's set up a tent and started a small campfire that crackles and pops, its pumpkin-colored embers glowing like miniature spaceships. This kid can do practically anything better than the rest of us. It makes me feel a little jealous, but I also feel sorry for him too because he's such a nerd.

"Get naked," he says.

I laugh. I'm surprised Mr. Roboto jokes during a time like this. But he just looks at me with placid eyes that convey dead seriousness. His funny bone is back at his lab, I guess, probably hanging out with the cobra and his half-bio spider.

"What?" I say. "Are you kidding?"

"You need to hurry up. Get naked inside the tent and lie on top of the open sleeping bag."

"But why?"

"The potency of the brew weakens with time," Bennie says. "Body heat generates more energy and makes yage last longer."

Genin eagerly casts off his snowsuit and peels his shirt from his broad caramel chest. Verity nods at me to do the same.

"It's fucking freezing out here," I say. "Let me have a drink first."

Verity reaches for the canteen over Bennie's shoulder, but Genin stops her. "Ant gloves first," he says, a smile on his face. He looks down on me by an inch or two, having gone through a growth spurt that Barbara claims is the result of her homecooked meals—but I've noticed Dr. Evelyn studying him as if she knows something about Genin we don't.

"I am *not* putting on ant gloves," I say, daring Genin to go against me, our eyes locked in a stupid alpha competition.

"You must," Genin says, deadly serious, as if he's just swallowed an entire volume of sacred scrolls. "The ant venom raises your adrenaline and gives you courage and wisdom. And it will act as an antihistamine against any allergic reactions."

"How bad does it hurt?" I ask.

"It will be the most awful pain you've ever felt in this life," Bennie says. "Like being stabbed or shot. You must focus and breathe to get through the worst. Most can't."

Nothing could hurt worse than what Guy put me through in Cleveland. Whatever the ants dish out, I decide I can take.

Verity uses her bulky snowsuit as a screen against the boys' view while I undress and slip alone into the tent. I lie naked on top of the coolness of the sleeping bag and watch the fog of my icicle breath rise like a trickle of smoke into the dark creases of canvas above me. Is it too late to change my mind?

Bennie abruptly opens the flap, and I use an arm to cover my breasts and a hand for the other part, but he's entirely focused on the ant bucket and his yage brew. He doesn't even look at me—which would be creepy, but I thought thirteen-year-old guys lived to see girls naked. Of course, he isn't just any boy, he's a total putty head—and maybe even gay. He does, after all, keep a pink boa in his steamer trunk.

Genin steps into the tent after Verity. *He* stares at me—and gulps.

Verity swats him across the chest with the back of her hand and shakes her finger at him so he doesn't get any weird ideas.

I try not to look at his dick, but I can't help myself because, well, his thing is huge, landing mid-thigh, and flanked by curly black hair. I know Verity sees it too but tries to pretend she doesn't. She finally winks at me when he isn't looking and makes the same exaggerated fish gesture guys do when they tell tall tales about their big catch, the one that got away. Only she's not kidding!

Bennie switches on a dim lantern.

"She needs to kneel," Genin says. "I'll catch her from behind."

Bennie gives Genin a dark look, piercing him with tiny silver daggers, which startles me because his eyes are usually so molten-brown with flecks of gold or deep green placidity, particularly when he's focused on one of his experiments.

"Kneel for him," Bennie says nonchalantly, burying any anger toward Genin I thought I sensed.

I sigh heavily as I rise to my knees, looking only at Verity because I'm naked and can't look at Bennie. This is way too much exposure.

Genin slides behind me on his knees, his body a warm rock. The swooshy-floaty feeling I had that day in the dining room when we first met rushes back stronger than ever; heat fills my cheeks, and shyness creeps in. Maybe even a little shame. I wish Genin and I were alone. This is the same excitement I used to feel with boys before doing time at the Trail's End Motel, but more intense. I'm happy these normal, natural feelings weren't completely destroyed. If I'd chosen to keep carrying the pain of what Guy did to me, I'd be allowing him to control my head and body from the grave too. And I refuse to let that happen.

Verity sets up an altar covered with crosses, a small ceramic Buddha, black and purple candles, a miniature statue of the Virgin Mary, a few rosaries, some burning sage, and what she calls "enlightenment" incense. She sprinkles salt around the sleeping bag, then removes a joint from her backpack. Bennie lights it for her, and she inhales deeply. The heavy musky scent of burning rope and pine lazily wafts over us. She sinks back into the shadows of this built-for ten tent and softly chants while rocking her body in small circles, a joint in one hand and her cracked brown leather Book of Spells in the other—the one Barbara, twice now, has tried to hide or burn. And soon Verity is lost, like Saratu, in a world I only catch glimpses of in dreams or during hallucinations.

"Take a deep slow breath in and count to four," Genin says. "Now hold it for four. Release it slowly, counting to four again. Easy. Find a rhythm that feels natural to you. Navy SEALs do this to relax before a mission or to fight pain. Let's set our intention to travel together to the hole under the river."

I don't tell him that Reggie has already taught me this breathing technique but I'm not sure how we set an intention. "How do we do that?" I ask.

"We think about becoming one and going there together. And breathe. That's it. That's all we need to do."

I roll my eyes. He makes the gravity of taking a potent drug sound easy, and that makes me feel slightly better.

Genin breathes too, and it isn't long before we find ourselves in sync, my body melting into his, the two of us becoming one as our heat comforts me and drives out the cold. A gust of wind taps the flaps on the tent. My legs stop shaking, and I find this all a little less weird and almost natural even—like I'm on to something very special that only Genin and I understand and the rest of the world misses.

Bennie uses a clamp to pull what look like two leafy, wriggling oven mitts from his bucket.

"Hold up your hands as if you're giving praise to God, palms toward your face," Genin says. He speaks with an unfamiliar and mature tenderness.

Falling into the erotic and forbidden dreaminess of skin on skin, I do as he says, and brace myself for this psychedelic road trip.

He brings his hands under my elbows and tightly grips my forearms. "Keep breathing," he says. "That's it. You're doing great. I'm here with you. I'm not leaving. Understand? I'm here with you through the entire adventure. You ready?"

Sucking in a deep breath, I slowly count one, two, three…and nod.

Bennie slips the bullet-ant-filled oven mitts over my bare hands and clamps my wrists vise–tight, allowing nothing—hands, ants, or air—to escape.

"AHHHHHH-JIIIHH!"

Waves of fire-licking burns consume me. Pain. Intense. Too much. *Breathe.*

I jerk and shake, throwing my head in a circle. Lightning. Have I been struck? Beads of sweat spring up on my forehead, and a rush of fire hot redness zooms through my arms and legs, a thousand sparklers injected into my veins. Drumbeats. Faster. Heavy. An active volcano—

my heart. I push my head back against Genin's chest. He remains solid. Leafy herbs and liquid glide down my throat.

One, two, three, four. Hold. Breathe.

Drink.

One, two, three, four.

Genin and I tumble backward in the dark, sliding through an abyss of ultra-polished rock, leaving Verity and Bennie, and this world, far behind. Gold flecks from an unseen moon offer glimpses of endless shiny black slate glistening with water that seeps through porous cores and oozes trickles of silver-like syrup. A low steady hum fills my ears, and I see blips of patterns and colors—white, red, orange, gold, blue, purple.

And then we free-fall through darkness.

I blindly reach out to grab something, anything, but Genin pulls me tighter toward him, and we melt like candle wax until I can't tell where he begins and I end.

There. A light. A tunnel.

We speed-slide and slip through a curve of cave, which opens to flying over acres of endless cracked mud. Rising higher, we zoom through an exotic outdoor bazar where copper pots hang and clang among royal-purple textiles stitched with gold threads. Others are with us here too, like bubbles or atoms free-floating on the wind, controlled chaos, both apart from and part of us, an intelligence that existed before we did, a feedback loop that grows, much like a child, with information it gathers and stores beyond space and time. A few black-and-white goats wearing brass bells clop over dry earth before turning into crazy geometric patterns of light like a Spirograph on speed. We've entered a kaleidoscope tunnel.

Whoosh!

Genin is across from me now. There is no such thing as sin or shame here because there is no matter in this matter. He and I shrug and agree, mentally connected. We float in a deep cave with a smooth floor of what looks like milky glittered quartz. A soft glow emanates from a hole in the rock wall, leading to another cave.

I motion for Genin to make his way with me toward the light. Those fleshy feelings I had in the tent are gone, replaced by an intense feeling of knowledge and a deeper understanding of some unknown I could never explain in a human body. I know Genin feels it too, because I can read his thoughts. We're connected on the same vibrational cable, two brains in sync, intertwined as one—no longer human, but better.

We move together, our feet coming to rest on ground that feels like a plush towel fresh from the dryer. This lightness in both body and soul excites me because it feels so familiar, as if I'm home or close to home.

The cave is orderly and void of the dust, rust, and decay I expect. Gold chalices, swords, scales, herbs, polished stones, tools, leather goods, bones, precious gems, various globes of metal, iron, glass, and bronze wait neatly along shelves carved out of what looks like black granite. It's as if we stumbled into an obsessive-compulsive version of an Indiana Jones movie. But it also reminds me a little of Bennie's lab, except for a mass of completely dirt-less tangled roots dangling on the right side of this oversized cavern, likely from a large tree above seemingly drawing life from the cave rather than latched in soil.

And in the center, there they are.

Thirteen giant pale-blue-skinned mummies with long red hair, sit cross-legged in the deep trance state of long-preserved dead. They've barely decayed, suffering only slight pruning of skin; it's as if they sat down to die together only yesterday instead of millennia ago. Some wear long strands of white and black pearls with bright red cardinal feathers. Each wears a thick copper bracelet on a right wrist, and all are branded on their shoulders with tattoos of symbols we don't recognize. I memorize the tattoos.

Their palms face heavenward, fingertips barely touching, holding a sparkly cat's cradle of web-like threads, which are attached to a floating, glowing, metallic orb slightly above their heads in the center of their circle. It looks like some sort of balancing game.

"The giants we were told about in the Amazon had white skin, not strange blue like this," Genin says. "They look like warriors too. Who do you think they are?"

My head tops out at the shoulder of one sitting warrior. "I don't know," I say. "They look Native American, but I think they're much more ancient."

"Check this out." Carved into the rock behind Genin is a string of text and unfamiliar symbols. It makes no sense to us. "Why would Native Americans use a combination of Hebrew and hieroglyphics?"

"I don't know," I say. "Likely because they're *not* Native Americans, or at least not in the way we think. I can't read the hieroglyphics, but the Hebrew… 'Thou shalt not…' Wait. This looks like a condensed version of the Ten Commandments. I can't understand the rest—can you?"

"No," Genin says. "This doesn't make any sense. This place is like a vault for the world's ancient religions. And look over there—a Mayan calendar."

Bennie told Verity and me about all the religions of the world only having little pieces of a poorly deciphered story, a missing code. Is it possible that Genin and I have stumbled into some sort of psychedelic base camp for consciousness? Or does this space represent a holographic universe in recycle mode, a time loop for civilization? Or is it simply a weird warehouse of the world's religions brought to us by NASA—or maybe by the yage brew?

I feel strangely at peace, but I also feel close to some secret, some ancient knowledge I can't quite grasp—like a red balloon just out of reach before it floats away.

A light clicking noise from within the tangled tree roots snags our attention about thirty steps away from where the natives died in meditation. Genin and I walk-float closer (the gravity is a lot lighter here than turf-side). A soft glow, but not like a light, more like the gel of fireflies, blinks within the middle of the roots. I've never seen such a strange 'inside-out' sort of tree, but stranger still, it seems to be protecting something.

I touch one of the roots, as does Genin and green leaves suddenly sprout when we pull back our fingertips.

Peering deeper into the web of roots, we spy a complex mechanism with hundreds of meshing bronze, gold, and steel gears. This, whatever it is, appears to be a device made of ancient, modern, and future elements separated into three main fragments of light—screens and other stuff I can't explain because I've never seen anything like it. It has inscriptions and it's maybe three feet tall, three feet wide, and three feet deep—a clockwork cube with settings, a series of zeros, ones, and still other incomprehensible symbols that overlap, and magically switch places, appearing as if they're in two places at once. If I focus on a zero, the strange sequence abruptly stops as if it senses we're watching, and then reverts to even more complicated equations. There's a key type of device sticking out of the front of it too.

"What do you think this is?" I ask.

Genin shrugs. "Military? Maybe a weapon? Whatever it is, it's way beyond 1984."

"Phstteeeeee!"

Color swiftly stains Genin's cheeks, and I feel sudden overwhelming dread that makes me want to run. If I'm built with half-hybrid courage like Bennie claims, I'm having a difficult time finding any. And I no longer feel in sync with Genin or this thoughts—but far from him and alone.

"Genin, stand your ground. Whatever's here with us, it wants us to mentally separate. To divide and conquer us, I think."

Genin nods, lowers his head, and closes his eyes. "I'm with you," he says in Basque. I'm more than a little surprised he speaks the language Bennie and I share but I have no time for inquiries.

Looking back at the gadget, I thrust my hand between the entangled buckeye roots and snatch the key looking device, curling it in my palm.

A gust of wind sweeps over our heads, and a thunderous noise, a sonic boom, like the one I heard my first day at Plum Hook, causes cave dust and small pebbles to fall on the pale skinned mummies. Without warning, one of them opens his eyes, and there is no pupil, no iris— just eerie royal-blue colored bulbs of light emanating from his sockets.

The roots of the tree contract and tighten around the ancient gear-like device until it's sealed over. The once glowing globe in the center of the Indians that gave us light suddenly goes cold-steel dark.

I can't see.

Something pushes me—hard. I fall against one of the mummies. A thread soft as a spider's web lands on my upper arm and I instinctively brush it away—only to discover that it's actually a fine strand of razor wire. I've dropped the key too. *Damn it!* I feel around the floor of the cave but come up empty.

Standing, I accidentally swipe my blood dripping fingertips on the thigh of the mummified corpse. The same feelings of self-preservation and rage I felt that day in the motel room with Guy spring up, a bubbling geyser of everything on this Earth that lies far from compassion or peace and I feel emboldened by my fury rather than fearful.

Reaching through the darkness, concentrating on Genin, I mentally toss him into the circle of mummies, missing every thread, the same way I levitated the lamp in my bedroom. He'll be safe there, I think, within their circle of protection, a guess I'm making based on some of Verity's Pagan studies.

The floating orb above the mummy's heads begins to glow again.

The shadow of black wings flap and hover overhead. We look up.

Breathe, Sam.

One, two, three, four...

I'm knocked to the ground with another push so strong it forces the air from my lungs. A screech from this creature causes more rock dust to crumble over our heads.

I grab one of the tree roots next to me and hoist myself up.

But I'm not in the cave anymore. And it's not 1984, its November 1954. At least that's what it says according to the space rocket calendar on the wall of this...military base? A sign outside a window reads, 'Nevada Testing Site Area 23', Silo 57.

I float through this bend in spacetime unseen by the soldiers in funny uniforms that surround me, on a ghost tour of a storage locker facility—an old airplane hangar, I think, converted into a lab and not really a silo like the one Bennie uses—this one is barn sized and sterile. Suspended inside clear containers float seriously deformed corpses of kids stored in what I can only describe as sausage casing. I hear a bunch of guys—not a woman in sight (unless you count my phantom ass), speaking German, which is weird for an American military base that I assume is a big secret.

Whoosh!

I'm transported again through this weird time travel portal I've entered, this time landing in a futuristic looking spaceship where I witness a captain use nothing but his hands and mind to steer it — over a plateau in Peru. We've followed petroglyph maps made by the natives and soundlessly hover our large craft over a landing strip carved onto a long-dry lakebed. Large pale-skinned warriors and their chief emerge from the caves to greet us. They only have three long fingers. No thumbs or pinkies. They're heads are elongated too. They each make offerings and one of them hands me a strange looking key—like the one I just lost!

KABOOM!

Mushroom cloud.

I run with an unknown group of people wearing strange silver suits, but there is no place to go.

Looking up, there's a hole in the sky.

"Cover it up!" someone shouts.

Air sirens.

"It's too late. They're here," another yells.

Who is here? I look all around but don't see anyone who isn't running away or trying to hide. It's complete pandemonium as people panic and stampede and I too get swept away by this human tsunami.

"Fire!"

The ground under my feet cracks and turns black.

Many.

People.

Die.

Lungs explode, ash falls, and life in this realm, wherever I am, retreats. Bodies lie scattered, some forever preserved in instantly petrified poses of fear—but within the shadow of smoke, hovers an angel-ike being, a single tear drifting down his cheek.

"Bennie?"

Skin peels away from my muscle and bone like thin membranes of rotting onion to reveal that my 'soul' is made of light, wires and plasma. Now unprotected, I, too, fail, breathing my last gasps of freedom. The angel-being holds out his arms and I float into them, my circuits powering down...

Again, I free fall in a vortex of darkness until landing in some sort of underground lab. Here, scientists, engineers, and military people race around checking charts, looking at monitors. And eight stories below their feet—she's there! I see her!

Saratu!

I found her!

She floats—trapped in a huge amber-filled liquid aquarium secured by a gold frame. She holds her palm to the glass, says hello to me again as she did in the dining room my first day at Plum Hook. She sees me! I wave.

"I'll get you out of here," I say. "I promise." But I'm not sure how.

Saratu doesn't seem scared, perhaps even resigned to her fate, whatever that might be, but more importantly, why her? What is it about Saratu that captures NASA's interest? But how do I know this is *NASA*? I quickly search this weird room made almost entirely of cable, switches, and steel, until I spot a small seal stamped onto what appears to be an oversized computer similar to the one in Bennie's silo. It reads: *NASA PLUM HOOK FACILITY* 3.141592654, and beneath it is a fractal diagram of a circle, a small battle shield looking emblem with a smaller circle in the middle and I've seen this before.

Someone's coming.

He stops.

He looks around as if he senses but can't see me.

This man isn't a "he" at all, at least not in the human sense. He has a reptilian-like claw for one foot that can't be covered with a shoe! It taps the ground like fingers thumping a desk. He feels familiar to me and I stretch back into the far reaches of my brain to locate a memory but the effort leaves me blank. This creature-man studies Saratu as she bows her head. It's as if she empties her thoughts, so that neither of us are able to read her anymore. The man-beast tries to press a hand to the glass in front of her but curses when it shocks him and forces him to jump back.

No!

Without warning, I'm suddenly returned to the cave and feel as if I've been launched out of a cannon. I'm beside Genin within in the circle of blue Indians.

"Genin!"

I fling myself over him like a protective cape.

The cave roof abruptly peels back and some of the meditating souls of the mummies spiral up in swirls of white mist. Wings unfold on their ghost-like backs as they propel higher into the heavens. They use swords and silk-like threads to mend rips in the multiverse, stitching in celestial concert to patch every tear high above the lone tree in the cornfield. The river too, is parted above our heads and we marvel at the otters, beavers, frogs, and fish suspended in action, watching us.

All goes quiet.

"Be." Someone whispers.

Unexpectedly, an army uniform approaches.

The soldier's face is fuzzy, and I can't read his nametag. I feel sick. Everything in the cave becomes blurry and confused as the soldier moves closer. I feel myself fading too, like Genin.

"Dad?"

As fast as we fell into the cave, I'm sucked out of it, through the lights, tunnels, and diagrams, spinning head over heels.

I suddenly sit up in the tent, disoriented, hands black, blistered, swollen, and covered in Bennie's salve, realizing I've returned. And what a headache.

There's also a long, thin, bleeding cut up my arm.

Verity puffs breath down Genin's throat and breaks suction for a moment shouting, "Oh my God, wake up Genin! Please don't die!" Bennie pounds on Genin's chest. Tears pool in Verity's eyes.

"What happened?" I ask, shoving her aside to check on Genin.

My handsome Genin.

"He's overdosing," Bennie says. "I can't get a pulse. He's not breathing."

Genin convulses on the sleeping bag, his eyes roll back in his head.

"No," I say. "He's still in the cave. We've got to bring him back here!"

I push Bennie out of the way and thump Genin hard on the chest. "Wake up, you brave son-ofa-bitch! I'm back. Follow me." Then I shout toward the ceiling. "Dad!" I scream. "Please save him!"

A lightning bolt zips through the tent, searing the top off and blowing Bennie and Verity into a corner. They hold on to one another to keep from being sucked up like lint into the storm outside.

Genin convulses and foam bubbles from his mouth. I grab his tongue to keep him from choking on it but it's difficult to hold the grip because my hands are so swollen and numb. Bennie crawls back to us, dragging a clinging Verity with him, and thrusts his salve tin into my hands.

"What do I do with this?"

"Rub it on his chest and pray," he says. "I'm out of options."

"You fucking sent him down there with me because he's human, didn't you?" I'm seething, glaring at Bennie accusingly, ready to shred him like beef and not caring what he might be able to do to me in return.

Bennie offers me a sadistic, almost triumphant smile, as if he knew all along Genin would go with me on this psychedelic freak tour in some misaligned chivalrous attempt to protect me. Bennie already knew that no human should take this trip, and that's why he kept Verity sidetracked, building her altar, practicing spells, and he's likely withholding an anti-allergen to the yage. But—Genin spoke perfect Basque on our trip, which means he may be hybrid too. So, what happened?

"Give me the fucking anti-allergen," I yell at Bennie.

"I don't have one," he says coldly.

"You have an anti-poison for everything!" I yell over the growing gusts. "But not a yage overdose?"

The wind whistles through the tent above our heads and the hushed whispers of spirits speaking some unknown or dead language returns. Verity grips Bennie's forearm tightly as she mumbles some incomprehensible chant.

Bennie lowers and shakes his head. I want to pummel him.

"I don't want to be around you anymore!" I scream. "If he dies, this is your fault, and you're not my friend!"

Verity resumes her position beside Genin and thumbs her rosary, repeating Hail Mary's as fast as a vinyl record skips under a needle. I smear Bennie's herbal goo on Genin's chest, my swollen hands throbbing and now three times their normal size. The nausea from the yage brew overtakes me and I fight back the urge to vomit. It's no use. I retreat to a back corner of the tent and gag before completely hurling the yage brew up and out of my stomach. Within the low glint of the lantern, I see it; a key-looking device with an eye symbol etched into its end. I snatch it up, wipe the puke away with my hand, and shove it into my coat pocket.

Twigs break just outside the tent. Randolph howls in the distance. I smell the scent of old garbage and sulfur as the wind beats itself hard against the tent. Bennie picks up his bucket of bullet ants and slowly moves toward the whipping entrance flaps to step outside, the anger in my eyes pelting him almost as much as the ice rain that now rages around us.

Genin bolts upright. He breathes.

Thank God!

He blinks a few times, hacks repeatedly, then grabs me and won't let go. Verity bites her bottom lip, tears streaming over the rims of her eyes.

The tent flap opens again and this time, Reggie steps through. He surveys the scene. I suddenly remember Genin and I are both naked, and I pick up a corner of the sleeping bag to cover us—and to hide my inflamed hands, which thankfully are improving a bit thanks to the salve.

"What the hell is going on here?" Reggie yells. "I smell weed."

"I don't smell any weed," Verity says. It's a miserable attempt at coyness.

"Kid," Reggie says, "don't lie to me. I served in Nam. Weed was a daily serving of vegetables for those of us stuck near enemy lines. And you two put some clothes on. I don't even want to know. All of you get your asses back to the house. I've been out here looking for you for hours. Don't bother to pack this up either. Hell's about to break loose while you're out here playing house. Move."

"Hours?" I ask. "What time is it?"

"It's past *midnight,*" Reggie barks.

I look at Verity who nods. Christ! Have we been tripping for six hours?

"Where's Bennie?" I ask.

"Bennie? How the hell would I know? Haven't seen him. Do I need to tell Dr. Evelyn to get you some 'vitamins'?" Reggie counters.

"What? You mean birth control?" I ask. "No! We didn't do anything!"

"Mmm-hmm," Reggie says. "It's natural, I get it. But so is getting pregnant. Just remember, kids raising kids rarely works. Got it? If you need pills, let me know."

I feel icky and ashamed that Reggie thinks I was doing the nasty with Genin in front of Verity. I stare at the tent floor, too embarrassed to look at anyone and very conscious of my nakedness. When Reggie steps outside with Verity, Genin and I quickly dress, then follow.

It's dark outside except for the dim glow of three lanterns Bennie left behind. The wind works in tandem with snowflakes to redesign the landscape.

Blood seeps through the chest of Genin's coat. Color flees his face, and it's his turn to fall.

Chapter 23

THE VIGIL

Day three.

I stand vigil at Genin's bedside.

There's a permanent scar under his breastbone, the result of emergency surgery. He acted so brave, allowing only one fleeting micro-expression of fear as Reggie hauled him down the snowy path until two soldiers on night patrol spotted us and radioed for aid. Genin lost consciousness again. They poured a gooey substance Reggie called QuarDrops into Genin's wound, which stemmed the blood flow. I'm not sure why Bennie's salve didn't work. I used all that was left.

The suits and uniforms carted Genin away to the NASA side of the farm—against my protests, of course. Reggie held me back, dragging me to the house, my cheeks numb, my heart filled with worry. I felt so weak after returning to my body, I couldn't fight him. The long gash in my arm under my coat was throbbing too, which didn't help. At least my sore swollen hands were hidden under the bulky gloves that Verity had to force on.

I feel better now that Genin is back at the farm, but another terrible storm blows outside, the kind that downs power lines, strands people in their homes, and leaves store shelves barren of bread. The soldiers drive around in snowmobiles or small tanks. As I look out the window, I'm surprised to see the shadowy figure of Bennie, hands stuffed in the pockets of his ski jacket, looking back at me through a swirl of snowflakes. Warmth flows through my chest and I close my eyes to feel him say, *I'm sorry*, his arms around me. But the feeling is too big for his frame, more masculine, centered, protective—and arousing. That's a surprising, unexpected feeling, and I struggle to shake it off.

When I open my eyes again, there is no one outside. Just tiny tornados of ice crystals. I pull the curtain shut with my now-healed hands, the swelling and blackness gone, along with the slice in my arm. I wish hearts could restore themselves as easily.

Genin stirs and moans, and a tan, muscular leg covered in dark hair pokes through the tangle of white sheets, suspended on the ledge of the bed like one of Tetana's log bridges she told me about in Nepal. I retreat from the window to Genin's bedside. He's definitely one fine specimen of human—damn near perfect by physical standards. If he weren't still so weak and attached to an IV, I might take advantage of the situation and him.

"Nemain," he calls.

"Who?" I ask.

He sits up feebly, wobbling, and looks at me confused. I move to his side.

"Where am I?"

"Back at the farm. In your room," I say. "Look. They're monitoring your vitals with this machine. I suspect everyone will come running in here soon—this thing has an alarm to tell them when you're awake. Who's Nemain?"

Genin shakes his head, looking confused. "I don't know."

"You got sliced pretty good, from back to rib cage," I say.

"How?" He asks. "What time is it?"

"Seven twelve p.m."

"What day is it?"

"Friday."

"What happened?"

"You remember the cave?"

Genin shakes his head. I'm disappointed. He has no memory of our trip together. At least not at the moment.

"Sam," he says, a look of complete bewilderment on his face, "where were you born?"

"Cleveland. Why?"

"No."

Genin sinks back into his feather pillow, then reaches out and lightly circles his fingers around my wrist as I sit down beside on him on the bed. He looks at me warmly. "Your birthplace sits in the middle of three habitable planets…you and some others rolled down the slope of a perfect right triangle to get here."

"Shhh," I whisper in his ear. "That's not Cleveland. They've got you doped up on morphine and God knows what else. Rest."

"I love you," he says. "Kiss me, angel."

My heart leaps, but I also realize it's the drugs Genin's had pumped through his system. No way would he act so mushy, otherwise. I wonder if I could shoot him up with pain killers every day? Still, hearing someone say 'I love you' is a wonderful sound and I file it away in a tiny area of my brain where I keep the good stuff.

And maybe I will take a tiny advantage of this situation. I lean toward him, our lips getting close. The lamp beside him flickers.

"Did you know that your dad is…" Genin trails off.

I lean forward. "My dad is what?" I ask.

As expected, the door bursts open and a cavalry of white lab coats appear, along with Dr. Evelyn and Major Lynch leading the charge, each trying to elbow the other out of the way. Another doctor pushes me away from a now-sleeping Genin.

Chapter 24

GAME OVER

"You get us all killed," Rakito says, his African accent getting heavier with his mounting concern.

All of us foster kids sit quietly in a circle, legs crossed, in the privacy of my room. Priyanka clutches Rakito's arm with long caramel fingers to calm him, which is unusual because peace and humility always seem to flow naturally from him.

Verity grips the book of spells she brought to the tent a few days ago, using a free finger to twist a tight curl floating along the side of her face.

Pa Ling and Fensig, dressed in the same fatigues as Genin, ooze testosterone-loaded bravado.

Genin made a full recovery and seems stronger—vibrant and more determinedly macho than ever. He's never mentioned his drug-induced "I love you" to me or said anything more about my "home" or Nemain—or my dad. And he doesn't seem to understand Basque-Enochian when he's conscious either—at least he acted so when I tested him.

Tetana studies me in her measured yet confident way, with understanding in her eyes, beneath too-short bangs, the spirit of a calculated warrior, I sense, brave and steady.

My suggestion—the one that Rakito thinks will get us all killed—is that we sneak into the NASA side of the farm to rescue Saratu. It took me a few days, but I slowly warmed up to Bennie again. He's here too, surprisingly. I had no choice. I need his brain power and knowledge about this place—but I haven't forgotten what he did to Genin. Bennie told me yesterday that I'm 'not privy' to the details of the rivalry that exists between him and Genin, but when I pressed him to explain, he declined. I've already walked everyone through the plan Bennie and I created; now I have to maneuver around their doubts and convince them to help us, at the risk of treason or death, on this snow-bound August night. No doubt the blizzard is brought to us, as Bennie pointed out to me in his lab, by rips and tears of this universe leaking into another realm, or another realm leaking into ours, one that's now oozing into this reality—and threatening us all.

Everyone now knows too, that our government and its private subcontractors are conducting tests on kids. But we've deliberately withheld a lot of details—like the fact that Bennie and I are Camaeliphim. And the naked psychedelic trip Genin and I took below the river to see giant blue-skinned Indians with red hair. We've told everyone Genin suffered an accident with an electric fence by getting too close to the NASA side of the farm. Unfortunately, that cover story isn't doing much to help our cause right now, and I realize these kids are smart, which cripples our hope for a full 'buy-in.'

I scan our motley crew. Bennie looks more tired than he did in the tent, the dark circles under his eyes now turning from light gray to puffy black. It worries me that he might have cancer or something, but if that's the case, why wouldn't he just use the salve? His illness perplexes me because I thought we, as Camaeliphim, were almost indestructible, like buckeye trees.

Bennie's been silent in our little meeting so far—the same old quiet Bennie. But now he takes charge, pushes our plan, fighting his exhaustion. "If we don't make the effort to rescue Saratu," he says, "these experiments will grow uglier. All of us will be plucked into the DOE's lair until we're drained as test subjects. Then they'll move on to others."

"You can talk?" says Tetana. She leans in for a closer inspection as if he's a statue that suddenly came to life. The others look just as surprised, but Bennie doesn't explain. There are more important questions at hand.

"Why us?" Priyanka asks. "Why not let Dr. Evelyn and Reggie handle this with Sergeant Major Lynch? They're planning to separate us soon and move us out of here anyway."

It's true. Barbara confided to Verity that Dr. Evelyn was ordered to shut down her experiment and all of us are to be reassigned to different foster homes. Evidently, Dr. Evelyn and Dr. Sterling offered to purchase a private piece of property and take legal custody of every one of us but were told by "authorities" that this was not an option.

We're being 'decommissioned' as Reggie might say. According to Priyanka, some of the suits blame Dr. Evelyn and Dr. Sterling for the Saratu fiasco—though I suspect this is simply the start of a Dennison discrediting campaign to cancel both doctor's clearances. I overheard Lynch saying that the soldiers are tired of "babysitting" because the Dennison's can't seem to do their job. There's a lot of yelling behind closed doors these days, and Barbara spends more time kneeled in prayer than ever.

"No way," Genin says. "They're adults. They'll duck and cover. Besides, even if they get us out of here, we aren't safe."

"What do you mean?" Fensig asks.

"Nobody is safe," Bennie answers. "Unless we shut them down, it will be death by methodical divide and conquer, hanging each of us separately if we fail to work together. They have figured out that gathering us here was a mistake because we gather strength from one another."

There is an awkward silence as everyone stares at Bennie, lingering on the doom and gloom of his words, but also likely wondering what he means.

"It's up to us," Genin says to break the tension and offer hope. "Plum Hook Bay is a Grimm's Fairy Tale. The doctors and Reggie don't have the manpower to fight a bunch of well-funded Captain Crooks and their industrialized military goons. They'll bury their heads in manuals looking for solutions that don't exist. If the DOE plays pinball with us, it's game over. Tilt." He slaps the granite floor with his bowie knife, which makes Verity jump.

"We aren't talking about busting in there with bombs," I add. "We only want to create a distraction, so they shut down the reactor long enough for Saratu to escape. The grid she's on uses nuclear fusion to keep her caged. It's a test lockup."

I hide my suspicions from everyone—except Bennie—that some Watchers have already crossed over and are hidden by Nephilim who pass as full humans working for our governments. If I can shut down the reactor, I believe it will briefly open a parallel tunnel to let in some Dominions too, that might be able to help us—and Camael. I know he's here. He has to be. This land, the way it sits on the globe, at the exact center of a universal "black hole," under electromagnetic fields that skew everything, is a perfect hiding place for an outnumbered Dominion angel with a price on his head.

"Dis nuclear fusion you discuss, can be good ting, no?" Rakito asks. "It conserves energy and is often misunderstood."

"Yes, it can be, in the hands of the right people," Bennie says. "Unlike fossil fuels, it's usually completely contained and burns no waste. Unfortunately, unfettered and mismanaged tests rip holes the size of Texas in our ozone layer. Scientists are paid large dosh to write papers blaming the holes on people using too much deodorant or hair spray, which is ludicrous. The problem with humans is that they don't consider consequences until *after* they blow things up. They also strap strangers into experiments that make *Helter Skelter* look like the ice cream man."

"What is dosh?" Tetana asks.

"Money," Priyanka answers. "It's common British."

"Actually, it's a term used more in Scotland," says Verity.

Rakito frowns and shakes his head as if he's both disgusted and trying to force a headache loose. I can tell that his character will prove too strong for him to turn his back on Saratu, my fox, the planet, or any of us. He rubs his close-cropped haircut with his hand as his wide-set eyes flicker over every person in this room. Finally, he puts his hand in the middle of the circle and we all, except for Jade, place ours on top of his in a multi-colored stack of solidarity.

"What do you want us to do?" Rakito asks.

"This is dumb plan," Jade says. She stands, leaning in my bathroom doorway, fists clenched, arms folded across her chest.

"Do you have a better idea?" I ask. I didn't even want to bring her into this, but Bennie's convinced she'll be useful.

She pushes up the sleeves of her dark-gray sweatshirt, her eyes looking like a cold and stormy sapphire ocean. I half expect to see glaciers floating in the reflection of her pupils. Of course, she's about to put a kink in our plan. Jade throws rocks as a hobby.

But to my complete yet unregistered surprise, she slaps her hand on the top of our flesh pile.

Chapter 25
SPECIES ENHANCEMENT

Three helicopters swoop low into the NASA side of Plum Brook, blowing snow and blinding the soldiers on the ground, just as Bennie predicted. Pa Ling and Fensig motion for Jade, Bennie, and me to move into position on one side of the Westinghouse building, where amazingly, the government left yet another loophole for us to slip through, compliments again, of too many bureaucratic chiefs zealously guarding their "bigot lists" and failing to share their "need-to-knows".

Tetana plays night watchwoman on the ledge near the perimeter of this place, ready to shoot a flare as a signal for Priyanka and Rakito to get word to Verity that it's time to run as fast as possible back to the house to call media and the local sheriff. The authorities outside the gates won't be able to do much except get nosy but raising outside public suspicion might help keep these military bozos preoccupied with crisis control.

Jade's bow and arrows rest snug across her chest under a ski jacket. She reminds me of a winter warrior, her inner rough edges worn smooth under the camouflage of white face paint and a fuzzy headband that covers her nearly pointed pale ears. Both of us carry loaded pistols tucked in our waistbands; she stole them from Sergeant Major Lynch's shed. He'd have our heads mounted to targets if he knew I picked the lock so she could lift his favorite Sig Sauer.

I brought my compass, along with Barbara's and Bennie's buckeyes, for good luck. Barbara told me once that Christians called buckeyes "the eyes of God." After everything I've gone through, I'm beginning to think maybe God exists, ready to touch the lives of those who dare to have faith.

Or maybe I've just spent too much time with Verity. Geez, that girl yaps on and on about Allah, Jesus, Ishtar, Yahweh, or whatever she decides to call God from one week to the next.

But what if she's right? Or what if God is all and none of them at the same time, like Bennie once suggested? Maybe God is the 'soul tonic', as Reggie says, which holds humans together—some intelligent vibrational force impossible for any beings to ever fully comprehend? Bennie once told me about this Max Planck guy, a physicist, who said that everything from here to infinity is comprised of frequency and energy—but the mystery scientists haven't been able to figure out is what holds it all together. Maybe God is the mystery that binds all of us together.

Alternatively, Bennie seems to think that God is an energy force progressing through space and time using electrical charges rather than gravitational pulls. But I don't know what to think. Maybe *we* are God—and we beta-test Earth, like mad scientists, hoping we don't fuck it all up too much.

"Hey, zombie poop," Jade says to me. "Wake up."

I blink and nod. Jade rolls her eyes at me. We have to be precise and work fast or we won't make it through the only entrance.

The whirling snow acts as a heavy cloud that conceals everything except bright helicopter lights. Bennie said every other Thursday at exactly six thirty p.m., a general catches some military jet called a Voodoo back to Washington, DC. I peek around the comer of the building we're huddled beside, but I don't see the guards that stood there just a second ago.

Someone grips a firm hand over my shoulder.

Shit!

It's only Genin. He's disarmed one of the guards and wears the poor guy's uniform. It's the most predictable trick in movies, but surprisingly, it works. Although Genin's uniform is a bit loose and too short at the ankles, he looks like an Army officer. I imagine he's a general and briefly flirt with the fantasy of being a general's wife. My heart flutters a little at being so close to him again, but at the moment I don't have the luxury of getting as gooey as a melted Mars Bar. Besides, what if *I* want to be the general someday? Ladies make good generals too.

Bennie, Jade, and I slip through the first chain-link guard gate, and Genin gets us through the second with a credit-card-looking piece of plastic that he swipes through a little slit, popping the door open. We find Pa-Ling and Fensig just inside. Bennie pulls out a handheld device and uses his thumbs to punch a bunch of stuff on a blue screen, bringing up a map.

"What is that thing?" Genin asks, mesmerized.

"A GPS," Bennie says.

"What's a GPS?" I ask.

"It's an abbreviation for 'global positioning system.' It tells us where we are and where we need to go."

"That little thing?" Fensig says. "How?"

"The military sent twelve satellites into space this year to detect the launch or detonation of nuclear devices all over the globe, using special sensors and atomic clocks," Bennie says. "This instrument leverages those satellites to give precise coordinates of where we are on the planet. It's really accurate right now, but I suspect that will prove a problem someday and governments will be forced to move those clocks off center to make everything approximate. What they don't know is that I got into their systems and mapped this place exactly."

"That thing looks like something from *Star Trek*," says Pa-Ling. "Too bad it's not a phone, Walkman, and a device to order pizza and play Pac-Man too! Where'd you get it?"

Bennie looks almost impressed by Pa-Ling's suggestion, and though I wouldn't swear to it, I think I see Bennie's eyes spark like he has an idea of something to build. "The U.S. government is always approximately fifty years ahead of the public on technology. I stole a discarded prototype off one of the trucks headed to the Huron County landfill. They actually bury government junk just outside of Monroeville in public dumps. I rebuilt it and tapped into NASA's computer networks—but they don't know I'm in there. They can't develop their own technology as fast as I learn to beat their systems. That will always be a problem for governments. Fighting technological intrusion will become a new kind of war in the future, I think."

I shiver a little. "So, if you can find your way around this maze, what stops them from using the same technology to come after us?"

"I scrambled their signal," Bennie says. "Unless we're visually spotted, they won't know we're in here. The added bonus is that nobody except ultra-level-clearance people gain admittance to this part of the facility, so it remains virtually empty except for three rotating scientists, a doctor running some clandestine LSD testing program, and a couple of engineers. There may be a guard or two, but they aren't military or CIA."

"Who are they then?"

"I don't know," Bennie says. "I don't think they're human."

Everyone stops what they're doing and looks at Bennie.

"What do you mean?" Genin asks.

"Epigenetics," Bennie says. "The U.S., U.S.S.R., and British governments whitewashed a bunch of Nazi scientists' backgrounds after World War II and forced them to carry on their gruesome experiments in their new countries—under assumed identities. Let's just say they created some creatures that would frighten the boogeyman and send Satan running for the gates."

Genin looks at me and Jade. "These chicks are not going down there with you alone," he says. "I won't allow it." He puts a protective arm over my shoulder.

I slide away. "Thanks, Tarzan," I say, "but this Jane can take care of herself."

"And we need you up here, Genin," Bennie says.

I feel a slow ember of evil growing in the center of my soul. I felt the same thing in the field before the storm, and when I wanted to murder Jade in the ditch, and when I killed Guy with my bare hands. Maybe it comes to me when I need it. Right now, it's up to me and the others to prevent this biotechnological virus among us from spreading.

Bennie turns to Pa Ling, Fensig, and Genin. "You three better get back outside before the snow dies down."

I scope out this fortress. I'm willing to bet the president of the United States couldn't even gain access here. And NASA people likely don't know what's really going on way down below their feet either. And neither does the Army, I'd guess, at least not completely.

How a few high-ranking beasts manage to forge so much power and influence under government noses, using tax dollars, boggles my mind. A fading part of my psyche wants to run, but another part, the part that stretches up from the bubbling tar of my lost memories, wants justice, even if it means dying, which might not be a bad option if the world is at risk of being obliterated by a bunch of bureaucratic Bezaliel-hybrid ass wipes anyway.

Genin slips his arm around my waist, pulls me to him, and plants a perfect kiss on my mouth so fast I'm barely able to compute what's happening even with a GPS thingy. He pulls me into him tightly and I feel my feet leave the ground. "You stay safe down there, Wonder Woman."

Bennie slaps a rope over his shoulder and abruptly turns away looking completely disgusted, or maybe even angry. This is where I think Dr. Evelyn and Verity may be wrong: I can't always read people— or should I say, hybrids.

Jade, Bennie, and I put on the oxygen masks Bennie pulls from his backpack, and we step further into this covert crucible. We can't take the elevator because Bennie says, not only do they have cameras, the elevators don't go as far down as we need to get below the surface. But behind a wall, buried in the rock, is an old hand-cranked lift once used to lower supplies back when this place was a munitions factory during World War II. According to Bennie, it was converted to a top-secret testing lab in the 1960s. But what it boils down to is, we're supposed to lower ourselves in complete darkness a little more than a half mile down, using pulleys, ropes, and cables, while standing in a petrified wooden cart not much bigger than a pencil holder.

Jade and I look at each other as if Bennie is crazy for asking us to get in a swinging bucket that's probably about as safe as poking a knife into an electrical socket, but we've come too far to go back. We climb into the basket, and a freezing whoosh of air hits me from below, but I can't see anything in the black. Bennie secures our waists to the cart with leather straps, then pulls a rope.

Oh, hell no!

We soar down so fast that Jade and I reactively grab each other. I lose my voice just like I did my first day at Plum Hook when I heard the sonic boom and buried my head in Barbara's chest. The freezing wind in this highway to hellhole warms quickly, but that does nothing for my stomach, which is stuck in my throat. Beads of sweat pop up on my forehead like unexpected pimples and my armpits leak. I can't see anyone or anything, even my basket mates, and my heartbeat throbs in my ears until I feel my eardrums pop. I take a deep breath and hold it to the count of four before exhaling and doing it again, imagining Genin's arms around me. I hear a zipping sound. Is a cable about to snap?

And just like that, we stop.

It's still pitch black in the shaft, but Jade and I silently push off of each other.

"Jesus holy shit, Bennie?" I say. "What the fuck?" My words sound garbled and muted behind the oxygen mask.

"We only fell for 9.8 seconds," he says way too matter-of-factly. "Stop being babies."

When I'm able to see again I'm going to slap him upside the head.

Whack!

Too late. Jade somehow found him in the dark and got in a good crack. For once I'm on her side.

Zap! Bzzzt. A plasma-like mini-lightning strike briefly lights our faces, leaving behind a smell like burned wood.

"Ouch! Shit! You prick!" Jade yells.

I undo my belt and grope for Jade in the dark, but I get lightly shocked when I touch her arm. Apparently, Bennie just gave her some sort of electrical jolt. Now *that's* a toy I'd play with.

"Not now," I say, tugging blindly on Jade's arm to hold her back from smacking him into next week. "You can kick Bennie's ass later. He still has to get us out of here."

"Da," she says.

I wait for Bennie to light a torch or something, but he turns on his GPS device and uses it to scan the wall instead. Briefly, the faint bluish glow on his face illuminates a handsome man a few years older. The swift vision reminds me of someone I used to know, or once had a dream about. But it disappears as quickly as we dropped down this hole.

Bennie pulls a long three-digit hand out of a small basket he's brought and I gasp. He pushes it up against the rock wall, and it moves slightly—a door. A splinter of soft light sneaks through. He pushes harder, and the door swings open. We step through.

We're at the junction of three wide tunnels. Concrete floors sit beneath smooth stone walls that rise to about fifty feet above our heads. Lantern-like sconces covered in iron mesh hang every few feet along the walls, and tight clumps of steel pipes run the length of the tunnels, both overhead and along the floor, their hisses and moans an industrial reminder of the cold functionality way down here beneath everything that is warm, green and alive up above.

Bennie removes his oxygen mask and says we can do the same because it's pressurized on this side of the rock.

"Where are we?" I ask.

"Under the nuclear reactor," Bennie says.

"Which direction we go?" Jade asks.

"I don't know," Bennie says.

"You don't *know*?" I ask. "You said your GPS thing mapped this place exactly."

"It does, but not this far down. I knew this place was here, but GPS is useless so far below the surface. Granite blocks the satellite signal. I've never been here because it took me a while to figure out what and where it was."

"What is it?" I ask.

"An ultra-top-secret lab." Bennie replies. "It taps the nuclear power from NASA's underside."

"*Under* a nuclear reactor?" I ask. "Isn't that more than a little dangerous?"

Bennie nods. "Perfect hiding place. It offers the best form of protection from prying eyes, don't you think? And that's not all. Everyone involved in building this part, from the engineers, soldiers and architects, to the scientists and federal agents—they're dead."

An involuntary chill gallops through me. "Dead as in old age and natural causes?"

Bennie shakes his head. "I don't think so."

"So, what we do now?" Jade asks.

"We pull the pistols out of our waistbands and each travel down a different tunnel until we find something," Bennie says.

"Wait a minute—that wasn't our plan," I say. "You said we were going to hold the engineer at gunpoint and make him shut down the reactor so Saratu could escape."

"We are. Whoever finds that person first should commence with our plan."

"And what if they find *us* first?" I ask. "And suppose one of us does find this person, how do we alert the other two without getting the entire U.S. Army involved?"

"We don't," Bennie says. "People without clearance aren't allowed down here and nobody above ground realizes this place exists. We're on our own. And if one of us is captured, you can bet we won't ever again see the light of day. No one will look for us either because technically we don't exist. Our lives, now owned by the government, have been reduced to an official paper trail that will lead straight to an incinerator, where some overworked sap will dispose of any traces of our existence under orders, and not ask any questions because he or she won't have a 'need to know'."

Bennie stares into my eyes just the way he looked at me through the window on my first day at Plum Hook, as if he can see what's inside me. I stare right back, and through his eyes I see the reflection of a fast-moving horror show that would make Stephen King's *Carrie* look like a Cabbage Patch Doll. Kids, including Bennie, have their ankles chained in cages so small they can't stand up. If he's able to occupy space in my head this way, using it like a movie theater, how much of me does he know? And how much does he still hide?

I turn my head to focus on the pipes, trying to wipe the vision from my brain. There's an energy field down here humming so strong that I'm able to read Bennie's thoughts and see them too—like my mom. I understand now, the double-edged sword of this ability—how it could be used as a cure or a curse.

"Bennie, we might die today, no?" Jade asks, a softening in her eyes. Hmm. Maybe the ice on her heart is melting a bit down here too.

"We might die today," he says.

"Then I die strong," Jade says, her cheeks flushing pink in the dim light.

For the first time since I've known her, intense emotional pain vibrates from her skin, onto mine, her hurt bouncing along my arm like tiny sparks. *Cages. Chains. Needles. She screams "NO!" She tries to hide behind a nurse, this child she once was. There is no place to go. She's dragged into a room, forced to drink. A man rips off her hospital gown*—I look away from her to stop the flow of her private horror. I've seen enough. Most humans couldn't endure what Jade went through, surrounded by Bezaliel monsters—sadists who exploit the human body and psyche for "species enhancement." That awful day in my motel room was a walk in the park compared to what Jade endured in the Ural Mountains of the U.S.S.R. She was traded here as a child.

"Jade?" I ask. "Were you kept at a facility in the Ural Mountains?"

Tears make a desperate attempt to form in Jade's eyes. She turns them off like a faucet. She nods and angrily looks away.

Chapter 26

THE BEAST

I clutch the handgun near my hip as I creep down this dimly lit tunnel of reinforced steel and concrete. Luckily there are no cameras under this reactor, just cobra-like hissing steam and trickles of liquid I hear but can't see, hiding inside the walls.

I move forward cautiously, one soft, slow step at a time, further into what I believe will be a short-lived future. To my surprise, I'm not afraid of being dead. If I won't even be aware of being dead, how bad can it be? It's the dying part, I fear. But if I do die today, and there is such a thing as heaven, I'm not exactly the cloud-hopping, harp-plucking type and I have a strong suspicion that the angels who guard the gate would turn me away and point me in the opposite direction.

A faint moan echoes from somewhere ahead. How I detest unexpected surprises. It forces me into a tug-of-war between a mind that says *don't panic* and a human-hybrid body that screams *Run!* Thank God I have this gun, even if I am the lousiest shot in class.

The sound grows.

The tunnel opens into a wide, round space that's been turned into an office. Ticking clocks take up almost every bit of wall space, each set to a different time. Under a large desk is a metal dog cage.

I cautiously step closer. *This can't be.*

Something whimpers.

A girl in a tattered, grimy, too-big, outdated, ruffled floral dress crouches in the cage, chained at the ankles, huddled against the bars like a frightened lab monkey. Her head is shaved, and her eyes look out at me in fearful wonder. She looks about eight years old.

Who would do such a thing?

As I kneel beside the cage, I gag from the smell of waste in the bucket beside her. She retreats nervously to the farthest, darkest corner of her hold.

Two pairs of footsteps make their way toward us. I can tell by the cadence of their gait that it's not Bennie and Jade. *Shit.* Low heels, maybe like men's dress shoes, scrape concrete. One uses a cane. I scramble under the big desk, beside the cage, and put a finger to my lips, willing the girl in the cage to be quiet. I hold up the gun to show her. Anyone allowed down here must know about this girl, and if they're cruel enough to chain up children, I have zero issue planting bullets in their bodies.

The girl studies me, odd and silent, pale arms mottled with needle marks, lesions, and scars, her cheeks sunken enough to practically hold water, which she looks like she needs.

"*Chun me gon na bho 26,*" one says.

Bodies? What bodies? Area 26? He's speaking Basque-Enochian and for some reason they moved bodies from Area 26 to NASA Plum Hook Bay. They mention some Silver Horn mine in Nevada and how they simulated a nuclear explosion in 1983 to force an evacuation so they could house aliens!

"*Dòra ganaich,*" says a second voice. "*Habin ribbah shin blep. Dar riis latha doon phlanaid mu heire adh.*"

He hates this planet? At least I think that's what he said. This language mutates so quickly I'm barely able to decipher this particular dialect. He also said he can't wait until the day "this dump", meaning Earth, is remodeled to accommodate "their kind".

"*A 'doy lay a' brok neeboo bo?*"

He says humans, especially women and girls, are fair game for "recreation."

I stifle an urge to puke.

The little girl puts her finger to her lips to shush me, then tightly squeezes her eyes shut and covers her ears with her hands.

The wrench in my gut makes me realize I've taken on this girl's pain internally, all of her trauma and deprivation—but also her high capacity for love and forgiveness. I feel her energy, as if she feeds on the good memories of her past, to nourish her soul even as she slowly decays.

A low whistle howls through the cave, bringing with it a chilly wind.

Four trouser legs line up almost side by side, along with one shiny black cane boasting a rubber seal stopper. If I had an axe, I'd cut down both of these creatures at the knees, snap the cane in two, and drive each splintered end right through their hearts like a vampire slayer.

Wait.

What the hell is *that*?

One man's foot is shoeless—and not really a foot at all, but rather a scaly, reddish reptilian appendage. Black claws tap the floor like manicured fingernails on a desk, just like they did during my yage trip! Saratu must be close. But what is this thing, this creature, hovering over the desk? And will it smell me? And does it have a reptilian head?

What I can't discern is if this probable epigenetic hybrid always existed? Or did someone else, maybe the government, play God, and accelerate evolution—or Creation? This creature seems ancient to me—from another time—or place, I don't know for sure, but that's how I *feel*. Humans, unfortunately, don't give much credence to *feelings* as evidence.

Another wave of déjà vu sweeps over me; that a million full moons ago, humans were more advanced than they are now, but had help destroying themselves—a few survivors forced to begin again with outside aid—and a stern warning from other realms to, this time, handle their share of energy with care. Seems humans may be incapable of listening.

A shiver of rage runs through me—a desire to drain the blood of the beasts standing above me. It's also tempered with reason and patience, a slow-drip percolator of balance between stalk and slay. Where is my fear? Not that I want it back.

I will myself to remain still, silent and unseen. But if that fails, I *will* kill. Bite first. That's a good rule for life, as Jade says.

Studying the caged girl, I realize that her head isn't shaved after all, but shiny because her hair fell out. She doesn't have eyebrows either, which makes me wonder if they've exposed her to radiation. Half-moon dark circles rest under her eyes like Bennie's—and Cameron the Cop's. She's definitely malnourished. The lesions on her arms, loss of weight, and apparent weakness stand as indicators she'll be dead within weeks, sooner if she's lucky.

She coughs blood into the sleeve of her dress. A deep pang of sorrow sucker-punches me in the gut. She'll never know what it's like to kiss a boy, go to prom, or hold her first baby. I wonder too, if she's ever been outdoors. Was she born here?

The creatures decide to share scotch and cigars in some lounge a long walk away. I listen until their foot-claw steps fade and disappear.

"How many more like you are here?" I ask.

The girl says nothing; she seems to have lost the ability to speak. Perhaps she's too severely traumatized; or maybe she has brain damage. But she points across the room to a row of six filing cabinets. Looks as if these 'doctors' keep track of their pet projects the old-fashioned way, handwritten, for quick destruction. Without evidence, anyone lucky enough to escape will be laughed off, discredited, or found dead. Suicide, mental illness, and "freak accidents," I'm discovering, serve as convenient excuses for shadowy governments to cover up a multitude of murderous sins.

I open one of the file drawers.

Each file is thick, like mine back at the farm, and some date all the way back to 1952. There are names of projects, subprojects, operations, and plans. Long lists of dates, drugs, and doses, along with case numbers, are bound into small books. But two folders immediately catch my eye: they're labeled *The ALPHA* and *the OMEGA*. I thumb through them and discover each is a type of subject programming. The ALPHA is used to increase physical and mental ability, and the OMEGA a self-destruct brain chip that causes a person to commit suicide or develop amnesia. Most of the paperwork is signed by a Dr. L.W. Greene, though a few sheets are signed by a Dr. S. Gottlieb.

The girl rattles the bars of her cage and points to the next file cabinet.

"You want me to open this one?" I ask.

The girl nods.

It's locked. From the desk I grab a letter opener and carefully poke the tip into the lock. It refuses to click. I stand back to study the metal cabinet. I kick it hard in the same place I used to kick Mrs. Myer's cabinet, because they look almost exactly the same. It blows open like Aladdin's cave. I chuckle at my success and the typical bureaucracy of strapped governments taking security short cuts and buying cheap filing cabinets.

"Be…" the girl says.

"Are you trying to tell me the name of the doctor?"

She shakes her head. "Be."

"You want me to go to the letter B?"

She nods, leans back in the cage, and closes her eyes.

I thumb through the files, calling off names. "Bailey? Barrett? Betsy? Bonnie? Benjamin?"

She rattles the cage.

"Which one?" I ask. "Benjamin?"

She nods.

I open the file. My heart practically stops.

Benjamin Q. Bathurst.

A photo of a much healthier-looking and younger Bennie greets me. He's outside somewhere, a park I think, smiling beside a little girl, younger than him, with dark curls. The file says the doctor bought these children from their alcoholic uncle in London when Bennie was six and Brigdhe, his sister, was three, after their parents were killed on holiday outside of Oxford in a countryside car crash.

Bought? What does that mean, the doctor *bought* these children? How does that type of transaction take place? Did they exchange money for kids like purchasing clothes from a store? The file doesn't specify where they're from but a typo on Bennie's birthdate makes him thousands of years old and I softly chuckle (because he sometimes acts like he is), before glancing at Brigdhe, who looks at me strangely.

I thumb through the pages but find no legal adoption papers or court documents, nothing that indicates any type of caseworker, counselor, or other foster-care worker was involved. All I can find is something that says the doctor gave two bottles of gin and five hundred dollars to "acquire the specimens."

I wonder if Bennie realizes his freedom and soul were traded at such a pittance.

Another sheet in the file says that Bennie is a genius beyond any intelligence yet encountered on this planet. He was the youngest ALPHA ever programmed, and after two years of 'training' was dumped back at Oxford, in the United Kingdom, with directions to assassinate a target: Dr. Evelyn Dennison, Director of the University of Oxford's Psychiatry and Biomedical Research Center.

What? Why? Why would DOE want Dr. Evelyn dead? And why *isn't* she dead? Why haven't they killed her here at Plum Hook?

I read this fucked-up file about as fast as my heart now beats.

It seems that Bennie refused to kill Dr. Evelyn, even though he'd been offered his sister's freedom if he'd follow through. He murdered his handler instead—shoved the guy into a wood shredder. (I knew that little shit had it in him but can't say I blame him a bit.) The incident got cleaned up by the British government and labeled a horrible landscaping accident, and Bennie disappeared into the UK countryside, where somehow, he put himself in a position to be *adopted* by the Dennison's.

I consider how well he and Dr. Sterling get along, but I'm surprised they actually legally made him their son—but what about Brigdhe? I scan the adoption papers. There's a raised seal on the last page that I don't recognize and most of its contents read more like a truce agreement than an adoption. I don't understand what the majority of it means because parts are redacted with heavy black ink and other parts are written in strange code-like symbols, similar to the ones Genin and I saw with the weird gadget in the cave, the one secured by tangled tree roots near the blue-skinned Indian mummies.

I turn back toward the cage with a sinking realization. "Oh, my God. Bennie is your brother."

The girl—Brigdhe—nods. A lone tear drifts down her hopeless angelic overly pale face.

Bennie must have known the doctor had his sister, or that she'd be so traumatized and sick that any normal life beyond this cage would be nearly impossible. I also wonder if Dr. Evelyn realizes Death slithers beneath her feet when she's on the NASA side of the farm? Did Bennie tell her, or Dr. Sterling? Is that why they're here?

Now I understand why Bennie's been working himself to exhaustion and wouldn't hang out with the rest of us. He had bigger, more brotherly things to concern himself with. His sister is the pawn. He's dangling on the thin hope of saving her.

"Ye-kne-hm? Ah-ah-li-ve?" Brigdhe stutters, her not quite English voice hoarse and raspy, as if she's trying to clear years of cobwebs from her throat.

"Yes, I know him," I say. "You don't have to talk. I know it hurts. Your brother is alive and here with me. I thought we were here to shut down the reactor, but now I know it was really to find you."

"N-o. N-o. Ga. G-o." Brigdhe sways back and forth in the cage, growing upset.

"I can't. I'm not leaving you here with these monsters. And I'm looking for a friend too."

I search for a file on Saratu. Nothing. I look for the names of other Plum Brook classmates but find none.

I've got to find Bennie and Jade and warn the Dennison's.

Brigdhe points at me.

"Me?" I say.

She points to the file cabinets again.

I understand. The thick file Dr. Evelyn handed me in my room, and the new one she created, may not be the only ones I have.

It doesn't take long for me to find my name, buried right behind Bennie's. How could I miss this the first time? With shaky fingers, I peek into the musty scraps and folds of a life I can't remember.

PROJECT TRAIL'S END.

It's written in big, bold letters, daring me to look.

I find my case number and the date my microchip was implanted. My "re-birthday" occurred when I was only ten months old. I was already running too, much to the astonishment of a pediatrician, who called in other doctors. I was immediately tagged as an ALPHA candidate; my blood type being added to a government registry, against the protests of my mother, it says here.

I flip through pictures of me at school, at the mall, with boys, drinking beer in the park, skateboarding, stealing from stores, and even some of me alone watching TV at various foster homes. I see pictures of my grandmother taking me to church, her beauty salon, and Bob's Newsstand. Someone took a picture of her in the hospital before she died from cancer, and she's propped up in bed, smiling, like she knows whoever's behind the camera. Then…

Rosie.

Her name stares at me like a laser beam boiling my eyes. Our own government erased her criminal history on DOE's orders and allowed her to run untouched, selling boys and girls to the highest bidders—often high-ranking officials. Sometimes people were drugged and placed in compromising positions with kids for later access to state secrets.

What I wouldn't give to be back in Mrs. Myers's dingy office right now, ignorant, rebellious and about to go to juvenile jail for stealing.

There is no mention of Dr. Awoudi, Cameron the Cop, or the Dennison's. A copy of the case file Mrs. Myers kept in her office is here, but Dr. Awoudi's name, and the tests he administered, are absent. It would seem that Septum Oculi might have gotten in the DOE's way, although there is absolutely nothing in these files to prove that. And if they did, how did they know about me? And why snatch me away from the DOE and then keep me so close to them?

According to this report, other blood will make me very sick and could even kill me. Consequently, it seems that any future pregnancy I'd have might pose a risk because my antibodies will attack the child I carry as if it's a foreign threat. The doctors also write that I'm a walking weapon, capable of going off at the wrong place and time. They'd hoped to test my capabilities at the motel, 'off the grid', in the event that I was killed…or killed my rapist.

A new project label glares from a folder stuffed into this one: Operation Third Eye.

There is a date for my mother's death—the day I was born! The file claims she died in childbirth. Did I kill her? But I remember my mom!

It occurs to me: Was the woman I remember really my mom? Maybe she was never my mother at all, but a copy—a ruse to cover my real mother's death. I hold tears in check. I'm also more than a little confused, because Reggie said she was in protective custody. Would he lie to me?

Feeling sick, I snap the folder shut.

I spot a small cloth newspaper bag hanging on the back of a coat rack. Jesus, they kidnapped a kid right off of his paper route, too? Fuckers. Still, I'll use the bag. I shove my file, Bennie, and Jade's, into it and sling it across a shoulder.

Above the filing cabinet hangs a large keyring, but instead of keys, it holds a bunch of plastic cards like Fensig and Pa Ling used to swipe open the gate to this place. I lift the ring off its hook and kneel down beside Bennie's sister.

"Do any of these unlock this cage, Brigdhe?"

She snatches the ring from me so fast I fall backward. She may be weak, but she's still a little flash like her brother, and she's got spunk. I like that. She thumbs through the cards to find a red one with number 57 on it (of course) and taps it repeatedly, shaking as she hands it back to me through the bars. I swipe, and just like that, Brigdhe is free.

But not really. She may not be behind bars anymore, but she's still a prisoner, I suspect, to her horrible memories, destroyed flesh, and soon, to death. Could Bennie's salve save her?

"The-rs mo-ar," she says as she crawls across the floor. "Oth-ers."

My shoulders tense. I don't want to hear this. "Can you show me?"

She nods and tries to walk but can't. I bend down and tell her to climb on my back, which she does. Her stench overwhelms me, and I have to breathe through my mouth to avoid the scent of overripe hybrid.

Brigdhe points to tell me where to go. Soon I'm walking down a hall that smells like an old folks' home or a hospital—a mix of bleach, medicine, and piss. To either side of us, metal doors with little windows stand at cold, silent attention. Cells. I peer through some of the windows. Some cells are empty. In others, there are kids and teenagers, crammed six to a room not much bigger than a broom closet. All of them appear to be in a state of shock, in a drug-induced stupor, or worse—they're dead—in varying states of decomposition, as if being studied to see how fast they'll rot. Some kids are missing arms or legs, or both—one wears an eye patch. Some are chained to a cot or a chair. They wear pea-green jumpsuits and blue paper slippers.

"Do you know which card unlocks each door?" I ask.

"Ya." Brigdhe's voice is weak.

"Is a girl named Saratu here?"

"N-a."

"Is Saratu dead?"

"N-a."

She slips off my back, head slung down, then lifts her face and smiles in a way that only a completely insane person could do. To my surprise, she runs down the hall and back again as if I've just slipped her a speed injection. She stops, faces me, looks into my eyes the way Bennie always does, and goes into a sort of trance.

Did someone flip a switch on her microchip? I back up, ready to fight.

She speaks, and this time, her voice is strong, like a woman's, and seems to channel through her than be 'of her'.

"*Suffer the children, and forbid them not, to come unto me, for of such is the reign of the heavens,*" she says. "*And she made from one woman every nation of every race to live on all the faces of the infinite galaxies, having determined allotted periods and the boundaries of their dwelling place, that they should seek God, and perhaps think and feel their way toward her and find her. Yet she is actually not far from each one of us.*"

I wish Verity were here to help me out with this psycho holy babble. It sounds sort of like Biblical scripture, but it's off—slanted feminine.

"Is Saratu God?" I ask.

Brigdhe looks at me as if I've lost my mind. Then she shakes her head. So, Saratu is not God. Whew. But she's not dead either. Glad we have that solved.

"*See that they do not despise even one of these little ones,*" Brigdhe says. "*For I tell you that angels always see for the face of my Mother. And the angels cast down, the ones that abandoned their proper roles, these she will find and keep in darkness, bound with everlasting chains for eternal judgment.*"

"Um, okay," I say. "You see, the girl that's usually good with all this holy roller stuff? I left her back at the big house. So, I'm not sure if you're trying to give me a message, a sermon, or a riddle. You'll have to be a little clearer."

Brigdhe reaches out to take my hand. "Big sister, you go." She points to the last door on the left.

Did Brigdhe just channel Saratu? I remember. Back at the house, I agreed to be the big sister.

Brigdhe smiles, her eyes soulful and friendly, alive with compassion before her face fades once more into sickness and despair.

I think about what she said. That we should "think and feel our way" toward God and find her, as she is not far from each of us. What does that *mean*?

Brigdhe collapses on all fours, lifts her head, and releases a cross between a high-pitched howl and a half bark. I know this sound. Some kids look out of their tiny windows, but nobody bangs on the doors or yells. I suspect noisy behavior has been beaten, micro-chipped, or radiated out of them.

Brigdhe falls back on her knees and motions back down the hallway in the direction from which she came, as if she's beckoning something to come forward. I press up against the wall, gun ready, in case she's summoned some genetically modified mole rat with razors for teeth. This piddly gun I can't even shoot now seems like a laughable and inappropriate defense against creatures I once thought only existed in horror movies.

Where is Scooby Doo when I need him?

Chapter 27
SCRAM

A fox winds its way, like a serpent, toward us, a dead rat dangling from its mouth. It drops its catch in front of Brigdhe, and she lightly scratches the fox's ears. It sniffs the air with its little nose, then tips its head toward me. It jerks back in surprise, pounces up and down in excitement, then bobs at my feet.

"Hope?"

I swoop the fox into my arms and nuzzle my nose in her fur. She smells like freshly cut grass and pine. She wags her fluffy black-tipped tail, yelps excitedly, then licks my face and wraps her tail around my forearm.

"How?" I say. "Where have you been hiding? She looks so healthy. How is this possible?"

Brigdhe shrugs. "Friend. Brings food."

She snaps off the head of the dead rat with her teeth and spits it on the ground. I have to look away when she crunches on the corpse, slurps its blood, and scoops out the insides like she's sucking an oyster from its shell.

Hope wiggles free from my arms, returns to Brigdhe, and uses her teeth to tug lightly at the hem of Brigdhe's faded floral dress. Brigdhe wipes her blood-stained mouth with the back of her hand and crawls after the fox, which leads her to the last door. I follow.

Brigdhe rises to her feet in front of the door and puts her palm on the wall next to it. She uses another card from the keyring to swipe the door open. She collapses into a crumpled heap on the floor in front of the door, so I scoop her over a shoulder in an army carry like I've seen Reggie do with sheep and Genin. I've got to find Bennie quick.

Hope bounces ahead of us, looking back now and then to make

sure we follow, and maybe to make sure that we don't get lost. Bennie called this fox my soul guide. Maybe she's supposed to keep me on the path—but to what, I'm not sure.

The lights here are dimmer than the cellblock, and the walls carved from porous limestone. Water oozes through, like condensation on a soda can, giving the rock a slick, chilly, sheen. Wolf spiders dodge behind sconces, their hairy legs sounding like the ticks of a thousand clocks—or guns. I shiver.

Brigdhe smacks the wall with the flat of her hand, and I realize that arachnids are part of her menu too. Desperation and neglect have taught her to hunt like an animal. I marvel at her resilience and respect her spirit. I wonder if I'd have fared even half as well.

Up ahead I see a small, square light. It's a window carved into a heavy steel door. I lean Brigdhe against the wall and move forward alone.

I don't stop to think.

I kick open the door.

The lizard doctor and his henchman have Bennie cornered by a metal railing in some weird room that is nothing but machines, cable, steel, grates, glass and flashing lights of all sorts. Jade stands next to the doctor, confusion lightly sketched on her face. A low hum buzzes overhead, and so may florescent lights glow above that it's almost like daylight way down here.

I've stepped onto some sort of vented and circular metallic balcony. I hide behind a large seamless cylindric titanium tank suspended over a vast hole in the ground by thin electrical wires producing sparks. Everyone stands on the *other* side of this balcony grate, which blocks our view from both sides. Looking up, I'm in awe about how wires so thin are capable of holding a vat this size. I quickly glance into the abyss below and see, feel, or hear nothing. It's the blackest darkness.

"Wir haben firma," the doctor says. *We have company.* Now he speaks, German?

"Ja Doktor," the other man says.

I crouch low, the way Reggie taught me. The buckeyes pinch my hip in one pocket while the compass in my other vibrates wildly. I steady my weapon. Breathe.

Hope unexpectedly howls. Wait. That's not Hope. It's Randolph. How'd Bennie's wolf get in here? I'm pretty sure the damn thing didn't ride down a mine shaft.

I hear someone coming toward me and they're not tiptoeing but stomping—on a mission—and I'm it!

Shit!

I'm in trouble. I believe that whatever is looking for me will show zero mercy down here. And there he is—a black-eyed-half-hybrid Nephilim. A cold snap tracks up my spine as our eyes meet. Intense hatred. I can't kill him, I don't think. But there's little time to think, only to react. I raise my gun and aim for the cranial vault of one of the doctor's cohorts, like Sergeant Major Lynch taught us. Slowly, I squeeze the trigger.

BAM!

Holy shit! Guns are loud without earplugs! And I got him!

Is there really a difference between a cranial vault and a nut sack, anyway?

The Nephilim screams almost as loudly as Guy did that day in my motel room, and this half-human falls to his knees, clutches his crotch, slips over the rail, and falls into the abyss.

I listen for a 'thud' sound but there's silence. That can't be. Everything has a bottom—pools, rivers, barrels, minds…and then… below…the whispering voices I heard in the field rise again—along with low howls and one blood-curdling groan, but still no crunching plop to indicate that this no good, onyx-eyed hybrid that I just shot, hit rock-bottom.

Swirling wisps of black smoke ascend out of the hole to dance and pulsate into transparent tentacles that arch, point, and tiptoe over and around the room, looking for something.

My memories grow stronger, zooming into view and retreating again to blend with this world, like a gasping portal to another place—a murky ocean with limited visibility and trapped within a shell that is this human body.

"And so, it shall be done to him, fracture for fracture, eye for eye, tooth for tooth. Just as he has injured a person, so it shall be done to him…"

"Scatha?" the lizard doctor asks, curiously eyeing me over.

I don't move. This Nephilim piece of shit seems to know me—but I'm not sure how that's possible.

"Have we met?" I ask.

As Bennie predicted, Nephilim and Camaeliphim hybrids find one another repulsive, and similarly poled, like magnets. This is why I experienced gut-tightening hatred toward Jade the first day we met. Nephilim infected her with their blood, another half-assed, ill-thought-out experiment. But –she isn't quite one of them. The soulless, half-hybrid genes they stuffed into her may be skewed toward mayhem, but I think she's a salvageable human.

I'd also like to think that between Bennie and me, we could take Jade and the doctor—but she likely also has a microchip to go along with her battle-loaded blood, and the Nephilim doctor is far more evolved than we are as fledgling Camaeliphim.

I take stock of my arsenal: a dying trauma victim who eats spiders and imbibes rat blood, an unreliable fox, a narcoleptic wolf, and a creepy autistic hybrid. Again, I'm on the short side of a fair fight and pretty much fucked. Hmm. What would Reggie do?

I step out from my hiding place and drop the gun. It won't do me any good anyway—this creature can't be destroyed by something as rudimentary as a bullet. He requires a sacred exorcism sort of handling, in the form of a miracle, which I could sure use right about now.

Now that I see him better, this Nephilim geezer looks like a 1960's throwback. He's balding, with slick gray hair at the temples; too-thin tie; perfectly pressed white shirt and black suit. He should be playing the accordion for a polka party at the Bronson Conservation Club instead of serving as the master of ceremonies for this covert cluster.

This creature's glaring and unearthly reptilian claw foot would definitely raise human alarm if he were top-side, and blow the Nephilim's cover, unlike me or Bennie, and likely others 'out there' who definitely look more human than this one. Thankfully, my flaw, it seems, courses inside—through my blood and is much less noticeable.

His black claw foot taps the grated floor, and his eyes, observant as a deadly cobra biding his time before he strikes, reveal a calculating hybrid capable of great damage. He stares into me and I at him.

I remember you, you worthless fuck.

The creature smiles but it's definitely not a pleasant, happy to see me again smile—it's more of a 'today is your day to die' kind of grin. Our brains line up in sync and he uploads our vile connection to one another. Yet if I lean away from him, I too, fall into the abyss, like his former cohort, which I'm guessing is what this creature hopes. I press my body forward, meeting him 'eye for eye' and this I learn, is the Safety Dance of which Bennie speaks—stay put, stand firm, and lean into someone's head through direct eye contact to avoid becoming their prey.

Unpleasant childhood memories flood my brain like a fissure slicing Earth, ready to swallow me up. I close my eyes to keep the pain from seeping through too much. But it isn't so bad. Something blocks the pain and it's…it's…peace? How could I be feeling peace? I open my eyes and curiously look around.

Lizard man watches me. Experiencing "emotion" is not impossible for him, but rare for his kind. If I remember correctly, he requires ever larger doses of negativity, like using too many drugs, to achieve the same high. His genetic makeup is also primed to foster efficiency through intense algorithmic logic. But since he's bred with human in him too, the Watchers aren't able to completely eradicate his roots, so to speak—and are left to contend with faulty wires of feelings that unexpectedly spring up. How awful it must be to require greater depths of depravity in order to *feel* something.

"You overrode your microchip," the doctor says. "Impressive. You and Bennie were the only two hybrids able to do that—but it is how we found you—and the others."

Others? Are the kids he kept in cells also hybrids? All of them?

The doctor holds his palms toward the silver bucket and slowly moves his hands in opposite directions, as if opening invisible curtains, but nothing happens. Is Saratu in there? I don't feel her but maybe the titanium blocks our ability to transfer energy. If she is in there, I have to figure out how to shut down the SCRAM button (an emergency kill switch for a nuclear reactor) that Bennie taught me about—which also turns off the lock on her liquid-filled prison.

"I will counterbalance whatever fate—good or bad—you choose," I say. "Just as my kind were created to do, from a power far greater than you and yours, you worthless immoral traitor."

I look around for Hope or Brigdhe but see neither.

The doctor smiles and runs a finger from Jade's temple to her chin. "You're no match for me, simpleton. I own you."

He'll flip Jade's switch, if he hasn't done so already.

Behind both of them sits the SCRAM button on a control panel—big, round, red, and corny. Keeping it simple for the humans, I suppose. But humans don't usually get down here—so why a SCRAM button *below* a reactor?

"Mr. Gottlieb?"

The lizard doctor looks unpleasantly surprised. "I'm Doctor to you." His face darkens and an evil shadow skitters across the wrinkles on his cheeks. His bright blue eyes ice over to concrete gray, then go black and he blinks, revealing red pupils.

Just as I suspected—ego and pride are humanized into him, and this is a weakness, as far as I'm concerned. He's been on Earth too long, absorbed by the frenetic consumeristic energy of Raga. She eventually sedates and then cannibalizes unprepared beings—particularly the ones who don't bolster themselves with Planck force, the energy Bennie claims balances us all, regardless of our home realm. I've got no time to waste. I need to 'off' this thing and find this Raga chick.

"He's a liar, Jade," I say. "He's not who he claims to be. But he *has* made you a superior human. You are capable of overriding his control."

Jade doesn't budge an inch except to look at me, helpless, locked in place. I really have to spend a little more time learning modern technology so I can fully understand how humans and hybrids become prey to such gadgetry. That is, if we make it out of here intact and alive—and that's certainly far from a given.

The doctor shows a flicker of smugness, but I also sense a little worry before he recovers.

I've been here before. True, my memories are skittish, like a blinking TV screen that can't quite hold the picture but all of this is familiar.

This Nephilim has been drinking. Scotch. Oban. 1976. The half empty bottle sits on a desk behind him, a horrible substitute for clarity. I wonder if this is why Dr. Evelyn allows us to drink—to keep our minds dull and distracted, under control—or perhaps to offset the microchip?

And so, it is…

Hybrids are a product of the divine in nature, under the purview of God, for life on a planet like Earth, where matter has been purposely slowed to solid form in order to protect The Word, also made solid here, and therefore, disabled from being removed from this realm.

Hybrids and humans may relish playing God and reverse engineering nature, but eventually, we must all return to the realm in which we are born, for recharging. But hybrids are capable of straddling many worlds, and it seems we sometimes forget the Golden Rule of realm roving and the unique gifts we possess, which makes us in many ways, more powerful than angels—because we can take on two forms, solid or supernatural.

This Nephilim's power came to him compliments of a deliberate and calculated manipulation of a bureaucratic maze, where systemic weaknesses were exploited—like discovering holes to scramble through. His conviction that he's bred into elitism is something no drugs, genetic modification, or blood transfusion will ever cure. He reached the pinnacle of his conscious horizon millennia ago and thinks if he tinkers enough with the ignorant and clueless, he'll crack the code of everything.

I remember.

There exists an emptiness between our worlds, his and mine—a 'nothingness' that connects us, but maintains a safe distance, designed by nature, because two dimensions are never supposed to converge the way they have done here on Earth, a planet that keeps the scales of balance between our realms.

"Brigdhe, no!" Bennie yells.

Brigdhe springs out of nowhere and charges toward the Nephilim from behind a row of computers. The hybrid easily grabs her arms before he spins her around to face Bennie. Brigdhe is weak, but there's a dark flash in her eyes, which tells me that she too, possesses a determined streak, like Bennie and me. I notice too, the pain and despair suddenly carved into Bennie's face, and it makes me want to weep, and hug him for eternity.

The doctor laughs. "I think she's hungry."

"Please," Bennie says. "I've worked to give you everything for which you've asked. You have money, power, credit for my inventions, and influence. Let her go."

"What?" I ask. "What are you talking about?"

I stare at Bennie in disbelief and shock. The Nephilim laughs. The doctor did know Bennie was here above him, working his ass off in a lab, night and day, to save his sister? Why not use his power like he did when he lifted me off the ground with his mind in Silo 57 and kill this thing? Shit. He can't. Nephilim's thrive on decay.

"Let her go," Bennie says in a voice that doesn't sound like him at all, but waaay scarier and forceful.

"No," the doctor says. "It's fun to scare the girls. And you haven't yet given me the key to eternal life."

"Be careful what you wish for," Bennie says. "You don't want such a curse."

Brigdhe collapses in the doctor's arms. He drops her to the floor and backs up a few steps, even closer now to the SCRAM button, blocking my view. Bennie runs to his sister's side and cradles her.

"Benjamin Brilliant, there you are," Brigdhe says, a smile stretching softly above her chin. "I knew I'd see you again." She reaches up to touch his face with shaky fingertips.

"It's me, Brie." Bennie reaches into his pocket and pulls out his tin of yage salve.

She stops him. "No. I've seen mum and dad in my dreams. They're lovely and look well. They say hello and miss you. They told me to tell you that they're only a thought away." She puts her hand over his. Bennie uses his other to wipe a tear from his face. "I did the Safety Dance just like you taught me. I got it right. Did you bring me Cutie Pie? Did you?"

Bennie reaches into his pocket. He pulls out a silver box and hands it to her.

So, Brigdhe evidently is familiar with Cutie Pie too.

"Kill her, Jade," the doctor says, looking at me, a crude smile hooked on his lips. "She's in my way."

Jade loads an arrow onto her bow, stretches the string, and raises her arms toward me. She won't miss.

I leap at her, but feel the sharp arrow painfully pierce my side.

A gush of bluish blood with golden flecks falls through the grate as Jade and I engage in battle. I punch her hard in the center of her face. She staggers backward, surprised. I think I broke her nose. Blood spurts from her nostrils, and the pain I know she feels from having her microchip short-circuited gives me the gift of time. I swipe the bow from her hands, and my loaded newspaper bag stuffed with heavy file folders hits her in the side and knocks her off balance. She recovers and I'm slightly grateful she didn't fall over the edge like the other creature I shot.

Brigdhe lifts the sparkly spider from its box and nods at Bennie. She turns and crawls a few inches closer to the doctor.

"Please," Bennie says to the doctor. "She holds the gift of eternal life. It's all I've got. You know you have the upper hand down here and we've failed in our mission."

The doctor grins at the disheveled child at his feet. As he bends to take the spider from her hand, she raises it up to him, the eyes of Cutie Pie studying everything about this Nephilim hybrid. I hope it's being transmitted, uploaded to Bennie's computer in Silo 57 for Dr. Sterling to study if Bennie is right, and we fail to make it out of here. The Nephilim inspects the bioelectromagnetic scientific marvel offered to him as I wonder more about our "mission" and who or what Bennie really might be.

Brigdhe smiles sweetly at the doctor. "Look at me," she says.

He stares into her eyes, and all evil seems to fall away from him, against his will.

Wow. I feel it too, just as I did in Saratu.

I didn't expect compassion could ever wield such power.

"I forgive you," she says.

An overwhelming feeling of warmth and enlightenment seeps forth from Brigdhe, and it lifts the hairs on my forearm as softly as being tickled by spider webs and permeates the room. Without warning, she hugs the doctor, crushing the spider into her chest.

"No!" The doctor yells.

He tries to wriggle free from her, to grab what's left of Cutie Pie, but Brigdhe opens both of her arms wide, palms up, head raised toward the sky, and leans backward over the railing until she and the Nephilim topple over it and into the abyss. The black wisps of smoke floating through the room immediately dive in to follow them.

Bennie sobs uncontrollably as he clutches the railing, staring into blackness. "No." He whispers. "It wasn't supposed to be this way."

I can't reach the SCRAM button.

Losing blood.

I need to save Saratu.

Compass vibrates.

Buckeyes pinch my hip.

I fall to my knees.

"Please, God," I pray. "Help me."

Bennie's hand is on my side. He swipes all of the salve he has left in his tin onto my wound.

I rip the string from Jade's bow as she jumps on my back. Hope and Randolph growl and bark over us. Each uses its teeth to take hold of one of Jade's pant legs. They pull her off of me and drag her across the grate. She screams and kicks at them, yet they hold firm as a white mist gently settles over her back.

I rise.

Still weak, I pull one buckeye from my pocket, wobbling, the room spinning, feeling like a grain of salt in a rolling tumbler. Shadows duck and roll along the wall, wisps of black ribbon that sift through a crack in the seam of Bennie's multiverse.

No! I must keep them from entering this world and altering realities.

A primal war scream shatters my thoughts—the cry of the Valkyries, long-forgotten sisters.

Blue light suddenly envelops the ominous black shadow spirits, encasing them like seashells over snails, and I hear the clash of swords, sparks, and a vibrational hum under our feet. A classical tragedy unfolds in a series of invisible crescendos, hushed whispers of spirits over our heads, speaking a long-dead ancient language I half understand, suddenly awakened from sleeping somewhere cold—the abstract painting, bold, splattered, scuttling across the canvas of space, a zodiac of clanging, rebel warriors that leave me straining to see, stuck inside a muddled half-human mind, until...

Nemain.

A spirit but not a spirit, here but not here—her energy so powerful, assertively compassionate, and full of knowledge, she's as close to me as a mirror. A series of infinite reflections rush to the shoreline of my mind and open the floodgates to my memory, eyes open. But I don't dare touch. It's beyond my capacity, bound as I am by this blood I carry—this basic human blood, the unparalleled original cosmic building block of life. I am not yet ready to join her where she must remain, in our counter-realm.

Nemain slices a darkened shadow with one glint from her celestial sword, powered by the energy of stars she's somehow captured and contained, or perhaps borrowed—yes, borrowed.

"Do it now," she says to me telepathically.

I reach for a buckeye in my pocket and take aim at the SCRAM button.

"You sure this will work?" I ask.

She smiles—and I remember Barbara's words about Native Americans believing that hetuk seeds are the eye of God.

Maybe I need to believe too.

I focus—set my intention.

Breathe.

I finally understand. The connection I have to this planet is my ability to take solid form, to think, feel, and survive—like a human. I float about two inches off the ground and send the buckeye hurtling toward the red button.

Direct. Hit.

A long, moaning crack snakes its way from ceiling to floor. A misty rain of dust powders Bennie, Jade and me. The lights dim and flicker before buzzing so brightly the bulbs burst and the liquid cage holding Saratu glows, trembles, and shatters, its contents spilling over into the abyss. Warm ripples of air warp our space and I grab hold of one of the steel railings, but now it's too hot and I yank my hand away.

I strain to see, expecting Saratu to emerge from her stainless steel and tempered glass cage. But there is no Saratu. She isn't here. I'm confused. My yage vision showed otherwise. This can't be right. Our entire plan was based on her being here. Disappointment and concern wash over me like the heat.

Jade stands there wide-eyed and frightened, a new look, a human look, a broken spell to go with her broken nose, microchip, and seriously wounded spirit. Bennie keeps staring at the hole in the ground below us in a trance-like state. I gently nudge him and he looks at me and blinks—a small smile creeping across his lips.

"You did it," he says.

Twelve kids find their way to us, confused, frightened, and clinging to each other. I'm not sure how they opened their cells and there's no time to ask but can only assume that once the doctor fell overboard with Brigdhe into the abyss, it may have deactivated their microchips.

A few pieces of industrialized architecture fall from the ceiling, followed by crumbling cement.

"Jade," I say. "This place is going to collapse. We have to get everyone out."

The ground rumbles again, louder this time. Thunder, lightning, and orbs of plasma zip around the underside of the reactor and over our heads, chasing each other, sometimes colliding and exploding, sparks raining down on us. Sprinklers engage above our heads and cracks split the walls further apart. Loud sirens and flashing red lights add to the mounting chaos.

Jade suddenly blows past me, out the door the kids came through. It's every lab rat for herself, I suppose. I should have known not to expect too much from a 'bite-first' kind of kid who's likely a double-agent anyway.

I focus my energy on visualizing Dr. Evelyn's face and hope she mentally picks up my message from way down here, like a pollen granule on the wind. Bennie showed me a book once, written by some former Apollo 11 astronaut and physicist named Dr. Edgar Mitchell. He claims that thoughts have the ability to travel faster than the speed of light. I hope this Dr. Mitchell dude is right.

"Bennie!" I yell into the ear-shattering cacophony. "We have to go!"

I look around but don't see him.

I'm not sure which way to turn to get out. I pull the compass from my pocket. It glows. I shake my head and ask the compass, "Are you sure?". I shrug and look at the kids.

"Follow me."

I head north through a large crack in the wall that split open about as easily as an egg and it leads to a cave system. Hissing whispers, the ones we heard that day while harvesting vegetables, return. The kids hold on to one another, all twelve of them. I feel responsible for getting them to safety—but how? We're trapped. The cave is a dead end. I don't know what to do.

I check my compass again. It points to a solid wall.

"What the fuck!" I yell. "Get us out of here!"

Without warning, the ground collapses beneath our feet, and we slide down at least twenty feet on loose soil and rocks before being dumped into another cave, the soft flow of dirt protecting our fall like nature's mattress. No one seems hurt, but it's dark. I can't see anyone so I don't know if we all made it through and there's no time for a head count.

A blast of cool air blows through, and we disturb a nest of bats.

Wait.

Hope.

My fox smelled like the outdoors—and where there's bats, there's a way out! We walk blind, bats pelting us in their disturbed confusion. Kids scream and whimper, the wolf howls, and my fox lets out a frightened yelp beside me so I lightly pet the top of her head to reassure both of us.

"Everybody shut up!" My voice echoes through the cave, but I get my wish. I pull the compass from my pocket. In its light, I see that the flying creatures around us aren't bats or dark spirits or even military bioelectromagnetic flying gizmos.

They're cardinals!

"What the hell?" I ask to no one in particular—bewildered by so many red birds in one dark space.

"Everybody hold hands," I say. "Single file. Now."

Verity once told me that cardinals mean angels are near. I want to tell her how wrong she is, because today has been nothing but chaos, horror, darkness, and death. Yet I can't help but feel an overwhelming peace for the moment, my distress easing, and I'm still breathing so maybe in some freakish way she's right.

I calculate we've walked a mile, slightly upward.

Running water.

The hoot of an owl.

More cardinals.

A small hole overhead reveals glinting stars and I feel a small gush of fresh air.

I clear away dirt over our heads, pitching clumps of rocks, fresh snow, and earth over my hair to enlarge the hole. I grab one of the kids by her arm and give her a shove upward.

"I'm going to hoist these other kids to you," I say. "Every kid who goes through the hole helps the next one up, got it?"

I don't know how many of them understand me, but this plan works, and soon we're all aboveground, under the cover of the lone tree in the cornfield. I inhale a breath of cool air as if taking a drag on a cigarette. This must be how my fox and Randolph and maybe Bennie too, traversed both sides of NASA so quickly and often unseen.

I make sure we're still all together but there is no Bennie. Then I remember; some kids got left behind in their cells, their souls extinguished before I knew them. They couldn't be saved. I bow my head. For a brief moment I ache for heaven to be real, a reward for the hell they suffered on Earth, compassion settling deep into the folds of my heart. I hope that there's more—more to us than the temporary vessel we all someday shed, whether we be human or hybrid. Nobody should be forced to go before their time. I'll have to bring that up at the next Ormian Council.

Keep walking, Sam.

I still have to get twelve half-starved, sick, and too lightly dressed kids to the house so they can get warmth, food, and medical care.

It's so cold.

The stars fade to make way for daybreak. Fighter jets zoom overhead. I hear warning sirens in the distance. Soldiers yell. It's pandemonium on the NASA side of Plum Hook.

I stumble along, leading a parade of exhausted, malnourished, fucked-up, and mostly silent kids. I tie my wiry copper hair into a knot behind my head and shake off slivers of ice. I gather up a handful of snow to quench my thirst. We're so close to the house.

And that's when I see them.

Twelve extraordinarily giant Native Americans with pale blue skin, covered in pearls, copper armbands, and red feathers, their tattoos like charcoal drawings against fresh snow, stand across the field from me, bright blue eyes and red hair glinting in the rising sun. I almost miss the well camouflaged furred white creature standing behind them.

A warrior raises her spear, smiles, and points it at me. And through them comes Saratu, clad in her usual sheet and smiling as if walking among celestial warrior beings just comes naturally for her.

"Saratu!"

The lead warrior's comrades bow their heads, put hand over heart, and turn together, slowly, to disappear in the forest. I know her. She's Lozen, sister of Victorio—cunning battle strategist and guardian of the twelve gates that guard the Portals of Ninmah.

Whoosh!

A bright ballet of lights inflames the sky like bottle rockets leaving a trail of sparkling gold dust. A gust of wind sweeps through the forest, bending treetops and shaking loose new snow. Black helicopters churn overhead. We've been spotted.

The helicopters land in the field, further flattening frozen crops.

I regather the others and make it to the yard before I stumble and collapse.

Kids swarm over me. One clears the snow around my head. Another covers me with a dirty hooded sweatshirt. A man lifts me.

"Cameron?"

"Shh. I knew you'd do good, kid."

His eyes. So blue, with flecks of green and gray that occasionally flicker into pools of liquid black ink. The navy-blue veins of his neck, like Arctic ice cracks, have receded, along with the worry and weakness he seemed to carry when we first met on the streets of Cleveland. He seems almost happy. No more dark circles under his eyes.

"Who are you?" I ask.

"You ask too many questions. You'll get through this."

"Riiight." I say. "Grownups lie."

"Hybrids do too," he says, looking down on me with a light smile.

"I'm so tired."

"You need iron."

I roll my eyes at him but am too weak to do much else.

Daylight grows stronger.

I grow weaker. I need to recharge in my realm.

I search for Bennie in every face but in the chaos and confusion, I've lost him. Dr. Evelyn is here now. I smell her perfume. Chanel No. 5. Dr. Sterling is with her too. He looks more worried than I've ever seen, his warm eyes red and wet.

Cameron is gone.

"Bennie," I say. "Where's Bennie?"

Reggie barks orders at soldiers. Sergeant Major Lynch is in full rescue mode, yelling at them to bring stretchers. Someone pokes a needle in my arm.

"Shhh," Dr. Evelyn whispers. "Good girl. You found the others."

Genin leans over me. "Hey, princess. You done good." He kisses my forehead and takes my free right hand, the one without an IV.

"Where's Bennie?"

Bennie.

Bennie.

Bennie!

I call for him in my head, but he doesn't answer.

I can't *feel* him anymore.

Dr. Evelyn cuts the newspaper bag from my shoulder and looks inside. She pulls out a folder, flips it open, quickly thumbs through. She blinks in disbelief.

"Oh my God," she whispers. "Colonel? You've got to see this."

Hope and Randolph peer sheepishly at the commotion from behind a fallen log about twenty feet from where I lay. I try to point— but I can't move.

My vision fades due to man's forced pharmaceutical darkness, the shitty kind that always forces the body and brain into involuntary suspended solitude.

Chapter 28

GOODBYE BENNIE

Stepping onto the veranda at Plum Hook Bay, I admire once-tended gardens that now grow wild and creep toward the forest. Reggie always said that plants could communicate, that we could use them to do all sorts of things such as read people's intentions or offer a hedge of protection against terrorism by using and recognizing the small electrical charges they emit.

Tangled vines twist and coil, their bright green tendrils stretching toward the wilderness, a silent and painfully slow photosynthetic attempt to flee this once guarded house belonging to "the government". Tractors sink in their muddy tracks, faded by the sun and covered in speckles of rust among labyrinth rows of overgrown cornfields; both have been left to the horses, now wild, that roam throughout these ten thousand plus acres.

It will be sunset soon.

I walk the wooded path I've walked so many times before, past Sarge's grave, where I lay wildflowers and clear away debris. Poor fella. I still think about this dog, how he lost his life two years ago. And it still makes my heart hurt because I have few answers and zero closure. I'm learning that sometimes, more often than I care to admit, I won't get answers either—unless I have a 'need to know.'

Randolph and Hope keep me company, circling each other, pouncing and playing as we make our way through the woods to Silo 57. The animals look plump and healthy, with shiny coats, and don't seem bothered by the radiation here, which I find surprising. I figured that they too, like Sarge, would be long buried by now. The radiation doesn't seem to bother me either. I'm immune, as Bennie predicted.

Running my fingers along the top of a bush, Katie comes to mind. I still don't know exactly who killed her and I think about her less as time passes, which sometimes bothers me because it makes me feel a little guilty for letting her memory fade. Dr. Evelyn told me that it was Mrs. Myers who used part of her retirement savings to purchase Katie's headstone. I told Reggie that I wanted to personally thank Mrs. Myers for that someday.

Reggie shared that Dr. Awoudi left the Cuyahoga Juvenile Justice System a few days after I did and he hasn't been seen since. Dr. Awoudi is 'off the grid', taking a well-deserved break from Septum Oculi—or so I've been told. Since there is no "need to know," none of us do.

Cameron the Cop carried me to safety when I collapsed near the house after I emerged from the cave system with the rescued kids. Yet Reggie and Dr. Evelyn both claimed Cameron was never there—had never been to NASA Plum Hook Bay. The kids also told Dr. Evelyn that I was never carried by anyone either but flew. For whatever his reasons, Cameron the Cop chose to remain incognito that day and made himself known only to me, so I guess everyone else has "no need to know."

For now, at least, Earth feels balanced. It gives me hope.

Speaking of Hope…

My fox plays in the field with Bennie's wolf just ahead.

I'm eighteen now. I'll live and work among humans, under an assumed *legend* (a cover story), subject to all the rules and regulations of this planet.

Humanness is still quite a bit of a foreign concept for me. These solid beings seem very keen to exchange their spirit for convenience and an unexamined life. It's as if most of them (but not all) purposely apply brakes to their "take off" and voluntarily plummet into mediocrity. Yet nearly all of them hope to be 'rich and famous', to earn power sans accountability. I find this perplexing, because humans, just like angels, aliens, and hybrids, are all forged from stardust. If humans had more faith, they could soar to incredible realms far beyond this provincial but promising planet. Unfortunately, I suspect that the specious charms of

Raga both blind and corrupt them.

What I find most annoying is that humans add to their handicaps by standing in lines for almost everything—groceries, clothes, bathrooms, accolades, attention, hope—gobbling up "wants" until they meet the end of their linear time lines much quicker than they should due to what Reggie swears is laziness and reliance on "processed food".

As Bennie once said too, humans are asleep even when they're awake—clueless about how to tap into the earthly energy which surrounds them and mostly blind to cosmic greatness, placated and doped up with technology, compliments of the Bezaliels who've learned how to remotely control them through the Nephilim, using gadgetry and greed.

Mayra, the Raga, is still out there too—and what part Dr. Evelyn still plays in this drama remains unknown. Is Dr. Evelyn foe or friend? I intuit that we need one another, she and I, at least professionally, and I'm sure I will someday cross paths with the good Doctors Dennison again—I feel it *in my bones,* as humans sometimes say.

The Dennison's returned to Oxford, England—or so I've been told. I do not feel *that* in my bones. I think they're somewhere else. And, it would seem that lying, particularly among Earth beings, is just as much a part of the human condition as their limited but noble exercise of occasional truthfulness.

Breathing in the scent of pine trees, I touch some leaves on a tree. I've always felt the energy of trees but now I'm able to see their auras too, just as I do in people. The soul of Sarge surges through the willow tree where his form was buried, revealing small golden orbs of energy that hang like new fruit, until they bounce around. The wolf and the fox seem to sense it too and stretch and wag their tails.

It's a pity that NASA Plum Hook Bay has been "decommissioned" by the government. Scientists claim it's no longer fit for human habitation. Politicians argue otherwise, until they're challenged to pitch tents on this side of the fence. They all decline. In fact, the day the reactor died, every human behind Plum Hook's fence jumped it, leaving behind eyeglasses, half-filled coffee mugs, packs of cigarettes, guns, ammo, and office supplies. Everything in the house and on the farm was left "as is", like someone stepped out for a moment but will be right back—to this wide-ranging radioactive time capsule.

I don't know what Plum Hook's contamination might later mean for humans, or what it means for the animals trapped behind the fence now, or the people still living in nearby Sandusky. But I do know that Mother Nature, with help from the Weavers, was able to set her seasons right, and it no longer snows in August. I guess people will decide to worry about this place only if and when it causes another problem— one too late to fix—as humans seem to prefer defensive reactionary pursuits over sensible planning.

There have been news reports of extra-tall blue people guarding the fence at night too, and locals swear on their Holy Bibles that they've seen White Bigfoot. Maybe a little dose of the supernatural, paired with governmental warnings of heavy radiation or being shot at, might be all it takes to keep feeble-hearted humans from trespassing. Effective 'false flags' Reggie calls them. But it's the few brave humans I worry about—the ones like Genin and the other foster kids, now all adults, that I could train to be mighty warriors against the Nephilim.

Rakito left Plum Hook Bay first. He joined the Peace Corps for a long-term mission in Nepal. Rakito is a special type of warrior, one who cultivates healing and calms fears using weapons of intelligence and compassion. There are not enough of his kind on Earth, a being who does not require explosions, applause, or violent camo covered victories to find his sense of worth.

Priyanka cried for days after Rakito left, and a few months later, she joined him. I heard from Verity, who heard from Tetana, that Rakito and Priyanka secretly got married with Barbara's help because Priyanka got pregnant, which royally pissed off Dr. Evelyn. I can't imagine two people meeting as kids and then living out their lives together. It seems like a lot of hardship and missed adventure. I hope they make it but the odds aren't in their favor.

Tetana joined the Air Force. Reggie made that happen. She's set to become one of the first female pilots to ever fly a fighter jet, which

I think is pretty cool. She's stationed at Lackland Air Force base in Texas doing eight weeks of basic training before being assigned her first station.

Verity's departure bothers me most. She got into Harvard and plans to study law and comparative religion. We've promised to stay in touch as much as possible.

Pa Ling and Fensig signed up for the Marine Corps. They wrote to say they're training together in the Carolina swamps for some Special Forces group. Fensig said Pa Ling actually befriended an alligator he swims with, one he named Jade, which doesn't surprise me after he told us about his pet shark, Loki, in Indonesia—and Jade seems like the perfect name for a scaly cold reptile.

Speaking of reptiles…

Without warning, Jade was unexpectedly sent back to Moscow when Congress axed the foreign exchange spy program for foster kids. Someone *accidentally* forgot to keep Project Blue Bird in a clandestine black ops budget and made the CIA/Dennison training program a public line item under Section 23 of a secret omnibus funding bill. The press had a field day over that well executed slip and fall.

Genin channeled his inner Rambo and left ahead of the others (except Rakito) for the Navy. He's written a few times, mostly as he went through basic training. He signed up to try out for a BUD/S program at a special warfare training facility in Coronado, California. I assume he's getting through okay because he already passed phase one, and he told me if he got into phase two, I wouldn't hear from him—and I haven't. Sometimes I think about the kiss we shared and wonder if anyone will ever make me feel that way again. It makes me smile. Every. Time.

Our trespassing into the NASA side of Plum Hook Bay forced the CIA to throw some other project, *M.K.-ULTRA* under the bus, to take heat off of the DOE after Verity called the cops that night. The *Washington Post* broke the MK Ultra story and won all sorts of awards.

Media, police, and protestors camped outside the gates of Plum Hook long after that day. Nobody important got out of here unscathed until *"the people"* got some answers. The DOE fed a few fake news facts to journalists it semi-trusted, to counter our reporters. Thanks to Reggie, they never could figure out from where the leak came.

Nobody, not even the government, knows about the other files I took from Dr. Gottlieb's green metal filing cabinet, the ones I've hidden for later—or the key device I have also hidden well. I'll need this key when I collect the codes Bennie told me are scattered all over this planet.

Reggie, through Sergeant Major Lynch, had Saratu airlifted over the fence the same day the reactor died. He assured me that I did indeed rescue her and she's tucked away in a very safe place that has nothing to do with governments. I can only hope she's the guest of a lost tribe somewhere deep in a jungle or desert. The truth is, she's probably being studied in yet another secret lab and I have no "need to know," but I *will* find her again.

I try not to think too hard about all this change. Whenever another kid leaves, it feels like my grandma dying all over again.

On the positive side, I've been accepted into the School of International Affairs at George Washington University in Washington, DC. I'll then transfer to another CIA-managed "farm" called "Langley" in Quantico, Virginia. After graduation, I'm off to the Army as an officer. Reggie made that happen too. He says if I do well, I'll be chosen as a logistics officer for an outfit called Delta Force, where I'll work as a covert CIA case officer, which he called a NOC (a person having "no official cover.") He claims it's dangerous work, but the perks are a hell of a lot better than getting stuck with diplomatic credentials at some foreign embassy where loudmouths are relegated, the ones who try too hard to sound and act more important than they really are. He added that NOCs also receive enough money to buy closets full of red heels, cool clothes, fancy cars, and anything else I might need to appear 'legit'.

I suppose I should be happy about getting all the stuff I ever wanted without having to steal it, but "stuff" doesn't appeal much to me now. What concerns me more is that I'll be forced to make new friends and

I'm not sure how I feel about that. Pure humans mostly annoy me and I find it hard to trust them.

Yet when I think about existing in their slowed form, a being made mostly of solid matter, the whole idea is sometimes boggling, until I remember I'm a Golden Blood. Will I manage here?

But the biggest thing I think about almost all the time is Bennie. A piece of me went with him when he disappeared. We were connected, Bennie and I, both psychically and physically, by our blood. I know Bennie from another time, one that isn't linear, and those memories hide on the dark side of my brain that rarely sees sunlight. If I think about our connection directly, it can't be felt. If I go about this new life, I pick up glimpses of Bennie that enter the periphery of my soul, ones that leave behind faint traces of love I'm able to temporarily claim but never completely capture.

And there are others here too, like Bennie and me. I will find them.

Sometimes I pretend that Bennie and his sister are reunited along some parallel universe in Bennie's lab at Silo #57, and he shows Brigdhe experiments while she holds his spider—or that they're running through these fields and woods of Plum Hook, their eyes no longer darkened by the deepness of their despair.

Standing on the ridge, I look across the vista to Lake Erie, and make a wish to see them one more time, even if it's a hallucination. And sometimes, though rarely these days, Bennie shows up in my dreams to tell me it's okay—that he's only a thought away...

I'm not *legally* supposed to be here, to lay flowers in front of Silo 57, pay respects, or sit among the trees and visit. I sneak through, past and above the heads of the unlucky and clueless soldiers ordered to stand watch. Hope helps me bypass through the loopholes around this place.

After a good summer rain, part of the river near NASA's retention ponds runs rust-red. The animals won't go near there, and despite what I suspect is contained contamination, the fox and the wolf are better off behind this fence where they have a plentiful supply of wild rabbits, mice, birds, deer, and woodchucks to feed to their new broods. Maybe they'll keep Bennie's spirit company too.

I climb onto the roof of Silo 57. It's carpeted with sod that was laid by soldiers to bury its contents and our story from history. Time and Nature will cover our existence and exhaust curiosity-seekers—or simply erase the memories, take them off air. Lights out.

Death, too, will force memories to fade.

The only sure thing in this world is that there exists no sure thing—because change forces the hand of everything. Impermanence filters through the heavens to infiltrate even the tiniest quark, the Ni, a perfect balance of frequency, vibration, and energy held together by a force no one can find, but that most call God.

Bennie's dark matter was never about gravity. Humans fail to make sense of their world because they've taken the wrong path to what is really an electrically charged and connected cosmos, where all planets and stars are strung together like a universally endless highway of glowing streetlights, abuzz with every bit of information ever exchanged.

I reach into my front pocket and pull out Bennie's shiny buckeye. I examine it like I did the first day Barbara handed me hers. The *Hetuk*—the eye of God—nearly impossible to destroy.

I softly pitch this final memento into the sod on top of Silo 57, and I remember dropping a coin for good luck into the Boy and Boot Fountain in Sandusky's Washington Park the day Reggie took Verity and me there. Reggie told me that a tornado destroyed the park in 1924 but the boy with the boot statue survived. Maybe that's what happened to me. I got caught in the path of a tornado but I'm still here.

The buckeye trees and the pines softly sway a few feet away. The sky is clear today.

I read in the Plum Hook library that Ohio arborist Daniel Drake once said back in the 1800s, that the deepest girdling does not deaden a buckeye tree. Even if cut down, it sends out young branches as a message to the universe that there is great power in a seed, and life is not so easily conquered.

The buckeye seed cracks, then sprouts its young thread-like branches to spread in every direction, to tightly embrace Bennie's lab. I float down from the roof to get out of the way and let nature conduct her business.

A red cardinal swoops onto a pine branch a short distance away. He wobbles his head, watches, and chirps before flying off again toward the river, his beautiful red wings gliding on a light breeze as he scouts another place to settle. I swipe a tear from one cheek, but another lands on the ground beside the silo. I place a hand over the buckeye roots now covering the building, as if checking for a pulse—maybe even hoping for one. Nothing—except the whisper of a nearby tree communicating with the grass, root systems, bacteria, bugs, and other trees around and under it.

Breathe, Sam.

You'll play the piano again, someday, Bennie said to me in the library.

Maybe today.

Heartache hurts. So too, my head.

I study the racecar-red heels on my feet as I sit with my fox. My shoes fit better now without lace trimmed bobby socks. And it's quieter than usual at Plum Hook Bay. I don't see anyone—not even a soldier or a black suit. Where are the kids? There's beautiful green grass and rust pine needles under my feet. And I still have no idea how this life caught me. I fly fast—even in heels—from a lot of things.

"OUCH!" I smack at a sudden bug bite on my right bicep, but instead, drive a small yellow arrow tip further into my skin.

I scan the wood line but see nothing before my head is pharmaceutically forced down and the pine needles blur into a puddle of rust. A breeze combs the small hairs on my forearm before it sweeps across the tree leaves and I stagger—dropping to my knees.

A chill.

Hybrid down.

I fight the poison trying to close my eyes.

Red birds circle overhead before they disappear through a cloud portal and a sunbeam warms my face.

"Goodbye, Sarge."

"Goodbye, Brigdhe."

"Goodbye, Bennie."

Huron River   Plum Hook
Ohio

Made in the USA
Columbia, SC
07 January 2020